DEADLY SILENCE

Jodie Larsen

AN ONYX BOOK

ONYX
Published by the Penguin Group
Penguin Putnam Inc., 375 Hudson Street,
New York, New York 10014, U.S.A.
Penguin Books Ltd, 27 Wrights Lane,
London W8 5TZ, England
Penguin Books Australia Ltd, Ringwood,
Victoria, Australia
Penguin Books Canada Ltd, 10 Alcorn Avenue,
Toronto, Ontario, Canada M4V 3B2
Penguin Books (N.Z.) Ltd, 182–190 Wairau Road,
Auckland 10, New Zealand

Penguin Books Ltd, Registered Offices:
Harmondsworth, Middlesex, England

Published by Onyx, an imprint of Dutton Signet,
a member of Penguin Putnam Inc.

First Printing, December, 1997
10 9 8 7 6 5 4 3 2 1

Copyright © Jodie Larsen Nida, 1997
All rights reserved

 REGISTERED TRADEMARK—MARCA REGISTRADA

Printed in the United States of America

Without limiting the rights under copyright reserved above, no part of
this publication may be reproduced, stored in or introduced into a
retrieval system, or transmitted, in any form, or by any means (electronic, mechanical, photocopying, recording, or otherwise), without
the prior written permission of both the copyright owner and the above
publisher of this book.

PUBLISHER'S NOTE
This is a work of fiction. Names, characters, places, and incidents either
are the product of the author's imagination or are used fictitiously,
and any resemblance to actual persons, living or dead, events, or locales
is entirely coincidental.

BOOKS ARE AVAILABLE AT QUANTITY DISCOUNTS WHEN USED TO PROMOTE
PRODUCTS OR SERVICES. FOR INFORMATION PLEASE WRITE TO PREMIUM MARKETING DIVISION, PENGUIN PUTNAM INC., 375 HUDSON STREET, NEW YORK, NEW
YORK 10014.

If you purchased this book without a cover you should be aware that
this book is stolen property. It was reported as "unsold and destroyed" to the publisher and neither the author nor the publisher has
received any payment for this "stripped book."

DEADLY PORTRAITS

Less than five minutes into their operation, Evan and Tony found their first target. A perfect match. Sitting alongside the jogging path near a redwood picnic table was a young mother who gently pulled and pushed the side-by-side double stroller as she talked quietly to a friend.

In the stroller were two children facing each other. The little girl giggled and played, entertaining the baby boy. Both had blond curls and light eyes. Years of experience led Evan to estimate the girl's age between twenty and twenty-five months and the boy at two to three months.

A convenient row of bushes provided perfect cover as Tony eased himself into position. He slid the lens cap off, focusing the camera with practiced precision. Beside him a photography manual entitled *Capturing Earth's Treasures* lay open. To any passersby he appeared to be casually photographing nature. But in reality the powerful telephoto lens pulled the children so close to his eye, he would have sworn he could jerk their precious blond curls with a twist of his fingertips. . . .

DEADLY SILENCE

① SIGNET　　　　　　　　　　　　　　　⬤ ONYX　　(0451)

HAIR RAISING THRILLERS

- ☐ **THE LOVE THAT KILLS by Ronald Levitsky.** A shattering novel of lawyers in a web of sex, drugs, and death ... "Compelling and provocative."—*Washington Post* (403746—$4.99)

- ☐ **SAFELIGHT by Linda Crockett Gray.** One man wanted to kill Rikki. One man wanted to save her. But the only one she could trust was herself in this novel of a beautiful woman dazzled by love—and stalked by death-lust. (173171—$4.99)

- ☐ **THE GIRL IN A SWING by Richard Adams.** "Astonishing ... sublime eroticism and gruesome nightmare ... an absolutely terrifying ghost story, as gripping and psychologically penetrating as anything in James or Poe. Richard Adams has written with marvelous tact and narrative power, a strange, beautiful, haunting book."—*The New York Times Book Review* (163060—$5.95)

*Prices slightly higher in Canada

Buy them at your local bookstore or use this convenient coupon for ordering.

PENGUIN USA
P.O. Box 999 — Dept. #17109
Bergenfield, New Jersey 07621

Please send me the books I have checked above.
I am enclosing $_____ (please add $2.00 to cover postage and handling). Send check or money order (no cash or C.O.D.'s) or charge by Mastercard or VISA (with a $15.00 minimum). Prices and numbers are subject to change without notice.

Card #_____ Exp. Date _____
Signature_____
Name_____
Address_____
City _____ State _____ Zip Code _____

For faster service when ordering by credit card call **1-800-253-6476**

Allow a minimum of 4-6 weeks for delivery. This offer is subject to change without notice.

For my father, Larry Larsen—
the strong, silent type

And my mother, Pat Larsen—
the most generous woman I've ever known

ACKNOWLEDGMENTS

I would like to express my sincere appreciation and thanks to everyone who helped create this book. The following are only a few of the special people who have helped me time and again:

Sherrie Dixon of Esq. Literary Productions—my constant source of encouragement and friendship.

Marilyn Prosser and the other Tulsa County librarians—generous people who never fail to make research a pleasure.

Tulsa's writing community and booksellers—for welcoming me with open arms and words of wisdom.

Audrey LaFehr, John Paine, and all the talented people at Dutton Signet—for making a dream come true.

Ben Gorrell, Julie Smith, Joy Ondracek, and Sharen Swagerty—the most loyal running buddies in the world.

Mark, Amanda, and Jonathan—who fill my life with the best inspiration in the world—love and laughter.

Prologue

As he jogged through the serene park, Evan Peterson evaluated the cool October day. A westerly breeze swept over the lush jogging trails on the outskirts of Savannah, pushing the few remaining clouds toward the ocean. Following the path, Evan twisted through a thick grove of trees, brushing strands of Spanish moss out of his way as they swayed in the gentle wind. Although another man would have relished the abundance of nature's blessings, Evan merely gauged the effect the pleasant weather would have on the work ahead. When he emerged at the edge of the park's vast playground, he slowed to a brisk walk to quickly survey the children playing in the area.

Sucking in a deep cleansing breath, he felt the last shreds of nervous energy being replaced by a familiar thirst. It was a powerful feeling, the need to dominate, to prevail at any cost. In a matter of seconds he could change the destiny of any of the children before him. Smiling, he knew once again that he was still invincible, a predator among his prey.

Evan hardly noticed the striking young woman leaning over the stroller blocking the path ahead. It was the object of her attention that caught his practiced eye. The baby. A perfect baby. In a second he unconsciously tallied the child's attributes: large blue eyes with thick, dark lashes; brown curls; plump, healthy body. Her mother's soft Southern accent seemed to float in the wind as she pulled the child into her arms.

He could have easily touched the girl's silky hair as he passed by, but he resisted, content to memorize her features instead. As his eyes probed her face, she visibly tensed, as if she knew the threat he posed. An involuntary shudder ran through him. He was certain he must be imagining things. The child could not have possibly sensed the danger, yet he was sure he had seen an instinctive flash of fear cloud those big blue eyes the instant before she turned away.

The jogging trail ended at the adjoining parking lot, where Evan stretched and discreetly watched. He could see the little girl struggling to be free, until finally the woman yielded and set her daughter on the playground. Without a glance in his direction she ran away, launching a full-fledged assault on a nearby array of heavy ropes forming a gigantic man-made spider web.

Even from a distance Evan could hear the child giggle as she clutched, swayed, and pulled herself to the center of the web. He found himself tempted to turn around and stare again, but he would have to wait. His very existence depended on being unseen, overlooked—another face in the crowd.

Without hesitation he opened the car door and slid in the front seat beside Tony Montegra. As usual, only a slight nod acknowledged Evan's arrival. After a few silent moments he simply stated, "My package didn't include the specs."

Unfolding the cream bond paper, Evan read aloud the target information. "Caucasian. Blond hair. Blue or green eyes. No sex preference. Under two acceptable, under four months preferred."

"Business as usual?" Tony mumbled.

Evan nodded as he tossed his spare set of keys to Tony, and deposited the set he received into his own pocket along with the spec sheet. The extra keys were insurance against this park's chief disadvantage—parking lots on each end of the stretch of playgrounds.

Even though Evan and Tony worked together on jobs only two or three times a year, they communicated silently and efficiently. Over the past fifteen years they had learned to understand the slightest glance or hand gesture. Whereas every aspect of Evan's life was controlled and precise, Tony preferred to wing it, to attack challenges as they came.

The men were opposites in every way, from their backgrounds to their appearances. Born and raised on a struggling farm in Iowa, Evan had watched his parents work themselves to death— literally. When he was left alone at eighteen, he sold everything, moved to Manhattan, and swore he would never live in poverty again. After only a week his destiny was set when a friend introduced him to Tony Montegra.

Tony was a dark, brooding young man who had a similar hunger for a better life. The oldest of five children, he had been like a father to his brothers, helping his single mother as much as he could by prowling the streets of Los Angeles with his friends. She never asked where he got the money he gave her, she only cried and hugged him. When he was seventeen, a store owner shot his best friend. Tony escaped with a bullet-grazed shoulder, and a valuable lesson. That night he left L.A. for good.

Learning how to survive first in Chicago, then in Manhattan, Tony quickly turned his street sense into a livelihood, alternating his crimes between the two cities. A reputation for discretion and solitude soon landed him several "positions," including a chance to be on the ground floor of an elite organization where minimal work held the promise of maximum wealth. Within the first year he realized that the complex nature of the assignments required he work with a partner once again. The thought turned his stomach until he met Evan Peterson.

As they stepped out of the car, in unison Evan and Tony reached behind their backs, switching on the small battery packs that powered their line of communication. Voice-activated, state-of-the-art mini-microphones were concealed under the collars of their jogging suits. The risks they took demanded the best equipment money could buy.

Evan casually walked away from the car, knowing Tony would remain behind to scrutinize the light settings on the camera for several minutes. Perfection was essential. Crisp, bold colors with sharp images comparable to professional studio portraits were the only acceptable product. If the negatives weren't perfect, they had wasted their time and energy. Wasted time meant someone else might get the job. Losing the job meant losing ten thousand untaxed, unrecorded dollars a month. Each.

Lengthening his perfectly tuned body into a runner's stretch, Evan waited until he heard Tony's voice in his earphone say, "Program one engaged."

Striding easily into a soft jog, Evan muttered, "First pass underway." He rolled through each step, his footfalls practically silent on the winding path as he passed the children snagged by the spider web. None of them seemed to notice him. Relieved, he continued on, graciously nodding at each passing jogger and waving to children as they played on the vast array of nearby jungle gyms and swings.

Less than five minutes into their operation, Evan and Tony found their first target. A perfect match. Sitting alongside the jogging path near a redwood picnic table was a young mother. As she gently pulled and pushed a side-by-side stroller, she talked quietly to a friend.

In the double stroller were two children facing each other. The little girl giggled and played, thoroughly entertaining the baby boy. Both had blond curls and light eyes. With years of experience Evan estimated the girl's age between twenty and twenty-five months and the boy at two to three months.

A convenient row of bushes provided perfect cover as Tony eased himself into position. He slid the lens cap off, focusing the camera with practiced precision. Beside him a photography manual was open to the section titled "Capturing Earth's

Treasures." To any passersby he appeared to be casually photographing nature. But in reality the powerful telephoto lens pulled the children so close to his eye, he would have sworn he could jerk their precious blond curls with a twist of his fingertips.

Ten minutes and three rolls of film later, Evan and Tony began their wait. The second phase of the game was always more dangerous, but a lot more fun. Most of the people lounging in the park were enjoying a relaxed morning, but Tony's patience was wearing thin as time crept slowly by. Finally he whispered, "Phase two is really dragging. Are you still clear?"

He heard Evan's response. "Yes. Everything okay with you?"

"Doing great. Just bored stiff. How long do you think they're going to sit on their butts and talk?" Tony muttered.

"One of the brats will throw a fit soon. Just wait. We've been in position over an hour. I'm sure the little linoleum lizards won't make it much longer."

Tony flexed one leg without visibly moving. He was resting on a park bench, his face partially covered by the manual on photography. "I hope you're right. I'm not sure how much longer I can stay this way. My friggin' back may break."

Snickering, Evan softly said, "Looks like we're in luck. The little girl just smacked her baby brother."

Both men discreetly watched the two women hug, then push their strollers in opposite directions down the sunlit path. As Tony followed, the slender woman in her early thirties stopped several times, pointing at birds and flowers as she described them to her children.

"They're heading right at you. Sit tight," Tony whispered.

Evan saw the woman pushing the double stroller approach his new location. Even though he was wearing a wig and stage makeup, he turned his face away, leaning into a long cat stretch as they passed. He knew this particular path wound through two small hills and another playground before it ended at the parking area. After watching them crest the first hill, he cut across a grassy knoll, then sprinted to his car.

Two minutes later, Evan was behind the steering wheel of a rented blue Caprice. The hat was gone, a different wig was in place, and a shirt and tie had appeared from under the jacket of the jogging suit. When the mother and her children walked within inches of him, Evan appeared to be exactly what he was—a professional.

Dropping in behind her as she pulled her minivan into the busy street, Evan was close enough to clearly see the mother's reflection in her rearview mirror. *Such a perfect little world she lives in . . . If she only knew*, he thought sadistically. *Would she run? Cry? Offer herself in place of her kids?* The last thought nearly made him laugh out loud.

Using their radios, Evan and Tony expertly tailed her by alternating streets, tag-teaming their quarry. When she stopped at the grocery store, Evan jotted down her license plate number so they could run a check on it, if necessary. Fifteen minutes later, they saw her emerge from the store, balancing the children and a sack of groceries. As she headed back to her car, they moved into position.

Traffic had picked up slightly at noon, making it a little tougher to negotiate Savannah's busy streets. Both men were relieved when she finally turned into a newly constructed neighborhood. Brightly colored flags marking model homes and vacant lots were sprinkled near the entry, but the minivan didn't slow until it approached a block already filled with new houses. Toys were scattered on porches, and several children stopped on their bikes and trikes to wait for the cars to pass.

"She's pulling in," Tony said.

"I'll get the address. You get the name on the mailbox, if there is one," Evan said.

As he drove past the two-story colonial home, he noticed everything—flawless new landscaping, crisp white paint against hunter green shutters. Maps and plans would be prepared later. *If* an order was placed.

Stopping around the corner, he closed his eyes to commit the scene to memory. Every detail of the house was clear in his mind, and he would bet the second-story front windows were the children's rooms. Evan opened his eyes at the sound of Tony's voice.

"Did you see it on the mailbox? Nelson. Their names are George and Mary Nelson."

"I love it when they make it easy," Evan laughed. "So easy."

Six hours later, a taxi stopped outside the sleek Manhattan office of Paradise Promotions. Evan quickly paid the driver, unlocked the office doors, and dropped his luggage inside. He immediately locked the door again, even though it was well past time to open. After traveling all night, he was in no mood to handle questions from ignorant tourists.

He glanced around. Everything looked normal. Waving stripes of lavender neon bordered the slate gray marble of the countertop. Scattered about the room were meticulous displays of brochures and pamphlets. Vacuum trails in the plush emerald carpet and the sparkle of the crystal tabletops were the only evidence that the cleaning crew had come and gone.

Walking to the back of the suite, Evan unlocked the door to a darkroom by keying in the disarming sequence on the keypad. Smiling, he thought of the surprise unauthorized visitors would receive if they were stupid enough to try to enter this room. Initially, he considered the level of security ridiculous, but after so many years he was used to the extreme precautionary measures. In fact, he wouldn't have it any other way.

Evan's movements could easily have been choreographed. His motions were precise yet graceful. Experience flowed from his fingertips, reflecting his personal need for perfection in every act. In only a few minutes, the negatives were processed and seventy-two close-up pictures of two rosy-cheeked, happy babies hung drying. He washed his hands thoroughly, started to leave, then stopped. Evan was drawn to one particular picture of the baby boy. Against the soft Georgian landscape he appeared to be smiling at a wispy cloud above, dreaming of a better life.

In the darkness of the room Evan greedily caressed the child's cheek. There was no doubt about it. The boy would sell quickly. A second trip to Savannah would be on his agenda soon. He could bank on it.

Chapter 1

"I heard you moved to Oklahoma City, but I didn't actually believe it. What happened to working for the good of all mankind, saving the poor souls of Little Rock?"

Nick Hunter broke into laughter as he recognized his childhood friend Jim. "All mankind repossessed my car. Then they threatened to kick me out of my apartment. Court costs were eating me alive, and you know as well as I do most of the clients I represented couldn't afford to pay."

Running his hand across the top of his elegant mahogany desk, Nick glanced around. It was still hard for him to believe he actually had a corner office on the top floor of one of Oklahoma City's finest buildings. Thick burgundy carpet, flame-stitched wingback chairs, and original Indian oil paintings were a far cry from the hole in the wall he'd worked out of just a few weeks ago. Sighing, he added, "Jim, I was damn lucky a firm as profitable as Kellars and Kellars would even give me the time of day, much less offer me a chance to work into a partnership."

"Top of your class probably didn't hurt your chances . . ."

Nick heard the hesitation, felt the tension in his

friend even though they were hundreds of miles apart. "Everything okay, Jim?" he asked.

"I don't suppose you're allowed to do favors for old buddies? Freebie, of course. Unfortunately, some of us are still wallowing in it, so to speak."

Rolling the chair back, Nick stood and walked to the edge of the floor-to-ceiling window. "Depends on what you need. I had to sign the standard agreement when I came to work here. I'm not allowed to represent any cases, or even give legal advice, to non-clients without approval of the senior partner, Will Kellars."

"If that's the guy in those TV commercials, you've certainly got your hands full. They've got style, but when you lick the chocolate coating off, the stench is still there."

"I thought you wanted a favor," Nick grumbled as he plopped back into his chair and spun around.

"I do."

Nick knew asking for anything wasn't easy for Jim. He was the kind of guy who preferred to keep his problems to himself. When Jim finally spoke, his voice was lower. "First, I need your promise. Peg and I haven't talked to anyone about this, not even our parents."

"Jim, anything you tell me will be strictly confidential. You have my word."

With a sigh, Jim began: "The last five years have been hell. Peg and I've seen every infertility specialist within a thousand miles, gone through hundreds of tests, Peg's had two surgeries. We've burned up every cent we'd ever saved and then some, trying in vitro fertilization plus every new procedure you can imagine. Nothing's worked."

Nick groaned. "I'm really sorry, Jim. I know how much the two of you want children. Peg would make a great mother."

"Which is where you come in . . ."

"Oh, no. You're not gonna try to rook me into any kinky donor-fatherhood-by-test-tube deal, are you?"

"Hell, no! You think I want my kid running around looking like Stretch Armstrong? I can just picture the poor child. Seven feet tall with a mane of blond hair and that lady-killer smile of yours. Don't worry, your gene pool is safe. We need *legal* help."

Nick was relieved as he said, "I'm only six foot six, not exactly considered a giant these days. What kind of help do you need?"

"Peg's found a woman who says she'll have our baby for us. We have seven embryos still frozen at the Midwestern Fertility Center, but the doctors won't implant into another person, much less an unrelated person. Too many legal hassles, they say."

"I can imagine."

"That's what we need you for. First, to get the center's attention. Those are *our* frozen babies, not theirs, and we should be able to control their destiny. Second, to handle the paperwork on the surrogate. We don't want any complications down the road, and we know you're the best. You've got a good heart and the ability to cut through the bullshit."

"Damn, Jim, when you ask for a favor, you

don't pull any punches, do you?" He swallowed hard, wanting to help his friend. Yet he hated the thought of asking Will Kellars to take on a pro bono case. Actually, he hated the thought of asking Will Kellars for anything at all.

Angela Anderson crouched on the floor of her office at Kellars & Kellars, her head almost touching the underside of her desk. As usual, she wished she had on jeans and tennis shoes instead of a silk suit. It was virtually impossible for her to work in the cramped space without hiking her skirt to an indecent level.

In less than five minutes Angela removed the computer's metal plate and spread various parts neatly across the floor of her office. After installing the latest system upgrade, she admired her handiwork, then acted with practiced precision to reassemble the machine.

Just as she was tightening the last screw, a deep voice muttered from her doorway, "Damn! She's *never* here!"

Bolting upright, Angela's head thudded painfully against her desk. She gently massaged the new bump as she leaned back and called, "Who's there and what the hell do you want?"

Crawling out from under her desk, Angela twisted until she could see the incredibly tall, handsome man in her doorway.

Sheepishly he said, "Sorry about that. Are you okay?"

It took a second to catch her breath. She cleared her throat and muttered, "Luckily, I have a very hard head." Pointing under the table, she explained, "I was adding a new chip that'll double my machine's processing speed."

Following the man's admiring gaze, she glanced down. With tingling cheeks Angela self-consciously tugged the short, tight silk of her black suit, coaxing the skirt back down her thighs. Catching a wisp of hair, she realized her French knot was sagging at the nape of her neck. With a quick shake, her shoulder-length auburn waves were free. "I'm usually not such a mess, really . . ."

Nick extended his hand as he said, "I shouldn't have barged in. By the way, I'm Nick Hunter. I've been working here for a couple of weeks now. I was beginning to think Angela Anderson was a figment of everyone's imagination."

"Believe me, even though I've been gone, I've heard all about *you*, too." Angela's official title was director of public relations. A fancy name for someone in charge of writing advertising copy and handling press releases for the law firm as well as its larger clients. Officially, an outside consulting firm, CompuCorp, was in charge of all computer operations, but everyone in the office knew Angela was the fastest person to troubleshoot problems. "I was attending an advanced management course, Public Relations in Mass Communications, in St. Paul," she added.

Raising his eyebrows, Nick said, "Sounds intriguing."

Angela cocked her head and eyed him, trying to decide if he had a sense of humor or not. Smiling, she said, "You really should get out more if you actually believe that." She rubbed the growing bump on her head. When she looked up at him, a spark in his blue eyes seemed to reflect genuine concern. Moving closer, she tilted her face as though she were looking at the noon sun. "Don't even think it," she warned.

Smiling, he gazed at the top of her head as he innocently asked, "Think what?"

She replied, "You were wondering why they let kids work here, or who I'm kidding wearing high heels. . . . Believe me, I've heard every vertically challenged joke there is."

"And I've heard them all on the other extreme." Patting the top of her head, he asked, "Are you sure you're okay?"

"Believe me, it would take more than a little blow to the head to keep me down. Let me guess. You need an urgent press release. Which congressman got hauled in for DUI this time? Or did some socialite break a fingernail?"

He laughed. "Nothing that easy. My computer's gone crazy. Can you help me?"

"I'll try." She moved closer to him and whispered, "Unofficially, of course. I believe proper procedure is to contact CompuCorp, the highest-priced firm in the city."

As she walked beside him toward his office, she noticed the confidence in Nick's quick stride. For once the rumors she had heard had been true. He actually was young, good-looking, and sensitive. Approaching his office, they could hear a steady beep. "Is that your machine?" Angela asked, slightly amazed.

Nick meekly answered, "Unfortunately. I must have hit the wrong key. I ended up on the WKE screen."

Turning to him, she asked, "The *what*?"

"The WKE screen. That's what it said. I didn't know what it was, but it looked interesting. So I sort of . . ."

Grinning, she asked, "Tried to get in it?"

Nick sheepishly nodded his head.

As they entered his office, Angela suddenly stopped.

"What's wrong?" Nick asked.

Hesitating, Angela stammered for a second, then said, "Nothing. Really."

"I know. It's a little overbearing, isn't it?"

Staring at the room, she said, "I . . . I just wasn't expecting you to be in Rick's old office. It just threw me off for a second, that's all."

With raised eyebrows he asked, "Rick? As in Rick Kellars?"

She nodded. "Kellars must really like you. No one has had this office since his son died." Walking to the far wall, she admired a beautiful oil painting of an Oklahoma field ablaze with Indian paintbrush.

Glaring at his computer, Nick asked, "Could you please make this thing be quiet?"

Angela looked at the ominous message: ACCESS DENIED—PASSWORD INVESTIGATION UNDERWAY. Smiling, she said, "No problem."

"Really?" he asked with a touch of awe.

Sliding into his chair, she reached over and gently pushed the Power button on the base processing unit, turning the machine off. The electronic whine spiraled down to silence as the screen faded to black. The beeping stopped. Everything stopped. She waited about ten seconds before pushing the Power button again. The setup program whirled through its system checks before Nick's normal sign-on screen appeared. With a flourish worthy of a magician's assistant, Angela exclaimed, "Ta-da!"

Nick's brows furrowed in mock disgust as he mumbled, "I could've done that myself."

"And next time you will. Let's see if we can re-create the problem. What were you trying?"

"I wanted to check for any outstanding or recent cases the firm has handled involving adoptions or the use of surrogate mothers."

"So you went from the Main Office Shell to Caseload Directory?"

"That's what I did, or rather, it's what I was trying to do."

Expertly she typed the entries needed. Together they scanned the listings, finding nothing in either area. Angela stood and looked curiously at Nick. "You know, considering the Kellars' family history, I doubt if the firm handles any cases in those areas."

"I don't suppose you'd care to expand?"

She lowered her voice, saying, "Not here."

Nick glanced at his watch and said, "I think I owe you lunch. Why don't I meet you at the elevators in five minutes?"

Angela hesitated for a few seconds, then called over her shoulder as she walked away. "Sounds great."

"Wait!"

Stopping in the doorway, she twirled back around.

Pausing, he shook his head and said, "Never mind . . ."

"Afraid we'll look ridiculous together?"

Shaking his head, Nick answered, "Of course not. I was just surprised to finally be having a business lunch with someone from the firm. Since I came to work here, the other lawyers have been rather distant, like I'm the carrier of some deadly disease."

Angela laughed, but was too embarrassed to tell him the reason why people were avoiding him. Instead she said, "It probably has more to do with this office than anything else. Mr. Kellars wouldn't have put you here if he didn't have some serious long-term plans for you. The others are just jealous." And, after having met him, she realized it was with good cause. Nick appeared to be brighter, wittier, and more persuasive than all of them rolled together, even if he was a little different.

Rolling his eyes, Nick muttered, "Great. Should I be flattered or worried?"

Turning to leave, Angela smiled and said, "Probably a little of both."

Nick waited patiently in the posh foyer of the twenty-second floor, admiring the large brass letters acclaiming KELLARS & KELLARS over the hand-carved mahogany doors. While he waited, he studied the huge portrait hanging inside the reception area. It was an impressive painting, depicting a distinguished Will Kellars seated at his desk with his son, Rick, standing by his side. Rick's hand rested confidently on his father's shoulder, as if they were eternally linked. Although they looked nothing alike, both men had the same insolent aura.

Turning around, he ambled across the hall. Equally impressive was the entry to the other office on the floor, a travel agency called Pampered in Paradise. Glancing through a glass panel on the side of one door, he was struck by the collection of breathtaking photographs displayed within. Crystal blue waters licked white sand beaches. Coral canyons exploded with colorful life beyond imagination.

Nick was immersed in daydreams of paradise when a ding, announcing the impending arrival of an elevator, forced him to focus his attention back on reality. As if on cue, the elevator door slid open the moment Angela arrived.

"I'm curious about the Kellars family—" Nick stopped abruptly as Angela shook her head and held one finger to her lips.

When they emerged into the sunlight, she finally explained, "Never, ever say anything inside that building that you wouldn't say directly to Will Kellars' face. Never."

Nick stared at her as they briskly descended the steps in front of the building. Shrugging, he said, "Okay. Where to?"

"How about spaghetti?"

"Love it."

"I usually walk. It's only a few blocks to Bricktown, an old industrial area that's been renovated."

Smiling wryly, he gently touched her arm as he said, "I'll try my best to keep up with you."

Angela showed Nick the shortcuts through

downtown Oklahoma City, pointing out various landmarks along the way. When they reached an old brick building, he eyed her suspiciously.

"Trust me," she said.

The overwhelming aroma of Italian spices as they entered the restaurant was a welcome pleasure. After her eyes adjusted, Angela led Nick to a secluded booth, away from the chatter pouring from the kitchen.

Halfway through his heaping plate of meatballs, Nick asked, "Why the cloak-and-dagger routine in the elevator?"

"The place is bugged," Angela stated flatly.

"So call an exterminator," he joked, although she had piqued his curiosity.

"Very funny. I'm serious. I'm surprised he didn't tell you when you interviewed. Mr. Kellars is very open about the level of security he maintains. All phone calls are recorded. He gets computer printouts of outgoing telephone numbers and how long each call lasted. Our floor is the only one in the building that uses an independent, bonded cleaning crew. You saw what happened when you tried to enter that program. Even though you never accessed anything, your attempt was reported within minutes. I guarantee it."

"You've got to be kidding."

Angela merely shook her head and held his incredulous stare.

"But what could he possibly be so worried about? I've never heard of espionage in a law firm," Nick asked.

"Information leaks. He always wants the element of surprise. Of course, that's just my opinion. Some people think his motives are less than pure."

Shrugging, he said, "I have to admit, I thought long and hard before accepting this job. My gut feeling said run, but everyone I asked said Kellars and Kellars was reputable, with a growing client base. Believe me, finding a law firm these days without a black cloud hanging over its head is almost impossible. How long have you been there?"

"Six years. It was crazy, really. I was working at the *Daily Oklahoman* in advertising when *he* called *me*. He said he'd heard I was bright and that he needed an in-house person to make sure all the press-related concerns of the firm were handled appropriately. When he doubled my salary and threw in four weeks paid vacation a year, I'd have been crazy to turn him down."

His eyes locked on hers. "Ever wish you had?"

Angela's gaze darted about the room. She couldn't remember the last time she had confided in anyone, much less a co-worker. Yet she sensed Nick was different. Surprising even herself, she openly replied, "Sometimes. It's nerve-wracking work. Kellars demands perfection. One hundred percent performance at all times. I have nightmares about forgetting to put a blank tape in my recorder before a meeting."

Nick abruptly stopped eating. "You record meetings?"

Out of habit, she glanced over her shoulder before answering. "It's a plan his secretary and I devised." Angela pulled a slim micro-recorder out of the pocket of her suit jacket and looked at Nick as though she was trusting him with her most valuable secret. "Of course, Mr. Kellars doesn't know. We found out a long time ago that when he gives orders, he expects them to be followed *precisely*. This way we don't have to worry about remembering every detail." She removed a tiny headset from her other pocket. "When we're safely back at our desks, we listen with earphones so no one knows."

Nick hesitated, carefully weighing the wisdom of Angela's little secret. Finally he said, "Very clever. I may have to acquire one of those myself."

Her voice was so quiet he could barely hear her as she replied. "Just promise you'll be careful. We never take them out of our pockets. We change tapes in the ladies' room. They go home with us every night. It seemed like a game at first, but it's become a key element to survival."

"I don't know about the ladies' room part, but the rest I can handle." Leaning forward, he whispered, "Aren't you taking all this a little too seriously? It's only a job."

She shrugged. "I guess it would appear odd to you. Even after all these years it still seems pretty bizarre to me. Working at K and K is just different. The corporate games are subtle but easy to recognize. People either accept them or go elsewhere. Besides, I'm spoiled. I like being able to pay for my mother to stay at Shadybrook. She has Alzheimer's and needs special care. It's expensive, but worth every penny."

"Ever feel like you're in the wrong job? Don't take this wrong, but you seem like you're overqualified to just write press releases."

Angela laughed as she explained. "I double-majored in marketing and computer science. When I got out of college, I had the typical grand illusions most new graduates have of starting my own business. I thought I could work a few years at the newspaper, save my money, then start a computer store. Not like the hardware stores you see everywhere, or those places that sell IBM's and Apple's next to the washers and dryers. I dreamed of a place where average people could come in, and for a reasonable price they could get a computer plus actually learn how to use it in their own home. Things have changed since then. Now I'd teach people how to surf the Net, use a fax-modem to order pizzas, the fun stuff."

Nick was enjoying the food, nodding as he listened.

With a mischievous grin she continued, "I wanted to make *anyone* feel at home on a computer, even giants with wayward fingers. . . . Seriously, I thought a degree in marketing would help me get my dream off the ground."

"Then your mother got sick?"

Staring at her food, she softly answered, "Yep. And Will Kellars made me an offer I couldn't refuse, so to speak. Sooner or later I guess we all have to do a reality check. My job at K and K may be boring, but it's stable and pays well." Her demeanor suddenly stiffened, her voice more guarded as she added, "You have to understand that Kellars is a very generous boss in many ways."

Clearing his throat, Nick asked, "Does the defense rest?"

Angela cocked her head, countering his quip with a deep sigh. "Nick, I'm just trying to give you the benefit of years of experience. It's a well-known fact that at K and K, loyalty only counts if it's forever."

"Are you trying to scare me?"

"Of course not." She pushed her hair back and added, "I'm making sure you know the ground rules. K and K is like any other company. If you do three things, you'll be fine."

"I'm almost afraid to ask. What three things?"

"Work hard. Mind your own business. Kiss Kellars' ass every chance you get."

"I've never been good at bootlicking," he scoffed.

She smiled and thought how sexy he looked with a sparkle of rebellion in his eyes. Leaning across the table, she lightly touched his hand. "So learn. Do what the old guy asks. After all, that's why you were hired, right?"

"Actually, I thought it was for my legal expertise."

"I'm sure it was, within the realm of Kellars' opinions. The other lawyers say he dictates court strategies and defense tactics like everything else in the office—which does have certain benefits."

"Such as?"

"If you do what he says and you lose the case, he won't hold you personally responsible."

Nick pushed his empty plate away, settling back against the hard wood of the bench. It was several seconds before he said, "A friend of mine called this morning to ask me to do some legal work.

Are you telling me Kellars already knows about our conversation since my office is bugged?"

"No. All I know is that he says our conversations are taped to protect the firm from being sued. Maybe he just tells people that so they'll be on their best behavior. If tapes really are made, I have no idea if anyone ever listens to them. Maybe they check them only when there's concern about a pending lawsuit. They may archive the tapes or record over them the next day. My bet is they don't exist. Only Kellars knows."

"But why go to such extremes?"

"Where were you four years ago?" Angela asked.

"Finishing up law school. Probably studying for the bar."

"Didn't you ever read newspapers or watch any television? You'd have had to be dead to miss the national media frenzy on Rick Kellars."

"I worked two jobs and carried eighteen to twenty credit hours a semester. The instructions on a package of No Doze were about the only thing I ever read that didn't directly relate to law school."

"Rick Kellars was the managing partner."

"I've seen the portrait in the entry. I always assumed it was his late son."

"That's right. But what you apparently don't know is that Rick was his *adopted* son, and that he was constantly in trouble. According to the rumor mill, Kellars started recording everything back then, to make sure Rick stayed in line. After his son was murdered, Kellars almost lost it. He drank constantly for almost two months before he snapped out of his depression. I've never seen a man more devastated. I'm sure that's why the firm doesn't handle adoption or surrogate-mother cases."

Nick started to speak, but Angela stopped him by sliding out of the booth. "I understand your curiosity, but it's a long story"—she glanced at her watch—"which will have to wait. I'm meeting Kellars in less than fifteen minutes, and I don't want to be late."

In Chicago, Tony Montegra threw his duffel bag on the foot of the bed, causing the bulge under the covers to moan and roll over. His gun was in one hand, pointed directly at the top of the groaning lump. For a second Tony considered firing first and asking questions later. As he imagined blood splattering across the designer goose down comforter that had set him back over five hundred bucks, he decided to make the bastard get out of his bed.

Calmly, coldly, Tony said, "Whoever the hell you are, you'd better crawl outta there with your hands in the air, or your brain is gonna have an out-of-body experience."

First one hand crept out, then another. An unruly mop of black hair emerged atop a handsome young face grinning from ear to ear. "Nice way to greet your baby brother, Tony."

Easing the gun to his side, Tony finally breathed again. "How'd you get to Chicago? And how the hell'd you get in here?"

Mocking him, his brother snapped, "I've

learned a few things. . . . Where'd you get the money to live like this?"

Staring back, Tony's teeth clamped down as he studied the man before him. When he'd left Los Angeles, his brother was just a kid, but now he was almost twenty years old. "Answer my questions first, Roberto. Does Mama know where you are?"

"Hell, no." He laughed, oblivious to the gun dangling at his brother's side. "She's been on my ass for months. I couldn't handle it anymore. I hopped on a bus and came to live with my generous big brother." He rolled out of bed, revealing his muscular six-foot frame. Wearing faded Jockey shorts and socks riddled with holes, he gestured with his arms as he added, "I'd have shown up years ago if I'd known you won the friggin' lottery. And to think, Mama was sure you were sending us every spare penny you had."

Memories of his mother and brothers were overwhelming Tony as he mumbled, "You can't stay here, Rob. Go home. I'll even pay for your airline ticket."

Roberto was a young image of Tony, and obviously practiced in playing for sympathy. With pleading eyes he asked, "Give me a couple of weeks, will you, Tony? It won't kill you to let me hang here for a while. I'm even willing to find some school. You know, one of those on TV where they teach you a trade. I could be driving trucks or welding in no time. I promise, I'll stay out of your way. You'll hardly even know I'm here."

Tony hesitated, his face hard. Finally he said, "If you stay here, you'll go by my rules." He watched his brother's face light up, clearly proud to have won the initial battle. "First, no one knows you're here. You come and go like the wind, unseen. Understand?"

Grinning from ear to ear, he nodded and answered, "Invisible wind. Got it."

Waggling a finger like a schoolteacher, Tony said, "Second, you never use the phone. Never answer it. Never make calls from it."

"Right. No phones."

"Last. You keep your ass out of trouble. The last thing I need is a bunch of cops snooping around here."

"No cops. Clean ass. Shit, I should've come here years ago." Eyeing Tony speculatively, he asked, "I don't suppose you'd consider cutting me into whatever deal you've got going?"

Tony merely cocked his head sideways and stared at his brother. He grabbed his duffel bag and headed toward the bathroom, grumbling, "I work alone. Always have. Always will. Don't ask again."

FBI agent Lesley Jaggers had spent a sleepless night at headquarters, searching the same computer records and files she had read a hundred times before, praying she would finally find something, anything she might have missed. If the pattern continued in the long string of baby-snatching cases, the "Serial Snatcher" was sure to strike soon. The thought turned her stomach, making her wonder why she had chosen what was surely the worst profession on the face of the earth.

Harsh fluorescent lights reflected her own

image in the small screen before her. Pushing a wisp of long sandy hair away from her eyes, she tried in vain to work it back into the loose braid that hung to the middle of her back. Not wanting to see her drawn and haggard image for another second, Lesley stood and stretched her lean five-foot-nine frame, then walked across the hall to stare at the huge map on the wall of her boss's office. Numbered flags marked every city where a snatching had occurred. Beside each flag was the date of the kidnapping.

So far no city had been hit twice, no ransom notes ever sent. They were always expert break-ins—scarcely any evidence and never a witness to be found. According to the Bureau's statisticians the pattern of occurrences were random in location, yet it was impossible to ignore the striking similarities. Each time a child had virtually vanished into thin air.

Lesley walked slowly back to her desk, trying to control the fury that raged deep within her soul. If it were only directed at the bastards who were responsible, she might have been able to shrug it off, to go home and rest like everyone else on the task force. But this case had become her own living nightmare, and the anger and repulsion she felt were directed inward. She was a highly trained FBI agent, one of the people responsible for stopping such inhumanly cruel acts. She had done every single thing by the book, scrutinized every shred of evidence, yet they still had no leads.

With a sigh Lesley stared at the calendar pinned

to the gray wall of her cubicle. In a matter of days another family would be torn apart. She wasn't sure she could bear the deadly silence that consumed a home with an empty crib again.

Chapter 2

At nine o'clock the next morning, Nick paced anxiously in the reception area outside Will Kellars' office. Kellars' secretary, an attractive older woman named Marilyn Blake, seemed to be doing her best to ignore him. He guessed she was transcribing a letter from the tiny earphones nestled in her ears as she lightly tapped on her computer's keyboard.

After what seemed like an eternity, Marilyn glanced his way with a smile and said, "You can go in now, Mr. Hunter."

Nick grabbed his notes and scooted past her desk, saying, "Thanks." When he opened the ornate double doors, he hesitated, still in awe of the executive suite. He was just as impressed this time as he had been when he interviewed with the firm a few months ago. Besides the sheer size of the room, the furniture and antique books in Will Kellars' office were worth a small fortune. Sunlight poured in the wall of windows, making every treasure sparkle. On the opposite side of the room was a massive wall of bookcases, the center of which framed a mirror lit by spotlights.

Trying to stay focused, Nick cleared his throat and looked at his new boss. "I won't take much of your time, Mr. Kellars. I appreciate you fitting me into your busy schedule this morning." Nick paced in front of the imposing desk, as intimidated as he had ever been by anyone. Lying awake most of last night, he had worried over every detail of this meeting. What to say, what not to say. Cancel, or show up and sweat. Was an old friendship really worth the risk?

"Sit down. You're making me nervous." Will Kellars sounded old and tired, but his eyes contradicted his voice. They were dark and hard yet sharp. Age had not dulled his ability to dominate with a single confident glance.

Although Kellars wasn't a large man, through his custom suit Nick could see his shoulders and arms were still muscular. In fact, had it not been for his expensive clothing, he could easily have passed for any working-class man. His thick head of wavy gray hair and the weathered lines of his face added an edge of hard-nosed experience to his authoritative demeanor.

Turning away from the comfortable wing-back chairs directly in front of Will Kellars, Nick sat in one of the solid oak chairs by the small conference table. He needed distance, not only from Kellars' stare, but from his own nerves. "I know you're wondering why I asked to see you."

"Not really. Every new lawyer we hire goes through this. Establishing territory. Laying down ground rules, like wild animals. If you're like everyone else, you either want to handle something more difficult, take on a challenging pro bono case, or renegotiate some fine point in your employment contract. Am I right?"

Nick was caught off guard. Even though he was slightly embarrassed by the predictability of his request, he still reacted swiftly. "Yes, sir. You scored a direct hit with point number two." He pushed down the urge to ask if eavesdropping on his phone conversations had anything to do with narrowing the lineup of possible motives.

"Ah, yes. After all, you do have a history of siding with the underdog. I must warn you, though. I'm here to make money, not to hand out talent for free. And that's what I consider you to be. Talent. Raw talent."

"Thank you, sir. There may be a way for the firm to profit indirectly from the case I'd like to handle. It could provide a substantial amount of publicity."

"And what if you lose? What will counterbalance the negative publicity?"

"I won't lose."

Kellars paused as a smile crept over his face. "Good. Self-confidence is a necessity around here. Let's hear your opening argument." Will clasped his hands behind his head, leaned back, rested his shoes on the corner of his desk, then closed his eyes.

Nerves tingled in his feet as Nick stood up. At least he didn't have to battle Kellars eye to eye. He wiped his palms on his slacks, took a deep breath, and began: "Although the surrogate-motherhood question has been addressed by the courts, to my knowledge the ownership of human embryos has not been decided. Cryopreservation techniques can now maintain a viable human being indefinitely. Sooner or later the courts will have to decide who has jurisdiction over that life."

Will Kellars remained still, but slightly opened one eye.

As Nick took another deep breath, he was certain he had made a good first impression. Trying to keep his momentum high, he continued, "At issue in this case is the control of human life in its most basic form. An embryo. Frozen and waiting for a womb to nurture it. To give birth to it. My clients produced this miracle. Their own eggs and sperm created this potential life. Yet they are being denied the right to control its destiny. Yes, without the medical facilities and brilliant doctors at Midwestern Fertility Center, this miracle could not have happened. This life would not be in suspended animation. But the point is, it did happen."

Nick paused for emphasis, waiting as if before a jury, letting every word sink in before he continued. "The center was created to help people exactly like Jim and Peg Downfield. To give them the chance to have a child of their own to love. Although the doctors have tried repeatedly, Peg and Jim have failed to produce a child."

Nick eyed Kellars, but could see no sign of how the man felt. "They have one last chance. A generous woman has offered to carry this miracle in her womb for them. To sustain its life for nine months. To hand a beautiful child into its parents' loving arms. Emotionally, biologically, in every way possible, the child will be theirs. It will merely have spent its first few months being nurtured in a different womb.

"But the management of the Midwestern Fertility Center refuses to allow this last chance for the miracle of life to happen. Under the terms of a contract Jim and Peg signed prior to the use of Midwestern's medical facilities, management has the right to control the implantation of fertilized embryos. Implantation in anyone other than Peg is forbidden.

"Unfortunately, Jim and Peg are not blessed with the ability to foresee the future. At the time they signed the contract in question, they had every right to believe they would be one of the many couples to successfully conceive and give birth to a baby. To believe otherwise would have left them without hope.

"Hope is all they're asking for now. Hope, and a chance to give life to one of their waiting babies." *And I hope I didn't just talk myself right into typing up my own resignation . . .*

Will Kellars sat up, watching Nick and waiting. Neither spoke for several minutes. Nick continued to pace slowly back and forth, as he had done during his entire speech. Part of him was relieved the worst was over, while the other part continued to worry.

Finally Kellars muttered, "Midwestern Fertility Center is in Arkansas, Nick."

"Yes, sir," Nick answered slowly, waiting for the kick he was sure was coming.

"In case you haven't noticed, son, you're not practicing in Arkansas anymore. Last time I checked, you were in Oklahoma."

"But I'm still licensed in Arkansas," Nick answered, relieved that Kellars at least had listened to his pitch.

Another long silence. "You expect national coverage of this case?"

"Not initially. The first few stages of publicity will probably be confined to Little Rock."

"Which will not benefit this firm."

"True. But in the long run—"

Will stood up, straightening his jacket as he butted in. ". . . they will make your life a living hell. Trying a case from out of state is practically impossible. Not to mention expensive. Very expensive. Don't get me wrong. I think you'd win. No jury in the world would turn down a heartbreaker case like this based on some stupid piece of paper called a contract. Juries like to sink their teeth into an issue, not interpret the meaning of some pile of legal mumbo-jumbo."

Nick was pleased. Even though he had lost the battle, he had not come away bleeding. "So you want me to pass on representing my friends?"

Kellars began fiddling with a file on his desk. It was obvious their conversation was over as he said, "Afraid so. Too much risk for too little benefit."

"Would you mind if I referred the case to a friend from law school? I'd like to offer to confer with him whenever he needs help."

"Confer all you want on your own time. Just don't take the case yourself. Emotional involvement in any case is trouble, and you're obviously too close to this one. I'm paying for talent, not trouble."

Nick felt the hair on the back of his neck tingle,

but managed to keep his voice steady as he said, "I appreciate your point of view."

"I have to admit, that was one hell of a speech you just gave. I've really been impressed with the work you've done since you joined us."

Relieved, Nick nodded and replied, "Thank you."

"I've been trying to decide who to put on our most important client. Rumor has it he'll be needing a lot of our assistance in the near future. You've just convinced me you're the man to handle it."

"Which client would that be?"

"Senator Holt," Kellars snapped.

Trying to control any outward appearance that could be perceived as objection, Nick asked, "Would it be too forward to ask why he's going to need so much legal assistance?"

Kellars walked around the side of his desk, leading Nick to the door. "Let's just say he's like a raccoon being chased by a bunch of hound dogs. It's only a matter of time before they get him treed."

Stopping just before the door, Nick asked, "Does this have anything to do with the rumors I've heard about his problems with the attorney general, Susan Stover?"

Kellars grinned and nodded. "She's calling a press conference just after lunch today to announce her office is beginning to conduct a formal investigation into Senator Holt's personal and campaign finances."

Nick wondered how Kellars could already

know about the upcoming press conference, but only asked, "Have you talked to the senator yet?"

"I wouldn't exactly call it talking. I merely listened while he blew off steam. His wife, Alice, was even more agitated than he was."

"Has the attorney general specified any particular reasons for the investigation?"

"Just a lot of gibberish about his rather extravagant lifestyle, and the apparent lack of accounting control exercised during his campaign. Sounds like the senator made an enemy of someone on his staff, but it's hard to tell. Stover could be blowing smoke. It's not exactly a secret how much they dislike each other."

Shaking his head, Nick said, "She wouldn't have anything to gain from making false accusations."

"On the contrary, she'd get lots of free publicity. She and the senator are on opposite sides of almost every fence, both politically and personally. This way she smears his name even if he hasn't done a thing wrong. For some reason people remember bad publicity long after the issue has faded. Come election time, there will still be that seed of doubt she planted, even if she never proves a damned thing."

Stepping out the door, Nick shook his hand. "Thank you for the opportunity. I'll do the best I can."

"You'd better do better than that, son, or Stover will eat you for lunch and I'll be dessert."

Annissa Jamison walked from her office into the reception room of Pampered in Paradise, searching for the box of brochures scheduled to be delivered. She knew the door chimes would have alerted her if anyone entered the office, but nevertheless, raw nerves demanded she check again. The glass reflected her own image, and she ran her hands down the new dress she wore, admiring the luxurious texture of the crimson fabric.

She studied her reflection for several seconds, touching the wrinkles that creased the smooth sable skin around her catlike eyes. People always described her as exotic. Her Jamaican heritage had given her the grace and beauty of a black panther. Even after so many years away from her homeland, words still rushed from deep within, her native accent refusing to be totally lost. Concern furrowed her brow. Age was taking its toll. Though she was still slim, strength was rapidly leaving her limbs. She wished she could wash away the years as easily as she rinsed away the gray that invaded her ultra-short black hair.

The office doors flew open just as she was turning to wait inside her office. "Package for Pampered in Paradise," the young delivery man called cheerfully as he placed the oversized carton on the desk and bolted back out the door.

Annissa stared at the box. Knowing she shouldn't risk straining her back again didn't make moving the heavy carton any easier. Taking a deep breath, she heaved it to her chest. Balancing on high heels, she felt the strain on her ankles, on her back, as she carried the package into her office and dropped it onto the conference table.

A bookshelf lined the far wall, its center a huge mirror lit by tiny spotlights. Staring at it for several seconds, she wondered whether she had the strength to carry the package any farther. At any time he could be watching, and opening the box here would be dangerous. Reaching into her purse, she pushed the button on the black box that dangled from her key chain. The paneled wall beside the bookcase popped open, revealing a hidden office behind hers. She walked inside. The hum of computers, scanners, and high-tech color copy machines filled the room. One-way mirrors on each end showed she had nothing to worry about. His office was empty.

Going back into her own office, she sliced open the box with her brass letter opener. Inside were thousands of brochures bringing the islands of the Caribbean to life, as well as tourism books on the different countries. After unpacking several layers, she found it—an elegant book on Jamaica. Carrying it into the hidden office, she slid the paneling closed behind her.

As she flipped through the book, the scenes of tropical paradise quickly passed, leaving only page after page of beautiful blond-haired babies whose eyes matched the blue of the ocean she had left behind so long ago. Touching the portrait of a little boy, she was amazed at the superb work Evan and Tony had done once again.

A long time ago part of her soul had been sickened each time a baby's image crossed her desk. But over time she had learned to view the part she played as a job, a way to make money. The children weren't real to her. They were pieces of paper, images captured on film, files to be tracked and maintained—just work.

Staring at the glossy picture, she wondered what had become of all the children they had handled. Her stomach twisted as she thought of her brother, Jax, and how so many years ago he had manipulated the entire family into this despicable scheme. *What's the sly devil look like now?* she thought. *Has time cruelly etched the years into him? Does my sister still wait on the manipulative little bastard as though he's a king like she did when we were children?*

"Deep in thought?" Will asked.

Annissa bolted upright. His voice broke her concentration, sending the book crashing to the floor. "Will . . . I didn't hear you come in."

Resting his hands on her shoulders, he said, "That's rather obvious. What are you doing?"

Stooping to pick up the book, out of habit Annissa glanced toward his office, then to hers, to be certain the secret panels were both closed. Standing, she answered, "Looking over the latest shipment from Paradise Promotions." Turning away from him, she set the book down and flipped to a picture of the boy. "As you can see, they've done excellent work."

Kellars barely noticed the child. Instead, he wrapped his arms seductively around Annissa. She tensed when she felt his teeth on the back of her neck, then began to relax against him. Feeling his hand move toward her breast, she said, " 'Tis a new dress, be gentler this time."

Evan had never been to Lincoln, Nebraska, before, so it took him a little longer than he had anticipated to find the address. When he finally

DEADLY SILENCE

located the house on Woodscrest, he quickly turned into the drive and parked.

Rushing to the front door, he rang the bell and took a deep breath. Brushing and straightening his charcoal gray suit, he checked his reflection in the sparkling glass. His posture was perfect. Broad shoulders, head held high. The short, straight dark wig fit precisely, as did the green-tinted contacts. Down to his flawless manicure he matched the part perfectly.

A woman opened the impressive door, her nervousness apparent from the way she clung to her husband's side. Both were in their early forties, impeccably dressed, obviously affluent.

He held out his hand and greeted them in a carefully practiced Midwestern accent. "You must be Dee and Larry Garvey. I'm Wallace Webster with the PLACE Foundation. I must apologize for being late. I had a little trouble finding your beautiful home." They both vigorously returned his handshake, then led him inside the formal living room.

As Evan listened to them ramble, he mentally calculated the value of the antiques and furniture. In less than a minute, he was convinced he could risk giving them the presentation. "If it's all right with the two of you, I'd like to begin by sharing some background on our organization. PLACE was founded over twenty years ago." He handed each of them a large full-color brochure. "As you can see, our name stands for Promoting Loving Adoptions and Creative Education, which is exactly what we do. We provide a critical service for confused or misguided teenagers in need of help.

"As I'm sure you know, teen birth rates are skyrocketing, and the adoption process can lead to an information and organizational nightmare. It can be brutal for both the scared young mother as well as the couple seeking the child. PLACE was designed to circumvent many of the typical problems. Our teenage mothers know their baby will go to a loving home; our prospective parents have the security of knowing the unborn child has been protected from alcohol and drug abuse, as well as the risks associated with prenatal cigarette smoking and improper nutrition."

Evan watched their eyes, searching for any sign of suspicion before he continued. "First of all, we insist on total confidentiality on both sides of our agreement. Once a teenager approaches us with her problem, she can be certain no one else will ever know she even had a child, unless she chooses to tell them. In order to make certain of this, the prospective parents are screened thoroughly, and the adoption process is private in every way. We even ask that friends and relatives not be told that the child is adopted."

As Evan expected, an apprehensive glance passed from Dee to Larry, but he proceeded quickly as he always did. "We are very selective about who we accept into our program. As you know, every step of the process is by referral, and we were happy that your doctor chose to confide in you. Besides physicians, in over twenty years we have established a large network of teachers, counselors, and clergy members who refer cases to us. We do not advertise or promote our program in any way, since that would impair the level of confidentiality we can maintain.

"Our center is set up like a college dormitory, with the mothers in residence. We have strict ground rules that the girls must agree to before they are accepted in our program. No smoking, alcohol, or drugs are permitted on campus. Proper nutrition and check-ups are required, including prenatal vitamins and additional supplements if designated by one of our staff obstetricians. We provide all clothing, food, etc., for them, and they are required to attend either high school equivalency classes or college-level courses. If they care to, they are allowed to maintain minimal contact with some of their old friends, but disclosure of their location is prohibited. To minimize suspicion and gossip, most of the girls say they're staying with a relative for a while."

As he caught his breath, he knew these people were just as gullible as so many he had seen before. It never ceased to amaze him how blind perfectly intelligent people could be. "Although most of our costs are covered through donations and the adoption fee we charge, we also ask that the girls perform simple jobs. They assist with kitchen and cleaning duties, plus they can volunteer to aid the teachers. By doing this, they not only learn to be responsible citizens, they gain valuable job experience that can later be listed on a résumé. Does our program sound like something you'd be interested in?"

Dee scooted closer to Larry and looked hopefully in his eyes. Her Midwestern accent was heavy as she nervously answered, "Yes. It sounds as though both the girls and the children benefit."

Outwardly Evan smiled, but inside he prepared to plunge the invisible knife deeper into his victims, then twist it with glee. "They do. Most of our cases are managed in one of two ways." He opened his briefcase and handed an elegant book to them, filled with page after page of stunning photographs. In the first section were photos of teenage girls. They were all in classrooms. Each wore the same type of maternity jumper, but some were noticeably in the latter stages of pregnancy. "As you can see, these girls are due over the next seven months. If you choose to sponsor one of them, your child will be available within days after it is born."

They continued to flip through the book, until they reached Section II. As soon as they turned to the picture of the first baby, Evan continued, "These children are available, but the mothers did not seek our assistance early enough in their pregnancy for sponsors to be found before birth. Because we insist on secrecy, placement of these children is a little more complicated."

Larry and Dee had stopped on a picture of a baby boy with curly blond hair and deep blue eyes. "No one would ever know he wasn't ours," Dee whispered. "He looks just like the pictures your mother has of you when you were a baby." She anxiously looked at Evan. "Could we have him?"

"As I said, the older babies create special difficulties. In fact, I'll be honest with you. Our primary problem with finding homes for these children is that most potential parents aren't willing to make the sacrifice we require, which is rather substantial."

Dee squeezed her husband's hand and asked, "Such as?"

Evan seemed hopeless as he shook his head and said, "One or both of you would need to go out of the country for several months so that no one will suspect the child isn't yours. I know it's a lot to ask. After all, everyone has some sort of business to attend to, and it's very disruptive."

"But I don't work," Dee said hopefully.

Perking up a bit, Evan said, "We do have cottages available in several locations, but if your professional or personal obligations require your constant attention, then . . . Of course, I'll have to see if he's still available."

Dee's eyes begged her husband, while her fingernails dug into his arm. Finally he said, "We'd appreciate your checking on him for us. We'd be *very* interested in having him."

"Wonderful!" Evan looked at Dee. "I understand you have a long history of miscarriages."

Dee nodded shyly.

"I'd like you to do two things. First, you'll need to start telling people you're pregnant. Tell them you're starting your fourth month, and that you've kept it a secret until you were certain this time things would work out. I have a package of foam pads in my car that will make you look the part. Move up one size every two weeks." He smiled and added, "Second, I think you'd better buy a book of baby names and get busy decorating a nursery."

Dee beamed. "The nursery has been ready for years, and we don't need a book. His name will be Larry." She hugged her husband as she wiped a tear from her eye. "Just like his dad."

Annissa twisted the cord of the telephone as she spoke, hopelessly tangling it. Dealing with unfamiliar people always made her nervous. "Are the Garveys potential candidates?" she asked.

"Swallowed it hook, line, and sinker. They never even asked about price," Evan replied. With the phone wedged between one shoulder and his ear, he peeled a layer of latex makeup down his forehead until it snapped off at the tip of his nose.

"They can afford it. According to the background check we ran, they're worth millions."

"Everything I saw backs that up. I'll let them sweat for a day, then call and tell them we've started processing."

"Good. I'll contact Tony. Meet him tomorrow night in Savannah. Same location. Contact me once the package is en route to Jamaica."

Annissa hung up the phone slowly. She knew this feeling would pass, as it always had in the past. But lately, every job seemed to take more out of her, as if each child they stole carried a piece of her soul to hell. She rubbed her arms, suddenly feeling a chill run through her bones. Maybe she was just getting old.

Too old to be managing an international kidnapping ring.

Chapter 3

It was another beautiful day in Savannah when Tony strolled up the sidewalk of the Nelson home. Although it was much warmer than before, he still smiled in anticipation.

Like so many others, the Nelson house was an easy mark. Burglar alarm stickers were plastered on the front windows. In a new neighborhood like this one, alarm companies loved to give their sales pitch to potential home builders as well as any prospective buyers. In a matter of minutes they usually revealed every type of installation option possible, specifically detailing the most common in the neighborhood.

Tony's uniform exactly matched those worn by the city water department employees. The bushy black wig, mustache, and dark contacts made him virtually unrecognizable. As expected, he had timed his visit perfectly, just before the children's nap. He could hear the baby crying as he rang the doorbell and waited.

Mary Nelson answered the door with a child resting on each hip. She looked like any mother of two small children just after lunchtime—ready for a welcome break.

"Mrs. Mary Nelson?" Tony asked before she

had time to speak. He kept his eyes glued to his clipboard as if he were double-checking his information, barely glancing up to greet her.

"Yes?" Mary asked. She bounced the children, trying to settle them more comfortably on her slender hips.

As he flashed a duplicate of a city I.D. badge, he said, "I'm with the water department, ma'am. Here to check the quality of the water in your neighborhood. Did you happen to read the article in the Sunday paper a few weeks ago about our program?" There was never any article, but he was sure she'd never know. Young mothers seldom had time for the luxury of reading an entire newspaper.

The baby was crying even louder, while the two-year-old squirmed to get down. Over the howling she replied, "Sorry, I must have missed it."

"It's really nothing to worry about, ma'am. Seems some of these new housing additions aren't using the proper type of pipe and nontoxic glue between the meter and the interior plumbing lines. Cutting corners on building expenses, I guess. We're just spot-checking to make sure the fluoride level is acceptable, and that there's not any lead or toxins in the water." Tony hated the sound of his faked Southern accent, but it was a necessary part of the role. He continued in his best drawl, "It's especially important for a family like yours. I'm sure you know how dangerous ingesting even small amounts of lead can be."

Mary was obviously disturbed by the thought of her children being exposed to lead poisoning.

Shifting away from the door, she said, "I'm sorry. Do come in. Things are always a little hectic around here this time of day."

"I can see your hands are full, so don't mind me a bit. I just need one water sample from downstairs, and one from upstairs. I'll be out of here in under two minutes."

She pointed over her shoulder. "The kitchen is through that door, and there's a bathroom at the end of the hall upstairs."

"Thanks. If it's okay with you, I'll just show myself out when I'm finished. You've got enough to worry about."

She called over her shoulder as she turned away, "That would be great. Will I be getting a report?"

"Only if the chemical levels are unacceptable. If you don't hear from us within a week, everything tested just fine, ma'am."

Tony withdrew two small plastic bottles from his jacket and headed off. He memorized the layout of the house as he walked through, noting the types of window contacts for the burglar alarm and where the control pad was located. It looked like the standard mid-line alarm installation he had expected to find in the price range for this type of home. Once upstairs, he slipped into the nursery. In seconds he flipped open the lock in the middle of the window, disconnected the burglar alarm contacts at its base, and hid a tiny listening device under the baby's changing table.

After he filled the sample bottle with tap water from the bathroom sink, he purposely stomped loudly down each stair and called, "I'm finished, ma'am. Thanks for your cooperation!" Two seconds later he pulled the front door closed behind him and walked confidently down the street. He was sure the next delivery would be headed out of the country soon. Very soon.

Just as the elevator arrived, Nick glanced at his watch. If he left his office now, he'd be at Senator Holt's office fifteen minutes early. He watched the elevator doors slide closed again and decided to kill the extra time by checking out the extravagant offices of Pampered in Paradise across the hall. His parents' thirty-fifth wedding anniversary was only six months away. Maybe he could finally afford to do something he had dreamed about for years—send them on a trip they would always remember.

Entering the office, he was overwhelmed once again by the photographs. Emerald isles set adrift on blue horizons, volcanoes nestled against rain forests, waterfalls cascading into crystal pools, kaleidoscopic reefs—paradise, indeed. No one was seated at the reception desk, so he meandered around, studying the photos, leafing through brochures. Finally, an elegantly dressed black woman came rushing out. He guessed she was probably in her late fifties, but it was hard to tell. She seemed very guarded, and an aura of tension surrounded her, detracting from the gracious facade.

"Can I help you?" she asked, her voice heavy with the lilt of the Caribbean.

Her accent caught him off guard. "I . . . I was just wondering about a trip . . . for my parents, that is."

Politely nodding, she said, "Ah, yes. And which of our contented clients recommended you to our firm?"

Shrugging, Nick answered, "No one. I was just passing by and thought I'd stop in."

The woman's face instantly dropped. Rather bluntly she stated, "I see. Well, I'm afraid I won't be able to help you. Pampered in Paradise operates strictly on a referral basis."

Nick was shocked. After staring at her for a second, he cocked his head and asked, "But this *is* a travel agency, isn't it?"

"Why, yes. Of course it is," she replied.

"And you won't even tell me what kind of vacation packages you have available?"

She started to turn away as she haughtily snapped, "I'm afraid that would waste both your time and mine."

Nick touched her shoulder, and when she was facing him once again he asked, "So what exactly is the deal? Is this reverse discrimination at work? Do you only book trips for black people?"

Annissa's deep, quiet laughter broke free as if it had been buried for centuries. Once she finally composed herself, she explained, "I'm sorry if I've seemed evasive. You see, Pampered in Paradise owns secluded cottages located on various Caribbean islands. We cater to a very exclusive clientele. Money is no object for our guests. Paradise books private jets, chauffeurs, chefs. Anything a person could want.

"Our clients usually travel for extended periods, sometimes six months to a year at a time. We insure they experience the true culture of the country they choose to vacation in. Every detail is arranged, from special menus and private scuba lessons to personal trainers and fitness experts. Complete confidentiality and satisfaction is guaranteed. We've never had a complaint."

Nick was captivated by the smooth way her words tumbled free from her lips. It was easy to see how beautiful she must have been when she was younger, because she was still captivating. He smiled and said, "So I guess you don't have a nice five-day cruise I could send my parents on?"

She shook her head, but she was smiling as she said, "No, sir. I'm afraid the shortest trip we arrange is four weeks. Any less than that could hardly be considered a vacation."

He stepped back and shrugged. "Then it looks like I won't be going on any vacations for a long, long time." Nick turned to leave, adding, "I appreciate your assistance. Mind if I take a brochure to dream about?"

With a twinkle in her eye she answered, "No problem."

As he waited for the elevator, he heard the dead bolt slide into place as she locked the office doors. Obviously, Pampered in Paradise didn't need his business, or anyone else's for that matter.

Nick stiffly sat in the overstuffed chair in the reception area of Senator Holt's office, arguing with himself for the hundredth time since he had been assigned the Holt case. His logical side kept trying to convince his ethical side that he could fairly represent a man he had detested for years. Holt epitomized everything Nick had always fought against, from his political views to the extravagant way he and his wife, Alice, lived.

Hearing footsteps, Nick was surprised to see the senator walking toward him. The man was even more impressive in person than he was on television. His gray hair had natural waves, and his golden tan made him look younger than his sixty-three years. Nick stood, extending his hand. "Senator Holt, I'm Nick Hunter with Kellars and Kellars."

Glancing into the large office, he noted the distinguished atmosphere. Light paneling set an elegant background for stately portraits of former Oklahoman elected officials and a framed copy of the state charter. The pale blue flag of Oklahoma hung beside an American flag on each side of an immense walnut desk.

After vigorously returning Nick's handshake, Senator Holt said, "Mr. Hunter, I've heard glowing remarks about your hard work and talent. I hope you're ready for a battle. My wife and I have no intention of putting up with this kind of slander."

So far Holt was everything Nick had expected, which made it even harder for him to say, "I'll do what I can to help. First, we need to minimize the media coverage. From what I've researched, though, Stover has the right to proceed with the investigation, and the taxpayers have the right to follow its progress."

"Do what you can, and then some. I've played the legal bullshit game for years. I know how it works." He stared at Nick as though expecting him to understand his insinuation, then added, "So, what can I do for you today?"

I'd have guessed you invented the bullshit game, Nick thought as he opened his briefcase and took out his legal pad. "I've been reviewing your files. I've prepared a rather long list of questions."

"Fire away."

"Don't you think we should wait for Mr. Kellars to arrive?"

"Will called a few minutes ago. Said you were capable of handling all this without him. I'm sure we won't miss him anyway. Now that Angela Anderson, she's a different story altogether." Holt gestured lewdly. "You should have packed her along just for us to look at."

Nick hesitated before he replied. "Somehow I don't think she'd appreciate that comment. As your legal counsel I feel I should warn you that in light of the frenzy of sexual-harassment charges, a man in your position should choose his words very carefully."

Senator Holt threw back his head and laughed. "Don't get me wrong, son. From what I can see, she's done a damn fine job on all my publicity. Kept me out of hot water for years, first with my campaign and now on this investigation. She runs interference better than most linebackers. Problem is, I'm always too distracted by those short skirts of hers to pay much attention to what's coming out of her pretty mouth. I guess I'm just lucky Alice handles those decisions."

A sharp rap at the door solved Nick's problem of how to tactfully change the subject. He was quickly beginning to see why the senator had such serious problems. Susan Stover, the state attorney general, appeared to be out to get him. Maybe his down-home style of chauvinism had influenced her decision to investigate his campaign contributions.

A tall blond woman entered the office. Nick immediately recognized Alice Holt from pictures he had seen in newspapers and on television. She was one of the few high-profile women in Oklahoma, seen constantly at her husband's side at every fund-raiser and social event imaginable. Fifteen years younger than the senator, she thrived on living in the political limelight.

The senator roughly put his arm around her, squeezing her shoulder against his. "Nick Hunter, this is my wife, Alice. Nick's the latest of Will's pack of professional manipulators. He's working on the damned Stover investigation for us."

Nick was surprised at the senator's bluntness as he politely shook Alice's hand. "Pleased to meet you," he said. She pulled away from her husband, moving closer to Nick. Her perfume assaulted his senses, and something about the inviting tilt of her face toward his made him back slightly away as she spoke.

"And I thought manipulation was more an amateur sport. I never knew I was up against professionals," she said.

"I'm sure you're in a league of your own, ma'am," Nick said with only the slightest edge of sarcasm in his voice.

"Call me Alice," she replied, then turned her attention to her husband. "I've finished reading the report on the groundwater contamination caused by saltwater disposal wells in Creek, Osage, and Noble counties. You'll need to issue this statement." She laid a typed page in front of the senator, who signed it without reading it.

With calculated confidence Alice lightly brushed Nick's arm as she walked past him to leave. She was almost out the door when she turned and said, "It was truly a pleasure meeting you, Nick. Let's have lunch sometime soon."

Nick turned back to the senator, who either expected his wife to openly flirt with people, or who wasn't paying enough attention to notice. Nick walked over, snapping open his briefcase. "Shall we begin?"

"You bet," Senator Holt barked as he sat down at his desk.

"First of all, I want you to understand that I need to know the truth, even if you feel something you say might be incriminating." Seeing the gleam in Holt's eyes, Nick pushed down the urge to leave and flatly added, "I can't defend you unless I know exactly what the attorney general might be able to dig up."

The senator cocked his head and laughed, then said, "I suppose the best defense is still a good offense."

Annissa stood behind the one-way mirror, watching Will Kellars. She knew as soon as he finished meeting with the law firm's young public relations woman, he would come to her to discuss their progress on the latest case. Pacing back and forth, she noticed how the pretty woman leaned slightly forward, as if hanging on his every word.

More important, she watched how Will played the charming father figure to his captive audience. It made her want to storm in and slap him.

Years ago she had been the same. Trusting Will Kellars above anyone, even though he refused to be seen in public with her. Growing more and more dependent on the money, until life didn't seem worth living without it. Will Kellars had bought her, just like all the desperate couples who had bought stolen children.

Finally, the woman walked out, leaving Will alone. Annissa automatically checked her makeup and smoothed her dress, then pressed the button by the mirror to signal him she was waiting. She watched as he locked his office door, then came over to the secret panel. When it opened, Annissa was still pacing, but for once it was herself she was impatient with, not Will.

"How did it go?" Will asked, his eyes avoiding hers.

Annissa could tell by the tone of his voice that their meeting would be purely business today. With relief she answered, "Quite well. Everything is lined up for tonight. The Garvey couple is ready to leave for the islands on a moment's notice. We've already received their wire for the first fifty thousand. Evan and Tony expect to have the Nelson baby to the Florida Keys by six a.m. As long as the weather holds, Maya will pick him up by boat there, as usual, and then she'll fly him from Miami to Jamaica tomorrow."

Will grabbed a pamphlet and leafed through it. "Any more problems with the new immigration agent?"

"No. Your suggestion worked perfectly," she snapped. His domineering attitude irritated her today. He might be able to manipulate the other people he worked with, but she knew every one of his tricks and she had long ago grown tired of playing his games.

Ignoring the abruptness in her voice, he asked, "How about Customs in Jamaica? Still accepting five hundred each?"

"Of course," she answered coldly.

Walking back to the panel, Will shrugged and said, "Sounds like you have everything under control, Annissa."

"Don't I always?" Once the panel was closed again, she unclenched her fingers and rubbed her aching joints. Her hands were trembling as she went back into her own office and sat down. *Why do I put up with this? He uses me in every possible way, and I just keep coming back for more.*

"You've been awfully quiet lately." Angela poked her head into Nick's office, waiting for a response.

Leaning back, he rubbed his eyes. "Busy. Holt has enough legal problems to keep ten lawyers up to their asses in alligators for months." He threw his hands in the air. "But lucky me, I get to tackle it alone."

"Not anymore. I met with Mr. Kellars this morning. I've been assigned to work with you on the Holt scandal. Obviously, I can't help with the legal technicalities, but he thinks we'll both be able to do a better job if we stay informed."

Nick smiled broadly. "Sounds great to me. What's protocol around here for teamwork?"

"Got me." Angela walked behind Nick's desk so she could whisper. "I've never worked with anyone besides Mr. Kellars. Except for Rick, when he was alive. Kellars has never named another partner since Rick died, so everyone in the office pretty much reports to him. Not on paper, of course. The organization chart shows a wonderful chain of command. But in reality he controls everyone like puppets."

Nick stood up, his shoulder within inches of hers. Gazing down at her, he asked, "So how can I help you?"

The masculine smell of his cologne and his nearness unnerved Angela, so she scooted back around and sat in one of the chairs in front of his desk. Leaning forward, she grabbed a crystal paperweight with a gold legal insignia inside and studied it as she said, "God only knows how hard it is to keep the press off Holt's trail right now. They're staked out at the courthouse just waiting for someone to sneeze. If you could warn me before any legal filings, I'm sure it would make things easier."

"No problem." He wondered if she shared his opinion of the Holts.

"And what can I do to make your life simpler in exchange?" she asked.

Several lewd thoughts crossed his mind, but Nick answered, "I could use a good sounding board. Someone to talk over details of the case, so I don't go off on some crazy tangent and lose sight of the real target. Right now I'm working twelve to fourteen hours a day. By the time I stumble into my apartment at night, I'm not sure which legal path looks best."

"I'm a great listener, but I don't know how much help I'll be at keeping you on track. My only legal knowledge is from osmosis. After six years of listening to all the technical gibberish around here, a little has worn off."

"From what I've seen, you could probably pass the bar easier than some of my law school buddies." He added, "But talking things over should be all I need for now. Sometimes saying things out loud is enough to make a puzzle magically fall together. How about testing it over dinner?"

"Tonight's one of the nights I visit my mother."

"At Shadybrook?" he asked.

Angela's face softened as she realized he remembered their earlier conversation. "It can be really depressing. Half the time she doesn't recognize me; the other half she thinks I'm still a child."

"That must be really tough," he said with genuine concern.

"It is." Hesitating, Angela decided to break one of her rules and asked, "How about dinner tomorrow at seven?"

Nick eagerly said, "Name the place."

She jotted down her address and handed it to him. As she headed for the door, she wondered if she had just made a mistake. Coworker relationships were always trouble. Stopping, she reminded herself that Nick was different from the other men she worked with, and that having a male who was just a friend might be a welcome change. Turning back around, she smiled and said, "I make a killer veggie lasagna. Bring the wine and a loaf of French bread and we're set."

Shaking his head, he sighed. "This may not be such a great idea. I haven't had a home-cooked meal in months. It may kill me."

As she walked out the door, she called back, "This place will kill you long before my lasagna has a chance!"

Evan and Tony sat in their rented cars several blocks away from the Nelson house. The Savannah night was unseasonably warm and humid, and both men were eager to wrap up their work as quickly as possible.

The tiny listening device Tony had planted the day before was working perfectly, picking up everything from the slight squeak of the rocking chair to the whisper of the ceiling fan. Evan could easily picture Mary Nelson rocking the baby boy as she sang the lullabies that floated into the car. Last night she had nursed him at midnight, and then he had slept until dawn. They had based their schedule on the assumption that tonight would be the same routine.

First, Evan checked the buckle on the child safety seat he had purchased that afternoon. Confident it was secure, he examined the belt of tools around his waist. The array of precision instruments were at his fingertips, ready if needed. He took a deep breath, the tension building inside him. At exactly one-thirty he edged the rented navy sedan closer, turning onto the quiet street. Tony listened and watched from the north corner, ready to warn Evan of any trouble. Stolen license tags temporarily covered the rental plates, just in case anyone noticed either one of the cars. Even the weather seemed to be cooperating as a line of clouds drifted across the moon to steal the night's shadows.

The folding ladder silently snapped together and slid into place below the front window. Evan's skin-tight camouflage clothes, gloves, and mask made him practically impossible to see as he scaled it as smoothly as a serpent. Approaching the window with extreme caution, he aimed his tiny flashlight at the lock. The beam revealed that his worries were for nothing. The window was still unlocked. Shining the narrow beam at the sill, he saw even better news. The alarm contact was as Tony had left it—disarmed.

Calmly, he slid the window open and crawled inside. He searched the room, his eyes already adjusted to the dim light. It was exactly as he had expected. He could hear the baby moving slightly in his bed, the sound of his breath rhythmically flowing in and out. Overhead, the ceiling fan whirled peacefully around.

After crossing to the dresser, he followed the cord of the baby monitor to the wall. With great care he eased the plug out of the socket. Next, he retrieved the listening device planted under the changing table and slid it into his pocket. Now all he had to do was grab the baby and go.

Outside, leaves began to rustle in the growing breeze. Bright blue and red curtains started to frolic in the wind from the open window. Soft shadows reflected from the night light to the ceiling and back again. The cool evening breeze rippled in, caressing the baby's cheeks and bringing life to the mobile above his head. Dangling black, white, and red balls danced and bobbed above the crib.

First, a mere whimper escaped from the baby as he slowly awakened to find his familiar surroundings disturbed. Within seconds it escalated into a confused, frightened wail.

Every muscle in Evan's body tensed. His hand immediately flew to the side of his utility belt. A slight tug at the Velcro allowed his fingers to wrap around a loaded pistol. He had always known it would come to this, so he was surprisingly calm, his grip steady.

Backing away from the crib, he prepared for the worst.

Chapter 4

Evan could hear the creak of the wood floor as Mary Nelson climbed out of bed to answer her son's cries. In an instant the window was shoved closed and he positioned himself behind the nursery's open door. As an afterthought, the baby monitor was plugged in again. He stood up just seconds before Mary shuffled tiredly past, only a hollow wooden door separating the two of them. His index finger grazed back and forth along the trigger as he waited.

"What's wrong, sweetie?" Mary whispered as she leaned over the crib and noticed the swaying mobile. "I didn't know you could reach your toys. Did they scare you?" The baby continued to cry. Evan could see nothing from where he was, but he could sense her movements as she lifted the boy out of his crib and carried him to the rocking chair.

For several minutes, his crying continued. It was a desperate cry for help, but soon the safety of his mother's arms calmed him. She rocked and sang to him until he was fast asleep. With practiced grace she eased him back into his crib, resting contentedly. Standing over him, she made certain he wasn't going to stir again before she turned to leave.

Evan never moved. He hoped Tony had heard enough through his headset to know what had happened and knew not to risk any communication. Even the slightest sound would jeopardize everything. When Mary finally walked out of the nursery, he breathed deeply for the first time in over fifteen minutes. Just as he started to move, she walked back in, freezing him instantly. She picked up the baby monitor and switched it on and off. Puzzled, she leaned down to check the plug. Her face came within inches of his foot. Any motion would betray him, and he was ready to kick her backward and shoot if necessary.

Finally she left. Before she could get back to her bedroom, he unplugged the monitor again. This time he waited. Ten more minutes made him reasonably certain she wasn't going to return. Normally, no drugs were needed to acquire a child. The routine was extremely fast, and most babies were so soundly asleep they barely stirred. They were usually in the car before they made a sound. But this was definitely not a routine job.

In the back of his belt was a small vial and cloth. Before leaving his hiding spot, he eased them out. The ether made his eyes burn as he sprinkled it onto the soft material. When he emerged, he immediately placed the cloth over the child's nose and mouth. *So much for whining, you little brat. I don't tolerate interference while I work.*

A few seconds later he picked up the limp baby. Evan suppressed the urge to toss him out the window and leave. Instead, he cradled him in one arm as he nimbly worked his way down the ladder. When he climbed into the car, he roughly slung the infant into the seat and muttered, "Selfish little bastard. You almost got your whole family killed." As he drove away, he took a deep breath and said, "I'm out, Tony."

"Man, you really had me worried. That's the closest we've come in years."

Evan's agitation was clear as he said, "I couldn't get the frigging ladder. You'll have to swing back and pick it up. And pull the window closed while you're at it."

Tony hesitated, his voice calculated as he asked, "How's the package?"

"Unconscious. I'll meet you outside the airport car-rental agency in twenty minutes."

"I'll be there," Tony said. "You sure the package is in good condition?"

"My nerves are shot. I wasn't taking any chances." Evan glanced at the apparently lifeless child and felt a surge of sadistic satisfaction. "He'll wake up after a nice long nap. It should make the rest of the night a lot easier."

"What are we gonna do if you hurt him?" Tony asked.

Evan snapped, "Easy. Find another one just like him."

Agent Jaggers wound through the urban fringe of Savannah, assessing the peaceful area. By the time she turned into the Nelsons' quiet residential neighborhood, a sense of urgency began to rise in her chest. She rolled down the window of the rented car to gain strength from the refreshing air, but instead caught the scent of the ocean on the breeze. How did the bastard pick who to take and where? Why did he choose to snatch *this* child from *this* particular house?

The late afternoon sun cast long shadows from children playing happily in their yards, scrambling up and down the street on tiny three wheelers and bicycles. Yet several things were wrong with the ideal suburban image. In this neighborhood every mother's eyes tracked their children like radar. She could almost feel those eyes trailing her car, suspecting the worst from every stranger. Add the three police cars parked in front of the Nelson house, and the picture became one of harsh reality.

Even though she'd been working the Serial Snatcher case for over six years, maintaining professional distance was getting harder and harder. Lesley took a deep, calming breath before she rang the doorbell. She smoothed her light denim dress, which she hoped would put the Nelsons more at ease than her usual business attire. In spite of the look of horror in Mary's face, Lesley calmly said, "Mrs. Nelson, I'm so sorry to bother you. I'm Agent Jaggers. I phoned earlier."

Mary's eyes brimmed with tears, her face swollen from hours of crying. From past experience Lesley knew the fear and agony the Nelsons were feeling. Every time someone came to the door, or the phone rang, it could bring news. Horrible news or wonderful news. Lesley quickly said, "I'm sorry, Mrs. Nelson. We don't have any new information yet. I need to ask some questions."

"I'm so sorry. I'm not normally this rude. Come in."

Mary Nelson looked like the other mothers—haunted by a nightmare come to life. Strands of blond hair had fallen out of a makeshift ponytail. She was wearing an oversized T-shirt and faded jeans. Lesley followed her inside. "Please call me Lesley. If you don't mind, I'd like to go over some more questions with you and your husband. I know it's hard, but sometimes things that seem totally unrelated to the crime really are important."

Mary shifted the weight of her little girl to the other hip. Since the kidnapping she hadn't let Heather out of her reach. Heather seemed to understand that overnight everything had changed. She laid her head on her mother's shoulder and sucked her thumb. "My husband is out searching with the police, but I'll try to help you."

They stopped in the kitchen. Pulling out a notepad, Lesley asked, "First of all, I need you to keep a list of any strangers who seem particularly helpful in trying to locate Jamie. Can you do that?"

"It's been on the news all day. We've already had calls from people offering to help search for him." She nodded, a sob catching in her throat. "Do you think the person who did this might call here?"

"Pedophiles are very sick people. Some like to watch the pain they've inflicted on the family." Lesley could tell Mary was about to start crying again, so she quickly added, "But we don't know what we're dealing with yet."

"I know what we're dealing with! Someone

took my baby. Right out of his crib!" Her voice was desperate as she asked, "If he's smart enough to do that, he won't get caught, will he?"

Lesley's voice was soothing. "We're going to try every possible way to find him. I've got people checking rental cars, flights, buses, and toll booths trying to find anyone who remembers seeing *any* baby late last night." Lesley wished she could tell Mary about the other kidnappings to make her feel less guilty, but the team couldn't risk it. If the public knew how long the snatchings had been going on, sheer panic would hit the nation. "Why don't we go outside and let Heather play while we talk? It's a beautiful day." Seeing Mary instantly tense her arms around the child, Lesley added, "I'll help you watch her." She opened her jacket enough to reveal the service revolver hanging in her shoulder holster. "No one is going to bother her. I promise."

Heather turned to her mother and smiled shyly. "Please play, Mom."

Mary eased Heather down, and together they slowly walked outside. The women sat on the redwood benches of a weathered picnic table while Heather vigorously assaulted the swing set. The backyard grass was freshly cut. Lesley stared at an overturned red wagon in the sandbox, then at the empty infant swing.

Refocusing, Lesley calmly said, "I've read the report you gave the police this morning. I want you to think back over the last few weeks." She dug through her purse, finally pulling a small pocket calendar out. "We're going to reconstruct every place you went, every person you talked to."

"I really don't go that many places." Mary's eyes never left Heather's. As she spoke, she perched on the edge of the bench as if she might need to spring into action at any moment. "With the children so young, it can be a real hassle trying to do even simple things like grocery shopping. It's amazing how much harder having two is than one."

Lesley wanted her to stay focused, so she quickly said, "Then it shouldn't be very hard. The most important thing is not to leave out anything you did or saw. Even something that seems totally irrelevant might be the lead we're looking for."

Two hours later, the sun was beginning to set. Lesley and Mary were satisfied they had covered every detail. Heather was exhausted, her head back on her mother's shoulder as they walked out to Lesley's rented Probe. Mary gently stroked her child's blond curls as she asked, "Do you have any children, Lesley?"

With a wistful look in her eye she answered, "Not yet. First, I have to find a husband, which isn't easy since I'm married to my job. I've always dreamed of having twins, though. A boy and a girl."

"I did too. But mine are almost like twins. They're only twenty months apart. We were so glad to have one of each. Especially since I can't have any more children. We felt very blessed. Until . . ."

Lesley gently touched Mary's shoulder as she said, "We'll find him, Mary."

Mary seemed to believe her. Just as Lesley started the car, Mary's face lit up. "Oh. I almost forgot. Last week a man from the water department came out. But he was only in the house for a couple of minutes."

Turning the engine back off, Lesley asked, "Why was he inside the house?"

"He said he needed to check chemical levels from the faucets."

"Did he go upstairs"—she hesitated, then added—"alone?"

Warily Mary answered, "Yes. But only for a minute or two. He really didn't stay long."

Lesley knew Mary sensed the skepticism in her voice. Her own stomach knotted with guilt as she realized what Mary was probably thinking. *What if he was the kidnapper? I let him in. I might as well have just handed my baby to him.* As Mary's tears flowed again, Lesley found a new determination from deep within. She knew she had to find Jamie Nelson. No matter what. Trying to be reassuring, she said, "It's probably nothing, but I'll go over to the water department right now and check it out. Did he have any identification?"

"Yes, but I don't remember his name."

Lesley reached out and gripped Mary's hand. "It wasn't your fault. Sometimes horrible things just happen."

"But why *my* baby?" she cried.

"I wish I knew. God, how I wish I knew."

Nick arrived at Angela's building looking like he'd stepped out of an L.L. Bean catalog. Wearing chinos with a bulky knit sweater tied around his neck, a soft denim shirt, and leather boots, he felt less relaxed than he appeared. As he hurried up the stairs to Angela's apartment, he balanced a bottle of wine, a loaf of French bread, and a bouquet of pink daisies in his arms.

Just seconds after he rang the bell, Angela threw open the door and waved him in. She was clearly engrossed in a story on the news. Nick followed her inside, noticing the cozy feel of her apartment. Like his own place, the living area was attached to the kitchen, except Angela's was large enough to accommodate a small butcher block island topped with tile. Both rooms were decorated in shades of peach, pink, and antique white, which gave the place a warm, open feeling.

"This is just disgusting," Angela muttered as she motioned for Nick to follow her.

As he did, he admired the tight black leggings and long purple sweater Angela wore. With her hair swept casually behind her ears, she looked beautiful yet comfortable. Nick slid onto the sofa beside Angela and watched the report long enough to ascertain that a baby had been kidnapped from his nursery in Georgia last night. The hysterical mother sobbed as she told of checking on him in the middle of the night, then finding the crib empty the next morning. The police had no suspects, no leads. Since a ransom note had not yet been delivered, they also had no motive. A snapshot of the adorable infant was splashed across the screen along with a plea for his safe return.

Grabbing the remote, Angela turned off the television. "I'm sorry, Nick. I didn't mean to ignore you. I just can't believe anyone could do something as cruel as stealing a baby from its own crib."

"I can't imagine what those poor parents are going through."

To snap herself out of the gloomy mood, Angela hopped up and said, "I'd better check on dinner." Since Nick followed her, she changed the subject by asking, "Where were you all day? I stopped by your office a couple of times, and you were always out."

Rolling his eyes, he answered, "In the law library."

"Is that as boring as it sounds?" she asked.

"Only until you slip into a coma."

Angela yawned, then said, "Speaking of comas, our dear friend Senator Holt must be in one. I went by his office today to ask him some questions on the Stover deal. His ability to skirt around the issues never ceases to amaze me. He never did tell me anything I could use. He kept changing the subject. Finally I gave up and left."

Nick shrugged and raised his eyebrows. " 'Skirting' around the issue may be your problem. He has the hots for you."

"Not!" she said emphatically as she pulled open the oven.

"I'm serious." Leaning over, he breathed deeply, thoroughly enjoying the almost sensuous aroma. "He told me so the other day. Said your short skirts were driving him wild."

"Nick, that's disgusting. He's ancient!" Angela whirled around, letting go of the oven door, which banged closed. "I can't believe the old coot even notices women anymore."

"He's not exactly married to a hag, you know," he said.

"So I've noticed. Rumor has it she's had more nips and tucks than Michael Jackson, but at least when you ask Alice a question, she has an intelligent answer. If I wouldn't lose my job because of it, I'd love to see Susan Stover prove her husband is up to no good. I can't believe people keep voting for him year after year."

Nick was relieved to hear they shared similar opinions of the senator. "At least you don't have to defend him, which is apparently going to be even tougher than I imagined."

Angela excitedly asked, "Did you find something incriminating in his records?"

His confidence wavering, Nick answered, "I spent all day trying to reconcile tax returns for the last three years to the documentation collected by the Stover committee on his estimated income. I'm getting damned frustrated. I can't tell whether it's my lack of tax expertise that's making it impossible, or if there really is a million-dollar discrepancy over the last three years."

"If I'm any judge of character, I'd guess there's a big discrepancy."

Raising the bottle of wine, he lifted his eyebrows in silent question. Angela responded by opening the cabinet above her head to extract two crystal wineglasses from the front of a perfectly straight row. It occurred to him how neat and clean everything was, even the high places were free of dust. After he uncorked the bottle and poured the wine, he walked over to sit at the kitchen table. "What've I gotten myself into?"

Angela hesitated, then began massaging his shoulders. After several seconds she answered, "I felt the same way once, and sometimes I still do. But life goes on." Feeling him tense under her fingertips, Angela added seriously, "It gets easier, Nick. Everything has a bad side *and* a good side. You'll learn to dwell more on the good and tolerate the bad. I promise. Right now I'd guess your long hours are to blame as much as anything."

Rolling his head back and forth, he muttered, "That feels so good."

Moving her fingers in slow, sensual circles, she replied, "You certainly are tense."

"Trying to dig up a million bucks tends to do that to me. Who does the accounting at our office? Maybe I could get Kellars' permission to have them help me straighten this mess out."

"No help there, Nick. All the firm's accounting is done by an outside CPA firm—Wood, Kruger and Etherton."

Turning slightly toward her, Nick asked, "Isn't that odd? With over seventy employees, you'd think it'd be more economical to hire people."

Angela shrugged. "I guess it's the same logic he uses for maintaining the computer systems. We could have a full-time computer department at our beck and call for what we pay them. Instead, CompuCrooks makes a fortune."

"Have you ever recommended CompuCorp be replaced by an employee?"

"Yes." She stood up and moved toward the oven. "Why do you think I told you one of the rules of survival was to mind your own business? That's basically what I was told when I suggested it." She pushed her head down and back, gruffly impersonating Will Kellars. " 'Your job is to take care of our public relations concerns. If I ever feel the need for your advice on our computer systems, I'll ask for it.' "

"No shit! Did he really say that?"

"Yes! I'm sure I looked like a deer trapped in headlights as I tried to back out his door."

Nick leaned back, grabbed the bouquet of daisies from their hiding place, and handed them to her. "I thought these might cheer you up. You looked pretty serious when I passed your office this morning."

Angela fleetingly wondered if he had an ulterior motive, but quickly decided she was reading more into a simple gesture of kindness than was really there. She smiled warmly and said, "Thanks, they're beautiful. I'm really glad we're working together."

"Me too. How'd your visit with your mother go last night?"

As she arranged the daisies in a vase, her voice was distant. "The visit was fine, but I'm afraid she's getting worse."

"I'm really sorry. Is there anything I can do?"

Their eyes held as she cocked her head and answered, "It's sweet of you to offer, but I can handle it." Nick could almost see the flash of memory hit her as she changed the subject. "You won't believe what I saw today!"

"Must have been pretty good."

"There was an older couple standing by the reception desk of Pampered in Paradise. You know, that travel agency on our floor."

"What's so unusual about that? Somebody must be able to afford the ridiculous trips they sell."

"I've worked at K and K for six years, and not once have I ever seen anyone actually go in there, except the black woman who runs it. She gives me the creeps. When I see her in the ladies' room, she won't even acknowledge my presence. I've never been able to figure out how they manage to stay in business with no customers."

He grinned, stuffing his hands in his pockets. "I checked out the place last week. Ross Perot is about the only person I can think of who could afford a vacation like that. They must do a hell of a job. Our friend Senator Holt is one of the shareholders. According to his tax return, he's raked in over a hundred thousand a year for the last three years from the place. And he owns only a third of it."

"Guess we're in the wrong business," Angela said with a look of disgust.

Nick watched carefully as she put the final touches on dinner, wondering what she would say if he asked her for a date. As if she could read his mind, she raised her wineglass to him and, with a warm smile, toasted. "To friendship!"

Annissa stared out the window, watching the sun slowly fall in the sky. A faint brown haze hovered over Oklahoma City's horizon, another reminder of how far she was from her island home, where the *doctor breeze* carried fresh, cool trade winds every morning.

Moving into the secret office behind hers, she closed the door and leaned against it. Resting her eyes, she rolled back the years until she was a child of ten. Her mother was scolding her for swimming around the end of the private resort piers to sell shell necklaces to tourists. Even though it was her brother Jax's idea, Annissa was the only one caught by the security guard. But when she pulled the wet ten-dollar bill out of her bathing suit, Tica's eyes widened in disbelief.

"How'd you get that, my child?" her mother whispered.

"A nice woman bought all my necklaces. She said I was skinny. What's skinny mean?"

"It means we'll eat like kings this week," she cried.

How she wished she could sit down with Tica and discuss this tangled mess. Her mother possessed an almost supernatural insight. A long time ago she had valued her opinion above all others, but Jax's influence was strong. His contagious youthful arrogance had convinced both her, and her sister, Maya, that they too could tempt fate and live a life full of risk, wealth, and adventure.

If Tica had known the truth from the beginning, she would never have allowed it to continue. But now she was thousands of miles away, dying of old age, or maybe because she actually believed all that *obeah*-black magic-*bushdoctor* crap. Annissa sighed. Maybe Tica was right. Maybe all their souls were already doomed to wander as *duppies*, forever trapped on earth because of their evil deeds.

"You look exhausted," Will grunted from across the room.

Annissa had been vaguely aware of him entering. She turned to watch him push the hidden panel back into place, noting the flawless lines of his tailored suit as he walked toward her. Even though he was still handsome, he seemed to have aged fifty years since his son died. She couldn't help but inwardly cringe at the sight of his wrinkled eyes and pale, sagging skin. Instinctively, her hand raised to touch the crinkles in her own flesh.

She suddenly wondered what would happen if Will died. The answer seemed too simple to be true. She would be free. Without packing a thing, she would get on a plane, leave this godforsaken place, and never look back.

"Well, what are you waiting for? I haven't got time to just stand around," he barked.

With an icy glare she said, "Do you ever listen to yourself? Last time I checked, I wasn't your slave." Her Caribbean accent was particularly heavy, as it always was when she was angry or tired.

Gritting his teeth, he asked, "Are you going to start that nonsense about quitting again? I thought we settled it six months ago." Seeing her stiffen even more, he walked to her and tried to take her in his arms. When she pulled away, he softly caressed her cheek with the back of his hand. "I'm sure you're still worried that our luck will run out, but it won't. You know better than anyone how careful we are."

"Careful isn't enough." Narrowing her eyes, she swatted his hand away from her face. "I know what you're thinking, Will. This isn't a mid-life crisis. I can't explain it, I just know we should get out while we can."

Exhaling loudly, Will started to leave. "I can see this isn't the time to handle business. Signal me when you've come to your senses."

Before he could get to the door, Annissa followed him and took his arm. Meeting his steady gaze, she said, "I've tried to get past this, Will. Really, I have. You just don't understand. All these years you've had a life. A real life. But what have I had?" She motioned to the room around her. "This place has been my world. I might as well eat and sleep here too, since you quit coming to my house years ago. You've always said we couldn't be seen together because of our connection to this place, but I'm not stupid. Interracial affairs are still taboo in your haughty circles, aren't they?"

As if he were speaking to a whining child, Will said, "Annissa, you know how much I care for you. Deep down, you also know that being seen together has nothing to do with skin color. Haven't I always made sure you had the best of everything?" Roughly pulling her to him, his voice was lusty as he added, "I still keep you satisfied, don't I?" Kissing her, he tried to hold her, but she broke away from him and walked over to the computer table.

Staring at the machine, she resisted the urge to wipe her mouth. "I'm sorry, Will. I can't right now." She sat down, and her fingers struck the keyboard hard as she typed the necessary commands. Pointing at figures on the screen, she coldly stated, "As you can see, the last purchase went flawlessly. Our Cayman account was credited with the remaining $325,000 yesterday."

"When are you going to record the intercompany disbursements?" he asked.

"This afternoon," she muttered.

"Who's bringing the cash in from the Caymans this month?"

Still staring at the screen, Annissa answered, "Your secretary. She's scheduled to stay at the corporate condo for four days."

"And the switch will be made on the jet?"

"Of course. She'll never know she had anything besides her own luggage. The cash is transferred to the secret compartment after the luggage is loaded but before the passengers board at MoBay airport."

"Good. I wouldn't want anything to happen to Marilyn. She's been a good worker. Very loyal, never complains."

"If you're worried about it, we can wait until the next week. Several of your staff lawyers are scheduled then."

"No. We need the cash now. Besides, what kind of Customs agent would stop a mouse like Marilyn?"

Jax leaned against the outside wall of Jamaica's MoBay airport enjoying the bright, warm day as he waited for Maya to clear Customs. From a distance he watched the usual throng of tourists pile onto busses, a Red Stripe beer shoved into their hands at the earliest possible moment. When he saw Maya emerge, he tossed down the piece of grass he had been chewing and headed for his van.

Maya was wearing a brightly striped sundress, and the infant she carried was wrapped in an equally bold blanket. As she crawled into the old van, she asked, "How's Tica?"

"As stubborn as you and 'Nissa," Jax answered. "I took her to a doctor, and she wouldn't even go inside. Why the delay?"

Maya shifted the baby in her arms. "Our Cuban contact warned me they were checking papers, so I decided to wait. You have a problem with that?"

Ignoring her, Jax started the engine and wildly pulled into traffic. As he blasted his horn he asked, "What's with the *baybee*? Usually my driving has them wailing at the top of their lungs by now."

A mild cloud of concern crossed Maya's face. "This one is quiet. Too quiet. When Tony dropped him off in the Keys, he warned me they'd had some trouble."

Jax laughed. "Tony probably enjoyed himself. He's never been one to avoid a little trouble."

Shrugging, Maya said, "Maybe I shouldn't have drugged this one before the flight. I don't suppose we could have a doctor check him?"

Almost ramming into the rear end of the slow-moving car ahead, Jax muttered, "You got that right, sis." He shrugged as he added, "You worry too much, Maya. That *baybee's* new parents will take him to the doctor. I'm sure they can afford it. In no time at all that *baybee* will have everything we never had, and then some."

* * *

Pressing the button on the speaker phone of his private line, he barked, "Will Kellars."

"Get me off that damned box!"

Instantly, Will grabbed the receiver and snapped, "Luckily, there's no one in my office. What the hell are you doing calling me here anyway? Especially at this time of day."

Shaking his head, Will leaned back in his chair and said, "Forget it. It's too soon. Our last delivery won't be complete for several months."

"I don't care. This one is personal. It'll be easier to pull off, since the target is known. All you need to do is find someone to take the package."

"This business is not your plaything. It would be dangerous to do another job so soon. The media might make a connection to Savannah."

"So do it a little differently. Your people are talented. Let them be creative. Just handle it. I'll get the specs to Pampered in the morning."

Will hung up and stared across his office at the large one-way mirror. Annissa would have a fit if he placed another order so soon, and for once he couldn't blame her. Kidnapping another child without a waiting period would be risky. Still, he was confident Evan and Tony could handle it. The real problem was all too obvious. In her state of mind, could Annissa deal with it? And if she couldn't, was it worth the consequences?

As he walked to the secret panel, he knew the answer. She would have to cope. She had no choice.

Chapter 5

Lesley wanted to kiss the ground by the time she pulled into a parking space at FBI headquarters. Her flight from Savannah to Washington, D.C., had been rerouted due to weather; then she found the battery in her car was dead when they finally landed at Dulles. Even though the lightweight jean dress had been perfect for the mild weather in Georgia, she'd practically frozen while waiting for the automotive club.

When she finally rushed into her boss's office, her words were rushed, her eyes bright with anticipation. "You're not going to believe this!"

Ed Collins was just shy of fifty, a slender man who rarely showed any kind of emotion. His expression was one of mild interest as he dropped his pencil and asked, "Believe what?"

Lesley answered, "I think we've finally got a break in the Serial Snatcher case. Someone in a city water department uniform, fake identification and all, showed up a couple of days before the kidnapping and gained entry to the Nelson house. I telephoned the Stigler family from six months ago, and the Johnsons from a little over a year ago. Both remember a public employee calling before the kidnappings. With the Stiglers, it was a building inspector with some story about faulty wiring being reported in the neighborhood. The Johnsons fell for an Environmental Protection Agency spot check of radon gas levels. We definitely have a pattern of an impostor accessing the homes in the weeks before the babies are snatched. Even the time of day matches. He's smart enough to come right before the children go down for a nap."

Slumping back in his chair, Ed ran his hand across his balding head. "Great! But now what do we do? Put out a bulletin on all people wearing uniforms or flashing badges?"

"Come on, Ed, give me a break." She began vigorously moving about the room again, unable to keep still. "What I need are composite sketches from each family. I know, I know. They're spread over the United States and Canada too." Her eyes pleaded as she asked, "Can you see about getting the composites for me? Even if the guy is wearing some sort of disguise, we may be able to combine the descriptions and come up with a reasonable sketch."

Narrowing one eye, Ed said, "How about just the last few years? The people aren't going to remember much further back than that anyway. Besides, why open old wounds?"

Across the room, Lesley's finger rested on Savannah, Georgia, where the twenty-second flag had been added to the map last night. "I'll settle for the last ten flags. I know we're getting closer, Ed. I can feel it . . . I thought of something else too."

"Still hot on your babies-for-sale angle?" he asked in his usual flat tone.

"There's no evidence to support the prevailing serial killer theory. Not one body has been found. Not one."

Ed slowly shook his head. "The network of people needed to sell babies would be huge, Lesley. In all these years someone would've cracked."

The phone rang, and Ed jumped to answer it. When he hung up, he said, "That was the lab. They found traces of ether on the crib sheet. The grass behind the nursery door matches the Nelsons' front lawn, so it isn't any help. Only prints on the plug to the baby monitor were the mother's. We can keep our fingers crossed on the strand of hair on the windowsill, but I bet you a hundred bucks it doesn't come through."

"Haven't we found ether before?" Lesley asked.

"Twice. Once the very first time. Then again ten years later." He moved across the room and pointed to flags at opposite ends of the map.

Pacing, Lesley was animated as she said, "So something didn't go down as planned this time. Maybe he's getting edgy in his old age. Losing his touch. I'll bet he was behind the door the whole time Mary Nelson was with the baby after midnight. How else could the grass have gotten there? Plus, she swears the monitor was plugged in when she left. She even checked the cord."

"You think we're dealing with a guy who's calm enough to wait for fifteen to twenty minutes without making a sound? I'm not sure any criminal is that cool, Jaggers."

"This bastard is."

* * *

Nick had just driven past the site of the Murrah Federal Building Memorial when he asked, "Have you ever noticed how quiet everything is around the bombing site? We were both talking a minute ago, then when it was in sight . . . silence."

Angela glanced over at him and replied, "Now that you mention it, you're right. This entire area has changed so much since then. It's not just that the building is gone, it's more like the air is still emotionally charged. In fact, it reminds me of the intense feeling around the Vietnam Veterans Memorial in D.C."

"It's good to know people don't forget. Maybe the memory of the pain can keep horrible things from happening again." Nick turned into a parking garage. As he politely helped her out of the car, he said, "By the way, nice touch, Angela."

"What are you talking about?" she asked, hurrying to keep up with him.

Looking down at her, he said, "The outfit. Navy slacks, matching blazer, even a silk tie. You'll be in great shape unless he mistakes you for a lonesome sailor."

"Very funny. It was your idea, you know."

"My idea?" he playfully asked.

"You're the one who said he couldn't handle short skirts." She tugged the thigh of the tailored slacks. "These are definitely not short."

Nick stopped and reached for his wallet. "I'll bet you he still can't handle it."

Angela kept walking, shaking her head. "I don't think I'll risk any money on a sucker bet like that. He may have gotten by with harassing women for so long, he doesn't even realize he's doing it."

"He realizes it. He just doesn't give a damn."

Senator Holt welcomed them as they entered the reception area of his office. After acknowledging Nick with a vigorous handshake, he slapped him on the back. "Make yourself at home. Take off your jacket and have a seat." Then he turned his attention to Angela and said, "And *you* can take off anything you like."

Angela reminded herself how badly she needed the money to pay for her mother's care. Although her fists hung docilely at her side, they were so tightly clenched the knuckles were white. She followed the men into the senator's private office.

Nick's cordial voice betrayed his underlying message: "Really, Senator. I'd appreciate your showing Angela a little more professional respect. She's worked very hard on your latest problem with Attorney General Stover, and I think I speak for both of us when I say we find your lewd remarks offensive."

"He means no harm, you know." Both Nick and Angela were startled when Alice Holt stood up from behind the wet bar in the far corner of the senator's spacious office. "You lawyers really need to learn to lighten up. What fun is life if you nitpick everything?" She giggled. "But then, what would lawyers do if they weren't nitpicking? No. Don't tell me. Run for political office!" She held up her fresh drink and added, "Care to join me?"

"Alice, I think you've had enough already." Senator Holt took the Bloody Mary from her hand and poured it down the drain. Staying at Alice's side, he turned to face Nick and Angela. "I suppose we should postpone this meeting for a while. I'll call your office to reschedule."

Angela and Nick both started to speak, but Angela was first. "Nick didn't mean to offend anyone, Senator. The information we're here to cover is urgent. You should respond to Susan Stover's latest allegations in time for the media to cover it on tonight's news. If you don't issue a statement, it will look as though you're backing down."

"Respond the way you've already prepared in that fancy presentation you were going to show me today. Mr. Hunter's right. You've done good work. I'll just have to trust you for now, won't I? I'll call you later."

Now it was Nick's turn. "But, Senator, I have a long list of questions on your personal investments, and we're running out of time."

"Call my accountants. WKE will walk you through everything I'm involved in. I'll call the managing partner and tell him to expect you." He walked over to them. He laid his hands on their shoulders and gently pushed them through the door. "Go. Now."

As soon as they were on the elevator, Angela slumped against the back wall and muttered, "Holy shit."

Neither spoke again until Nick squeezed himself behind the steering wheel of his Cutlass. Angela shot him a worried look as she asked, "Are you going to pack your desk as soon as we get back, or wait until the security guard can help? Mr. Kellars always assigns a guard to escort the people he fires out the door, you know. Wouldn't want them to slip a virus in the old computer system or anything, now, would he?"

Even though Nick was obviously troubled, he started the car and quietly said, "Come on, Angela, calm down. We're not going to get fired."

"For the record, Hunter, I am calm." Angela jerked out the tortoise-shell comb that held her French twist, freeing her auburn hair to fall on her shoulders. Slowly running her thumbnail noisily along the comb's teeth, she said, "I think I'm handling things pretty well considering we just got kicked out of Senator Holt's office. For insulting him, no less! In case you haven't figured it out, the senator is the biggest client of Kellars and Kellars. Oops, how could I be so stupid? I mean the biggest ex-client."

Shaking his head, Nick firmly stated, "He wasn't mad. He was just embarrassed. He not only stuck his foot in his mouth, his wife was making a total ass out of herself."

Angela stared at the comb, concentrating on the different sounds each tooth made. "So what else is new? If Holt gave a damn about being embarrassed in public, he would have divorced Alice years ago. She's always making scenes. But without her, who would make the decisions for him?"

Shrugging, Nick said, "Then he's used to covering for her and we have nothing to worry about." Glaring at the comb, he added, "Could you please stop that? It's making me nervous."

Angela grabbed her purse and shoved the comb inside. Looking out the window, she saw they were passing the memorial. She sighed, then looked at her own hands. When they were a block away, she quietly said, "I suppose I should handle damage control. I've been with the firm longer, so maybe he'll take the news better from me."

"What the hell are you talking about?"

Angela pinned him with an incredulous look. "Telling Kellars our side of the story before Hotlips gets us canned, of course."

"Please, Angela. Just go on like nothing happened. You don't know how people like Holt think. It would make him look bad to complain about what happened. What's he going to say? 'I was sexually harassing your head of public relations when that lawyer you just hired told me off'? Trust me. This will blow over without Kellars ever knowing."

"And if it doesn't?"

"I've only been at K and K a few months, but I suppose I still remember how to run a law firm." Nudging her, he smiled and added, "We'll start our own company. Our first case will be to sue K and K for unjustly firing us. Then we can go after the good senator for sexual harassment. If all else fails, I know of a great case on ownership and control of cryopreserved embryos. Tons of publicity potential. Huge settlement at stake. Living on macaroni and cheese for a couple more years won't be so bad."

"A couple more years?" she asked skeptically.

"Macaroni was a main staple of my diet before I came here. Partly because it's one of the few things I know how to fix."

Smiling in spite of herself, Angela said, "I think I can come up with a few other creative, inexpensive meals. Of course, all that starch probably made you a better lawyer."

"Are you accusing me of being stiff?"

Angela laughed. "I wouldn't touch that line for a million bucks. Would you like to rephrase the question, counselor?"

"I withdraw the question, your honor."

Angela put her hand on his arm. "Seriously, Nick. No matter what happens, I really do appreciate you asking him to stop making those tacky remarks. It was very noble of you. Professionally risky, maybe downright stupid, but noble nonetheless."

Shooting her a playful look, Nick asked, "So are you coming to my rescue next time his wife makes a move on me?"

"She's done that?"

"It's not her fault. I'm just irresistible." He flashed her a killer smile.

"Really? To women?" She turned to look out the window at the passing skyscrapers. *He is irresistible, damn him. In the last ten minutes, anyway. I just wish I could figure him out. He acts like he's interested, but he couldn't be.*

"You love to play games, don't you?" Nick asked.

Welcoming the change of subject, Angela immediately snapped, "You bet."

"Then figure this one out. Holt said I should contact his accounting firm, WKE. You said all of Kellars and Kellars accounting work was done by Wood, Kruger and Etherton."

Shrugging, Angela said, "Which could be abbreviated WKE. It doesn't surprise me that they'd use the same firm."

"So why would Kellars and Kellars have access to their independent accounting firm's computer program? Remember what the screen on my machine said when it locked up the day I met you . . ."

"WKE." She hesitated, then said, "Which could just as easily stand for Will Kellars Enterprises."

"No matter what, I'm not getting a warm feeling about all this, Angela. First, the senator owns part of the travel agency that shares the firm's floor. Now he just happens to use the same accountants. For both of our sakes, I hope this campaign investigation gets settled soon."

Evan opened the envelope with the key to his Porsche. His twitching eyelid finally relaxed as he saw the stack of hundred-dollar bills neatly tucked inside the piece of paper. Something was different this time, and his stomach tightened automatically with apprehension.

The money always came alone. Never before had even a scrap of potential evidence been delivered with the payment. He took a deep calming breath before unfolding the paper. It described a special package, the exact location of which was known. Preliminary photo sessions were not needed, since a satisfied purchaser would be arranged after the fact. The package was scheduled to be delivered in ten days. A bonus of $25,000 each would arrive if the transaction was completed utilizing a new technique on a timely basis.

Additional information and travel arrangements would arrive in two days.

Evan read the note twice, both times hesitating when he came to the phrase "utilizing a new technique." He and Tony had successfully completed job after job in the same manner. Precise timing was essential, as was planning. How could they possibly expect them to develop a new method in less than eight days? He knew the answer. They didn't care how the job was executed, as long as delivery occurred on time.

The heavy bond paper crumpled in Evan's fist as his foot pushed the accelerator to the floor. Evan knew Tony usually celebrated each successful job with a gambling spree in Monaco. He only hoped he hadn't left the country yet. Grabbing his cell phone, he dialed Tony's number. When he answered, Evan said, "I'm glad I caught you."

"Must be urgent," Tony mumbled.

Evan's voice was calm as he replied, "Could be. A special delivery. Interested?"

"What's the value?"

"Twenty-five each."

"I can handle it. Anything else?"

Evan coughed, then answered, "It requires an alternate method of procurement."

"Why?"

"Avoiding connections."

After a long hesitation Tony said, "I understand."

Evan hung up. Relief washed over him. Knowing Tony would be on board eased his mind about handling another job so soon. He was already thinking of intriguing new schemes. In fact, he was surprised they hadn't thought of modifying things earlier. Intricate, complex, yet efficient changes could throw the authorities off what little trail they consistently left.

Definitely easy money.

In Chicago, Tony cradled the phone and stared at his brother, who had been scrutinizing his every word. "Got a problem?" Tony asked.

Roberto grinned. "So I'm curious. Can you blame me?"

Standing, Tony walked over to him and said, "I like my privacy. Remember?"

Holding up his hands, Roberto answered, "I don't care what you're gonna do. I'll watch the place for you. Keep all this nice stuff of yours safe."

"When I get back, we're going to have a long, serious talk. Understand?"

Roberto merely shrugged, knowing he could convince Tony to let him stay. Besides, even if he kicked him out, a few more days in paradise were better than none at all.

Angela's hand was shaking as she checked her makeup in the bathroom mirror. Will Kellars wanted to see her—immediately. *Nick was wrong. Senator Hotlips squealed like a stuck pig. We're being fired! Shit.*

She tensely walked into the stall closest to the wall and slid the lock into place. Reaching into her pocket, she pulled out her recorder and ejected the tape. Flipping it over, she fumbled when she tried to snap it back in, juggling it with one hand before it plopped into the water and floated casually to the bottom of the toilet.

For several seconds she simply stared at the tape in disbelief. A bubble floated from it as it rested comfortably on the cold white porcelain. A nervous giggle escaped as she realized that even in her worst nightmare, her tape had never been flushed down the toilet. But she had no choice. She reached over and pushed the handle down, sure she was watching the little whirlpool carry not only the tape but her career down the drain, too.

As she emerged from the ladies' room, she practically screamed when she ran into Marilyn.

"My goodness, Angela. Maybe you should cut down on your caffeine. You're awfully jumpy."

"Marilyn, I need a huge favor," Angela whispered.

"Name it."

She patted her pocket. "My last tape just went down the toilet. Literally. Can I borrow one?"

Marilyn laughed, "I keep a spare microcassette in my top desk drawer. I'll walk back with you and get it."

"Thanks, Marilyn. You're a life saver."

The light skirt Marilyn wore seemed to float as she briskly walked. Her excitement was contagious as she said, "Did you know I'm supposed to leave for the Caymans in three days? I've waited five years for another shot at the corporate condo, and I'm finally in. It's paradise." She closed her eyes. "The beach is just outside the bedroom window. All night you hear the waves rolling in. At dawn, when the ocean is calm, you snorkel to the coral reefs just offshore and see millions of tropical fish. Then you lay in the sun and bake."

Marilyn glanced toward Mr. Kellars' door, then discreetly opened her drawer and handed the tape to Angela.

As Angela dropped it into place and pushed the record button to test it, she sighed, "I can't wait to go myself. I must be scheduled to go the week after you get back. That is, if I don't get fired today."

From behind them a deep, male voice said, "I saw that. Hand over that tape this instant!"

Both women whirled around. Nick laughed at the horror-stricken expressions on their faces.

Angela instantly relaxed, then whispered, "It's okay, Marilyn. I trusted him with our secret. He knows all about our little game." Pulling open the pocket of her navy blazer, she tucked the recorder inside.

"Young man, if you ever, ever scare me like that again I'll . . . Oh, never mind. Just be careful!" Pressing the intercom, she said, "Mr. Kellars, Mr. Hunter and Ms. Anderson are here for the meeting you requested."

They all heard Will's gruff reply: "Send 'em in."

"Are we the only ones coming?" Angela asked as she walked toward his office door.

Marilyn merely nodded and smiled.

Angela followed Nick through the immense doors, his huge shadow falling across her like an ominous cloud. Her fear was gone, replaced by bleak acceptance. She was ready to fight, or grovel, whatever it would take to keep her job. Walking away from Nick, she stopped in the sunlight streaming in the windows, her feet slightly apart, her arms crossed defensively. In her men's-style navy suit and tie, she looked like a twelve-year-old boy trying, but failing miserably, to convince everyone he was a man.

Will Kellars was standing by the bookcase mirror when they entered. Walking toward them, he said, "I suppose you're wondering why I interrupted your busy schedules."

Both of them nodded.

"I got a call from Senator Holt this morning. . . ."

Angela's glare at Nick said, "I told you so."

". . . He told me how pleased he was with the work you are both doing."

Nick grinned and raised an eyebrow, resisting the urge to gloat. Will Kellars walked over and seized an envelope from his desk. "The firm is buying you dinner. I appreciate the hard work the two of you put in every day. Without employees like you, Kellars and Kellars wouldn't be one of the top firms in Oklahoma." He handed Nick the envelope. "Just give them this, and the bill will be sent directly to me." He stared at them in the awkward silence, finally commanding, "You can go now. I'm sure you both have plenty to keep you busy."

Too stunned to say anything, they thanked him and left. Nick silently followed Angela back to her office. He leaned in the doorway until she finally asked, "Are you going to stand there all day?"

"Depends," he quipped.

"On how long it takes me to eat crow?" she snapped.

Beaming, Nick answered, "No."

"Then what?" she asked.

"I believe he wants us to have dinner sometime."

Against her better judgment, she muttered, "Fine."

Still grinning, Nick asked, "Tomorrow?"

Without looking up she replied, "Great. Fine. Whatever."

"Shall we go straight from here or should I pick you up at seven?"

"Seven." Pinning him with an insolent look, she added, "That is, if you can quit by then."

"Quit what?" he asked innocently.

"That 'I was right' attitude you've got going. Your baby blues are twinkling big-time."

He raised his eyebrows naively as he replied, "This happens to be my polite, sophisticated attitude."

Smirking, Angela said, "I don't like it. You look too damn smug."

"So you'd rather me be rude, crude, and obnoxious?"

She laughed since she couldn't even imagine Nick as anything but a gentleman. "Tomorrow night at seven. Polite is fine, but drop sophisticated." She stood up, signaling him to wait as she walked toward him with her hand extended. "Let's just get it over with now, instead of dragging it out. You were right. I was wrong. Your superior intellect has been proven."

Nick shook her hand, then kept it captured in his. "Thank you. But intelligence had nothing to do with it. Women don't think like men. If they did, we wouldn't have to balance juries so carefully." Releasing his grip slowly, he turned and walked away.

Angela wished he hadn't let go. She walked back to her desk and sighed.

Popping his head back in her doorway, he playfully added, "And by the way, these baby blues always twinkle at the prospect of having dinner with a beautiful woman. Especially a *free* dinner." He jumped sideways, dodging the pen she hurled at him. She heard it bounce off the far wall as he sauntered away.

Lesley stared at the computer-generated sketches lining the drab wall of the conference room. Ten drawings. Ten distinct hairstyles. Ten different men. Six had thin faces with high, well-defined cheekbones. Four had rounder faces, with deep clefts in the chins. Some had mustaches, some beards. Eye colors ranged from light blue to almost black. She stood and pulled them down one by one. Rearranging them, she hung them back up, grouping the cheekbones separately from the chins. The beards were hung near the closest set of eyes.

Turning to Ed, she said, "There's two of them. Look closely. These five could all be the same man. He's taller and thinner, probably between thirty and thirty-five. The other four could be the second suspect. Shorter, darker, a little older."

Ed leaned back and studied the pictures. After tapping his pencil against his cheek for several seconds, he shifted his gaze to Lesley and said, "It's possible. Not very likely, but possible. I'll send them to the computer lab and have one composite sketch done of each group."

Lesley stood, then began shoving papers into her briefcase. "Then I'd like to go back to each family and check to see if anyone saw someone matching those composites at the park before the kidnapping. That's our only other lead. Every one of the families had visited a park near their home within a couple of days of the snatching."

Ed slowly nodded. "We're finally making real progress."

"Thank God," Lesley said as she seized her briefcase and left. She had ten desperate families to contact, and many others who were still in emotional limbo. People who would give anything to have their babies home again. And somehow she was going to find a way to help them.

"Have you met Susan Stover before?" Angela asked as Nick drove toward the attorney general's office the next day.

"No. But I've been watching her on television and reading what she says in the newspapers for so long, I feel like I know her," Nick answered.

"She comes across as a real bitch," Angela said flatly.

Nick threw a stunned look at her. "I thought all women supported any female who managed to climb their way to the top."

She shrugged. "Not me. I support people who earn my respect."

After digesting her strong reaction, he replied, "You have an unusual opinion for a woman."

Smiling, she batted her eyes and in a soft Southern drawl said, "You mean a little ol' helpless woman like me?" Adjusting to her normal Midwestern voice, she said, "Nick, surely by now you've figured out that I'm far from helpless."

"Definitely." Still, he was certain he was treading on unstable ground, and he quickly changed the subject. "So why do you think Susan Stover is a bitch?"

Angela smiled, not missing his switch. "I've watched her work for years. Instead of playing her cards all at once, she loves to drag things out. I'll bet she has a scrapbook ten inches thick of all the newspaper articles her accusations have provoked. She loves to ruffle feathers, to be in the limelight. Plus, I hate to admit it, but I'm prejudiced. She's the daughter of the richest man in Oklahoma. She lives in a mansion. It just doesn't seem that she's had to scrape the bottom of the barrel like the rest of us to get where she is."

Nick raised his brows. "Sounds like a case of jealousy." He ignored the ominous flare of Angela's eyes and continued, "She's got a tough job. Put yourself in her shoes. She lost her husband before she was even thirty years old, so she still lives with her overbearing father. Suppose you were the attorney general and someone came to you who said they knew a certain senator was living way beyond his means. You'd watch for a while. You'd get reports on the luxurious home, the extravagant trips. Even allowing for freebies from lobbyists, it doesn't add up."

"So you make allegations that could ruin a man's future?" Angela's eyes sparked as she goaded him on. "Start a nice mud-slinging match with the public as spectators?"

Enjoying the game, he took a deep breath and answered, "No, first you go to them and ask for an explanation. Quietly. Then when they kick you out of their office, you hit the media full force."

Angela's eyes went wide. "Did she approach Senator Holt quietly, as you put it?"

Nick nodded as he turned into the parking garage. "I think so. I have a file of initial information that was accumulated by her office. I've checked all the newspaper articles, and nothing had been released to the public before Senator Holt got his hands on that file. Either she gave it to him before she publicly accused him, or he has contacts inside her office. And right now I'd rather not think about the ramifications of the latter possibility."

Through clenched teeth Annissa quietly said, "It's set for tomorrow morning."

"You've always done good work, Annissa." Reaching out to her, Will smiled. "I knew you could pull it off."

She didn't back down. Instead, she pleaded with him. "You know how I feel about this job. It's not smart. We could lose everything. And it won't end here. I'm sure the greed will keep getting worse. It always does."

"Who knows? I learned a long time ago not to second-guess people."

Annissa's eyes held his. "Look at me, Will. I'm getting too old to worry about this. When will it end?"

Will did look at her. He felt the attraction still

pulling him, even after twenty years. She was the same strikingly beautiful girl he had fallen for long ago. "We both know it's not that easy, Annissa. We've dug ourselves in pretty deep. I'm not sure there is a way out, at least for a few more years."

She softly shook her head. "I don't know if I can make it that long. I'm tired. Our luck can't hold forever. I think we should get out now, while we still can. I want to go back home. My mother's going to be seventy next month, and I haven't seen her in years."

"So take a trip. After this job we won't do another one for six months. I promise."

"And who's going to handle all the daily transfers? Are you planning to get the cash out of the jet when it comes back from the Caymans yourself? The people at the airport are used to my monthly inspections. First they'd wonder who you were. Then they'd wonder why you were snooping around Pampered's private jet. Don't you see, Will? As long as this business is going on, I'm stuck. I want out."

Will's soft gaze turned instantly vicious. "I've been patient with you up until now, but I'm warning you. Don't ever say that again, Annissa. Don't even think it. No one is indispensable."

Chapter 6

Tony rubbed his burning eyes, combing his hair back with his fingers. Coughing, his hidden mini-microphone carried his voice to Evan as he softly said, "Damn flu hit me in the middle of the flight. Thought I was gonna die before the plane landed. Since I can barely walk, much less think right now, I hope this plan of yours is foolproof."

Through the headset he heard the tension in Evan's voice as he asked, "Are you positive you can handle this?"

"Sure." Slumping into the seat of the stolen car, Tony added, "I just want to get it over with so I can go back to Chicago and die." Sun coursed through the dark windshield, dimly reflecting off his thermos as he tilted it to pour another cup of coffee. He was still trying to quiet his restless stomach as he watched the main entry of the target's house. A layer of sweat was forming under the heavy stage makeup and wig, causing his entire head to itch.

In an instant his physical misery was replaced by the primal instincts of the hunt. Adrenaline surged the moment he caught movement in the target's foyer through his binoculars. Tony watched as the girl emerged from the front door of the house, toting a backpack, a diaper bag, and the baby. He knew from the stats that she was only seventeen, but even if he hadn't known, he could easily have guessed her age by the bounce in her stride and the way her long, straight brown hair swung freely as she crossed the sidewalk to her car.

"She's on her way. . . . Pulling out now in a black Lexus," he said.

"We're clear at the stop sign," Evan replied. "You sure you're well enough to handle the action?"

"Of course. Let's get this over with." Tony put his hand on the pistol tucked inside his belt as he accelerated. Just as she rolled to a stop at the corner, he bumped the back of her car, barely hard enough to make her pitch forward against her seat belt. He cautiously pushed open his door and walked to where the two bumpers had collided. One taillight on the Lexus was broken, but the rental car looked fine.

Tony stayed near the back fender of her car, shaking his head and looking thoroughly disgusted with himself. He knew she could see him in her driver's-side mirror, and that he looked like every other guy on his way to work, his suit perfectly pressed, his shoes gleaming in the early morning sunlight. She would get out of the car sooner or later. So he waited and watched. She seemed to be searching for something, digging in her purse. *Shit! A cell phone!*

Thinking quickly, he smiled as he tapped on her window and then on his watch, indicating he was in a hurry. The driver's door of the Lexus slowly cracked open. "I'm calling the police to report the accident."

"Don't bother. I already did."

She hesitated for a moment, apparently considering when he could possibly have had time to place the call. It was the only opportunity he needed.

Her chestnut hair shimmered in the sunlight as Tony grabbed her by it and jerked her out of the car. Holding the dark gun barrel high, he watched the rush of terror replace the confusion in her eyes.

The girl pulled back, bumping against her car. He could barely hear her voice as she cried, "Take whatever you want. My purse . . . is in the front seat. I'll . . . I'll get it for you."

Tony relaxed slightly, certain she was paralyzed with fear. He eased his grip and demanded, "Don't move. Just turn slowly around and no one will get hurt."

She merely whimpered, quickly doing as she was told.

Tony lowered the gun slightly, reaching with his free hand to grab her arm. She slid sideways before he had a chance to lock onto her again, then whirled around, managing to slam her knee into Tony's groin.

For a split second Tony didn't know what had happened. The air blasted painfully out of his lungs, followed by an excruciating gulp as he felt his groin ignite. Furious, he recovered quickly but not before the girl clawed his face, her nails leaving a bloody trail as they ripped through the makeup to his skin.

Watching her eyes, Tony struggled to control her. A puzzled expression instantaneously changed to horror when his wig peeled off in her hand. Her next blow was a kick to his chest that knocked the wind out of him once again and scattered pieces of his communications equipment on the ground.

The plan had called for simply tying the girl up, but her violent reaction made Tony's next decision easy. Her first and only scream for help ended when his fist crushed her jaw, slamming her head against the car door. He shoved her limp body into the backseat of the Lexus, shut the door, and gasped for air. Jumping behind the wheel of her car, he slammed it into gear and sped off.

Annissa cringed when the phone rang. Even though it was after ten o'clock, she was seated in the secret office, working. Snatching the special line, she snapped, "Yes?"

"We've got a problem."

Recognizing Evan's voice, she relaxed a little and asked, "Did you get the package?"

"It's already on its way out of the country. But we had a slight snag this time."

Annissa icily demanded, "Define snag."

"The girl fought. We were interrupted before we could remove all the evidence."

"Such as?" Annissa asked impatiently.

"A wig, walkie-talkie, and thermos. The car had to be left behind as well."

"Can it be traced?"

"No way. Stolen tags, no serial number."

"Good." She hesitated, then asked, "What about prints?"

"It's possible they could lift Tony's off the thermos."

After a moment Annissa slowly stated, "Our procedure prevents leaving fingerprints. How could this have happened?"

Evan exploded, "You know as well as I do that you wanted this job done using a *different* procedure. Don't you dare try to throw this back in our faces."

"Enough." Annissa was silent as she realized her nightmares were coming true. She wondered how Will would react, then asked, "What about the mother?"

"Drugged and dumped. She won't remember much, if anything."

"And Tony?"

"Leaving the country indefinitely."

"Look for a replacement."

Evan sighed and quietly replied, "But we both know the chances of the police identifying him are minimal. The fewer people who know, the better. I'd rather wait and let this blow over. It would be safer for all of us."

"We don't pay for mistakes, Evan. None of us can afford it. Find a replacement, but don't give any details of the operation until later. And Evan, do it *now*."

Cradling the phone, she knew she had to tell Will. Without hesitation she dialed his number at home. A cynical smile crossed her face as she finished briefly describing the problems. She could almost feel the turmoil building inside him as he processed the extent of damage.

"You know I have to call," he finally stated.

"I suppose so," she replied.

"Thanks for not saying 'I told you so,'" he said. "If I could get my hands on that damned file of evidence, I would stop all this. You know that, don't you?"

Rudely hanging up before she replied, she said to herself, "It's too late now, Will." Pacing about the small room, she felt like a caged beast. Her old fears had been well founded. Now she faced the birth of new ones.

Hot water pounded his neck, slowly easing the tension of the day. Nick lathered his hair, looking forward to an evening out with Angela. As he rinsed the suds from his hair, he barely heard the phone ringing. Grabbing a towel, he wiped the burning soap from his eyes and rushed to answer it.

"I was hoping you'd still be there," Angela said.

"Actually, I'm standing here dripping wet. You're not going to back out on me, are you?"

Angela pushed the intriguing vision of him out of her mind. "No. But can you come a few minutes early?"

"Why?"

"Just come. Okay?"

"If you're trying to be mysterious, it's working. I'll be right over." He finished rinsing off and quickly dressed in his best suit, a black Armani he had found on sale. As he drove, Nick tried to guess what Angela could possibly want. He was captivated by her, yet his defenses were strongly in position. Last year he had dated a woman twice, then out of the blue she frantically called his apartment to tell him she needed his help—*immediately*. He arrived after a harrowing drive across town, only to find her handcuffed to her bed. She was naked, topped with oozing whipped cream, a few strategically located cherries, and a bottle of chocolate syrup was waiting on the pillow beside her. Not exactly subtle.

After parking next to Angela's car, he jogged up the stairs to her apartment. She opened the door before he even rang the bell. She was definitely not naked, and there wasn't a sign of whipped cream anywhere. Yet in some ways she was even sexier than he had imagined. The business suit she'd worn to work that day had been replaced by an elegant black evening dress that sparkled each time she moved. It was cocktail length, with a scooped neck. Only two spaghetti straps crossed the entire length of her bare back, and spiked black sandals made her legs look endless. "You look beautiful," he managed to say.

"Thanks. You look pretty outstanding yourself. Have you been listening to the news?" she asked.

"No."

Pulling him inside, she practically shoved him onto her sofa. "You're not going to believe this." Nick was watching her moist lips, waiting to see them move again. He wasn't the slightest bit interested in any news, unless it pertained to whipped cream, cherries, and chocolate syrup.

Angela explained, "Susan Stover's seventeen-year-old daughter was abducted in a car-jacking today. They found her drugged on the outskirts of town a little while ago. Her jaw was broken, but they think she's going to be okay."

Nick's appetite instantly vanished. "That's horrible," he said.

"It gets worse. Sandra's baby was in the car with her. Apparently, Susan Stover's grandchild has been kidnapped."

Nick shook his head as he thought. Finally he asked, "Do they have any leads?"

Angela grabbed a waist-length white jacket tailored from the same satiny material. As she slipped it on, she answered, "Not yet. Why don't we go? This whole kidnapping business is sickening. it's really putting me on edge, and I was hoping we could have a nice, quiet dinner together."

Nick purposely centered their conversation on other things as they drove to Nichols Hills. They talked about where she went to school, his basketball scholarship that disappeared when his knee was injured, a mutual love-hate relationship with skiing. By the time they parked outside the Coach House restaurant, they were deeply entangled in a discussion of irrational childhood fears.

As they walked in, their conversation immediately shifted, the romantic influence of their surroundings bringing new meaning to their evening together. Both Nick and Angela were impressed by the beautifully decorated tables. Single red roses rested across each linen place setting, tied in a ribbon of pure white silk. The waiters were dressed in black slacks, red cummerbunds, and crisp white shirts with black bow ties. The only illumination was from scarlet candles flickering in the center of each table.

Shortly after they ordered, Angela hesitated, absently turning her water glass by the stem as she asked, "He wouldn't do it. . . . Would he?"

Nick shook his head, caught off guard by the question. *"Who* wouldn't do *what?"* he asked.

Angela was suddenly embarrassed by her own perverted thoughts. Picking up her rose, she touched the crimson petals, relishing its delicate elegance. A blush crept over her face as she quietly said, "I'm sorry, I can't get the kidnapping off my mind. It dawned on me that Senator Holt would have a lot to gain if he kept Susan Stover's mind off his case for a while."

Nick stared at her for a second, then said, "Considering what we're working on, I think it's perfectly natural for you to try to connect the two. Unfortunately, I'm afraid it's a pretty big stretch."

They were interrupted by the waiter delivering the bottle of Sauternes they had ordered. She watched the pale amber wine splash into the wineglasses, then caught herself studying Nick's face. When the waiter left, Angela smiled and asked, "Are you *really* comfortable here?"

He looked at her, enjoying the evening immensely. "This is certainly superb, but comfortable?" He shrugged. "I would probably be more comfortable kicking back in a pair of sweats, if that's what you mean."

"I love this place, but I think we got a waiter who needs an attitude adjustment." Winking, she said, "Listen to this." She popped open her tiny evening bag and pushed the Play button on her recorder. They both laughed when they heard the waiter's squeaky, nasal voice haughtily reciting the menu, then discussing their choice of wine.

Nick chuckled saying, "You're dangerous with that thing."

"Definitely," Angela replied. She started to stop the recorder, but hesitated when she heard Will Kellars' voice describing what a great person Rick had been. He sounded different, his speech slurred. When Angela heard Marilyn's voice, she realized she had recorded over the tape she borrowed from her. Pushing the Off button she added, "I guess the tape I borrowed from Marilyn the other day already had something recorded on it."

"Kellars sounded drunk. He was talking about his son who died, right?"

"If he was, he must have been in a different world. Rick Kellars was one of the most disgusting people I've ever known. Besides being a druggie, he kept obsessing on innocent women. First he stalked them, then he tried to kill them. He belonged in an institution, all right. Not the fancy psychiatric hospital his father paid off. He belonged in prison."

"That tape makes him sound like a saint." Nick pushed the Play button again, and they listened together. Both of them felt slightly guilty, like small children eavesdropping at their parents' bedroom door during a passionate encounter.

Kellars' pathetic voice droned on, until he finally grumbled, "You know, I've hurt so many innocent people, I'll probably rot in hell." Nick's and Angela's eyes met and held as his last few words faded to static.

Angela's hand was shaking as she took a long sip of wine. Her eyes never left his as she lowered the wineglass and asked, "What could be more innocent than a baby?"

Lesley was dressing when she heard the news. In her agitation her fingers poked through two brand-new pairs of stockings before she gave up and pulled on gray wool slacks and a black cashmere sweater. Glaring at her reflection in her steamy bathroom mirror, she braided her hair so tightly that it made her head ache, then rushed to FBI headquarters.

After taking a deep breath, she walked into Ed's office. She couldn't help but notice the neat stack of files on his credenza, the mini-blinds tilted at their precise morning angle. He had on his weekend clothes, perfectly pressed khaki slacks and an Old Navy sweatshirt.

Calmly, maybe a little too much so, she said, "Good morning, Ed. Is this a convenient time?"

Ed eyed her and replied, "Sure. Have a seat."

She softly kicked the door closed, then walked to the window. Turning toward him, she asked, "I assume you've heard about the Stover kidnapping."

Ed said, "I officially opened a file at six this morning. I had the Oklahoma City police fax us the details. We're in the loop now, so we'll get updated as they progress." He tossed a stack of papers on the table. "We should find out more any minute."

Lesley quickly scanned the information, then said, "It's been over twenty-four hours since the child was taken."

"The grandmother is Oklahoma's attorney general and the daughter of some rich guy. He's throwing his weight around, ordering everyone in the country to find his great-granddaughter. Otherwise, we probably wouldn't be looking at it at all. The kidnapping pattern doesn't fit our guidelines. This was obviously a car-jacking that went wrong. Whoever pulled this job was sloppy, and we both know the guy we're looking for is definitely not sloppy. No one's ever been hurt before, and the mother of this kid was worked over pretty bad, then drugged out of her mind. Besides, it's too soon. The pattern is well established. Our next flag won't be popping up for six more months."

"I think I should go interview the family anyway."

Leaning back, he stared at her with narrowed eyes before finally saying, "I'll approve the trip, but I think you'll be wasting a lot of time and energy."

Lesley sighed. Even though she hated to admit it, she had a feeling he was probably right. But she still had to try. "Care if I run a couple more ideas by you?"

"That's what I'm here for."

"What kind of car-jackers carry high-tech communications equipment?" she asked.

Ed thought for a second before answering, "The

smart ones. Making sure their asses are covered so no one surprises them in the middle of a job."

Shaking her head, she said impatiently, "But most car-jackings are over in a matter of seconds. They should be able to simply *see* if anyone is coming."

"True. But why take a chance? Why not keep in contact?"

"In contact with whom? Car-jackings are usually random. Fast. In and out. The car-jackers would be together, so they could steal the car and get the hell out of there. Isn't that the point? If you already have a couple of cars, why steal one?"

"Could be a car-theft ring. We'll need to check with the locals. . . . But I can tell you think the Stover car-jacking was planned, and not just to get the car. You think they wanted the baby, possibly *only* the baby," he replied.

"If you're going to take the time to cover your ass, you'd probably know what your target is ahead of time."

"No doubt a rich, young heiress would be a good target. Except that they didn't keep Sandra Stover. And they haven't ransomed the baby. Yet." Ed was preoccupied as he slowly muttered, "Which leads to why we're here. Let's assume the baby was the target. Why suddenly change a pattern that's been successful for years?"

Lesley leaned back, feeling as though she'd just won an important battle. "Exactly. There would have to be some reason. Some special deal. If this is a kidnapping ring, they might have needed a kid . . . fast."

"Then why switch from stealing middle-class

babies to nabbing one of the almighty Stover family? If they knew who they were going to take, they must have known what kind of reaction they'd get from Samuel Stover. He doesn't exactly keep a low profile. For Christ's sake, his daughter, who happens to be the baby's grandmother, is Oklahoma's attorney general. It wouldn't take a genius to figure out the stakes were pretty high."

She was deep in thought. "Why would anyone draw that much attention to themselves unless that was the only baby they wanted?"

"Remember the old saying. Criminals are stupid," he answered.

Lesley was quiet for a second, then slowly shook her head. "Not if we're dealing with the same people as before. There's a reason they chose her. We've just got to find it."

The sky was cloudless and so blue it looked as though the plane could easily disappear forever, just like the baby girl nestled in Maya's arms. Gently, continuously, Maya rocked and hummed a Jamaican lullaby to her, even though the child slept soundly. The baby had logged many hours of air time in the last two days. Drugs pulsing through her tiny veins made her sleep deeply through the whine of the pressurized cabin.

Even though her brown curls had been shaved, a blanket was constantly wrapped around the child's bald head, masking her face from the other passengers. Dark makeup made it impossible to tell what race the child was, and what appeared to be a large strawberry birthmark on her forehead kept those who somehow managed to glimpse from staring too long.

Maya tensed as the captain's friendly drawl came over the speakers, informing his passengers they would be landing in Jamaica in five minutes. The weather in Montego Bay was perfect. Eighty degrees with a slight northern breeze. The island appeared below, its lush mountains flowing into the clear blue ocean. Huts and cottages marked the landscape, as well as a few sprawling plantations. Nearing the airport, tourists dotted the beaches; some even waved from their paddle boats as the plane passed just above them. Maya remembered how excited she had been the first time she saw Jamaica from the air. Now seeing it scared the hell out of her—every trip ended at Customs, where one slip could be disastrous.

As they taxied to a stop on the runway, eager travelers flooded the aisles, grabbing their carry-on baggage from the overhead compartments. Then they waited. Shifting nervously back and forth, the people in the airplane's narrow aisles paid no attention to the woman who remained in her seat, holding a quiet baby and looking out the window.

At last the stairway slid into place at the rear of the plane, and the excited procession of travelers headed into the large, open hangar that served as MoBay airport. Some successfully rescued their luggage from enterprising porters, dashing to wait in lines to clear Customs. As they began exotic vacations, Maya eased into their midst, just another Jamaican returning home. In seconds she slipped effortlessly through Customs with the baby. She knew if she checked inside her passport, the folded bills would be gone.

When she emerged from the airport, the baby began squirming under the heat of the blanket. Jax was waiting as planned, yet she could sense his agitation through the rippling waves of heat rising from the tarmac. From a distance he looked like every other native Jamaican. Laid back, casually dressed, in no hurry to go anywhere or do anything. But a closer look revealed a man with too many gray hairs for his age and a constant expression of mild panic that made his dark eyes dart restlessly about.

Maya slid into the old minivan, her dress catching on the spring growing out of the seat. "What's wrong?" she asked.

He grunted, "Tica's sick. *Bushdoctor's* herbs aren't working."

"Worse than last time? How bad is she?" Maya asked as she bounced the child on her knee. Out the window she gazed at a river that flowed from a mountain ravine. It was only an innocuous trickle, yet she knew a cloudburst could transform it into a torrent that would quickly flood the pitted tundra, effectively cutting them off from the rest of the island.

Jax answered, his voice carrying the boredom of repeating the same story once again. "She wants the family with her when her souls fly. She wants us to get Annissa, even though she knows Annissa can't come here." The baby was crying loudly, her tiny fists clenched in anger. "Shut up that one," he snapped.

Maya sighed and rocked the child as she said, "Can you blame her?"

Jax hesitated, deciding which way to handle Maya. Reaching over, he patted her leg. Trying to sound light-hearted, he said, "Sis, you know I'd do anything for you or Tica, but what she's asking is . . ."

"Dangerous." She leaned against him and added playfully, "So what do we do that isn't?"

Jax laughed, squeezing her tightly. "You always see things so bright. You're probably right, as usual." He shot a look at the crying child that reflected only a sliver of the violence coiled tightly inside him. "This one came too soon. What do you feel about her? Is she a warning?"

Maya shrugged and replied, "You know Tica is the only one who has the gift."

"You have it, you just ignore it."

"Maybe—"

"Shut up that one!" Jax repeated, his accented English heavy with impatience.

"She's hot and the sleeping medicine is finally wearing off. My little one is probably very, very hungry." Maya cooed as she made faces at the baby, trying to distract her. "Why don't you take us to Tica's house? Maybe I can change her mind about 'Nissa coming and feed the child." Jax beeped his horn and swerved around a car going too slow for his liking. Chickens ventured dangerously close to the roadway, yet were unfazed by the blast of air from the passing van.

"I wouldn't bring up 'Nissa if I were you. She thinks the *obeah* has harnessed the evil to her earthly spirit, and that her *duppy* will wander lost forever in the mists of the sea," he said.

"I don't believe in *duppies* or ghosts any more than you believe in the black magic of the *obeah*, Jax. Maybe we do have two souls, or maybe we all just die. Period. No soul floating up to heaven. No *duppy* to hang around and haunt the living. Just nonexistence." With the eyes of an adoring sister, she gazed at him as if she expected him to know the truth.

"It doesn't matter what we believe. What matters is what she believes. That much we all owe her, even Annissa."

"Annissa's managed to pay the bills all these years. Quite well, actually," she said.

Jax tensed again, unable to ignore the sense of impending doom he felt. "No matter. The time is over. Too many passed years."

"She only agreed to do what was best for all of us. It's not her fault. 'Nissa couldn't see the future, how it would all turn out, any better than we could."

"History, Maya. All that 'tis ancient history. Years have flown past us all, yet we ignore what we know's true. Evil took our house. Tica wants her family back before it's too late for her souls. Her passing will soon come." The baby's crying escalated. "Shut up that one, I tell you. Do it or—"

"Or what, Jax? You'll toss her out to sea? You like money too much. Too bad you can't get Annissa back and still keep the money coming, too."

Nodding, Jax grinned and replied, "How true." A few miles later, the child suddenly stopped crying. Slowly, in the peaceful new silence that surrounded them, a smile spread across his face. He was genuinely excited as he said, "You're brilliant, Maya. You solved our problem." Although he'd been plotting Annissa's return for two weeks, he loved twisting the truth, even if it was only to make his baby sister feel important.

"And how, exactly, did I do that?" Maya asked.

"We just have to get Annissa here, with all the money in the Cayman accounts. Simple, really."

Maya leaned over and kissed him on the cheek. "I knew you'd find a way, Jax. I just knew it."

"We're going to blitz the nation with our campaign. I want every soul to see Amber's face. I want them to feel our pain. We will find her!"

Susan Stover watched her father walk to the easel and draw as he spoke. She wondered if she would ever lose the feeling of awe he so often inspired as she listened to him.

"We'll need marketing to develop a slick media kit with photos of little Amber alone and with Sandra. Compile basic fact sheets with her date of birth, blood type, the birthmark on her forehead, footprints, hell, everything we know. A hot line is being set up by the phone company as we speak. We'll need volunteers to man the lines twenty-four hours a day. I'm putting up a $250,000 reward for her safe return."

Until now Susan had watched quietly from the corner of the room. Pushing her short salt-and-pepper hair behind her ears, she tried in vain to smooth the wrinkles from the deep purple slacks and blouse she had been wearing for two days. Dark circles under her light gray eyes silently declared her lack of sleep, but it was the deeper expression of controlled panic she suspected held everyone's attention. As soon as she raised her voice, all eyes focused on her. "Every television station will have to be contacted. Magazines and newspapers will need to be sent a kit, along with a plea to run our story. Sandra's jaw is broken, so she isn't well enough to do interviews. I'm planning to conduct daily press conferences. Any other suggestions or ideas?"

The voice from the back of the room was shy, almost too quiet to be heard. "Posters. In grocery store windows, malls, post offices. We could even do billboards."

"Excellent idea," Samuel said.

"Anyone else?" Susan asked as she scanned the room.

"Direct mail to every pediatrician, emphasizing her birthmark," the head of marketing shouted.

She smiled and nodded. "That's good, too."

A hush fell around them again. Finally, Susan held her head high and tearfully said, "My father and I are so grateful to have you all behind us. Thank you again for being here and for offering your support, your personal time, and most of all your prayers. We just know Amber is still alive, and that we can find her with your help."

Samuel nodded in agreement as he followed Susan out of the room. They walked silently back to his office, both trying to regain enough composure to go on. Once inside the large suite, Susan walked to the window. Leaning her forehead against the warm glass, she softly said, "You should be proud. They all came to support you."

Sitting at his desk, he slumped back and closed his eyes. "And you, too," he said.

Peering outside, Susan was sure the beautiful Oklahoma day was mocking their misery. "What now?" she asked.

"I'll stay here in case anyone has any questions. You'd better get back to Sandra. She needs you."

Susan looked at her father, noticing the lines etched deep in his face and the way his breath seemed to catch every minute or so. She wanted to hug him, and for him to hug her back, but she knew it was no use. They never touched, at least not any time she could remember. When her husband had died so soon after their marriage, her father had been a pillar of strength, no tears, just acceptance. He opened his house to her, and she ran back home, never meaning to stay for good. *You get on with life, Susie, that's how you get past these things,* he had told her. And he was right.

They had lived well for the last seventeen years, a comfortable coexistence in a mansion big enough to hold several families. Yet sometimes she wondered if she even knew the man sitting a few feet from her. Weeks would go by when their hectic schedules kept them apart, and even when they were together they rarely talked about anything personal. Conversations always revolved around politics and business.

Susan considered why it always seemed to take a family crisis to throw them together, why they didn't communicate on an emotional level. "Dad?" she softly said.

He opened his eyes in silent question.

The weary expression on his face made her realize that, once again, it wasn't the right time to close the gap between them. Their eyes held as she merely asked, "Is everything going to be all right?"

This time Samuel Stover offered no shrewd lessons on life. He merely shrugged and looked away.

Chapter 7

Pampered in Paradise's corporate jet taxied to a stop just outside Hangar 38, as it always did. Annissa watched and waited inside, her manicured nails tapping a reggae beat on the glossy metal of the small airplane she stood beside. Across the tarmac a dark green field of winter wheat rippled in the mild breeze.

The mock navy airline uniform Annissa wore fitted snugly. White braid lined the cap covering her short hair, exactly matching white lapel and shoulder piping. As the plane taxied to a stop, she felt a gust of warm air flatten her skirt against her thighs, then whip back to puff it forward.

When the jet's door opened, she leaned closer to the airplane, resting in its cool shadow where no one could see her. Four passengers emerged, tanned and cheerful, toting their luggage past the hangar to a waiting limousine. Moving to the side of the huge structure, she observed them loading their bags and crawling into the elegant comfort of the backseat.

When the pilot emerged she was halfway to the plane, a large black leather briefcase dangling from her shoulder. "Is she ready for inspection?" Annissa cheerfully asked.

Nodding, he tipped his cap and replied, "As always, ma'am."

"Any problems on the flight to report?"

"Smooth as a baby's behind."

Annissa's step faltered as his words penetrated, but she controlled her panic. He couldn't possibly know. She smiled and said, "Then it shouldn't take long." Reaching into her briefcase, she withdrew a clipboard, complete with checklists for cleanliness, upholstery, kitchen stock, bar selection, and appliance inspections. Darting up the stairs, she called back to the pilot, "I should be finished in ten minutes. Then you can take her for refueling."

As always Annissa's pen swiftly checked off the boxes, indicating everything on the plane was in working order. Moving through the passenger compartment, she pulled the shades on the windows one by one as she passed, ostensibly to preserve the velvet cloth that covered the plane's twelve seats. When she reached the set of plush benches in the center of the plane, she slid in, bending low to pop open the secret compartment below the window seat. One by one she removed rolls of money, counting twenty in total. She slipped back off the bench, looking into her briefcase. Two hundred thousand dollars. Enough to take her far, far away. But not enough to support an entire family forced to live in seclusion and hide for the rest of their lives.

The sound of footsteps startled her, and she whirled around in time to see Marilyn running breathlessly down the aisle toward her. Annissa froze as a sickening dread exploded inside her.

"Oh. Excuse me, I didn't mean to interrupt you," Marilyn politely said.

"No problem." Annissa caught her breath and tried to smile convincingly. "You really startled me. I'm just doing our routine post-flight inspection. Can I help you?"

Marilyn giggled, her smile warm as she said, "I love your accent. It was so relaxing to listen to the voices of islanders drifting nearby. I wish I could have stayed there forever."

Annissa was becoming impatient. The last thing she wanted was for Will's secretary to recognize her. She continued to smile but curtly asked, "Did you forget something . . . ?"

"Oh, my, yes. My hat. The nice man on the beach made it while I watched. It even has a little hummingbird sticking out of it." Marilyn reached up. As she snapped open the overhead compartment, her purse bumped Annissa's briefcase. A fat roll of cash tumbled out, rolling onto the plush carpet between their feet.

Annissa looked down to avoid making eye contact. She knew grabbing the money too quickly would make her seem nervous or guilty, so instead she acted as though nothing unusual had happened.

Embarrassed, Marilyn felt the blood rush to her face. "I'm such a klutz. Let me get that for you."

"Really, it's no problem," Annissa replied, thankful the woman had apparently taken advantage of the plane's open bar.

Marilyn shook her head wistfully. " 'No problem.' I love the way you people talk."

Both women simultaneously stooped to grab the

money, Annissa being the quickest. In one swift motion the roll was back where it belonged and the briefcase was zipped closed, concealing the rest of its contents.

"Goodness, I hope you have a bodyguard. It's not safe to carry around that kind of money. Especially a delicate woman like yourself."

"I'm careful." She patted her briefcase. "After I get off duty I'm going to book a trip of my own. I've been saving for years."

Marilyn's silly hat now rested on her head, the hummingbird bobbing as she walked toward the exit. "If I were you, I'd go to an island in the Caribbean. It's paradise there, you know."

Unless you're a stupid young girl with grand ambitions, Annissa thought, but replied, "For some. I hope you enjoyed your trip."

"More than I dreamed possible. This is a fabulous plane. I can't wait to go again."

Annissa walked down the stairs with Marilyn, waving as she bounced away. She signaled the pilot when she passed through the hangar. As soon as she was safely inside her car, she locked the doors and leaned her head on the steering wheel.

I knew something like this would happen! First the Stover kidnapping in our own backyard, and now Will's secretary seeing a cash pickup. It's time to get out! If I don't, I'll spend the rest of my days rotting in jail.

As she glanced at the briefcase on the seat beside her, her anger grew. *A measly two hundred thousand. The safe at the office has three times that much, and there's millions in the Cayman accounts.*

Fifteen years of my life are gone, and what do I have to show for it? I can't travel, hell, I can't even go say good-bye to my mother before she dies.

I have as much right to that money as anyone else, and I'll be damned if I'll leave without it!

As Annissa sped away, she never noticed the car that weaved through traffic, following her.

The computer screen glowed in Angela's face, the blinking cursor waiting patiently for her to type the press release Senator Holt needed to make first thing in the morning. She sat with her legs crisscrossed at the desk in the corner of her bedroom, still wearing the same jeans and sweater she'd pulled on early that morning to visit her mother.

It seemed that every Sunday she promised herself she would find time to simply relax, and every Sunday something interfered. More often than not it was work. Trying to write a statement about the Stover kidnapping for a man she thought was despicable, maybe even underhanded enough to have planned the kidnapping himself, made her want to scream.

She quickly shook her head and combed her hair back with her fingers. *Stop thinking like that!* she told herself. Holt might be a lecherous old coot, but he was definitely not a kidnapper. Reaching down, she grabbed the Sunday paper and read the cover story for the third time, trying to find the right phrasing for the senator. Words that could communicate sorrow and outrage over an unspeakable crime. Words to support a woman who was trying to destroy his career. Words she knew were a pile of shit. She threw the newspaper back on the floor and forced herself to write, just in time to be interrupted by the doorbell. "Who is it?" she called.

"It's Nick."

Unlocking the dead bolt, she slid off the chain and threw open the door.

Nick was holding a large pizza box and a four-pack of wine coolers. "Hungry?"

"Starving. Come in." The pizza was almost level with her face. "It smells wonderful."

"Super Supreme, hold the red sauce."

Scrunching her nose, she led him into the kitchen. "No sauce? Weird. Very weird."

Nick slid the pizza onto the butcher block and smiled. "Try it before you complain."

"I have a phone, you know."

"Not one that's working. It's been busy for almost an hour. The operator said it was off the hook."

Angela popped up and ran into the bedroom. Sure enough, the receiver was slightly ajar. She returned it to its cradle and returned to the living room. With mock irritation she said, "You were right, as usual."

"Did I interrupt anything important?"

"Just the press release for Hotlips about the Stover baby kidnapping. But I've been going around in circles for hours. My heart's just not in this one."

Nick twisted open two wine coolers and held one out to Angela. "I spent all day studying his files. Everything adds up. The accountants have a reasonable explanation for every penny. It seems he has a lot of generous friends loaning him limos and private jets, buying extravagant gifts. All stuff that is hard to prove, and even harder to disprove. Looks like the rest of Stover's case is circumstantial."

"I thought you were off about a million dollars," Angela said.

"One of WKE's many accountants whipped out several deals. Some sort of return of capital investments that don't show up on the tax return like normal deals. Besides, a lot of Stover's case is based on contributions by Holt's friends to his campaign. I can study his personal finances till the hogs come home and never see the other side of the equation. Of course, neither can Susan Stover without convening a grand jury."

"I thought she was going to."

"Supposedly this week. But I have a feeling the kidnapping may slow things down. We'll just have to wait and see."

One side of her mouth curled as she shook her head. "The timing is almost too good to be true, isn't it?"

Nick took a long drink, then set the bottle down. His expression bordered on worry as he agreed. "It is an awfully big coincidence. Stover's personal life goes crazy about the same time her professional target practice pays off."

"I'm too suspicious, aren't I?" Angela asked.

"Not necessarily. I've thought the same thing. In fact, I've even wondered if we should try to find out for certain."

* * *

The Stover mansion was exactly that. A mansion. The main house rested behind ancient trees and a sprawling landscaped lawn. On the north side, the tennis courts were completely shielded by shade trees. A running track looped about the outer grounds, but it was the swimming pool that impressed Lesley the most. The second-story balcony overlooked the sparkling water. Olympic size, yet lined by gracious curves, the shallow end was separated by a gently arched bridge of crisp white planks. A magnificent fountain pulsed along one side, its basins overflowing in five small waterfalls that flowed across a line of steps.

"Pretty, isn't it?" Susan Stover had entered the room and stopped next to Lesley on the balcony. The first thing Lesley noticed about the woman was how her hair perfectly framed her face, highlighting strong, prominent cheekbones. Her pale blue jumpsuit was flawlessly accessorized, right down to her shoes. She was an imposing woman, but certainly not because of her size, since she wasn't much over five feet tall. It was her gray eyes. Although they were striking, they were far too serious.

"It's a beautiful pool. In fact, your entire home is extraordinary." Lesley extended her hand and accepted Susan's frigid handshake. "I'm Lesley Jaggers. I phoned a few hours ago from the airport."

Susan was cordial yet stiff. It was obvious her nerves were tautly stretched. "Nice to meet you. Sorry, my hands are always cold. Stress and old age, I guess."

"Don't worry about it," Lesley said.

"Sandra will be in soon. You do understand that she can't talk very well. Her jaw was broken in several places."

Nodding sympathetically, Lesley said, "I'll ask only a few questions. I'll try not to upset her."

Susan turned her attention back to the pool. She seemed distracted, almost annoyed by Lesley's presence as she said, "This has been quite an ordeal."

"Our team's investigation will be very thorough," Lesley said with conviction. "I'd like to help you find Amber as soon as possible. In fact, nothing would please me more than solving this case."

"We'll do anything you ask," Susan replied. "Anything."

Sandra Stover walked slowly into the room, her grandfather helping her onto the sofa.

"This is my father, Samuel Stover, and my daughter, Sandra. This is Agent Jaggers with the FBI."

Lesley quickly sized up the girl. She was quite pretty, or would be once her face healed. Baggy clothes covered an ultra-thin figure. Her brown eyes were dull, either from medication or despair. As they extended their hands, Lesley said, "Please call me Lesley. I'd like to ask you a few questions, Sandra." Handing her a spiral pad of paper and a pen, she added, "You can write down your answers if you like."

Sandra nodded. The bruises on her face had begun to heal slightly, leaving her cheeks swollen and masked in various shades of green, yellow, and purple.

Samuel Stover spoke, his voice as commanding as his demeanor. "I'd like to speak to you alone first if you don't mind."

"Not at all." She followed him into the hallway, stopping in front of an enormous vase of fresh flowers backed by a huge antique mirror.

Samuel stuffed his hands in the pockets of his twill pants. "I have a team of the best investigators money can buy on this case, and I'd like you to keep them informed of any leads you might have. I've already told my head man to send you copies of everything we have. Can I count on your cooperation?"

Lesley didn't envy the man, or any of the wealth he had accumulated. His power had obviously come at a high price. Her voice was understanding yet firm as she replied, "Mr. Stover, the FBI will do the best we can to locate Amber. We would be very grateful for any information your team could provide, but you have to understand, our files are confidential. They cannot be shared with civilians. You'll just have to trust us."

Samuel Stover crossed his arms. "Well, in that case I think you should keep your little talk with Sandra short and sweet. I doubt she'll be able to tell you any more than you'll find in the notes I've already furnished to the police. Don't upset her." He turned and headed back into the room, the conversation obviously ended.

Lesley followed him in and pulled an armchair close to Sandra. Flipping open her briefcase, she set up a tape recorder, even though it was only a formality. As planned, Lesley began talking quietly to Sandra, her voice comforting yet confident.

DEADLY SILENCE

Hours spent the night before phrasing questions that could be answered easily with only a nod of the head paid off quickly. Sandra began to relax, Samuel quit pacing violently across the balcony, and Susan leaned against the back of the couch, gently stroking her child's long brown hair.

"That's all the questions I have for you right now, Sandra. But I'd like you to look at a couple of pictures before I go." Lesley walked over and pulled the twelve composite drawings from her briefcase. "I need to know if you've ever seen any of these men. Not just the day you were attacked, but at any time. Even in passing, like on the street, in a car, or even at a park. Okay?"

Sandra nodded. Lesley handed her the stack. The first ten pictures were the individual drawings from the various families. The last two were the new sketches she had asked the computer artist to compile from the others. Sandra flipped past each of the first five, stopping to stare at picture number six.

"Do you recognize him?"

Sandra scrunched her eyes, looking puzzled.

"Maybe?"

She nodded. Lesley pulled that photo out. Number seven and eight went by, but number nine stalled her again.

"Another maybe?"

She nodded. Number ten passed. Number eleven passed. Then she flipped to number twelve, a composite drawn based on the four men with rounder faces. Immediately, Sandra's eyes grew wide and she jumped up, almost colliding with

Lesley. Muffled noises filled with excitement tried to escape from Sandra's lips but couldn't.

"Do you recognize him?"

She nodded furiously.

"Use the paper to tell us where you've seen him before."

By now everyone in the room had gathered around the couch to watch as Sandra quickly jotted:

Hit my car. Hurt me. Took my baby!!!

Samuel grabbed the composite, shouting, "Let me have that picture! I'll have this jerk's face plastered on every newspaper first thing in the morning. We're gonna catch the bastard!" He stormed toward the door.

Lesley started to follow, calling after him, "Mr. Stover, that's government property. You'll need permission to print it from my supervisor."

There was fire in Samuel's eyes as he paused in the doorway. "Young lady, hasn't anyone ever told you that possession is nine-tenths of the law?" A second later he was gone.

"I don't understand what you're so upset about."

Annissa spun around, immediately confronting Will Kellars eye to eye. He tolerated her glare, knowing from experience that Annissa's temper was short-lived.

As Will expected, the fire in Annissa downgraded to a burning gleam deep in her black eyes. But her arms were still crossed, ready for a fight.

"Now I have even more reason to leave the country. Your secretary saw the money. I'm sure she recognized me."

"As well she should. We book all our international trips through Pampered."

"And you think it's normal for people to carry around rolls of hundred-dollar bills? She can't be that stupid. No one is."

"You're overreacting. Marilyn told me herself she had the time of her life. She was probably three sheets to the wind when they landed. She never said a word about seeing you or the cash."

Annissa walked over, grabbing the Monday morning paper. She held the front page under his nose. "And what of this? This sketch looks an awful lot like Tony. Someone might recognize him."

Will's expression darkened. "Unfortunately, by now he's dead. A nasty fire seems to have started in his apartment, so even if someone recognizes him, what harm could it do? There is no way he can lead back to us."

She wanted to scream, *Dead? If they killed him, they won't bat an eye when it's our turn!* Instead, she merely pleaded with him, "Don't you see, Will? Everything is falling apart. Kidnapping was bad enough. Now we're accessories to murder!"

In a placating voice he replied, "Every business has minor setbacks occasionally. Things went smoothly for several years, and now we're going through a rough stage. Just wait."

"I can't do this forever, and neither can you. When will it all end? Haven't enough people suffered at your hands?"

Will froze, pure hatred pulsing in his gaze. "Is that what you want? For me to admit that I *like* hurting people? That I don't do this for the money alone?"

With great difficulty she held his vile stare.

Shrugging, he looked away. His tone was so light it was even more threatening as he said, "I guess after all these years I owe you that. Sure, I enjoy watching these sniveling parents suffer. People who can't love their kids should have them taken away. There are plenty of people out there who'll give them the time and attention they need. Damn right, I wish someone had stolen *me* when I was a baby. Adoptive parents give a damn."

For years Annissa had suspected that money wasn't Will's true motivation, but it was still disturbing to know the truth. "Then let *me* out, Will. I'm sick of the whole business, especially now that we're dealing in murder."

Ignoring her plea, he moved so close to her she could see only his eyes. "Just shut up and do your job."

She stepped back, bumping into a table as she asked, "What about Stover? He's got everyone in the nation looking for that baby."

"Well, he won't find her, will he?"

"No. But the reward scares me. A quarter-million dollars can turn up a lot of stones."

"Are you worried about Evan?"

"No. I think Evan is reliable. But it wouldn't hurt to cut him a bigger bonus. Just to be sure."

"Fine. Send him fifty thousand."

"He'll be suspicious if he doesn't get Tony's share as usual."

"Tell him to contact us when he has reestablished Tony's whereabouts. That we'll forward his share directly to him."

"I hope he buys it," Annissa muttered.

"He will. His greed runs deep."

"It's nice to see all of you this morning." Senator Holt studied the group of reporters milling around outside the Capitol Building. A strong south wind whipped fiercely about, creating technical nightmares for the television crews. The senator's black Italian leather shoes and charcoal suit contrasted with the white hair on his temples, making him look distinguished, downright powerful.

As he pulled the speech Angela had prepared from his pocket, questions began flying. He held up his hands, patiently demanding silence before he spoke. "I'd like to read my statement first. Unfortunately, I won't have time to answer many questions today. We have a full agenda to address."

Before he could continue, a particularly brash young reporter shouted from the back of the crowd, "Do you think the kidnapping of her granddaughter will prevent Susan Stover from convening a grand jury this week?"

Years of political experience made Holt's answer flow easily from his lips, his demeanor calm and reserved. "The Stover kidnapping is truly a tragedy. My heart goes out to the entire family, and I pray the child will be located soon. The effect on convening a grand jury is quite irrelevant. If one is ever convened, I will be happy to cooperate in every way possible. I have nothing to hide. My life is dedicated to serving the people of Oklahoma."

Alice Holt watched from the steps behind him, immensely pleased with how her husband had fielded the first question. He read the prepared statement flawlessly and, in spite of the reporters' protests, excused himself graciously without answering any additional questions. He walked casually to stand next to his wife, and they posed for a few cameramen. Suddenly their expressions turned cold, although the cameras continued to flash. Susan Stover was walking directly toward them.

Susan's unexpected arrival at the Capitol created a feeding frenzy for the media. Reporters who had begun packing away their equipment immediately switched gears. They swarmed in disorganized clusters, thrusting microphones in her face, some of which were no longer even connected. Flash bulbs temporarily blinded the attorney general long enough for the media crowd to form a circle, blocking her path into the building and trapping her next to Senator Holt.

"Attorney General Stover, could you tell us how you're feeling right now?" several reporters shouted.

Susan glanced toward the senator, who seemed to be content, at least for now, for her to be in the spotlight. She forced back an unexpected resurgence of tears and focused herself. "Worried. But we are doing everything in our power to gain control of the situation. I'm sure you all saw the sketch of the suspect in this morning's *Daily Oklahoman*. We're very pleased with the progress we've made in the case in such a short time."

"Do you think the kidnapping is for revenge? Maybe one of the people you helped put away when you were the district attorney?"

Susan was sickened by the thought, especially since the police had mentioned the same theory. But she kept her chin high, responding boldly, "Without question I have made my share of enemies, not only in my position as attorney general, but also during the ten years I served as district attorney. You all know that I've not only fought on the prevention side of the crime issue, but also on the management side. I've helped develop prevention programs for the metropolitan area and spearheaded crime-fighting initiatives. If this horrendous act of violence was conducted by someone whom I have offended in my fight against crime, then I can only say that I hope they will reconsider their motives and return Amber." She wiped the corner of her eye as she added, "She's an innocent child, and certainly not the person who should suffer the consequences of someone else's actions."

"What about Amber's father? Where is he? How does he feel about this?"

Susan silently thanked God that the reporter had been tactful enough not to use the word illegitimate. Her daughter's teen pregnancy had been the cause of many hours of anguish, and she blamed herself for spending more time at her job than with her daughter—a trait she must have inherited from her father. The fact that she wasn't with Sandra now sent another wave of guilt into Susan's already aching heart. Her voice quavered as she answered, "Amber's father loves her very much. He is extremely concerned, as we all are."

"How do you feel about the amount of money your father, Samuel Stover, is spending on the rescue campaign?"

From behind her Susan heard Senator Holt clear his throat. She suspected he was having a hard time keeping quiet. She answered, "My father has worked very hard in his life to attain his wealth. He built Stover Enterprises from the ground up, working day and night to accomplish his dream. How he chooses to spend his money is no one's business but his own. Personally, I'm grateful to him for all the emotional and financial support he's giving us during this ordeal. Now if you'll excuse me, I have work to do."

"Since Senator Holt is here to discuss the issue, are you planning to proceed with the grand jury investigation of his finances?"

From the corner of her eye she saw Holt moving forward as she answered, "If, and only if, my office uncovers enough substantive evidence to convene a grand jury, then it will be done. I've scheduled a meeting this morning with my staff to discuss the progress on the case." Turning to recognize him, she stiffly added, "I'm sure Senator Holt will continue to be cooperative and we can wrap the matter up swiftly."

Holt put his arm around her in a fatherly gesture. "Of course I'll cooperate, and I'll do anything I can to help you find that little girl. Oklahomans stick together, even if they are on opposite sides of the fence."

Susan weakly smiled, thankful when he let go of her.

"So you'll know by this afternoon?" a reporter shouted.

"These things take time. In fairness to the senator, we will be double-checking our information before any further action is taken. As I said, I have work to do. Excuse me."

As she walked away, she ignored the cruel string of questions being shouted, even though they felt like knives plunging into her heart.

Have you received a ransom note? Is the rumor we've heard about the psychic leading you to the body true? When can we speak to you daughter, Sandra? Is it possible Sandra herself is in some way responsible for her disappearance? . . .

Chapter 8

A bead of sweat trickled down Angela's forehead. As discreetly as she could, she brushed it away with the back of her hand. For the last fifteen minutes she had waited patiently, listening to Will Kellars talk on his phone about an upcoming trial. Sunlight bathed her seat at the conference table in his office. Initially, the warmth had been relaxing, lulling her into a peaceful state of mind. Now it felt like it might easily suffocate her. Taking off her suit jacket, she carefully draped it over the back of her chair. Trying in vain not to eavesdrop, she absentmindedly tugged the neckline of the sleeveless white silk shell, allowing the puffs of cooler air to revive her spirits.

Finally, Will hung up, instantly turning his attention back to their business. Without missing a beat, he resumed exactly where he had been interrupted. "I'll need the new commercial to cover the exact reasons why estate planning is essential. Use a techno screen with bullets highlighting last will and testament preparation, living trusts, proper witnessing and execution, hazards of probate, complicated asset allocations, tax ramifications, and benefits to survivors. Emphasize the burden they'll be to their loved ones and relatives if they pass on without a will."

He paused, his brow furrowed in deep thought. "I want a shot of a grieving widow shaking her head at all the paperwork. Assets tied up senselessly. All it would have taken was a simple trip to see their attorney. We can close showing children whose parents died without a will, relatives fighting over who has to care for them. Wards of the court. With them in the background, a judge will explain to the audience that their fate lies in his hands instead of those who loved them most. People should be terrified of dying intestate by the time we're through with them."

The buzzer on his phone interrupted again before Angela could speak. Marilyn announced, "Senator Holt on line three, sir. Would you like to take it?"

"Yes." As he reached for his phone, he nodded to Angela. "This may take a few minutes. I'll have Marilyn buzz you when I'm finished."

Angela responded immediately. She gathered her papers and pulled his door closed as she left.

"Is your meeting going well? You look a little flushed," Marilyn said.

"Fine. I was in the hot seat, literally. After all these years I should know better than to sit at that conference table when the morning sun is beating down." She lowered her voice. "I just hate having to be so close to those eyes of his right off the bat. Unnerves me too much. It's like he's burning holes through my soul."

Marilyn grimaced. "I know. I'm glad he uses a dictaphone most of the time. At least I don't have to sit there and take dictation with him breathing down my throat." She looked at her phone, noticing the light on line three blink off. "Don't leave. Looks like it was a short conversation. I'm sure he'll be back with you in just a second."

Angela noted Marilyn's deep, golden tan. "You look gorgeous. How was your trip?"

Softly closing her eyes, she visibly relaxed and said, "Fantastic. I've never been so at ease in my life. You are going to love it. This time next week you'll be basking in true extravagance. People waiting on you hand and foot. Whatever food or drinks you want, whenever you want. Even the airplane is first-class. You don't even feel like you're flying in that private jet Pampered in Paradise owns. It's more like floating."

Angela eagerly replied, "I've heard it's luxurious. Are there really sofas and velvet-covered reclining chairs? Video games and VCR's to watch movies?"

Marilyn nodded as she said, "Not to mention the open bar and full-size rest room. I was pretty tipsy by the time we landed. Almost ran over that weird woman who runs the travel agency across the hall, Ms. Jamison. I forgot my hat, and I must have scared her to death when I ran back to get it. She looked like she'd seen a ghost."

Puzzled, Angela asked, "What was she doing there?"

"I guess she inspects the plane after every trip, since she had a clipboard with checklists. She needs to be more careful, though. A frail woman like that has no business carrying around the kind of money she had with her. She accidentally dropped a roll of cash." Marilyn held up her hands, gesturing the size of the roll of bills. "Hundred-dollar bills, no less, at least that's what I could see."

Angela swallowed hard, instantly suspicious. "Did you ask her what . . ." The buzzer interrupted them. Will Kellars' voice boomed, "Get Anderson back in here."

Marilyn tossed her head to one side. "You're on. Break a leg."

Angela walked back into his office, carefully seating herself in the chair farthest from the direct sunlight.

Kellars had put on his jacket and was standing behind his desk, obviously getting ready to leave. "So, are we clear on the new advertising campaign strategy?"

"I think so. I do have a couple of questions."

Pushing the cuff of his shirt back to reveal his Rolex, he nodded and said, "Fire away, but make it fast."

"First of all, what time frame do you prefer the spots to run, and when do you want them to begin?"

"Six weeks from now. Our initial target audience will be housewives. Contract for commercial time on all the talk shows and soap operas. We want these women nagging their husbands as soon as they set foot back home in the evening."

"And the secondary campaign?"

"Older men. Check the latest demographics to see when the best pull would be on men between fifty-five and seventy. My guess is local newscasts, maybe the weather channel, but who the hell knows anymore?"

She continued to scribble on her yellow legal pad, and asked without looking up, "Technical assistance?" Angela was usually assigned a lawyer who was responsible for evaluating any complex questions that popped up while they were preparing advertising campaigns.

"You seem to work well with Hunter. He can refer you elsewhere if necessary. He's expecting you tomorrow afternoon at four."

"I'll get right on it." She stood, picked up her jacket from the nearby chair, then draped it over her arm as she collected her other things. The recorder in the pocket clicked off, its noise muffled against her abdomen. To Angela it sounded like an explosion, and she visibly paled. With wide eyes she looked at Will, expecting an interrogation. But luckily, he seemed unfazed as he studied her.

"How's your workload, Anderson? You look worn out."

With great control she managed to hold her voice steady. "Nothing to complain about."

"You're scheduled for a vacation soon, right?"

She swallowed hard and nodded.

"I just found out there's an open slot on the chartered flight. If you can be ready in the morning, you can have a nice long, refreshing trip." He glanced down at his watch again, then added, "But you'd have to leave early tomorrow. Can you clear your calendar that fast? I know twenty hours isn't much lead time for a vacation, but as efficient as you are, I'll bet you can do it."

A thousand reasons why she couldn't go flooded Angela's mind, but she knew better than to turn down an act of kindness by Will Kellars. Prudence demanded she at least inquire about her most important business assignments, so she asked, "What about the new estate campaign? And the Stover-Holt issue? If a grand jury is convened, the senator will need all the help we can give him. This probably isn't the best time for me to leave."

"Conscientious employees never think there's a good time to leave. The new advertising campaign can wait a week. Stover doesn't have enough to go to a grand jury. Besides, her heart isn't in her job right now. She's got more important fish to fry with her grandchild missing. Nick Hunter can field any of Holt's emergencies, so it looks like you're clear. On your way out, have Marilyn rearrange your itinerary. Relax and have a good time, Angela. You deserve it."

The Porsche's high-performance engine was silenced when Evan turned off the key and slowly pulled it out of the ignition. As usual, he sat outside the post office for several minutes, making certain no one had followed him. Satisfied he was alone, he jogged up to the building. He almost stopped dead when he saw her face. The reward poster for Amber Stover hung on the main entry door. Directly under the huge color photo of the smiling baby were the words, $250,000 REWARD FOR SAFE RETURN.

The impact of the sizable reward soaked in. Rewards were common in this line of work, but a quarter million was by far the largest in his experience. He hoped no one involved would be shortsighted enough to try to cash out.

Stepping into the busy foyer, he blended easily with the other hurried men and women. The key turned effortlessly in his box, popping open the steel door. Glancing inside, he slowly dragged in a breath of air, hoping it could clear his mind. Two envelopes were waiting. Two. Not one.

Surely Tony hadn't found a reliable hiding place outside the country already? As casually as he could, he walked back out and slipped into his car. Several blocks away, he pulled into a vacant parking lot and opened the largest envelope first. Flipping through, he counted the bills. Fifty thousand dollars in cash. Nothing else. So far, so good.

The second envelope ripped easily open. Inside was a typed message:

> Performance evaluation revealed excellent level of execution. Owner very satisfied. Original bonus amount discussed has been doubled. Will transmit partner's share when permanent forwarding address is received and independently verified.

After reading the message twice, he rubbed his temples. The fifty thousand was all his. Tony would receive payment only when they could verify his location. *How in God's name did they think they could verify the address of a criminal undercover in a foreign country?*

The answer was so simple it made his stomach turn. They had no intention of ever paying him, which could mean only one thing—Tony was dead!

Nick was surprised to see Angela appear in his office doorway at six o'clock in the evening. She looked anxious, even hyper, yet still gorgeous standing in stocking feet, wearing a canary yellow suit. Without high heels she seemed very small and fragile. Nick suppressed his urge to walk over and hold her, bury his head in that gorgeous hair. Clearing his throat, he managed to say, "It's Tuesday. One of your visit-Mother days. What are you still doing here?"

"I'm running late. Mom will have to understand. I need a huge favor."

"Anything."

"Kellars offered to extend my trip to Jamaica! I'm leaving in the morning." She continued, in spite of the shocked expression on Nick's face, "I've put together this file on possible press releases and statements Holt might need to make while I'm gone."

Nick stood and held up his hands. "Slow down. When did all this happen?"

She walked over and laid the file on his desk. "A few hours ago. I know this is my work, but Kellars thought you could handle any emergencies that might pop up while I'm gone. I'm sorry to rush out, but I have a thousand things to get done and I'm running out of time."

Grinning, he playfully ordered, "Then get your butt out of here! And drink some sinful island concoctions for me!"

She turned around, then looked back, her

brown eyes drinking in one last look at him as she said, "It would be more fun if you were going, too."

"True." He winked at her coyly. "But if I went, I wouldn't let you take work with you."

"Speaking of which, I have to go!"

Nick watched her bounce out of his office. Her energy was contagious, even invigorating. He flipped through the file she had left on his desk. Virtually every possibility for the upcoming week was covered. With reluctance he admitted to himself he would miss her.

The phone rang, and he quickly answered, "Nick Hunter."

"Hey, Nick. Just thought I'd touch base with you."

Nick recognized his friend Jim's voice. "How's the cryopreservation case coming? Are you famous yet?"

"Hell, no. At this rate the surrogate we have lined up will be too old to even have a baby once we do get control of the embryos. Peg and I'll be in some nursing home, trying to remember how babies ever got made in the first place. That lawyer you referred us to is doing a fine job, though. It's just a case of a minnow attacking a whale. They have all the money in the world to stall with, and they know time is running against us."

"I'm really sorry I couldn't help you myself. Jason called me the other night at home. Filled me in on all the filings. You're right. They're creating a paperwork dragon, betting you won't be able to hang onto its tail."

"They're wrong. We'll drag 'em down with us.

Stuff some fireworks up that dragon's blistering little butt while we're at it, too. We've talked to several other couples who go there, and they agree. One might even join in the lawsuit."

For a moment Nick longed to be back on his own. He truthfully said, "God, I wish I could take your case. What's funny is that six months ago I would've killed for a case like this. How's Peg holding up?"

"Fine. Working two jobs doesn't leave much time for self-pity. Anger and hostility, but not self-pity."

"She was never the 'poor me' type. She'll be leading a protest any day now. Give her my best."

"I will. Now that you've settled in, how do you like your fancy new job?"

"It's fine. Interesting cases. Things are different here, though. I've never worked anywhere quite like it."

"Anything in particular?"

"Nothing I can pinpoint. Sometimes I feel like there's some big joke, and I'm the only one who doesn't know the punch line. Or like everyone's talking behind my back. I must be getting paranoid in my old age."

"Hotshots always do. The further up the corporate ladder you climb, the more people will want to stab you in the back. Success is something everyone wants for themselves, and most of them don't particularly care to have a lot of competition standing in their way."

Intrigued by Jim's take on the situation, Nick nodded and asked, "So you think I'm a threat?

That's why they treat me like I have leprosy or something?"

"You're a ringer if I ever saw one. The ladies fall all over you, and the clients line up at your door because that extra oxygen you get to your brain makes you brighter than the rest of us. You couldn't be more of a threat if you carried around a friggin' shotgun and waved it in their faces."

"Not here. Only one secretary has looked at me sideways, and I think she forgot her glasses that day. And the only woman I'm interested in treats me like I'm her big brother."

"Thank God. Now I can tell Peg you've lost your touch and to forget about you. You made my day, buddy."

"Glad to be of service."

"Thanks again for all you've done on our case. We really do appreciate it."

"I'll call you in a couple of weeks." Nick hung up. Suddenly he felt very alone. It was a disturbing feeling, and no matter how hard he tried to shake it, it wouldn't let go.

By the time the alarm clock rang at five a.m., Angela had been staring at it for over an hour. She knew she should get up and get ready to leave, yet she wanted to stay in her own bed, under her own covers, for as long as she possibly could.

Pretending, she thought. *Everyone thinks you're so in control, when deep down you're just a chickenshit.* All night she had worried about traveling to Jamaica. Alone. What would she do for a whole week with no one to talk to? Tourists were discouraged to go on excursions unaccompanied by a local guide. She could hire someone, but how would she know who to trust? Like all third-world countries, the vast disparity between the lavish tourist sites and the poverty of the rest of the island was fuel for violence. She wished again Nick could accompany her. Share the sights with her. Just be with her.

He had called last night at eleven o'clock to wish her a safe trip. Talked about some little things, nothing really. For an hour their voices had passed casually back and forth. Comfortable conversation, the kind that old friends and lovers fall into—where each one already knows what the other one will say, finishing each other's sentences. Angela would have kept talking all night, but she knew Nick didn't understand. Couldn't understand. He'd probably never been scared and lonely a day in his life.

Rolling out of bed, she showered and dressed. At precisely nine a.m., the limo driver knocked on the door to her apartment. He carried away her luggage as she ran from room to room doing a final household check. But when the dead bolt slid into place, a knot clenched her stomach.

The feeling of dread had been growing all night, and now was impossible to ignore. She stared at her apartment door, pushing down the odd sensation that nothing would ever be the same again.

Even though she didn't want to go, it was too late to turn back now. The limo was waiting.

Jax spotted her the moment she stepped out of the Pampered in Paradise jet. In skin-tight jeans and a denim shirt knotted casually at her waist, she looked incredibly young and, even better, gullible. Being pretty helped. Watching her slender body bask in the sun would certainly make the time pass quickly, even though it would be a temptation he would have to control. But most of all he chose her because she looked so damned virtuous, in a wonderfully naive way.

By the time she passed through Customs, he knew her name, address, and where she worked. The moment she emerged from the long, hot line, he was at her side, flashing a smile that had deceived so many before. "Welcome to Jamaica, pretty lady. Would you by chance be with the legal firm of Kellars and Kellars?"

Shocked, Angela said, "Yes, I am." Without meaning to seem rude, she tugged her itinerary out of her pocket to see if she was scheduled to be met at the airport. It merely showed her arrival time and the name of the hotel.

"Then come with me, please." Jax led her to his minivan, noticing how hesitant her steps were as she followed him. When they reached the car, he bowed and offered the petite American woman her choice between ice-cold bottles of Red Stripe and Ting, two Jamaican originals.

"Which one has a kick?" she asked.

He held out the Red Stripe beer and grinned. "My name is Jax. Kellars and Kellars has paid for me to drive you to your home away from home." To his surprise, she reached for the Ting. "Are these all your bags?" he asked.

"Yes." She was beginning to relax, inhaling long

breaths of ocean breeze. The sun sensuously warmed her hair, making her scalp tingle.

Jax grabbed her bags and threw them into the white minivan. "I'll be your guide while you're here. I'll take you anywhere you want to go, Miss . . ." Even though he already knew her name from the tag on her luggage, he didn't want to tip his hand.

"Anderson. But call me Angela." She glanced around one more time, wondering where the other people on the flight had gone.

Jax shrugged and smiled. "No need to worry. Pampered in Paradise works with my company. We are the only service they use on the island. You will be safe with me, no trouble, no bother. You can ride up front or in the back. Whichever pretty lady prefers."

His smile won her trust. Relieved, she said, "Up front would be nice. Could I ask you questions as we drive to the hotel?"

"*Irie*. No problem." He jogged to her side, opening the door for her as she slipped into the tattered front seat.

"First question. What does '*irie*' mean?"

Jax slid into the driver's side and grinned at her. "Jamaicans are a carefree people. *Irie* is our way of saying everything is fine, wonderful. It is a happy word. We hope you'll use it often while you're here sharing our island culture."

She took a long swig of the cool beverage. "Obviously a statement rehearsed many times. And what is Ting?"

"We make it on the island. From grapefruits. A grapefruit soda. You like?"

She nodded in approval as the cool, tart liquid quenched her thirst. The airport was open-air, no fans or air conditioning. Standing in line waiting to clear Customs had proven to be a sweltering experience. They swung into the heavy traffic, everyone driving on the wrong side of the road. Horns blared constantly, and she wondered if it was normal, or just a reaction to the domineering way Jax drove. Traffic signals seemed to mean very little, if anything to him. *If this is the taxi service the travel agency trusts, I'd hate to be in one of the bad ones.*

Jax smiled as he saw Angela shyly sink into her seat and buckle her safety belt. "Feeling better now?"

"Much. The airport was hot."

"Because you are overdressed, pretty lady." He reached over and tugged on the knee of her blue jeans. "In Jamaica, clothing should be like the ocean's breath. Light and airy."

"I'll remember that," she answered stiffly. His touch made her uneasy, reminding her of the bizarre premonition she'd had when she left her apartment that morning.

"You will be here but a week?" he asked, even though he already knew her departure date.

Angela nodded. She loved to hear him speak. He had a deep, resonant voice totally unexpected because of his gaunt appearance. English words seemed to be masked in his native language, like iridescent layers of a pearl. She had to listen carefully to understand most of what he said because of his heavy accent.

His eyes fleetingly met hers as he asked, "Are you traveling alone?"

She nodded, then instantly regretted it when she realized she probably shouldn't have told a stranger she was by herself.

Jax raised an eyebrow and smiled at her. "Jamaican men will be enchanted by your beauty. If you are alone, be strong."

Angela stared at Jax for several seconds, then asked, "Strong?" Self-defense wasn't exactly what she had been worried about.

"Relax. Jamaican men will respect you as long as you respect them."

Great. Just great. Why in the world did I agree to come here? "And how will they know that I respect them?"

He turned to her, a gleam in his eye. "If they offer you the priceless chance to spend the night with their *big bamboo*, you should firmly say thanks, but no thanks. Respect their manhood and they will respect your choice. That is, of course, unless you want to."

"Want to what?" she asked naively.

Jax answered with a wicked smile that instantly flooded Angela's face with color. He was still grinning as he pointed at the lush tangle of flowers along the hillside. "Jamaica is a beautiful place. I will show it to you, as only a native Jamaican can."

She couldn't explain why she felt comfortable with Jax. Even safe. Maybe it was his age, or his gentle voice, or the way he talked of sex as if it was just another of the island's treasures. Without hesitation she said, "That would be wonderful."

"Tomorrow you will climb the Dunns River waterfalls near Ocho Rios and shop in the open markets for John Crow beads, coral, alabaster, and jipijapa straw baskets. The next day you can tour Rose Hall. Maybe meet the ghost of the 'White Witch' who lives there. Rafting down the Great River will be next, then the beaches of Negril—"

"Wait! Wait! I only have a week!"

"And what a week it will be, pretty lady. You will know all the treasures of our country before you go home. You will tell your children's children about the beauty here."

And like it or not, you will help me save my family!

Chapter 9

Annissa hurried into work. In the last few months she had found it more and more difficult to arrive on time. Although she usually read her morning paper over her first cup of coffee at home, today it was tucked under one arm, since she'd overslept again. Unlocking the doors, she flipped on the lights, then dropped her briefcase and newspaper on her desk. After brewing a pot of coffee, she finally sat down, ready to begin the day.

As she grabbed the newspaper, it fluttered apart, falling open on her credenza. The image of Evan's face stared at her from just under the headline, FBI SEEKS SECOND KIDNAPPING SUSPECT. The hair was close, his features a little too harsh but still recognizable. But the eyes were perfect. Shrewd, calculating, cold. Definitely Evan's eyes. Quickly scanning the related story, she found no information on how the suspect had been identified. The same description of the kidnapping was recounted, the same facts listed for the tenth time.

Annissa cradled her face in her hands while she thought. Kellars would overreact, as he'd done with Tony. There was no way to keep him from seeing the paper or from watching the news. But she wanted no part of another killing. What could she do?

Suddenly she knew. Silently slipping into the hidden office, she checked Will's office through the one-way mirror. He was meeting with one of the lawyers, apparently engaged in a heated discussion. If she worked fast, she could be finished before Kellars could confront her.

After breezing through the series of security codes, she located the first file she needed. Scribbling down the phone number, she connected the modem and waited as the number dialed through. In less than three minutes, she had opened an account in Grand Cayman, under the name Elaine Patterson, in the account of fifty thousand dollars. Five minutes later, a one-way plane ticket was verified for Elaine Patterson, to be delivered within the hour to Paradise Promotions in Manhattan.

The last part of her plan was the most cunning, yet by far the most dangerous. She quickly dialed the direct phone line to Paradise Promotions, something she had never done before. Phone records could be traced, but in this case the risk was a necessary evil.

Evan was freshly showered, immaculately dressed, and ready to leave. He stood behind the counter, his morning espresso steaming in his left hand while his right hand busily jotted down a message to suspend cleaning of the office until he returned. The rest of his business affairs were ready for his short trip to Nova Scotia, everything temporarily on hold or farmed out to other agencies.

He was rushing out the door with his suitcase when the phone rang. For an instant he considered not answering it, but just after the answering machine picked up, he changed his mind. Grabbing the receiver, he mumbled, "Paradise Promotions, Evan speaking."

"Elaine Patterson needs to check with Federal Bank in Grand Cayman upon arrival. Tickets will be delivered momentarily. Further instructions to be transferred to designated box. Good luck." Click.

Evan never tried to respond. There was no need to. He knew exactly what she meant, every calculated word echoed in his mind. *What the hell went wrong?* was all he wondered.

Practically flying up the spiral staircase to his apartment, he threw open his closet. He peeled off the elegant suit he had worn for only twenty minutes, meticulously replacing it on its hand-carved walnut hanger. Grabbing another suitcase, he began tossing in the makeup and wigs he used for disguises. He kept out the kit of creams and stage makeup he would need to use right now, and headed into the bathroom.

Twenty minutes later, he came back down the spiral staircase, only much slower than before. His footing was always precarious at first, the high heels pinching his toes with each step. The airplane ticket had been dropped through the mail slot. Bending over, he plucked it up, flipping it open. He had less than an hour to get to the airport. Running his hands down the cashmere sweater and long, flowing skirt, he checked his mascara and lipstick one last time before he stepped out to hail a cab.

Elaine Patterson would make her flight as planned.

"We need to take care of Evan," Will muttered.

Annissa tugged a loose thread near a button on her scarlet jacket, then smoothed her short black skirt. Cocking her head, she put one slender finger to her lip and said, "Let me guess. A convenient fire, like Tony? Or are we going to just detonate the security system at Paradise Promotions? After all, why not destroy valuable personal property as long as we're murdering a loyal assistant?" Turning away, she added, "We only have a few hundred thousand dollars worth of photographic processing equipment at Paradise Promotions, but then again, that would make a nice insurance settlement, wouldn't it?"

Will glared at her, sick of her sarcasm. "You're overreacting, Annissa. Again."

She whipped around to face him, fury dancing in her eyes. "Like hell I am. Tony was murdered, his body burned beyond recognition just hours after the Stover kidnapping. Quite a coincidence, wasn't it? He never crossed us. Never demanded more money or risked exposure of the operation in any way."

"He got careless," Will stated flatly.

"I guess you never make mistakes. One hundred percent perfection, one hundred percent of the time. If I make a mistake, are you going to blow up my house? Or will my car explode when I put the key in the ignition? It's becoming quite a challenge wondering what method will be used to end my scrawny existence."

Without missing a beat Will smoothly lied, "You'd never be a target. You're far too valuable."

"So is Evan. That's why I've already taken care of him."

Will swung around, his face stopping within inches of hers. "You *what*?"

She never flinched or backed away. "You heard me. I made sure he doesn't end up singing backup for Elvis, like Tony did."

Moving away, Will's eyes were barely slits as he asked, "And how do you think you've accomplished such a feat?"

"He's already on his way to have plastic surgery. No one will recognize him once they've worked their magic. It's a very expensive, very private institution."

"Where?"

Annissa considered lying, but decided the truth was just as elusive to a man who delegated responsibility as well as Will. "Grand Cayman," she smoothly answered.

"Are you sure he'll get out of this country without being caught?"

She looked at her watch. "It's already past ten. He should be taking off in a few minutes. I guarantee you, he won't be caught. Evan is one of the smartest, most versatile people I've ever known."

Will rubbed his face with his hand, staring into Annissa's eyes. Slowly a smile began to light his harsh face. "You are a sly witch, Annissa. You always have been."

"Killing isn't part of the deal. I thought we agreed on that, if nothing else."

"We do. But now you're making decisions alone," he said, his eyebrows raised.

"I've been making decisions alone for years. How long has it been since you've been involved in the daily operations? How many times lately have you handled a problem with this building? Set up a PLACE presentation? Wired money? Made deposits? You may be the owner, but I'm the operator. Without me you'd be dead in the water and you know it."

Once again silence.

Through gritted teeth he finally spoke, "Why transfer fifty thousand dollars for Evan to use? Why not a million? Or two million?"

She defiantly held his malignant stare. "I must have been mistaken about your plans. I thought you wanted this operation to continue."

"As it must."

"Then I did what was necessary. The plastic surgery will cost twenty-five thousand dollars. Considering the temporary displacement he'll have to face, as well as the physical discomfort, I felt fifty thousand would be reasonable. Silence isn't cheap. Or perfection."

"Since when is one person worth so much?"

"Since Tony is gone. Evan is talented. In many ways."

"And you think Evan will fly to Grand Cayman, get a new face, and be back in the States in a matter of a couple of weeks? What makes you so sure he won't just disappear?"

She shrugged. "He could."

"Then you could run back to Jamaica. You'd both be out of the organization. Isn't that what you want?"

"No," she lied. Throwing a bold look at him, she stated, "I've decided my place is here. I've been gone too long to go back now. That's why Evan's return is crucial. He allows us the privilege of continuing the operation with minimum risk of exposure. It would take months to train someone to present the PLACE scam convincingly. We don't have months to spare."

The silence again. This time it hung between them like an ominous warning.

Will stood up, walking over to the door that led back into his office. "I'm glad to see you've come around. I think getting Evan out of the country was a good decision, Annissa. If anyone is concerned, I can honestly say he's out of the picture."

Angela's tan was deep and golden from the tropical sun. Blending in was easy. No one seemed to care about anything. No timetables, no deadlines, hardly any reminders that life was still slipping away. The rising and falling sun was enough indication of the passage of time, in some ways too much. Native Jamaicans lived life easier than Americans. They believed the pure water found inside coconuts guaranteed health and happiness. Judging from their carefree attitude, Angela wondered if they might just have the right idea.

Unlike most tourists, Angela woke each day as the first maverick sunbeams broke through her window shutters. Jax was right—dawn was the perfect time for snorkeling. The ocean was still, the beaches barren. Seashells drifted in with the evening tide and lay waiting on the sand. Spectacular conch shells were easily within diving range.

Jax drove her everywhere, showing her things she was sure no other tourist ever saw. He haggled with the locals for her, driving hard bargains on her behalf. Now, as she lay in the sun letting hot white sand trickle through her fingertips, she wondered what her trip would have been like if he hadn't taken her under his wing.

For some reason her mind kept mulling over something he had said yesterday when she asked about his family. At first he had answered in his carefree manner, telling about his mother, Tica, and his little sister, Maya. But as he talked, his gaze wandered, and he grew very solemn. His attention was focused more on the ocean than on her when he said, "Blood ties can never be broken, only lengthened. Even in death a bridge links our souls together. The good of one bleeds over, as does the evil."

Remembering his words sent gooseflesh over her arms and legs, the same way they had the first time he uttered them. She rolled onto her stomach, suddenly very uneasy about lying idly in the sun. The same feeling she'd had just before she left Oklahoma City seized her. Her palms began to sweat, and her heart pounded. Then she remembered. The work she'd so carefully packed was still waiting. That must be what was nagging her. But Jax was coming soon, since Angela had agreed to one last excursion to Montego Bay. She could work tomorrow—her last day in paradise.

Ignoring everything, she felt the sand mold to

her back. The soothing mixture of the faint reggae beat blended with the lapping of the ocean waves whisking her away. As sleep enveloped her, she dreamed of strolling across hot sands, cooling her toes occasionally in the surf. Then she reached the end of a private beach, where a large stone wall and pier blocked her way. Without a thought she walked into the water, sliding into the salty depths to swim around the barrier to freedom. As she climbed back out of the water on the other side, she saw him. She'd known he would come.

Nick was there waiting for her. His tall, lean body slick with musky tanning oil, his blond chest hair flecked with grains of sand. He was lying on his side, his long, muscular legs stretching well off the end of the brightly colored beach towel. When he saw her, his eyes held hers. She stood beside him. Silent. Waiting.

Beautiful, sculpted fingers touched her. His hands caressed her toes, then worked their way seductively up her calves, pausing to stroke behind her knees before they skipped higher. His mouth found the palm of her hand. As he tenderly kissed it, she knelt beside him, her lips finding his. The salty taste of the ocean mixed with the fragrance of tropical flowers to overwhelm her senses. For an eternity they explored each other.

He leaned away from her, his eyes the same color as the ocean behind him, silently seeking permission to dive into the forbidden waters. She answered by reaching one arm behind her back to tug softly the bow of her bikini top. It came free easily, falling into the sand. The rest of the bikini quickly joined it, as Nick ran his hands over each curve of her body. Teasing. Inflaming. Electrifying.

"Wake up pretty lady. You've been sunning too long." Jax gently tickled her toes. "Wake up! We've lots to do this day."

Angela slowly opened her eyes, not wanting the dream to end. Reality invaded immediately when she saw Jax standing over her. Even though he couldn't possibly know what she had just been dreaming, her cheeks flushed in embarrassment as she rushed to stand up.

He extended his hand to help her. "Forget your vial of sunblock, did you? Your face is as red as an *otaheite* apple. Hope that pampered American skin of yours doesn't burn easily."

Angela was shaky at first, holding Jax's hand for support. She quickly forced herself back to the real world, letting go of him so she could brush the sand off her arms and legs. "I'll be fine, Jax," she whispered.

But in reality Angela wasn't so sure. The dream had hit her hard, too hard. She could no longer deny how she felt. *Great*, she thought. *Out of the millions of men in the world, I've fallen for one who'll never want me.*

"Mr. Kellars. There's a person on line two who insists on speaking with you. His name is Carl Kramer, and he's with Associated Medical, Incorporated. Do you want me to take a message?"

His curiosity piqued, Will answered, "No, Marilyn, I'll speak to him." He punched the flashing light marked line two. "Will Kellars."

"I'm sorry to disturb you, Mr. Kellars, I know

you're a busy man. My name is Carl Kramer. Our company manages Shadybrook Rest Home. I'm afraid I have some rather bad news for one of your employees. We've been unable to contact her, and she listed your firm as her place of employment."

"Who are you speaking of?"

"Ms. Angela Anderson. Is she still engaged in your employ?"

"Yes."

"Do you know how I can contact her? This is urgent."

"She's not in the country right now, but I believe she's due back tomorrow evening." Annoyed, he asked, "Why do you need her?"

"Her mother passed away in her sleep last night. Her disease advanced quickly in the last few months. Such a tragedy. Can I count on you to notify Ms. Anderson as soon as possible?"

Will hesitated while he pondered the impact of the news on Anderson's workload, then muttered, "I'll handle it. Thank you for contacting us."

"We routinely take care of some of the disposal details, so to speak, but I'll still need to talk to her. Would you have her call me as soon as possible?"

"Certainly. Could you tell me, did her mother have a will?"

"I'd have no way of knowing. You'll need to ask Ms. Anderson."

"It's not important. Good-bye."

Will hung up. Marilyn could easily call the Jamaican hotel or send a telegram, but what good would it do? Angela would know soon enough. Too soon. He'd have Marilyn meet her at the plane tomorrow evening. Give her a few days off to wrap up her mother's affairs.

Damn, the new estate-planning advertising will probably run late. Why isn't anything ever easy? In the back of his mind he mentally noted to wait a few weeks, then tell Angela to draw up pamphlets to distribute to all the area nursing homes as part of the estate-planning media campaign. Smiling, he thought, *Even death can be profitable. I can't believe I didn't think of it years ago.*

Jax stared at his mother from the doorway of the small cottage where they lived, watching the specks of dust dance around her in the light cascading through the window. In her wildly colored cotton housedress, she didn't look ill. In fact, she looked as though she might get up, walk outside, and dance in the lush green grass. But as he looked closer, he could see the dress hung loosely on her skeletal frame. "Tica?" he softly said, hesitant to interrupt her.

She turned, her dark eyes barely open. A hint of a smile and a raised finger were his sign she was awake.

Jax wore no shirt, only baggy cotton pants that tied at the waist and ankles. Shuffling toward her, he said, "She's leaving tomorrow. So far everything is working perfectly."

Her voice was gravelly, quiet. "She trusts you, then?"

Jax nodded. "Ya, mon. And we were lucky. Very lucky. She is bright. Computers are her hobby."

A sly smile crossed her wrinkled face as she

came to life. One gnarled hand rubbed the other as she asked, "She'll deliver it?"

He shrugged. "I'll wait to ask until we're on our way to the airport tomorrow. She'll have less time to think about it that way. Such a worrier, that one."

Tica coughed, a wave of pain rushing through her body. Grimacing, she asked, "What if she refuses?"

Jax took her hand and smiled. "She won't. But if she does, I have her address in the States and phone number from her luggage tags. Her souls are light and free. I'm sure she'll help a friend."

"I hope you're right."

"Besides, I'll make certain she has quite a hangover from her last night. I'm taking her to see the fire-eater celebration up close. Free her inner spirit with a little *ganja*. If that doesn't work, I have the *bushdoctor's* potion to fall back on."

"Have you told Maya our plans yet?"

"No, I was waiting until we were certain exactly what they were."

"Can she get the cash from Grand Cayman?"

"With the right banking codes. Our Cuban friend won't bother her while she's on his boat, if that's your worry."

"Worries are all old women have, and *dunza*—money—brings the worst out in people."

"Pretty soon you will relax. I have been thinking of how to do this for years, and I couldn't have found a better person than Angela Anderson to help me pull it off."

"You always were my sly one, Jax." She grabbed his hand and squeezed. "I knew I could count on you. Walk good, son. Walk good *firstlight*—tomorrow."

Jax kissed her cheek and left, closing the door behind him. When he walked into the kitchen, Maya was coming in the screen door. "Did you get it?" he asked.

Maya's white cotton dress was damp from sweat. Nodding, she reached into her purse and pulled out a small package. "Here 'tis," she said, playfully tossing it to him. "He said to only use half."

Jax's heart almost stopped. Diving for the box, he caught it in midair and skidded across the kitchen floor on his knees. When he came to a stop, he stayed there, unmoving. His heart was pounding so hard he thought surely Maya could hear it.

She laughed and joked, "A little jumpy, aren't we?"

Jax never answered. He merely clutched the small package of explosives to his chest and sighed.

Chapter 10

Angela looked at the cloudy sky, hoping it wasn't a bad omen as she emerged from her hotel room. Last night's festivities had definitely taken a toll.

"Headache, pretty lady?" he asked as she edged toward him.

A silent glare was his answer as she walked carefully to his minivan, each step placed to minimize the impact of the vibration on her pounding head. Sunglasses covered bloodshot eyes. A wide-brimmed straw hat concealed a fully braided head of auburn hair, complete with beads that clicked against one another with each step.

Jax handed her four aspirin and an icy Ting. "These will help."

Her stomach protested at first but settled quickly. Each pothole threatened her sanity as they rode toward the airport. For the first time since she had arrived in Jamaica, rain fell in sheets onto the countryside. It matched her mood precisely.

She had no memory of having her hair braided, a feat that must have taken hours. Peering at Jax, she held a few tiny braids in her hand and asked, "Did you have something to do with this?"

"Beautiful, aren't they?"

"But how could . . . ?"

"Well, three strands of hair are carefully weaved—"

Slugging his upper arm, she snapped, "I know how to braid hair, you idiot. *Who* did it? And *when*?"

"I believe her name was Rosa. Right after you performed with the fire eater, of course."

Angela moaned, "After I *what*?"

"You had a wonderful time on your last night in paradise, pretty lady."

"If you say so." She slumped in her seat and moaned.

"It is fitting you will leave our country looking like an exotically beautiful native." With a wink he lightly jiggled the beads that covered her shoulders. "I was wondering if you could do me a favor, pretty lady."

Keeping her eyes closed, she replied, "Sure, Jax. Name it."

"Smuggle drugs for me into the States."

Turning her head slowly toward him, she pulled her sunglasses to the edge of her nose. Her stinging eyes contemplated his face while her brain processed his words. "Do *what*?" she asked. She had smelled marijuana, or as the locals called it, *ganja*, on the wind many times since her arrival in Jamaica. Maybe the locals didn't realize the penalty in the States for possession of controlled substances. Or that even Americans going home had to clear Customs.

Jax's laughter was loud and long, drowning the sounds of the pouring rain. He laughed so hard, tears streaked his face and he held his side. "Just kidding, pretty lady. My favor is not illegal, or dangerous." He lied quite well. "Just complicated."

"Go on."

"A long time ago, my mother, Tica, had a fight with my oldest sister. We haven't seen her in many years. As I told you, Tica isn't well now. She must make amends before it's too late. The eternal bridge she travels toward is weak. She fears it might break when she passes onto it, throwing her earthly soul into the great void. But you can help."

Rubbing her temples, Angela distractedly asked, "How?"

He bent over and pulled a large manila envelope out from under the driver's seat. "I have a photograph of the family, and notes from Tica and myself. I know what you're thinking—crazy islander, just stick it in the post. We cannot. She would send it back unopened, as she has so many of our packages. Forgive me for my intrusion of your privacy, but I noticed on your luggage that you live in the same city."

Angela tried to think logically, but her brain was busy convincing the rest of her body that it had to live until tomorrow. Her voice was barely a whisper as she asked, "So you want me to take this to her?"

"Yes. Hand it to her personally. To no one else. Her address is on the envelope. Look her in the eye and tell her, 'Jax sent me. The bridge must be rebuilt before 'tis too late.' " He screeched the van to a stop in time for a goat and its billy to cross the narrow road, knocking Angela's tender head roughly against the passenger window. "Can you remember that?"

Rubbing her new bruise, she said, "Sure. I'm hungover, not stupid. What makes you think she'll take the package from me?" Angela vaguely recognized that the address was in an elite suburb of Oklahoma City, one she knew little about. She stuffed the envelope into the briefcase by her feet.

"She is a very elegant, polite woman. She could never be rude to a stranger."

"But you haven't seen her in years. Maybe she's changed."

"Some things change. But Tica's wisdom and teachings are still in her heart. Refuse you she will not."

Nick was always impressed when he walked into Will Kellars' office. While he waited, he read title after title of the antique law and medical books, gently touching each leather binding. He was startled when he heard Will's voice behind him.

"That's a fine one there. I was reading it again the other day." When Nick turned to face him, he continued, "Did you know in the early eighteen hundreds they actually believed the reason people got sleepy in church was because of stale air? This medical book says that churches must be thoroughly aired out after each service to prevent the parishioners from getting droopy-eyed during the sermon. The stuffy air was supposedly what caused the people to get bored and drowsy, not the minister's rambling." Kellars laughed and slapped Nick on the back. "Quite a theory, isn't it?"

Nick couldn't help but smile. "I have to admit, I suffered from the droopy-eyed syndrome myself many times while I was growing up. Where did you get these antique medical books?"

"My father was a doctor, and so was his, etc., etc. These medical journals have been passed down for years. Needless to say, my father wasn't very happy when I didn't follow the family tradition, especially since I was an only child."

Nick wondered what had made him rebel against tradition, and what the price had been. "Why didn't you?"

"Pretty simple, really. I never cared to be around sick people."

"What about the law volumes? Some of these must be hundreds of years old."

Kellars' chest puffed out. "They are. I have a broker who finds rare books for me. He does an excellent job. Anytime you want to—"

Marilyn's smooth voice interrupted their conversation in mid-sentence. "Mr. Kellars, Senator Holt is here. He says it's urgent that he speak to you right away."

Nick stood up to leave, but Kellars signaled him to stay seated.

Kellars opened the door to his office and extended his hand. "Good morning, Senator. What a coincidence. Nick Hunter is here with me, and we were just preparing to discuss your case."

Holt stormed in, his voice indignant as he said, "That bitch just won't let up. A report came in a few minutes ago. Stover is going to convene a grand jury either today or Monday."

"According to whom?" Nick asked.

The senator replied, "A very reliable source. What's more important is that she is following through with her threat, even under the circumstances."

Kellars glared at Holt as though to silence him. "She's a strong woman. We felt this was a possibility, and we're totally prepared for it."

"I'm sure as shit glad you are. Personally, it turns my stomach. We've already dropped six points in the polls because of all this crap. Now it'll be front-page news again for weeks. Isn't there any way you can stop her?"

Nick found himself wondering exactly how far the senator would go when Will calmly answered, "At this stage in the game, that wouldn't be wise. We have all your information ready for them to examine. Every stick is in line."

Nick hesitantly interrupted. "At least everything we know about. Is there anything you haven't told us, sir?"

"And what the hell is that supposed to mean?" the senator asked.

Kellars shot a defiant look at Nick, who quickly answered, "If you have any involvements, financial or not, that could be discovered by a grand jury investigation, we need to know about them now. The last thing we need is to be caught off guard at a critical time like this."

Shaking his head, Holt answered, "Son, I've told you a thousand times. My campaign is legit. My life is legit. The only thing I'm guilty of is doing what every other politician in the United States does."

"Which is?" Nick asked.

Holt shot a look at Kellars. "Are you shitting me? You hiring greenhorns now, Will?"

Kellars slowly shook his head and smiled slyly. "Go ahead, Bob. Educate him."

After several seconds of silence, the disgusted senator sighed and said, "Riding on the tails of lobbyists, accepting freebies, vacationing in fancy resorts on taxpayer dollars because the sponsoring companies are considering bringing business into our state, trading a few low-level staff appointments for important political connections. Nothing earth-shattering. Or criminal, for that matter."

Nick knew all of those were true, but was glad to hear the senator admit them. Seeing the gleam in Will Kellars' eyes made him say, "Susan Stover will make things exactly like those you just mentioned seem criminal. It doesn't make any difference if every politician in the last two hundred years has done the same things. You'll be her example. Her way to stop corruption in our government by weeding out one member of the good ol' boy network."

"And which side of the snake's belly are you on, Hunter?"

Nick laughed. "Yours, Senator. But I think you should know exactly where we're headed. I'd guess this grand jury could be investigating for weeks, if not months, before they hand down any indictments. This is a complex situation. Most of what we're dealing with is very gray. A lot will depend on the personalities involved and their political allegiances."

"So what should I do?"

"Try to ignore all this for now. We'll handle it."

"And Angela will have a statement ready for me when the story breaks?"

Kellars quickly answered before Nick could respond. "Ms. Anderson won't be available for several days. She's had a recent death in the family. Her mother just passed away."

Shaking his head, Holt said, "Sorry to hear that. She's such a pretty young thing."

Nick felt like someone had slugged him in the chest. He found his voice had a hard time crawling out of his throat as he tried to speak again. "Angela left statements with me just in case the grand jury convened while she was gone. I'll fax you the press-release copy when you need it."

Senator Holt walked to the door and opened it. "My gorgeous wife is waiting in the limo, so I'd best be going. We're attending the opening of the new recycling plant today." Shaking their hands, he added, "You fellows keep up the good work."

Nick stood silently for several seconds, still reeling from the shock of Will's news. "I'm sorry, Mr. Kellars, I hadn't heard about Angela's mother."

Shrugging, he nonchalantly said, "Neither has she."

Nick couldn't believe anyone could be so callous. Controlling his anger, he said, "What?"

"She gets back today at six. When the nursing home called yesterday, it was too late to change her flight arrangements. Sometimes no news is good news. She deserved a vacation. Knowing a day sooner wouldn't bring her mother back, would it?"

Nick disagreed with the twisted logic, but just shook his head. "Who's going to tell her?"

"Marilyn will meet her at the airport."

Nick knew how devastated Angela would be, and he didn't want her to be alone. "Let me tell her. Since we started working together on the Holt case, we've become good friends."

Will propped his feet on the corner of his desk. "Fine with me. Just clear it with Marilyn. Are you as surprised about the Holt case going forward as I am?"

Nick crossed to look out the windows at the bustling streets below. "Not really. Although all the evidence I've seen is superficial. We've supplied verifiable documentation to contest all the allegations."

"Are you sure?"

"Positive."

Will looked and sounded like a typical law school professor about to catch an unsuspecting fly in his web. "And what does that mean to you?"

Nick knew all too well, but in the last few weeks he had tried to convince himself he was just being overly suspicious. "That we don't know what her real allegations are, what evidence she has up her sleeve. That the information we have possession of was provided or leaked on purpose to draw our attention away from the real issue."

"Spoken like a true lawyer. And what are we going to do about it?"

Their eyes met. "Push to find out the real situation as soon as possible."

"True. And how would you go about that?"

"Hire an investigator to talk to the senator's staff?"

Kellars shook his head.

"Susan Stover's staff?"

This time he nodded. "For openers. We'll discuss the next step when, and if, necessary. For now, you've got enough work to do to keep you busy for quite a while."

Nick started to leave, but as his hand closed around the cold brass doorknob, he turned back.

Kellars looked up, his pen stopping in midstroke on the page. "Something bothering you, Hunter?"

"I was just wondering why we didn't investigate sooner. It sounds as though you suspected we were barking up the wrong tree all along. Why wait until the last minute?"

Kellars sighed. Raising his eyebrows, he said, "Because I honestly didn't think Stover would follow through with this. I thought she would see the futility of pursuing the issue. Throwing tax dollars on what will be perceived as a personal vendetta won't look good on her record."

Nick nodded and left. As he walked slowly down the hall, he couldn't help but wonder about the timing of the Stover kidnapping. Kellars' surprise realization that Susan Stover's case might actually proceed made him equally uneasy. It was almost as if he had expected her to roll over and play dead.

Passing Angela's dark office, he stopped in midstride. Flipping on the lights, he went inside and leaned against the wall. Directly in front of him framed snapshots lined the credenza behind her immaculately clean desk. He'd never noticed them before, but now they practically grabbed him. Walking over, he picked up the first one. It was a picture of a smiling middle-aged couple, obviously Angela's parents many years ago. The next one showed Angela with her mother at her college graduation. The last was a professional portrait of a beautiful, vibrant older woman. Nick put the picture down and walked away.

Angela was relieved when she didn't recognize any of the other passengers aboard the Pampered jet. She took a seat at the very back. Closing her eyes, she breathed deeply, hoping everyone would leave her alone in her misery. Conversation was definitely not something she cared to undertake today.

By the time they reached cruising altitude, Angela was ready to work. She sorted through the stack of papers in her briefcase, deciding the estate-planning campaign was the most important. Kellars would expect it to run on time, even though he had granted a week's extension to accommodate her trip to Jamaica.

At first listening to the tape of Kellar's voice was almost painful, the words like bullets ripping through her skull. She pushed the Pause button on her recorder, lowered the volume, and swallowed three more aspirin. Sheer willpower forced her to concentrate harder, her subconscious relying on years of experience to pull her through. In minutes, she was writing his exact words with ease, her hangover curbed to a dull ache behind her temples. She wrote quickly, barely managing to keep up with his drawl:

"I want a shot of a grieving widow shaking her head at all the paperwork. Her assets tied up senselessly. All it would have taken was a simple trip to see their attorney. We can close with children whose parents have died without a will, relatives fighting over who has to care for them. Wards of the court. With them in the background, a judge will explain to the audience that their fate lies in his hands instead of those who loved them most. People should be terrified of dying intestate by the time we're through with them."

Angela lifted her pen, waiting while the tape played past Marilyn's interruption for Senator Holt's call, and her own exit from his office. She braced her pounding head for the loud click that always signaled a gap in the recording, and was surprised when none came. Then she remembered. It had been so hot that morning, she had left her jacket draped over the back of her chair. With the recorder in the pocket, *and running*.

Will Kellars' discussion with the senator lasted only seconds. Although Angela could only hear his side of the conversation, it was apparent they were considering attending a social engagement that evening. A few seconds of silence followed before a strange dragging sound, like someone pushing a heavy box across the carpet. Will Kellars' voice was lower, almost angry when he spoke next.

A woman with a familiar Jamaican accent replied.

"How many times do we have to go over this? Don't interrupt me during business hours unless it's an emergency."

"I'll let you decide. This just came in the morning post."

". . . So the Carters backed out? Nothing suspicious at least. We'll find another couple."

"Not in two weeks. That's when it's due. She's already in Montego."

"Quit panicking. Things will work out."

"Suppose we can find a potential buyer. Who will pitch PLACE? Evan will be out for weeks."

". . . You will."

"But I can't. It's been years . . ."

"So, start practicing. You were the first to ever do it. It'll come back in no time. . . . I have legal matters to handle now."

Angela rewound the tape and listened to the bizarre conversation again. Her head was spinning. How could someone have gone in Will Kellars' office without passing Marilyn's desk? It couldn't have been a phone conversation; she could hear the rustle of papers passing between them. Plus, the voices sounded the same, not hollow like one was being broadcast on a speaker phone. Someone else she knew called mail "the post," but who?

She flipped to a clean yellow sheet on her legal pad as the tape rewound again. This time she transcribed the entire conversation, pausing between sentences to make sure every word was copied correctly. When she was finished, she stared at the words, reading them over and over.

That same uncontrollable feeling of dread curled back around her chest. With a trembling hand she ejected the tape from the recorder and slipped it into her briefcase, where it couldn't be accidentally erased.

The rest of Angela's flight was spent trying to decide what to do next. Her practical side argued to forget the tape. It didn't make sense anyway. "Pitch place" sounded like an address for musicians, or some kind of baseball term, but not anything criminal. She knew she should go on with her life like nothing had happened. *Don't rock the boat, or you might just capsize it*, she thought.

But Angela knew that what she had heard would be impossible to ignore. The voices sounded too sinister to be speaking of anything innocent. It would haunt her day and night until she came up with a plausible answer. Angela stared out the window at the fluffy gray clouds below the wing. She tried eavesdropping on the conversation of the elderly couple seated in front of her. Nothing helped. She giggled aloud when one ludicrous thought crossed her mind: *Just walk in and slap the recorder down in Kellars' face. Ask him exactly what the hell he's up to.*

The captain's voice startled her back to reality.

He announced they would be landing at Dallas-Ft. Worth International Airport to pick up two passengers in less than an hour, and that the Customs forms must be completed before they could depart again. Everything was going perfectly, he said, right on schedule. He hoped everyone was enjoying their flight.

Angela leaned her head back as she listened, suddenly fighting an overwhelming wave of tears. She hated her senseless emotions. Tears had always flowed easily. Too easily. It was a trait she despised in herself and constantly fought to contain.

The most frustrating thing of all was that she had no idea why she was crying.

Lesley looked out the window of the study in the Stover mansion, admiring the terraced landscaping of freshly planted yellow and orange mums. Turning back to face the Stovers, she sighed and asked, "Anyone else?"

"No. I had my secretary pull all the files for the last five years. You have everything." Samuel Stover paced back and forth, his patience worn thin from endless hours of questioning. Lesley controlled herself, suppressing the urge to explain that enemies could not always be found by looking through files. People shunned years ago, a disgruntled ex-employee, or someone envious of their wealth, could be the kidnapper.

Except physically, Susan Stover mirrored her father's image in every way. Their carriage, aloofness, and powerful presence were identical. Lesley directed her attention back to Susan. "Has your daughter remembered anything helpful? Who might want to harm her or the baby?"

Susan twisted the gold chain around her neck, finally dropping it against the cream blouse. Shaking her head, she answered, "Nothing worth looking into. Of course, she had her share of disappointed boyfriends in high school, and some mild squabbles with jealous girls. But after she got pregnant, the rest of the kids pretty much ignored her. It seemed to drop her socially down to their level." Her voice took on a hard edge. "After all, there's no reason to be envious of someone who screwed up their life by getting pregnant at sixteen." Susan realized how bitter she sounded, and quickly added, "At least that seems to be how the kids see it."

Lesley caught the obvious resentfulness and chose to follow the lead. "And the father of her child? Could he have a motive himself? Or an enemy?"

Susan's eyes softened, her voice sincere as she said, "He's just a nice kid. We know his parents. Jason Janssen wouldn't hurt a fly. I doubt if he's ever said an unkind word to anyone in his life. He got in over his head. That's all."

"Still, he sounds like the fatherly type. Yet apparently he's chosen to be excluded from the upbringing of his baby. Why?"

A quick fiery glance shot between Susan and her father. Samuel chimed in, "He realized it was a mistake. He shouldn't have to pay forever for a night of passion. Should he?"

Lesley didn't miss the unspoken connection the

two of the shared. She quickly asked, "Would you mind if I talk to him?"

"He's very upset about Amber's disappearance," Susan answered.

"I realize that. Any father would be. I'd still like to talk to him."

"If you must," she sighed. Grabbing her gold chain again, she twisted it back and forth. After a few moments she asked, "By the way, did you turn up anything on Senator Holt?"

"We're still looking. He has an ironclad alibi for the day of the kidnapping, though. Witnesses saw him from dawn to dusk on the Senate floor."

"He wouldn't have done it himself," Susan responded sharply.

Lesley tensed at the verbal slap, then mentally reminded herself what the Stovers were going through. "His phone records look normal, too. Lots of calls to his lawyer's office. I suppose that's directly tied to your campaign-fraud allegations. I called the lawyer in charge of his case—she flipped back through her yellow legal pad—"a Nick Hunter. He said they've been working extensively on his defense since the first allegations were made. Even Holt's press releases are handled by his law firm. The rest of the telephone calls check out. Normal, everyday numbers. We examined his cell phone, his office lines, and his home."

"What about Alice Holt?"

"We checked her cell phone, too. Hairdressers, manicurists, nothing exotic."

"He could've gone to a pay phone."

Samuel interrupted. "Back off, Susan. They've

checked everything they can. Holt's not stupid enough to pull a stunt like this."

Susan whirled around, her eyes blazing. "Damn it, Dad, I think he is." A tear slid down her cheek. "I just don't know how to prove it!"

Chapter 11

Nick didn't want to miss Angela's return flight, so he arrived early. The sun was low in the sky, the wind brisk. Leaning against a hangar wall, he watched planes glide in as others soared, banked, and disappeared.

For years he had studied how to present complicated issues in front of a jury. How to make complex problems seem black and white. How to candy-coat the most vile materials so the jurors could still sleep at night. But he had no idea how to tell Angela about her mother. Now he wished he'd let Marilyn come along. Maybe it would have been easier with two of them to help Angela through this tough time. Of one thing he was certain: she would need someone who cared.

Nick swallowed hard when he realized a small, gleaming white plane was headed directly toward Hangar 38. As it drew closer, he could see the palm tree logo on the tail section, and the bright red and purple word PARADISE blazoned across the midsection. He should have guessed that anything associated with Pampered in Paradise would be first-class.

At first he didn't recognize Angela. She was the last passenger out of the plane, walking slowly down the shaky stairway. The bouncy stride he associated with her was gone. Large sunglasses covered a tanned face, and a huge straw hat made only the swinging ends of her braided hair evident. She wore an outfit obviously purchased in Jamaica, flowing white with splashes of tropical flowers. It was the overflowing briefcase that finally convinced him it really was Angela. He would recognize that soft black leather anywhere, even without her initials branded on the side.

"Angela!" he called.

She visibly jumped, then headed his way. Squeezing Nick's hand with her free one, she took off her sunglasses. "What are you doing here? The limo driver said he'd take me home."

Nick looked into her eyes. He could tell she'd been crying. A wave of guilt broke over him as he realized how relieved he was that he wouldn't have to be the one to tell her. Soothingly he said, "I wanted to be with you. I can't tell you how sorry I am." He pulled her into a long hug, his chest knocking her straw hat off. He caught it and held them both in spite of her effort to push away.

"What are you talking about?" She finally freed herself and searched his stricken face. "Oh, my God! We've been fired, haven't we? Hotlips blew the whistle, right? I knew I shouldn't have gone. I just knew it. I've had this horrible feeling that something awful was going to happen."

Nick paled, his eyes filled with sorrow. "I'm sorry, Angela. It's not your job, it's your mother. I thought you knew. You look like you've been crying."

Wide-eyed, she drew back and asked, "What about my mother?"

He looked down at his feet, then back at her, his own eyes brimming with tears. There was no need to say the words aloud. Her briefcase dropped from her hand, and Nick pulled her close to hold her. After a few moments he walked her to his car and gently helped her inside.

While the limo driver loaded her luggage into the trunk of the Cutlass, Nick hurriedly gathered the papers that had blown out of her briefcase and stuffed them back in. A quick glance showed several stray papers flattened against a cyclone fence by the wind, and he jogged over to retrieve them. Satisfied he had collected as much of her work as possible, he walked toward his car, briefcase in hand.

Even though his foot was within an inch of it, Nick never noticed the tiny tape that had fallen into a crack on the tarmac, or the Jamaican woman who was so cautiously observing them from deep inside Hangar 38.

Angela watched the landscape blur as Nick drove toward her apartment. Tears streamed down her cheeks. He didn't press her to talk. Instead, he simply rested his hand on top of hers—a reminder that she wasn't alone.

Finally, the questions inside her would not wait. "When did it happen?"

"Wednesday night."

She was too numb to wonder why no one had told her sooner. Her voice was heavy with self-loathing as she muttered, "While I was partying in Jamaica."

"Angela, it would've happened anyway."

She nodded, wiped her eyes, then asked, "How?"

Nick replied, "I stopped at the nursing home. She passed peacefully, in her sleep. They're pretty sure it was a stroke."

Angela turned toward him, her tear-streaked face a testament to her pain as she simply nodded.

Nick parked outside her apartment building. Taking her hand gently in his, he said, "I want to help in any way I can."

"I think this is one of those things I have to work through alone." She tried to force a smile but couldn't as he carried her luggage to the door. Unlocking it, she realized her uncanny sense of foreboding had been justified. In a strange way it was a relief. The worst was over. She led him into her apartment, throwing the bags she carried onto the bed. Her eye caught her reflection in the antique mirror over the chest of drawers. "I do need one thing, Nick."

"Just name it."

"Help me get these damn braids out of my hair." Hysterical laughter consumed her first, breaking loose the anguish inside. Nick took her in his arms and held her until the eruption subsided.

Hours later, when she'd fallen asleep in his arms on the sofa, he carried her to bed. He slid off her shoes and covered her with a soft blanket. Then one by one he slipped off the tiny beads and gently unwound each silky strand of hair.

* * *

Monday turned out to be as bleak as any day Angela had ever lived through. When she finally got back to her apartment, she was exhausted. She tossed the mail and newspaper on the sofa, kicking off the black high heels. As she made her way into the bedroom she scooped up the shoes, realizing how good the carpet felt against her aching feet. Tossing the shoes into the closet, she peeled off her dark suit and hung it in the very back, where, hopefully, she wouldn't have to see it for a long, long time. After shaking her hair free, she shuffled into the bathroom and ran a deep, hot bubble bath.

Turning the radio to a soft rock station, she hoped to push everything out of her mind. For the first time since she returned from Jamaica she had time to relax. And think.

The memorial service was over, the relatives gone. Her mother was settled peacefully between her father and her grandmother. Her few possessions from the nursing home had been either doled out or packed away. Although there were still details to take care of, nothing seemed urgent anymore. Numbness had settled in, replacing the stabbing emotional pain with a hollow, lonely feeling.

Angela slid deeper into the bubbles, until only her face remained above. Though the sound was muffled, she knew the telephone was ringing, interrupting one of her favorite songs. She slid up enough to hear the answering machine take the call. Bubbles oozed down her face and neck as she listened to Nick's deep voice echo through her small apartment.

He talked slowly, as if he expected her to pick up the phone any second. "Angela, it's Nick. Just wanted to make sure you're all right. I'll be at the office till about nine o'clock tonight if you want to talk. Don't worry about the grand jury. I had Holt issue the press release you wrote last week. Take care of yourself."

Angela sank back under the water. Susan Stover had apparently succeeded at taking the first formal step toward indicting Holt. Now Senator Holt would be driving them both crazy until he was either cleared or thrown in jail. She sat up, the bubbles tickling as they slithered down her wet skin. Patting dry, she tried to ignore the conspicuous bikini lines left by her new tan. She knew they would fade as quickly as they had appeared, and right now they were part of a memory she would just as soon forget.

After wrapping in a white satin robe, she erased Nick's message and settled onto the sofa to read the newspaper. Even though she was prepared for it, the front-page headline still shocked her. Both Nick and Will Kellars were behind the senator and his wife in the photo taken at the Capitol building. It was in full color, inset with a shot of Susan Stover smiling triumphantly. She recognized her own words quoted exactly.

Her guilty conscience kicked into high gear, easily conquering her common sense. What kind of daughter would act the way she had? Flying off to Jamaica when her mother needed her most. Not spending time with her before she left. Partying through the night on the day her mother had died. Now she could add shunting her work off on a friend to her list. At least she could stop the last one before it was too late.

She grabbed the phone from the end table and dialed Nick's direct line. He answered before the first ring died.

"Nick Hunter."

"You did a great job on the Holt case."

He sighed, sounding relieved as he said, "I'm so glad you called, I've been worried about you. . . . I was hoping you'd call. You deserve all the credit on the Holt announcement. I just faxed over the press release you'd prepared." His voice was stronger as he added, "How are you holding up?"

Just hearing his voice made her feel better. "I'm fine. Tired but okay. Relatives have a way of wringing you dry. Sometimes I wonder how long my aunts can live on one piece of family gossip. I must have heard about Aunt Lillian's secret liposuction twenty times, from twenty different people." She yawned, then added, "I was planning on coming into the office tomorrow morning."

"Don't rush it. Kellars said to take off as long as you need."

She rubbed her aching temples. "What I need is to keep my mind occupied. I have way too much time to think when I'm home alone, and right now I think about things that make me crazy. I'm just getting ready to sift through my briefcase." She walked over to her desk and pulled some of the wrinkled papers out. "It looks like a tornado hit it."

"Have you eaten?"

She suddenly realized how hungry she was. "No. For some reason the assortment of casseroles and Jell-O salads at Aunt Peggy's just didn't appeal to me this afternoon. I know we're getting in a pizza rut, but I'll spring for it this time if you'll stop and pick it up on the way over. Hold the red sauce, of course."

"Deal. Do you need me to bring anything else?"

She was still flattening out crinkled papers, unconsciously sorting them into piles. "No. I took enough work with me to last for days. Unfortunately, I haven't finished any of it. Or even started it, for that matter."

"With the grand jury investigation going on, I don't think either one of us will be bored for quite a while. I'll be over in a few minutes. Bye."

The phone line went dead, but Angela didn't think to say good-bye, or even to push the button to hang up the phone. Instead, she stared at the legal pad in her hand. A rush of anxiety overcame her as she reread the curious words she had transcribed from the mysterious tape of Will Kellars.

Thirty minutes later, Nick's arrival caught Angela off guard. When she opened her door, he was surprised to see she was wearing only a short satin robe. Her hair was wet, her feet bare. Except for the panicked, hollow expression in her eyes, she looked like a fashion model waiting for her turn to pose for the *Sports Illustrated*'s swimsuit issue.

Angela's perfect tan was highlighted by the contrasting white robe, which fell seductively open above the sash at her waistline. Sleek wet hair swept away from her face, framing naturally perfect skin and innocent brown eyes. Without makeup she seemed far younger and, surprisingly, even more beautiful.

She nervously darted away from the door, and him. Nick tried to suppress his body's obvious reaction to seeing her this way. Placing the pizza on the island in the kitchen, he forced himself to ask, "What's wrong?"

"For the last thirty minutes I've been searching for the damn tape." She motioned for him to follow her into the bedroom. "I dumped everything out of my briefcase and my luggage. After frantically tearing through the pile, I emptied my purse, too. The tape is gone!"

Nick could tell by her continued quick, sharp movements how upset she was. "What tape?"

"I'm sorry, Nick. I know this doesn't make a lot of sense. It's a long story. I'll tell you over dinner."

They went back into the kitchen. While she popped open a diet soda, Nick opted for a light beer. Once they were seated, Angela explained. "I took work with me to Jamaica, but I never got around to it until I was on the plane, coming home."

Rolling his eyes, he smiled and said, "Let me guess. This has to do with one of your infamous tape recordings of Will Kellars. Personally, they make me nervous, especially now."

"I know. He'd have a cow if he found out." She sliced a huge wedge of pizza, placing it on his plate. "Eat and listen."

"Yes, ma'am." He saluted her playfully, relieved to see some fire back in her eyes.

"The day I left, I was in his office and I got hot."

Nick's raised eyebrow earned him a kick under the table.

She slowed down. "I was sitting directly in the sun, and I started to sweat. So I slipped off my jacket and hung it over the back of my chair. When Kellars got a call from Senator Holt, I waited by Marilyn's desk for a few minutes." She stopped long enough to take a quick drink, her enthusiasm contagious as she continued, "My recorder was running while I was gone!"

"So what did Kellars do, plot an assassination with the senator? Are they planning to knock off Susan Stover before she causes any more trouble?"

Ignoring the sarcasm in his voice, she replied, "Hold on, I'll show you."

Nick tried not to stare as the slinky robe floated behind her, leaving little to the imagination. She disappeared into the bedroom and ran back out, legal pad in hand.

"I wish you could hear the tape, but I can't find it. My memory seems to be screwed up. Probably that damned hangover. I was sure I put the tape in my briefcase, so it couldn't accidentally get erased. But I can't find it now."

"Maybe it fell out on the runway."

She stopped, remembering her arrival. "Oh, my God! I'm sure it did. We could go back and get it." She looked down, suddenly surprised by her lack of clothes. "I'll get dressed."

"Hold on! It's rained for three days straight. The chances of us finding a microtape would be slim, even in broad daylight. What exactly was on it that's so important?"

Angela stuck the pad in front of him and waited while he read it. "He wasn't talking to the senator, Nick. Marilyn told me when the light for that phone line went off. On the tape, it sounds like someone else was in the room *with* him. It was a woman. A woman from somewhere in the Caribbean, maybe Jamaican."

"So?"

Angela's agitation was obvious. "So how did she get in there? I never left Marilyn's desk. In fact, I was blocking the way to the door."

"Are you sure it wasn't a speaker phone?"

"Positive. I could hear the papers rustling. Besides, she sounded normal. And there was this weird, rough sound. Like something being dragged."

Doing his best hunchback impersonation, Nick said, "The body. Drag the body to the window and roll it out, then hide in the liquor cabinet again, before *that short woman* comes back."

"This is serious, Nick."

He stood up. Resting his hands on her shoulders, he gently massaged her tense muscles. "Maybe she was in his bathroom. There's a door in the corner behind his desk that leads to his private john."

Angela wanted to succumb to the comforting warmth of his hands, but she couldn't accept his lame explanation. "So he has a strange woman in his bathroom at the same time he's talking to me about a new advertising promo? Sorry, Nick. That's a little too kinky for me."

He felt her relaxing, and wished they could concentrate on other things. One look at her eager eyes told him Angela had no intention of giving this up. He dropped his hands and picked up the legal pad. "It is peculiar, plus, from what this says, it sounds like she's interrupted him before. I wouldn't think she'd hide in the bathroom, especially on a regular basis. Are you sure she was Jamaican?"

"I don't know. To tell you the truth, I tried to forget about it after I first heard it. My head was pounding, my stomach churning, and I had this incredible sense of impending doom. I stuffed the tape in my briefcase and spent the rest of the flight trying to stop crying. With me, tears are like floodwaters. It's really a pain in the ass, especially in business situations."

"So that's why you looked like you'd been crying when I first saw you get off the plane. I'll never forgive myself for jumping to the wrong conclusion that night."

She walked over and hugged him. "Forget it. I honestly don't know what I'd do without you. You've been a lot more than just a friend, and I appreciate it."

He wanted to bend down and pick her up. Carry her into the bedroom and show her exactly how much more than a friend he wanted to be, but he knew she was far too vulnerable. Needing to distance himself, he quickly said, "Maybe I should look through that mess you've made. The tape could still be here."

"It's worth a try." She followed him into the

bedroom, watching as he sifted through the pile of notes and file folders. He carefully examined each one, making certain nothing was hidden. He stopped when he came to a large, sealed manila envelope. "What's this?"

"I'm supposed to deliver it for a friend of mine."

His head slightly tilted in question.

Angela continued, "I met a man, Jax, while I was in Jamaica. He was so sweet to me. Drove me everywhere in his van. That's what he does for a living, like a taxi driver here in the States. At any rate, he took me to all the beautiful island places that most tourists never get a chance to see. Every day he had some wonderful adventure planned. I can't wait to show you the pictures!"

Nick didn't bother to conceal his wariness as he replied, "I'm afraid to ask what he expected for payment."

Angela smiled and shook her head, "Nothing like that. Get your mind out of the gutter, will you?"

"Sorry." He tried not to sound too envious as he said, "It just seems odd that this man appears out of nowhere and occupies all your time, that's all."

Angela took his hands and squeezed them. "I appreciate your concern for my virtue, but Jax was just being nice. Besides, I paid him the going rate for drivers, and he was old enough to be my father. He was probably happy not to have to drive around a bunch of obnoxious tourists for once." She dropped his hands, teasingly adding, "On the way to the airport he asked me to smuggle drugs for him."

Nick never flinched. He just nodded his head, waiting for the punch line.

"He was joking, of course. His mother is very ill. Since his sister lives near here, he wanted me to deliver this to her."

"Could be drugs."

"It passed drug dogs in both Jamaica and again at Dallas-Fort Worth. They never even sneezed."

"Have you looked inside?"

Her brown eyes flared as she answered, "Of course not, it's sealed. Besides, why would I?"

Turning it over, he held it up to see if he could see anything. "Aren't you even slightly suspicious?"

"No. He was a *nice* man." She sincerely added, "*Very* nice. He made my trip magnificent. Why shouldn't I do a favor for him?"

He shrugged, his mental jury still wavering. "No reason. When are you planning on taking it over?"

"I hadn't thought about it. With Mother . . . and all. I guess I'll run it by after work tomorrow. I suppose you want to come along to protect me."

"It wouldn't be a bad idea, even though it's a pretty ritzy address. Would you mind?"

"No. It might be nice having my own bodyguard." Cocking her head, she smiled and added, "It's just so funny. You really don't fit the stereotype at all, Nick."

He froze, then stepped toward her. "What's that supposed to mean?"

"Everyone in the office knows. You don't have

to pretend with me." She grabbed his hand and squeezed it. "I'm your friend. Nothing else matters."

Glaring at her, he asked, "Everyone knows *what? What* doesn't matter?"

"That you're gay." Seeing the expression of disbelief on his face, she anxiously added, "It's no big deal. I couldn't care less. It bothers some of the guys in the office, but, hey, that's their problem. People can be prejudiced about the strangest things—skin color, religion, sexual preference. I can't understand why they don't see that we're all just people."

Nick was shaking his head, obviously contemplating her revelation as she added, "I have to admit, though, deep down I don't think I really believed it until the other night when you helped me with my braids. That was so sweet—definitely not something one of those macho creeps I've dated before would do."

Staring blankly at her, Nick applied the ridiculous idea to a whirlwind of memories. Suddenly, the puzzle started to fall together. Why the men's room cleared whenever he came in. Why secretaries were the only people to invite him to lunch. Why Angela was sitting across from him right now, half naked yet totally oblivious to his masculine presence.

"I don't suppose you'd care to share with me how this information was obtained?" he asked.

"Right after you were hired, one of the office gossips saw you going into a gay bar. I guess she'd hit on you your first day, and apparently you didn't respond to her. The rest is history."

"You're kidding, right?"

"Don't worry about it. Some people's lives revolve around tracking the latest business tidbits, and sleazier things we won't discuss. You were the hot topic in the copy room for about a week, then they moved onto bigger and better affairs."

He thought for a second. "As far as I know, I've never been in any gay bars."

She was beginning to realize the rumor mill had churned out another false story. She weakly answered, "It was Stetson's, on Main."

The name was vaguely familiar, then he remembered. "I met a client there the first week I was here. He picked the location, since I was new in town. Seemed like a nice enough place to me." He shook his head, a smile creasing dimples into his cheeks. "And by the way, I'm not gay, and that outfit you've been prancing around in all night has been driving me crazy."

Angela's face burned through all the possible shades of red, stalling on a deep color near the end of the spectrum. "I—I'm sorry, Nick. I should have known better." She suddenly grasped the lapels of her robe and pulled them around her chest. "I'll change."

"No! Er, I mean, no, please don't. You don't have to change now, Angela." He stepped back, giving her some room. "I didn't mean to imply I was going to rape you or anything. It's getting late anyway. I suppose I need to be leaving."

"I really am sorry," she said, but inside she was screaming, *He's not gay!*

Nick wasn't sure if the lingering twinkle in her eye was relief, but he hoped it was. "There is absolutely no reason to be sorry. I'm just glad you told me. Looks like I need to set the record straight, so to speak."

"I know someone who could help you." She cocked her head and smiled flirtatiously.

"And who would that be?" He looked down at the top of her head. "I have minimum height requirements, you know."

"Really?" She dragged the foot stool to where he stood, then stepped onto it. She was eye to eye with him when she finally spoke, her lips barely brushing his each time they parted. "Exactly how strict are those requirements of yours?"

Nick leaned his head away from Angela, trying to ignore the sensual fragrance of her hair that was pulling him like a magnet. "Strict enough to be careful. I don't believe in diving in until I check how deep the water is."

Angela heard what he said, but kissed him anyway. At first it was only her arms that closed around his neck, stroked his hair. Then it seemed as though a wall deep inside him broke down, and he returned her kisses, only deeper and more passionately. She felt a dazed mixture of raw emotions drenching her. Then just as suddenly as his wall crumbled, it returned. Harder and stronger than ever.

His voice was hoarse when he spoke, his eyes glazed with passion. "I can't do this, Angela. I want to, God only knows how much. But it isn't right. Not now. I'll see you at work tomorrow."

He held her for several seconds after he spoke, then sat her down like a precious vase. Angela was numb as she watched him walk through her apartment and out the door. So numb that she didn't move, she just stared at the door in disbelief.

Nick leaned against the door of Angela's apartment, wanting desperately to go back inside. He stood there, weighing his options until one of her neighbors came trotting down the stairs, walking her Doberman. The dog stopped near Nick's leg, bared its teeth, and growled. As the owner tugged its leash, Nick turned around and knocked on Angela's door.

"Who is it?" Angela called.

"It's me."

She opened the door, hiding behind it.

"I'm sorry, Angela. I didn't mean to run out of here like a scared teenager."

"It's okay." She motioned toward the living room. "Want to talk about it?"

After Nick walked in, she closed and bolted the door behind him. "I suppose this all seems pretty foolish to you," he said.

"Not at all. I hate to admit it, but I've been fighting my feelings for you for quite a while. Of course, I thought you were off limits, so I told myself it was a case of wanting something I couldn't have. Then tonight when you implied you might be interested . . . I guess I just overreacted."

Shaking his head, he reached out and touched her cheek. "No. I was the one who overreacted. I know how tough things are right now for you. I just don't want to be included in a part of your life you'd rather forget."

She moved closer, aware of the strength of his

warm leg against hers. "You could never be that. I already feel closer to you than anyone else. In case you haven't noticed, I'm pretty much antisocial. Men are not exactly knocking down my door." She laughed, then added, "Or women either, for that matter."

Returning her smile, he said, "I wouldn't say that. I think you've just been too busy lately to let yourself have any fun."

"Mother took a lot of my time and energy."

He reached over, gently brushing a strand of hair away from her eyes. "And you don't exactly have the kind of job you leave behind when you go home. Believe me, I know your type. In a lot of ways we're exactly the same."

She shrugged and asked, "Hopeless workaholics?"

"I prefer not to think of the situation as hopeless. Just temporary. I don't know about you, but I have no desire to slave away at my desk until I drop dead at forty-five from a heart attack."

"I haven't thought about it. My main goal was making sure Mother was comfortable. Now that she's gone, I guess I need to reevaluate my priorities."

"I decided before I took this job that I'd try it for two or three years, save as much as I could, then start my own practice again. Life is too short to spend twelve hours a day doing something you aren't passionate about."

"Passionate?"

He held up his hands, then said, "Don't worry, no correlation to tonight intended. Before, I've always buried myself in my cases, since I knew I was fighting for people who couldn't fight for themselves. I miss that intensity. That feeling that you're doing something that makes a difference. But, unfortunately, financial reality does have an impact."

Angela reached out and stroked his cheek with her hand. "You are, undoubtedly, the most complex man I've ever known."

Nick stretched his arm around her so her head rested comfortably beneath his. "I know you're tired and confused. And if you're anything like me, you're probably as frustrated as hell. But I think we need to go into this with our eyes open. No surprises."

She nodded her head, snuggling against his chest. "I do have one question."

"Fire away," he said as he ran his fingers through her hair.

"Are you always this calm and levelheaded?"

"Usually."

A long sigh escaped from deep within her chest. She sounded as though she were almost asleep.

"Do you have a problem with that?"

"Well . . ."

"Come on. What is it?"

"I was just wondering if you'd ever do anything impetuous. You know, something a little risky but a lot of fun. Crazy. Adventurous." She yawned, relaxing as his hands kept tenderly stroking her hair.

"Did you have anything particular in mind?"

"Secluded beach . . . hot oil . . . sensual . . ."

Nick knew she was falling asleep, so he pulled

her even closer. He held her for a long time before he carried her to bed.

When Angela walked into her office on Tuesday morning, she felt as though her entire life had shifted dimensions. She was going through the same motions, yet nothing felt familiar. Part of her wanted to run, to forget the old routines and break free. Find a new job in a new city, away from all the memories that painfully bombarded her wherever she looked. But the memory of Nick last night, the look of passion in his eyes and his gentle touch, created a promise for her future right where she was.

Forcing herself to unload the contents of her briefcase, she made a stack for each task, then sat and stared at them. Grabbing the handwritten notes of the mysterious tape, she rushed to Nick's office, happy to at least momentarily be away from her own office. Nick immediately waved for her to come inside.

"Ms. Anderson just arrived, Mrs. Holt. I'll put you on the speaker phone so we can all discuss the situation." Nick pushed a button and hung up. He quickly crossed the office to close the door as he welcomed Angela with a smile that was so warmly overpowering it made her blush. After making herself comfortable, Angela stated, "Good morning, Mrs. Holt."

"Good morning. As I was telling Mr. Hunter, Bob is feeling a bit under the weather right now. He asked me to call you and set up the press release about the Stover baby."

Angela gave Nick a curious glance. Nick walked

to the window as he explained, "Mrs. Holt, I don't think Angela has heard the news." He directed his next comments to Angela. "They found the body of a baby girl in the South Canadian River about an hour ago. They're trying to determine if it's Amber Stover."

The color drained from Angela's face, but she recovered quickly. "Mrs. Holt, what did you have in mind?"

"I thought we should issue some sort of statement." Her voice was firm, straightforward. "You know, sympathetic and caring. The state is in mourning. The usual bullshit."

Angela shook her head in disagreement. "But what if the child isn't the Stover baby? I think we ought to have positive identification before we rush into this."

"I agree," Nick added.

Her voice was even more callous as she snapped, "Just write something up and fax it over. I have an appointment to get my nails done, and some errands to run. When I get back, if the body has been claimed, then I'll have Bob issue the statement. It's a no-lose situation for you two. We'll be prepared for the worst, and you get to do what you do best—rack up some more of those outrageous legal fees. Good-bye."

Silence filled Nick's office. Angela sat staring at the phone, still wondering how anyone could be so cold and insensitive. She finally looked up at Nick, who obviously shared her views. "How am I supposed to write a statement without knowing what the coroner has to say? If the baby was murdered, we'd need to throw in an anti-crime statement. If she died of natural causes, it would be a different announcement entirely. What if it isn't the Stover baby? Isn't Alice Holt overreacting?"

When he turned to face her, their eyes met and held as he uttered, "I certainly hope so."

Chapter 12

"Susan, go wait in the car. Now. You're being ridiculous," Samuel Stover harshly demanded.

Susan knew she was probably the only one on the face of the earth who could directly disobey such an explicit command from him without worrying about future retribution. With her head held high, she slammed the car door closed and said, "I'm going, Dad, and there's nothing you can do to stop me."

Samuel adjusted the knot of his paisley silk tie and buttoned his navy jacket. Putting his arms on her shoulders, he shook his head, his eyes tortured as he explained, "You don't need this image burned into your memory. I know from the war. Trust me, it's something you never forget. Never. Remembering Amber as she was when she was alive would be so much easier."

Every time Susan thought she had her emotions under control, they seemed to creep back to haunt her. Her voice cracked as she said, "It may not be her."

"Even if it's a stranger, the face will haunt you. Besides, the description the coroner gave of the body they found was close. Too close."

She wiped a tear and stood straighter. After taking a deep breath, she said, "If it is Amber, then the sooner I face it, the better. I have to be strong for Sandra, like you were for me when I needed you."

He stared at his daughter, wishing he could change the world. It dawned on him that after so many years, he still didn't know how to face death. He wondered if he ever would, if anyone really could, then shook his head. "You make it sound like facing your granddaughter's death is something you can make happen with a snap of your fingers. You don't need to impress anyone, Susan. Being strong has nothing to do with this. Quit being so mule-headed and let me go in alone."

Tilting her head, she pegged him with sad gray eyes. "I believe being mule-headed is a trait I acquired directly from you."

"Unfortunately, that's probably true," he grumbled.

"I'm not trying to impress anyone. I think I'll be able to accept that she's gone if I can say goodbye to her."

He exhaled loudly, obviously frustrated as they started to walk inside. "That's a bunch of bullshit, Susan. Either way she'll be gone. But if you see her lying there, it will block out some of the happy memories you have of her. Memories you need to hold in your heart. I've never told anyone this, but I wish I'd never seen your mother after she passed on. It took me years to forget how asinine she looked. The mortician had caked so much makeup on her, she seemed more like a grotesque wax imitation, or a plastic doll. She didn't even resemble your mother. Her body looked exactly like what it was—an empty shell."

They rounded the corner of the dingy hallway, both stopping at a door with an ominous black-lettered sign that said, MORGUE.

Samuel cleared his throat and put his hands on Susan's shoulders. "At least let me go first. If you insist, I'll go back with you once we're certain."

Susan's confidence had suddenly waned. Her stomach was queasy as she nodded in approval. Samuel took her hand and led her through the door. He stopped in front of a group of tacky, old reception chairs, and pushed her into one before he disappeared into the inner door marked, IDENTIFICATION.

Minutes dragged by as Susan waited. As she nervously pushed at her cuticles, she noticed the odor hanging in the air. It was the same stench of formaldehyde she remembered from her high school biology class when they dissected frogs. Lifeless, stinking, dead frogs. *Amber can't be dead!* The thought of her grandbaby lying on a cold slab in the other room made her physically ill. She frantically searched the hall, finding the door to the ladies' rest room with only seconds to spare. As she knelt in front of a toilet, her gut clenched. *They did this because of me, I know it!*

Once she was finally finished being ill, she washed her face and stared at the pathetic image in the mirror. No amount of makeup would help, so she merely dried her face and left. When she emerged, her father was waiting, his eyes downcast.

"Well?" she asked.

With his hand gently pushing the small of her back, he guided her out the door of the morgue. His voice cracked as he whispered, "It isn't her, Susan. Thank God, it isn't her."

Jax found his mother in the kitchen, stooped over the counter preparing *ackee*. Her gnarled fingers worked to clean the thin red membrane away from the yellow lobes and black seeds. He watched her drop the fruit into a pot of boiling water and shift her attention to a breadfruit before she noticed him. "Need help?" he asked, knowing she would never let him lift a finger.

Her crooked teeth showed as she cracked a narrow smile and shook her head. Wiping her hands on her old apron, she turned her attention to her son as he said, " 'Tis almost my time to go. I handled everything for you and Maya. She knows how to handle the business while I'm in the States. When I send word, you'll have to go with her. This place won't be safe much longer. Are you sure you're up to all the traveling? Do you have plenty of herbs from the *bushdoctor*?"

With gnarled fingers working to untie the apron, she glared at him. "I have all I need of everything. Don't delay, Jax." Her eyes became even more intense as she reached out to dig yellowed fingernails into his arm. "And don't do more harm than good!"

He tried to ignore the impact of the threat in her eyes. "We could leave things the way they are."

Livid, she almost drew blood as her nails cut

into his flesh. "Never! I will not die knowing it hasn't ended."

Jerking away from her grip, he walked to the screen door and said, "Then I have to go."

She leaned against the counter, her hands twisting over and under themselves. Her voice was softer, more controlled as she asked, "How long will the last *baybee* tarry?"

"Until you leave. Then she'll need to be sent to stay with Thomas and Kay." Reacting to another threatening glare, he said, "They can be trusted. If it can be arranged, I'll pick her up when I get back from the States so I can return her. If not, I've left Maya instructions on how to dispose of her."

"Shame, Jax! The child is not a piece of rubbish. A little person she is, with pure souls. Like you and Maya once were, and Annissa, too!"

He glared back at her, his temper pushing aside any pity that was left in him. "You know I didn't mean anything like that. Maya will place her on a commercial flight to Florida. She's to leave a note that says where her family is located, then slip out. The airline people will find her and send her home. Easy."

"And what happens if some *bandulu*—criminal—finds her? Then what will you do? Be glad 'tis someone else's problem?"

"It's a good plan, Tica. Stop trying to imagine problems."

Her answer was a brief glare that ended when she turned away, fixing her gaze on a skittish doctor bird outside the window.

"I do the best I can. Besides, we'll only use it if

something happens to me. I plan on collecting the reward money, even though it will be one of the tougher tasks we face in all this. Maybe even impossible."

"I still can't believe you are trying to get *dunza* for that child from its own family. You know *dunza* isn't important anymore. *Dunza* is what got us into this mess in the first place!"

"It *is* important, Tica. We will have to move from place to place for the next few years, and it won't be cheap. You may need doctors. A quarter-million dollars will last a long time in the islands."

She turned around, walking toward him as she said, "I need no doctors, just my Annissa back home. I'll be free when the spirits of these *baybees* are off my souls and the souls of my children."

He knew arguing was hopeless. "I'll do the best I can. Maya will need to check with our Cuban friend every forty-eight hours for messages. I'll only call directly to where you are when it's absolutely safe."

She stopped and laughed. "Absolutely safe? Will we ever be safe again?"

"We haven't been safe in years," Jax seethed. "Besides, safe is an idea. Don't let it start bothering you now."

"Everything bothers me now. I suppose that's what happens to foolish old mistresses. They go crazy looking back at all the mistakes they made along the way."

"Everyone makes mistakes. Everyone has things they've done they wish they could change, Mama."

"Get out of my sight! *Everyone* doesn't live off

the suffering of *baybees* and their mamas, and I raised you well enough to know it." As he stormed out the door, she shouted, "Remember my words, boy. Don't bring more trouble on our heads than we already have!"

Nick buzzed Angela's office at six. When there was no answer, he thought about putting a note on her desk, but changed his mind when he realized she was already gone. Assuming she was still exhausted, he went back to his office to call her apartment. Leaving a message, he awkwardly said, "I'd like to help deliver your friend's package tonight. Hope you're feeling better. I'll come by later and pick you up."

In a way, he was relieved she wasn't there. It would give him the time he needed. He'd been thinking about the tape all day. Angela was too levelheaded to blow things out of proportion, and his curiosity was killing him. What he had planned for tonight was risky, and he didn't want Angela involved in any way.

He smiled as he thought of what she'd said about being adventurous just before she went to sleep. She'd certainly change her opinion once he carried out tonight's plan. Hopefully, he'd still be employed when he had a chance to brag.

After walking slowly through the entire office, he was certain everyone else had left for the night. From Marilyn's desk he buzzed the intercom into Will Kellars' office, waiting for a reply. Even though he had watched Kellars leave with Marilyn over an hour ago, he wasn't taking any chances that he might still be inside.

DEADLY SILENCE   235

Cradling the receiver of the phone, he swung around to face the huge doors. Taking a deep breath, he turned the brass doorknobs and pushed. Relief rushed through him as the doors easily opened. Before he walked in, he carefully removed the piece of tape he'd slipped over the lock that afternoon on his way to lunch.

Nick didn't turn on the lights. Instead he worked from the ample illumination provided by moonlight streaming in the windows and the glow from the small spotlights that brightened the mirror between the bookshelves. He walked briskly past the conference table and desk, stopping before the door he assumed went to Kellars' private rest room.

Taking another deep breath, he opened the door, walked inside, and closed it. After fumbling in the darkness for several seconds, he found the light switch. The fluorescent hum of the indirect lighting roared in his ears. It seemed loud enough for the entire building to hear, but logically, he knew that was ridiculous. He consciously relaxed his neck and shoulder muscles, hoping to calm his rattled nerves as well.

Another door was in the back of the small bathroom, and he pulled it open quickly, as if trying to surprise someone, or something. The only thing he surprised was himself. He felt ridiculous as he stared at several coats, one of Kellars' extra suits, and dozens of empty clothes hangers. One side held a pile of fresh towels, and the other was stacked high with spare rolls of toilet paper, bars of soap, and cleaning supplies.

He'd gone too far not to check every possibility,

so he pushed aside the coats and rapped on the wall at the back of the closet, listening carefully for any indication there was a hidden door. All he heard were echoes of his own knocks.

Echoes of a reckless, harebrained idea that could easily cost him his career if he got caught.

Annissa was working at the computer in the hidden room when she heard strange hollow thumps coming from the direction of Will's office. At first she thought they were from the cleaning crew, but after a glance at her watch, knew otherwise. It was much too early.

She walked toward the sound, which she could tell was coming from the far end of Will's office, near the bathroom. When she paused to listen more closely, the sound stopped as abruptly as it had begun. Like a curious cat, she went to the one-way mirror, searching for clues in the dark office beyond. Moonlight streamed in from the night, reflecting off the polished wood of Will's desk. She was about to go back to her work when a man's face suddenly appeared directly in front of her. An involuntary gasp escaped from her lips before she had time to cover her mouth. As quickly as he emerged, he disappeared, a huge, murky shadow against the starlit window.

A burglar! My God, what if he heard me in here? I need to call Will, tell him.

Annissa's legs wobbled like a newborn foal. She grabbed the countertop to stabilize herself, then made her way back to the chair near the computer. Her hands were like ice as she rested them against her face. She bolted upright when the pain seized her. It was piercing at first, like thorns ripping the delicate tissues deep inside her chest. It flowed like liquid fire through her neck, her breast, down her left arm.

Suddenly, her surroundings began to shrivel and drift. An odd sense of fascination overcame Annissa as the room grew smaller and smaller, until there was nothing left but a peaceful black void.

Nick switched off the ignition, noticing that strength was finally returning to his hands. He flexed them, testing their usefulness. Since he'd been in Kellars' office, he'd had a tough time quieting his raw nerves. At first he was sure he'd heard something from behind the bookcase, but passing time had brought reason and logic.

He stood in the parking lot for a while, breathing in fresh, clean air. Once he regained his composure, he headed to Angela's door. She answered quickly, wearing jeans and an oversized purple K-State sweatshirt. Excitement bubbled from her as she said, "Come in. I have great news!"

"Judging from the way you look, you must have won a lottery."

"No." She whipped the recorder out of her pocket. "I found the tape! It was at the airport, soggy but not broken. Listen!"

As the scratchy sound of Will Kellars' voice mixed with the lilt of the Jamaican woman, Nick realized that Angela had been right. When it was finished, he said, "I'm impressed. Obviously you don't plan to give up, so I'd better tell you what I just did."

Grabbing a beer from the refrigerator, she tossed it to him. "You look like you could use this."

After he took a long, satisfying swig, they walked into the living room and sat down. Sighing, he watched her expectantly as he said, "Twenty minutes ago, I broke into Will Kellars' office."

"Oh, come on." Setting her beer down, she stared at him in disbelief.

As he took her hands in his, their eyes met and held. "Seriously, I really did. All day I studied the transcript you made of the tape, and now that I've heard it, I'm glad I did. I had to know if there was another way into his office. It's like I've become obsessed with the idea that Kellars is not what he appears to be."

Angela's face reflected his mixture of trepidation and concern. "I feel the same way. . . . For six years I've been minding my own business, and now, all of a sudden, I think about him constantly." Angela's eyes were dark with worry. Leaning even closer, she squeezed his fingers. "So, was there a secret passage?"

"No . . . Well, maybe."

Cocking her head, she replied, "That's a lot of help. How'd you get in? Marilyn says the door is always locked, even if Kellars is just in someone else's office in the building. She says he even locks himself in sometimes, and he's never given her a key."

"This afternoon when I went to lunch with him, I made sure he walked out first. Then I slipped a piece of tape over the lock as I passed."

Toasting him with her beer, she said, "I'm impressed. You don't seem like the underhanded type."

"Just the gay type?" he grumbled playfully.

With an exaggerated quiver of her lower lip, she replied, "I said I was sorry about all that. Lots of people are gay. It's no big deal."

"I know. I know," he said stoically. "At any rate, when I went back tonight, the door slid right open. I checked the bathroom, but there's nothing in there except a coat closet. I even banged around to see if it was hollow, for hidden doors or panels. To tell you the truth, I felt pretty silly. Scared shitless but silly."

"Sounds very macho to me," she said, leaning closer.

"The next part isn't. I left the bathroom and stopped by the bookshelf, looking at one of those eerie pictures of his dead son. For some reason they keep spotlights on the mirror between his bookcases all the time. When I stepped in front of the mirror, it looked strange, like something moved besides me. And I could have sworn I heard someone. Now I'm beginning to think my imagination conjured up a ghost."

Her curiosity piqued, she leaned forward and asked, "What'd you hear?"

Wrinkling his face, he shook his head as he remembered. "It wasn't a word. More like someone gasping. Kind of a scared sound."

Angela was hanging on his every word. "Then what'd you do?"

He leaned back and shrugged. "What every sane lawyer would do. I ran like hell with my tail tucked between my legs." Watching her laugh, he added, "Really, I thought my heart was going to jump out of my chest. I'm still not quite back to normal. Mr. Macho, right?"

Reaching over, she brushed a wayward lock of blond hair away from his face. "Mr. Intelligent. What would you have done? Shake this person-ghost's hand and say, 'Pleased to meet you, I was just here to check out the plumbing'? Getting out of there was the smartest thing you could do."

"What if someone did see me?" She was so close to him he wanted to wrap his arms around her. He settled for savoring the aroma of her perfume.

"Even if they did, there isn't anything Kellars could do about it."

Distracted, he asked, "How's that?"

"*If* there is a secret room, and *if* someone in it saw you, and *if* they told Kellars, how in the world would he bring it up? It would obviously be connected to something illegal. Since you didn't find anything, they'd probably just assume you were curious and let it slide."

He cast her a sideways glance. "That's a lot of *if's*. Besides, they could always claim the security system was somehow triggered."

"True. We need to come up with some logical reason why you were in there."

"In the dark."

Angela sighed. "I didn't say it'd be easy."

"I was near the bookshelf when I heard a noise. I could always say the door was unlocked and I wanted to borrow one of his antique books. He's offered to loan them to me before."

"Sounds as good as anything I can come up with." Angela ran a finger down the side of his face, leaning until her lips were touching his. As she closed her eyes, she whispered, "I still can't believe you did it."

"Neither can I," he said, kissing her in reply. "And you thought I wasn't adventurous."

Moving even closer, she mumbled, "So far I really like being wrong about you."

Nick stretched his arms around her, wrapping her warmth against his chest. It had been a long time since anything had felt so right. Plunging his fingers into her hair, he stared into her exquisite eyes before kissing her deeply.

Angela responded with her hands, her lips, her heart. Crawling onto his lap, she pressed softly against his hardness, making him moan.

He leaned back. Lust was heavy in his voice as he mumbled, "We're moving awfully fast."

"I'm . . . I'm not sure I'm ready to . . ."

Taking her hand, he said, "So we'll slow down. I wasn't kidding before, Angela. I'll wait."

She smiled. "It's no wonder I'm falling for you."

"Really?"

"Really."

After a gentle kiss, he managed to walk to the front door and said, "I'll pick you up in the morning."

"Promise?"

"I promise."

After locking the door, Angela leaned against it for a long time. Her first thoughts were only of Nick, and how lucky she was to have him. Then darker thoughts crept in, as they often do in solitude. She could easily picture her mother, how excited she would have been to meet Nick.

As her stomach clenched, she started to work out her frustrations, attacking the dishes in the kitchen first. Hours later, she was finally exhausted enough to sleep.

Annissa's world emerged slowly. First she was aware of the hum of the computer by her head. Next, the lights became brighter, growing from tiny flickers to illuminate the room. Fluid shapes molded into familiar objects. Very carefully she tried to pull herself up. Knowing she needed immediate medical attention didn't help. She couldn't call an ambulance from inside the hidden room.

The phone seemed so far away, although it was only a few yards. By alternately leaning on pieces of furniture and cabinets, she managed to grab it without falling. With great effort she dialed Will Kellars' phone number. After twenty rings she gave up, momentarily exhausted from the attempt.

Leaning back, Annissa assessed each part of her body. A cold sweat covered her forehead, and shivers vibrated down her spine. Her legs were weak, but seemed to be gaining strength each minute. She flexed her left arm, which responded well. The ache in her chest had subsided, but the thought of that excruciating pain returning scared the hell out of her.

If she could just make it downstairs, she'd be all right. Dialing the phone again, she contacted a nearby taxi service. From deep within she gathered every ounce of willpower to stand.

DEADLY SILENCE

The first few steps were like those of an old woman's—back arched, feet dragging, hands trembling. She clung to the panel leading to her office for a minute to regather her strength. Once outside the hidden door, she fumbled for her purse and pushed the button to seal the secret entry.

As she walked into the reception area, the lush, spirited photographs seemed to mock her frailty. She was almost to the door when another stinging flash crept down her left arm, buckling her knees. She stayed there, kneeling and panting until the pain faded, then grabbed the doorknob to pull herself up.

Hunched over, she stumbled to the elevator and waited. She knew she could make it to the hospital if she just held on for a few more minutes.

The taxi was waiting as she crawled across the building's ornate lobby. The burly driver rushed to help, easily carrying her, then placing her gently in the backseat. Just before they turned into the hospital's emergency entrance, he glanced back at her and asked, "There some reason we're being followed?"

Annissa simply shrugged, the pain too intense for her to answer, much less care.

At two a.m. the deserted Manhattan alley was cloaked in darkness. The back door to the office of Paradise Promotions was relatively easy to break into, at least for someone with extensive field experience. Surprising Evan in his deepest stage of sleep might make things go smoother. Then again, Evan was extremely intelligent and would probably not participate willingly. Either way, preparations had been made. He would cooperate or die.

Walking toward the back room, the intruder noticed the keypad next to the door. He hadn't brought the proper equipment to tackle any sophisticated electronics systems right now. Instead, he concentrated on what he came for—Evan Peterson.

Lavender neon cast a haunting glow throughout the front office, illuminating the precisely arranged pamphlets. Each footstep was cautiously placed as he crossed the room, then step by step climbed the spiral staircase toward the loft. Walking softly across the thick carpet with his .357 leading the way, he scanned for movement while intently listening for the slightest sound. Every fiber in his body was ready to strike. Pausing outside the bedroom door, he cleared his mind.

In one swift motion he was through the door, beside the bed. An empty bed, in a room obviously vacated in a hurry. The intruder knew Evan never tolerated disarray in any element of his life, yet the bedspread was rumpled and several boxes were strewn on the floor.

A quick search of the loft turned up nothing very interesting. He chuckled when he saw the lipstick marks on the bathroom counter, knowing Evan would probably kick the bitch out for being such a slob, even if she was the sexiest woman alive. Overwhelming disappointment made his movements faster, less calculated than they should be.

With a glance across the front office, he appraised the sophisticated air of the place. Evan must have decorated it himself. His style was unmistakable. Just as he was about to leave, a blinking light under the counter caught his attention. Crossing over, he stooped, a gloved finger gently pushing the playback button on Evan's answering machine. Familiar voices filled the empty office.

When the tape was finished, he smiled and popped it out of the machine. The morning hadn't been a total waste of time. He knew where Elaine Patterson was, even if he didn't know who she was, or what she had to do with the network. He would find her, make her pay for what they had done.

After all, Grand Cayman was a small island, and the natives were very friendly. For the right price.

When Annissa awoke, she was in the emergency room, the harsh lights glaring down in her eyes. A nurse was inflating the blood-pressure cuff on her arm, while a doctor stood beside the bed, jotting down entries on a medical chart.

"How are you feeling, Ms. Jamison? I'm Dr. Sigl."

Dr. Sigl was a tall, slender woman dressed in a crisp white coat over green surgical scrubs. Sandy hair framed an oval face with high cheekbones and caring eyes. Nauseated and terrified, Annissa tried to respond, but her throat was so dry she barely managed to ask, "What happened to me?"

"You had a mild heart attack. Your preliminary blood work indicates you are also a borderline diabetic. Are you taking any medication?"

"No." The heart monitor blipped erratically as Annissa tensed. "What's that?"

Dr. Sigl handed her a small cup of water. "I want you to relax. Imagine you're strolling across the hot sand near the ocean. Think how good it feels to have cool water rush soothingly between your toes."

Annissa strained, wondering why the doctor had chosen those particular words. She closed her eyes as she was told, but instead of allowing childhood memories of the ocean to overwhelm her, she concentrated on how to get out of the hospital. Finally, the blip of the monitor began to sound like a metronome pacing a waltz. Annissa opened her eyes, certain one of her plans would work.

Dr. Sigl continued, "Much better. Do you have a personal physician you'd like us to contact?"

"No. I'll be leaving as soon as possible. Right now, as a matter of fact. I'm feeling much better."

Shaking her head, Dr. Sigl touched Annissa's arm and stared at her until she was sure she had her full attention. "I'm afraid that wouldn't be very wise. Even though you survived the first attack, we need extensive tests to determine its cause. We'll also do more blood-sugar work to ascertain if you should be on insulin. Plus, the damage to the heart muscle must be assessed. A cardiologist has been called to discuss the tests that will need to be performed. He should be here any minute."

"What's this for?" Annissa lifted her right hand, which held a tube connected to a bag of clear fluid.

"Your blood pressure was irregular when you

arrived. We've administered drugs to stabilize your condition and minimize damage to the heart muscles."

"Am I going to die?" she asked flatly.

Firmly gripping Annissa's hand, Dr. Sigl replied, "You definitely are not going to die. You're a very strong woman. Once the cardiologist determines whether you need surgery, we can discuss the changes you'll need to make in your lifestyle. Proper nutrition and exercise are essential for diabetics. And recovering heart-attack victims."

Alarmed, she asked, "Surgery?"

"It's possible. If your attack was caused by arterial blockage, or if there's been valve damage. I'm sure he'll go over everything with you."

"What if I decide not to have the surgery right now? Can it be postponed?"

Hesitantly Dr. Sigl answered, "Sometimes, but it would be very risky. I have to go now. I'll check on you once you're settled in the cardiac-care unit. It's an excellent facility, you'll be quite comfortable there."

Annissa watched her push aside the curtain and disappear. Her mind was racing. For once Will Kellars would have to understand, and help.

"How can you be perky at this hour?" Angela yawned, her body reminding her it was barely six a.m. Leaning against the back of the elevator, she studied Nick. He looked positively energetic, electrified by the same risk that made her want to crawl back under a stack of warm covers and hide.

"Perky?" He rocked back and forth, shaking his

head and grinning. "I don't think it's possible for a six-foot-six guy to be perky."

Angela let her eyes roam from his soft leather shoes, up his gray pinstripe suit, past his fascinating eyes, to the mane of blond hair on top of his head. Nodding, she smiled and said, "You're right. Perky isn't it."

With a smirk he added, "Perfect! I'll bet you meant I'm perfect in every possible way."

"And humble, too. What more could a woman ask for?" Nudging him, she tiptoed and whispered, "You look exceptionally sexy this morning."

Bending down, he asked, "Are you making another pass at me?"

Opening his arms, he silently invited her to enter his embrace as she replied, "Of course I am. Why else would I agree to meet you before sunrise?"

His arms wrapped around her as he whispered, "Because you promised to stand guard while I sketch the floor plan, remember?"

The elevator doors opened, and she reluctantly stepped out saying, "How boring."

"You didn't think it was boring last night."

Smiling seductively, she replied, "True. Very, very true."

Nick glanced around. Taking her in his arms again, his lips grazed her ear, and the soft tropical scent of her perfume made it hard for him to concentrate. "On second thought, since no one is around . . ."

Smiling, she slipped away and said, "Go see if you can discover that back entrance to Kellars' suite. Then we'll see about finding some secret rendezvous point."

Nick replied, "Warn me if anyone comes."

"How am I supposed to do that?"

"Cough or something—you're the creative one, remember? I won't take very long." Nick shrugged and smiled, then quickly nipped her earlobe.

"Nick!" she gasped, ducking away from him.

He winked at her, then headed down the hall, taking calculated steps so he could jot down the distances on his legal pad. Angela paced back and forth, trying to look as inconspicuous as possible, which she rapidly realized was absurd. At this hour, if anyone came, she would have to pretend to be leaving the ladies' room.

Through the window of Pampered in Paradise, the picture of the sun setting behind the mountains bordering Montego Bay caught her attention. Angela stopped beside the massive doors, peering into the travel agency's office. For several moments she stared at the picture, wishing she had never seen that island. She shook off the irritating notion that memories of flawless Jamaican sunsets had taken the place of her last chance to see her mother alive.

Turning around, she leaned back, pinching the bridge of her nose and tilting her head to help stop the invasion of tears that now accompanied even fleeting thoughts of her mother. Suddenly the large mahogany door slid open, spilling her into the reception area of Pampered in Paradise.

Barely catching herself, she stumbled into the dimly lit room. Half expecting alarms to ring and armed guards to jump out of the shadows waving machine guns, she froze. But nothing happened. Although the lights were off, the back part of the office was illuminated by morning sunlight streaming through the windows. She slipped back out the door, pulling it almost closed. As loud as she could, she coughed.

Nick walked up behind her, surprising her. "What's wrong?" he whispered.

Angela's hand flew to her mouth. "Don't sneak up on me like that! You almost scared me to death."

"You were the one who signaled," he whispered, his voice mocking.

"I know. I know. Look at this." Angela pushed open the door and walked inside. "Think we should check it out?"

"What the hell?" He shrugged, following her. "May as well go to prison for breaking and entering. At least I know a lot of good lawyers."

Angela shook her head, testing the excuse she had already planned to use if anyone came. "There was no breaking involved. We were merely making sure no one had burglarized the place so we would know whether to call the police."

Nick rolled his eyes at her. "You're the one who should've been a lawyer. That's some of the most twisted logic I've heard in ages." He studied the sketches on the legal pad in his hand. "Getting a good feel for this space will really help with these floor plans. Let's check her office first, since it should back up against Mr. Kellars' suite."

They pushed the door closed behind them, leaving the lights off. Once past the entryway, they were surprised to find only two offices and a small kitchen area. The first room appeared to be for specialized conferences. A big-screen television was in one corner, a videocassette player set on top of it. A small bookshelf held rows of tapes marked with various island names and locations. Overstuffed chairs lined the conference table in the center of the room.

"This must be where Pampered makes its sales pitches. Pretty snazzy, huh?" He picked up one of the oversized books lying on the table, flipping through the glorious pictures of the island getaways.

"Only the best," Angela whispered. "Wouldn't want those millionaires to feel uncomfortable for even a second."

Angela noticed Nick was pacing off the dimensions of the rooms as they walked, adding them to the sketch in his hand. They passed into the larger office, which was still considerably smaller than Kellars' suite. Decorated with imported furniture and exotic fabrics, it had an island flavor and a unique style—except for the mahogany bookcase that lined the far wall. In its center was a mirror, identical to the one in Will Kellars' office, right down to the tiny spotlights that always lit it, even in broad daylight.

Chapter 13

Annissa awoke to the sight of the young cardiologist's face directly above hers. She could easily have been his mother, which immediately made her feel ancient.

"Good morning, Ms. Jamison," he said pleasantly.

"Morning?" she moaned.

"Yes. I think it's about eight o'clock. Do you remember coming to the hospital last night?"

Annissa nodded as her mind cleared and the reality of her near death seized her. "The tests. What did they show?"

"That you're a lucky woman. We think you have very little damage to the heart tissue. After this afternoon's tests we'll know for certain about arterial blockage. You've responded well to the drugs they administered when you were admitted. Strong blood pressure, excellent prognosis. I'd say you're going to pull through this episode just fine."

She bolted upright, then fell back from the pain that shot through her. Weakly she asked, "This afternoon's tests? You want to do more?"

"Yes. Last night we performed an Ultrafast CT Scan. It's like a souped-up CAT scanner that photographs cholesterol deposits. It uses a computer to turn simple X rays into cross-section images. Its fast scanner was synchronized with your heartbeat via the electrocardiogram leads we attached near your collarbone. The tests were positive, but unfortunately, an Ultrafast CT can't determine what percentage of an artery is clogged. Our next step will be a stress test, and after that we'll decide whether to perform an angiogram."

Overwhelmed, Annissa asked, "Could I have another heart attack?"

"Anything's possible." He nodded toward the sophisticated equipment positioned by her bed. "But we'll be monitoring you. No need to worry, the nurse will know what your body is doing even before you do. Just get some rest, and I'll see you this afternoon." He winked and slipped out the door.

Annissa closed her eyes for several minutes, her mind unwinding the tangle of obstacles she faced. After she eliminated her alternatives, the decision was obvious.

She stared at the digital display of the machine beside her, wondering if the nurses had the power to keep her there without her consent. The on-off switch was well within her reach, so she clicked it off, listening to the hum of the machine wind down to silence.

Annissa anxiously awaited the expected crash of nurses and revival teams, but they never materialized. Carefully she removed the electrodes, then winced as she slid the needle out of the back of her hand. She grabbed a tissue, holding it in place to stop the small trickle of blood.

A paper sack in the closet held her clothing. In

less than five minutes, she was on the elevator, feeling much better than she had dreamed possible only a few hours ago.

Angela was waiting at her apartment door when Nick came up the stairs. As soon as she saw him, she anxiously asked, "This has been driving me crazy all day! What'd you find?"

Nick tugged an envelope out of the hip pocket of his blue jeans and handed it to her. As he followed her inside, she removed the sketch, unfolding the warm paper carefully.

She was amazed at its accuracy. Looking back at him, she asked, "How long did it take you to do this?"

He shook his head. "Only an hour or so. I tried to keep everything to scale. At least as close as I could using this morning's crude measurements." He pointed at the area highlighted in bright yellow. "There seems to be a relatively large space unaccounted for, about the same size as Kellars' own office."

Angela pinpointed the part of the map Nick had highlighted in red as she added, "Behind his bookcase."

"And behind Pampered's bookcase." Their eyes met and held, each pondering the illegal implications of a hidden office.

Angela hesitantly asked, "Could it be storage space, or maybe some kind of equipment area for the building?"

"Afraid not. I checked with the building engineer." Dropping the map to his side, he asked, "Do you have the transcript of that tape? Maybe it will make more sense if we assume the woman from Pampered came through some sort of secret passage."

"Sure, it's on my computer." She led him into her bedroom, where the machine was nestled in one corner. Angela sat cross-legged in her black jogging suit, obviously comfortable at the keyboard. After pulling up the file, they both studied the mysterious dialogue once again.

"How many people do you know who use the word 'post' to mean mail?" Nick asked.

"No one. Except in Jamaica. Jax called it that."

"That woman who runs Pampered is from Jamaica. What's her name?"

"Got me. It definitely could be her on the tape. Judging from your floor plan, she's the most likely one to have been able to get into his office through a hidden passage."

Nick was sitting on the floor behind her, his back resting against the end of her bed. He rolled to his knees and read the screen. " 'Pitch place' still hangs me up. Does this word processing program have a thesaurus built in?"

"Of course."

"Try it on 'pitch.' "

Angela moved the cursor and pushed the right buttons. The screen displayed a variety of terms, from fling and hurl to decline and slope. Nothing that helped solve the mystery. "Might as well try the dictionary function while we're at it," she said. She pushed another key and the list of definitions popped up.

"That's it!" she pointed to the last line on the screen where it said—*Informal. A sales talk.* "They're talking about selling something. Something that is due in two weeks, that was going to be sold to a couple." Angela's eyes widened, her hand involuntarily rising to her lips. "It couldn't be, Nick."

Nick relaxed his knees, sinking so his upper body rested on his heels. "A baby?" he asked quietly.

"No one is despicable enough to kidnap babies and then sell them." Her voice grew weaker as she asked, "Are they?"

"It would explain how so many children disappear without a trace."

"I thought most of those kids were kidnapped by their own parents. You know, divorce-child custody arguments."

"Some of them are. But unfortunately, some just flat disappear. No motive. No ransom. They're just gone."

"We have to stop them, Nick."

"I know."

Neither Angela nor Nick moved for a long time. They both were lost in dark thoughts of respectable citizens buying and selling kidnapped babies. Finally Nick said, "We could be wrong about all this. Maybe it's a big coincidence."

"True. But I just remembered the money."

"What money?" Nick asked, growing even more concerned.

"The day I accidentally made that tape, I was talking to Marilyn at her desk. She said when she flew back home from Jamaica on the Pampered in Paradise plane, she surprised the woman who manages it during the post-flight inspection. Marilyn was worried about her because she dropped a roll of hundred-dollar bills." Angela's eyes met his. "You know Marilyn, it would never dawn on her that someone carrying around a large amount of cash might be up to no good."

"You were on that plane. Did you see anything suspicious?"

Angela thought for a second, then shook her head. "No, but I wasn't exactly in top form, either. Coming back, I had a horrible hangover and, as you know, a bad case of the weepies."

"Did you have any delays in Customs at DFW?" he asked.

"None. We were through in minutes. As soon as the plane refueled, we were off again."

Nick ran his hands through his hair and sighed. "I didn't see anyone suspicious at the airport while I was waiting for you to arrive."

"Marilyn said she went back a few minutes after everyone left the plane because she forgot something. We probably didn't hang around long enough to see whoever it was that made the pickup."

"Or the drop. They could be moving something out of the country, too. You never heard anything unusual while you were on board, did you?"

"No. But music is piped in all the time. The only time you could hear the engine noise was when the pilot would come over the speaker to tell us about the flight."

Nick stood up and walked to Angela's side. "So we're working for a man who may be involved in kidnapping and money laundering."

"Maybe he's smuggling drugs, too."

"Why not? What else could go wrong?"

Angela answered, "I've been asking myself that ever since I got back from Jamaica. I was hoping the worst was already over, but there is one other problem."

Nick nodded. "I know. Does the Stover kidnapping somehow fit in? And if it does, what are we going to do about it?"

"I'd forgotten what a spectacular view you have."

Annissa stared blankly at Will Kellars' back. The sarcasm in her voice was unmistakable as she replied, "It's been a long time since you stopped by my home. I'm surprised you even remembered how to get here. I guess the idea of your lily-white friends thinking you might be romantically associated with a black woman isn't as humiliating as it once was. That's why you stopped coming here, wasn't it?"

Will turned away from the window, choosing to ignore her. He resisted the urge to point out the elegant way she lived because of him. From the crown molding that graced ten-foot ceilings to the Persian rugs at her feet, she was surrounded by luxury. "How are you feeling, Annissa?"

Annissa sat in a scroll-back chair, wearing a bold print caftan. She shrugged and muttered, "As well as can be expected."

"You should've stayed in the hospital."

"And I suppose you'd have handled the bank transfers? You don't even know which banks are involved, much less where to find the daily authorization codes or how to use them."

Softly shaking his head, he said, "One day wouldn't make that much difference."

"How would you know? You haven't got a clue what's required to run this operation. It's complicated. Very complicated."

"I was the one who paid for you to get that degree in accounting. Now I suppose it's your turn to teach me some of what you learned. This incident has made me realize that we have no backup system in place. We can start with the banking in the morning. You'll find I'm a quick study."

"You sound like you're talking about some piece of equipment that you toss into the trash when it breaks. This is a complicated network of people. It involves *lives*, Will. Yours and mine, as well as a handful of others. In case you've forgotten, what we do is illegal."

"And in case you've forgotten, it's what paid for all this." He waved one arm, sweeping the room. "Not to mention supporting your entire family in Jamaica."

"You never miss a shot, do you? Just once, could we have a discussion without your implied threats against me and my relatives?"

Embers of romantic sparks made his voice soften. "I need you at work, Annissa. Healthy, not dead."

Reacting to his familiar tone, she sighed. "I'm not planning on dying anytime soon. It'll just take me a few days to get things lined up so you can handle them. Then I'll go see a doctor."

"I'm not incompetent, you know. If you'll write down the banking procedures, I can help you deal with the routine things until you're back on your feet."

"So you've changed your mind?"

"About what?"

Dismayed, she shook her head. "My, my, how quickly they forget. It was your idea in the first place, Will. No written documentation. Memorize everything. No need to risk having evidence lying around where anyone could get their hands on it. Computers with security codes on top of security codes. Systems that erase themselves whenever the wrong keystrokes are entered. And after all that you want me to *write down* the bank-account numbers and wire-access codes for all the funds we have stashed in the Cayman Islands?"

"Okay, you made your point. If my office is clear when you get ready to do the routine operations tomorrow, buzz me and I'll come watch."

Annissa stared at him in disbelief.

Will snapped, "I'm not senile, you know. I can learn a few codes. Once you're feeling better, things can get back to normal. I'll arrange for someone to drive you for the next few weeks."

"I'd prefer to take a cab."

He was already walking across the room toward the door. "No. It's the least I can do. My private investigator will be here at nine. He'll take you wherever you need to go."

Suddenly remembering her trip to the hospital, she replied, "Make sure he doesn't follow me too close, Will. He may just discover things you never wanted him—or anyone else, for that matter—to know."

* * *

Angela poured Nick another cup of hot chocolate. It was almost midnight. Hours of pacing had not made coping with their predicament any easier. If anything, the longer Angela thought about it, the more complicated it seemed.

"I still think we should call the FBI," she mumbled into her steaming mug, softly blowing the remains of a marshmallow across its surface. After digging through the pile of newspapers to be recycled, she'd found an article on the Stover kidnapping case. At the bottom were two phone numbers. One was for the Stover hot line; the other listed a number for FBI agent Lesley Jaggers. Angela pointed at the newspaper article. "Maybe this Agent Jaggers could help. We could run what we know by her without making any formal accusations."

"Jaggers? She's the one who called me about Senator Holt's case. She seemed quite thorough. Asked good, solid questions. Unfortunately, I don't think I was giving her the answers she had in mind."

Lowering her cup, Angela asked, "Why would an FBI agent call you?"

"She said they were doing a routine check on the senator's phone bills and that he'd placed numerous calls to our office. At the time I thought it was probably connected to the grand jury investigation. It never dawned on me they would suspect Senator Holt of kidnapping the Stover baby."

Angela set her cup down so fast, creamy liquid sloshed over the sides. "That means the FBI may already know about Kellars!" she said.

He shook his head and gazed at her skeptically.

"I wouldn't get my hopes up if I were you. I seriously doubt they even suspect he's involved. If they did, they'd be crawling all over the office. I'm sure one of us would've noticed."

"We could call Agent Jaggers anonymously. Just drop a few hints."

Nick helped her clean up the mess, his hands brushing against hers. He firmly said, "Not without more proof. They would barge in with search warrants. If Kellars is smart enough to get away with this, he's smart enough to have covered his ass. They won't find a damned thing. And if this is all a big coincidence, even if we called anonymously, our heads would end up on the chopping block. Remember, we still have to work there."

"So how can we get facts to support this theory of ours? It's not like we can walk into his office and say, 'Excuse me, Mr. Kellars, would you mind explaining to us exactly how you kidnap children and sell them?'"

"True." Nick stretched as he yawned, then added, "But we can observe for a while. Now that we know what we're looking for, maybe we'll see something. I think I'll drop in on our lady friend at Pampered in Paradise. I'm pretty sure it's her voice on the tape, but I'd like to know for certain. Can I borrow your recorder?"

"Sure. Meanwhile, I can snoop around on the computer at work. So far no one has ever questioned me playing with the different programs. Maybe I can sneak another full-system backup out."

He took her hands in his, gently squeezing them. "Be careful, Angela. If only half of what we suspect is true, then we're dealing with some pretty shady characters. Even if the security isn't as tight as Kellars wants everyone to believe, there's no sense risking your job at this point. No one ever said a word to me about that WKE program alarm I set off, but that doesn't mean Kellars wasn't told. And the door to the computer room is rarely locked like it should be. Could be a trap, or a big bluff. Kellars seems to be a master of intimidation."

"And manipulation." She leaned closer to him, her head against the soft sweatshirt he wore. "I don't suppose you remember how you got to that WKE screen?"

Holding her, he quietly said, "I haven't a clue."

Leaning back, Angela looked up at him and said, "We could try it here."

"Are you linked to the main office computer?"

"I have a modem, but I don't think we want to try long-distance snooping. A couple of weeks ago the power went out, so I sort of brought home one of the tape backups."

Cocking his head, Nick said, "Sort of?"

"Okay, you caught me. It's not like I *stole* something. I just took out one tape and put in another." Ignoring the look he was giving her, she added, "At any rate, I brought home a tape that has all the office's programs copied." She sat at her computer, ready to work.

He held up his hands and laughed. "Slow down. Could you translate into English?"

Angela was in her element. Her eyes were sharp as she explained, "First, let's cover a network. Our computers at work are all linked to the one in the computer room. It doles out the files we need. That's why it's called a file server. The machines in our offices have hard drives, too. That way the information can be doubly protected. Understand so far?"

He smiled. "Every word."

She took his hands, pulling him down beside her. "Then let's cover maintaining the integrity of the system. At any time, a hard drive can fail. Because of that possibility there are two types of backups commonly used to ensure no data is lost. One type of backup just copies the information in particular files, not the actual programs themselves. You have to have a program to make any sense out of the information from that kind of a backup. But in a full-system backup, everything on the hard drive is copied or backed up."

"Which you would need . . . ?"

"In case your hard drive crashes and you lose everything, your data as well as your programs. From a full-system backup you can restore your information just the way it was before the system failed. Programs and data. Is all this as clear as mud?"

"You bet, let's give it a shot."

Angela turned, her face level with his. For several seconds they simply looked at each other. Then Nick softly kissed her and muttered, "There are a million things I'd rather be doing with you right now, but I suppose this is more important."

She sighed and answered, "How true . . ."

An hour later, Nick was asleep on her bedroom floor when she finally got to the same password screen labeled WKE. She started to wake him to tell him the good news, but he looked too peaceful to disturb. Like a huge hibernating bear, he was sprawled on his side with his face resting on one curled arm. She eased quietly out of her chair and spread a soft afghan over him.

By three a.m. she had tried every word linked to Will Kellars she could think of, from RICK to POWER. She flagrantly ignored the ominous warning that flashed each time she chose the wrong password. Almost ready to give up, she finally tried typing PARADISE. The colorful screen scrolled into an elaborate accounting program. She wasn't sure how to extract the important information, but she knew enough to highlight COMPANY SELECTION on the main menu and hit the enter key.

Angela was exhausted, so the list of available corporate records merely satisfied her curiosity enough to allow her to relax. She left the screen glowing the list of five choices, laid down on her bed, and let the rest of the world's problems slip by for a little while.

The private landing strip, somewhere in the Florida Keys, was bustling with early morning activity. The friendships Jax had maintained over the years with mainlanders had paid off well. No one seemed to notice the arrival of the small Piper as it bumped gently down the dirt runway, much less care about any of its passengers.

Doubt plagued him as he made his way to a rundown old motel. Either Angela had never delivered the package, or Annissa was going to be more of a problem than he had planned. His entire scheme depended on Angela. At first he had assumed she would be glad to help if he asked. But now he realized that he couldn't give her a choice. She had to cooperate whether she wanted to or not. Too many lives were at stake.

After resting for a few minutes, Jax rolled over and dialed the number. When Maya finally answered, a baby's cries and static made it difficult for him to hear, much less concentrate. "Did you arrange delivery of the ransom note?" he asked.

"Tomorrow morning, at the woman's office."

"Was it clean? Any possible way to trace it?"

"As pure as coconut milk," Maya snapped.

"Why's that one crying again? In all these years I never heard one cry so much. I'm glad I'm gone."

"You're lucky. Between Tica and this *baybee* I feel like screaming along with her," Maya answered, her voice on edge.

"It won't be much longer. Soon screaming *baybees* will be a thing of our past." He hung up, and fell back on the bed. The rest of the night he fitfully slept, his dreams tied to the days ahead.

The next morning, he rushed to catch an early morning flight out of Miami, only to find the flight delayed. Four hours later when they finally boarded, he was so jittery he could hardly sit still. He hated flying. His knuckles were white as turbulence plagued the flight from takeoff through the terrifying landing in Oklahoma City. The 727 commercial jet landed so violently several of the baggage compartments overhead popped open. Jax eased his grip on the armrests only after he forced his eyes open and realized he had managed to survive the ordeal. Of all the miles he'd crossed in the last few days, these had been the toughest. So far, traveling to the States was a miserable experience, one he never cared to endure again.

After claiming his luggage, he checked his watch. Clutching his suitcase, he ran to the nearest exit to hail a cab. "Downtown post, please," he said to the driver with a graceful accent.

Confused, the overweight driver answered, "You mean the VFW or the American Legion?"

"Downtown post," Jax repeated. When the cab driver's reflection merely stared blankly at him from the rearview mirror, Jax tried, "Mail? The downtown mail room?"

"You mean the post office?"

"Ya, mon, the post office. Still open, is it?"

"Let's see, it's almost four. We might make it in time. I'll put the pedal to the metal. Hang on."

Jax had no idea what the man was talking about, but he felt right at home bobbing and weaving through the late-afternoon traffic at high speed, even though to him they were driving on the wrong side of the road. He watched the passing homes and buildings with childlike curiosity. This was his first trip to the States, and it was fascinating. The people here were nothing like native Jamaicans. Stuffy clothes, tense attitudes, pale, grim faces.

He paid the cab driver and carried his luggage up the steps to the post office with him. Inside, he followed the signs to the rented boxes. Withdrawing his key, he found the one his Cuban friend had opened for him and unlocked it. His heart sank as he looked inside. The package he had mailed was nowhere in sight. Only a thin yellow slip of paper rested within the small metal frame. Nothing else.

He stood staring at it in disbelief until a mailman walked past. "If you hurry, you can take that slip to that window over there to get your package, sir."

"*Irie*, mon. Thank you much." Jax smiled, rushing to get in line at the pickup window. The woman behind the glass made him sign the name he was currently using, James Jackson, then handed him a small, heavy box wrapped in brown paper.

Jax checked his watch again. He would have to hurry if he was going to make it to Angela's apartment before she got home from work. He unzipped his suitcase and very carefully placed the package on top of his dirty clothes. The handgun and ammunition were essential to his plan. And so was Angela Anderson.

"Shit!" Nick growled when he saw Angela's clock glowing eight fifteen a.m. His feet were tangled in the afghan as he rolled over and tried to stand, making him flop on his side. After righting himself, he crawled to the side of the bed and touched Angela's cheek. "Wake up! We're late for work!"

Angela moaned, then slowly turned to look at him. Although she was under the covers, she was still wearing the black jogging outfit. Bolting upright when the fog of sleep cleared, she gasped, "Oh, no!"

As Nick ran to the bedroom door he yelled, "I'll

go home and change, then pick you up on my way back."

"Wait!" she called. "Before you go, look at what I found last night." Rolling off the bed, she staggered to the computer.

Nick quickly scanned the screen with her, reading the list of companies aloud:

> Wood, Kruger & Etherton
> W.K. Enterprises
> Kellars & Kellars
> CompuCorp
> Pampered in Paradise
> Paradise Promotions

"What *is* this?" he asked.

"The WKE program you stumbled on to that day. It looks like an accounting program, or a database for records of some kind. I didn't have time to get past this screen."

They exchanged a meaningful glance. "So Will Kellars *is* involved in Pampered in Paradise."

"Looks that way."

He pointed at the screen. "And CompuCorp. Isn't that the company who handles our technical support?"

"Yes. And a lot that isn't very technical. Remember, CompuCrooks? They charge the company a fortune, even if they just plug in a machine or troubleshoot a problem on the phone."

"And Wood, Kruger and Etherton is the accounting firm that handles both Kellars and Kellars and Senator Holt's financial affairs," she said.

"Can we get any more information out of this?" he asked.

"I don't see why not, but it'll take some time. We'd better get to work first." Angela grinned and winked at him as she added, "I'll call in for both of us. I'll tell them we overslept."

Laughing, he replied, "The rumor mill ought to have fun with that one." He kissed her on the cheek, then said, "I'll be back in thirty minutes." As he ran to the door he added, "Remind me to tell you the scheme I dreamt up last night."

Angela stroked where his whiskers had brushed her, her thoughts lingering on his touch. As she rushed into the shower, a strange combination of anticipation, lust, and dread made her shiver. Hot water flowed over her, but the warmth was only skin deep. Twisted, vicious thoughts of babies snatched out of their cribs and sold to strangers chilled her to the bone.

Susan Stover was obviously irritated. "What is taking the grand jury so long? We've put enough evidence in their hands to clearly show Holt should be indicted. Has anyone heard why they're holding back?"

Her young assistant sighed and answered, "They want to hear additional testimony. They've subpoenaed ten more witnesses." He handed her a file, waiting patiently.

"But the documentation is black and white!" she exclaimed.

He replied, "Apparently, so is the documentation from Holt's staff supporting their position."

"I'm sorry to keep doing this to you, but could

you bring the other files to me again?" As he turned away, she added, "I really appreciate the extra work you've done since all this happened with Amber. I don't know what I'd do without you."

At the door, he responded, "It's about time I paid you back for everything you've done for me. If you need anything, you just ask. Promise?"

Susan nodded. As soon as he was gone, she plowed her fingers through her graying hair. While she waited for the files, she decided to work on her In box, which was currently overflowing with unopened mail.

With a deep breath, Susan forced herself to concentrate on her work. Right now it seemed to be the only thing keeping her sane. She pulled the wire box toward her, grabbing the tall stack of mail that had accumulated over the last few days. Slicing effortlessly through each envelope, she worked her way down the pile. A manila envelope stamped PERSONAL & CONFIDENTIAL caught her eye. She opened the envelope, the serrated edges expanding to reveal a peek at the contents.

A glossy picture of Amber's beautiful face smiled up at her. Amber was on her back, her face beneath the *USA Today* banner bearing last weekend's date. Susan Stover stared at the picture, trying to be certain. The baby had short hair, not much more than a light coat of peach fuzz. She looked thinner than Amber, but still healthy. Then she saw it. A small red birthmark just above her kneecap was visible below the tiny white dress she wore in the photo. It *was* Amber!

In her excitement Susan never considered she

might be destroying evidence when she touched the envelope and what little it held. She pulled out the slip of paper and read the message, her heart pounding in her chest.

> No police, no FBI, or no baby. We are watching every move. Further instruction within seventy-two hours. Wire-transfer quadruple advertised reward amount immediately to Swiss bank listed below. Follow all further transfer orders precisely to guarantee safe delivery.

Tucking the photo and the note back inside the envelope, she stuffed them into her purse. A tear trickled down her cheek as she picked up the phone. By the time her daughter answered, she remembered the phone line was being monitored by the FBI. Even though it tore at her heart, she asked an irrelevant question and hung up.

In a flash she grabbed her purse and ran out the door silently screaming, "Amber's still alive!"

Chapter 14

Annissa hurried into the hidden office, anxious to complete her task before Will Kellars arrived. She typed in the access code words and entered the System Administration screen. From there she proceeded to disable the program function that would automatically erase all the files if the system codes were breached.

All night Annissa had worried about the consequences of Will Kellars touching her computer system. Only the accounting files were capable of being restored from a backup system designed by CompuCorp. All the adoption records were kept on her machine alone, and they would be lost if his archaic attitude toward technological advancement was any indication of how proficient he would be at a keyboard. Kellars was very intelligent, but nevertheless computer illiterate and as unrelenting as the tide. She knew he wouldn't give up the idea of helping her, even if she had just run a marathon.

Out of the corner of her eye, Annissa could see the lights in Will Kellars' office flicker, then glow steadily. She pushed a series of buttons, totally exiting the computer system before walking over to buzz him. He came in, carrying a steaming mug of coffee and munching a chocolate long john.

"I stopped for donuts on the way. Can I get you one?" he asked.

Annissa's mouth watered, but she knew she shouldn't risk eating high-cholesterol foods. "I'd better pass," she answered.

"Did Tate take good care of you this morning?" Will asked.

Annissa's accent was always heavy when she was tired, and in a thick voice she said, "He was very prompt, but he drives like a *duppy* from hell. That man should move to my homeland. He'd be very comfortable on the roads of Jamaica."

"I'll talk to him." He moved closer to her, his eyes full of lust.

Stepping backward, she shook her head. "I'm really not feeling very well this morning, Will. Could we just go over the codes?"

"What I have in mind is guaranteed to make you relax." His hand caught the hem of her light silk skirt, then roamed to the top of her stockings. Feeling her thighs tense, he leaned his head on her shoulder and whispered, "Come on, you know you want it."

I want it, all right. I want out of here. I want the goddamned money. But most of all, I never want you to touch me again.

"How are you holding up?" Nick asked as he passed Angela in the hall.

"As well as can be expected, considering the day got started a little off kilter. Nothing quite like being late to get the adrenaline pumping."

Catching the sly look in her eyes, he followed her gaze to the wide-eyed secretary obviously straining to hear their every word. Suddenly, she realized the double meaning "being late" held and blushed profusely.

Nick briefly wondered if her comment was intended to help restore his reputation. He said quietly, "Surely the rumor mill doesn't work that fast."

She raised one brow. "You bet it does. Susan, the head gossip, was practically stalking my office when I got here, waiting to get the rest of the scoop on our night of passion."

"So what'd you tell her?"

"That you were a perfect gentleman." Angela winked, seductively adding, "*Perfect* in every way, *all* night long. I threw in how exhausted I was, just for a kicker. She was practically drooling when she left."

Nick laughed. "I'm glad that's taken care of. We still on for tonight?"

Moving closer, she sexily answered, "I wouldn't miss it for the world."

"Neither would I. I think I have a way to get those facts we were discussing last night."

"Sounds intriguing." Out of the corner of her eye, Angela saw one of the secretaries straining to hear them, so she stood on tiptoe, brushing her lips across Nick's ear as she spoke. "We're being watched, you know."

He leaned down to whisper back, "I know. Kinda kinky, isn't it?" As they passed the secretarial area, he said loud enough for everyone to hear, "Angela, wear that little black outfit again tonight. You look absolutely stunning in it!"

Susan Stover ran past the guards in the entryway of Stover Towers. Her foot tapped impatiently as she waited for an elevator. Once inside, she anxiously wondered how the kidnappers could possibly be watching the entire family. There were too many of them. It would have been easy at first, when they all were huddled around the phone praying every call would bring news, but now they were spread all over town. Besides herself, they would have to watch her father, Sandra, plus a swarm of relatives and a handful of FBI agents posing as servants. It would take a small army of people. Even though she was certain they were bluffing, she had scrutinized her rearview mirror constantly on her way over, never catching a glimpse of anyone or anything suspicious.

When she reached the top floor, she stormed past her father's secretary, in spite of her ardent warning that he did not want to be disturbed for any reason. Susan stopped short just inside his door, shocked to see him slumped behind his desk, tears streaking his face.

"Did they find something?" he asked, his voice little more than a hoarse whisper.

Susan didn't say a word. Instead she opened her purse and with a trembling hand placed the picture with the note in front of him. His reaction stunned her even more. Since Amber's kidnapping he had been so strong. Now, as she watched more tears form in the corners of his eyes and heard his voice catch in his throat, she knew it had all been a facade. For the first time in her life, she realized that he was capable of emotion. Real, gut-wrenching emotion.

"My God . . . She's alive! She really *is* alive!" Wiping his cheeks with the back of his hand, he looked up at his daughter. "I'd given up, Susan. In my heart I thought for certain Amber was dead. I never thought we'd see her again."

Susan cautiously crossed the space between them, then hugged her father long and hard. "We're going to get her back, Dad. I know we will."

"Have you done anything? Called anyone?"

"No. I went home to tell Sandra, then I came straight here. You should've seen her, Dad. She smiled. Really smiled."

He was quickly regaining control, the emotional wall returning as he sternly commanded, "Promise me you won't tell anyone about the ransom. We can handle this. Amber's life is at stake."

"But . . ."

"Susan, I know you're the attorney general, and I know how it will look when the media gets hold of the story. They'll probably never catch the people who did it because we didn't run to the authorities. At this point, I don't give a damn what people think. And I don't really care whether they catch the bastards as long as Amber's back home, where we can protect her. What if these people really are watching? God only knows who we can trust and who we can't. A million dollars is nothing to me. Amber's worth all the money I have."

Susan's voice was hesitant as she asked, "You

really want to do this alone? Not even include the FBI? That Jaggers woman seems trustworthy. We could ask her not to discuss the deal with anyone."

He firmly replied, "What happens if something goes wrong? She'd be out on a limb. Probably lose her job. The FBI has strict rules of conduct. We can't ask her to risk her career for us. Besides, we're a pretty good team. We can handle this."

"So we keep quiet. You realize that means Amber's life is in our hands."

He held up the note, his eyes still moist as he flatly answered, "And theirs."

The third key Jax tried slid easily into the dead bolt on Angela's door. The locking bar opened as he slowly twisted the key in his hand. After glancing over his shoulder to make sure no one was watching, he opened the door. No alarms sounded. No dogs barked. With a sigh he slipped inside and locked the door behind him.

The sun had just fallen past the horizon, and in the twilight Jax could see the layout of Angela's apartment. The gun felt cold, foreign against the small of his back as he walked. The bedroom, full bath, large living area, kitchen, and utility room were just as she had drawn them in the sand the day he had quizzed her about life in the States. As he walked through the apartment, he noticed little things, a basket of shells he'd helped her collect, framed pictures of her family, a poem stuck to the refrigerator with a magnet.

As darkness fell, Jax decided to wait in the oversize closet of her bedroom until he was sure it was safe to come out. Pushing aside her clothes, he cleared enough space for his thin frame between the back wall and a black suit that still carried the scent of Angela's perfume.

He didn't have to wait long. In less than five minutes, he heard voices. One was Angela's. The other was definitely a problem. Reaching behind him, he slowly pulled the gun from the waist of his slacks.

Instinctively, his fingers folded tighter around the grip of the weapon. He was prepared for a fight.

"Curiosity's been killing me," Nick said as they walked into Angela's apartment.

"Me, too. Sometimes I feel like I'm going to explode if I have to spend another day weighing every word I say while I'm in that office." Jerking the pins from her hair, she roughly shook her head back and forth. "It's so . . . so frustrating! I thought of a thousand things we should look for in this computer program tonight, but I was afraid to write my ideas down. Even thinking in that building makes me nervous now. I'm definitely paranoid."

"No, you're just being smart. We've got to be careful while we're there. It's probably not necessary, but until we know what we're dealing with, let's both try to act natural."

"Easier said than done." Angela walked into the bedroom, tossed her jacket on the bed, and sat down at her computer. "Ready?" she asked.

"As ready as I'll ever be," Nick replied.

Angela expertly moved from screen to screen,

scanning each selection. In only a few seconds she selected printouts of the last quarter's transactions for each company. The inkjet printer on the desk next to the computer hummed to life. It whined, then began to spit out page after page of dates, descriptions, and numbers.

Nick grabbed the first document and read it. Intrigued, he said, "This shows intercompany transfers. Looks like WK Enterprises pays the other companies regularly. At least once a month there's a sizable cash disbursement the day after WK receives a cash infusion."

"And I'll bet I know where WK Enterprises gets its income."

"Somewhere in paradise?" he asked sarcastically.

She nodded. "Let's see if we can find anything else. I was hoping we could tap into their financial records, but it looks like we're only in a sub-ledger system of some kind. We need something solid that we can use as evidence."

Frustrated, he began pacing. "So far all this looks pretty legit. The other companies bill WK for services rendered. WK wire-transfers the money to them. Nothing very unusual."

"But what does WK do to make all this money? From what I've seen, we're talking between fifty and a hundred thousand a month. Clear. Not a bad business."

"Could be anything. Oil and gas. Mutual funds. Real estate. I wonder who owns the building we're in. I'll bet you a hundred bucks it's WK Enterprises. How else could Kellars arrange a floor plan like the one I sketched?" Nick asked.

"Good question. And why have a hidden office if what you're doing is legal?"

Nick sat on Angela's bed. With his feet still on the floor, he leaned back. After staring at the ceiling for several seconds he sighed and asked, "So how does selling babies fit in here?"

"I have no idea. Can you find any more on WK in that hunk of rusty microchips?"

She patted the computer gently, "It's okay, Turbo. He didn't mean it."

"You talk to your computer?" he asked cynically.

She turned, shooting him a nasty look. "Don't you?"

"Of course not."

"That explains it," she said bluntly and whirled back around.

"Explains what?"

"Why you're always fumbling on it. You have to respect your machinery. Treat it right and it will work with you, for you. My father taught me that when I was six years old. Of course, we weren't talking about computers, but the logic still applies."

Standing up, he walked over to her. "Knowing you, the discussion was how to get the perfect mix of oil and grease on your bicycle chain, or better yet, a basic dissertation on thermonuclear physics. I have a feeling you weren't an average kid."

As she worked, he softly stroked her hair. Her voice was softer as she said, "I didn't conquer thermonuclear physics until I was ten. Seriously, my dad knew he wasn't going to be around to help Mom and I. His disease progressed slowly. He had five years to set things straight. I guess he wanted to be sure we could take care of ourselves after he was gone. By the time I was eleven, I was pretty mechanically inclined."

Angela relaxed, reveling in his touch, until she saw something intriguing on the computer screen. Bolting upright, she exclaimed, "Oh my God! I think we *really* found something this time!"

Jax listened to everything they said, every muscle in his body ready to strike. Their words were intriguing yet extremely disturbing. They were obviously putting the pieces of the puzzle together. But why would they be suspicious? Maybe Angela had opened the package he sent to Annissa and somehow deciphered the plan. Maybe she couldn't be trusted after all.

Carefully calculating his slightest move, he edged to where he could see through the crack of the door. Angela was seated at the computer, directly across from him. Next to her stood a giant.

Jax knew he wouldn't stand a chance against that man in any sort of fight. Beneath the starched business shirt Jax could see the well-defined muscles in his back and shoulders. The guy probably outweighed him by a hundred pounds and was at least a foot taller, not to mention the vast age difference. He remembered Angela talking about Nick, her lawyer friend from work, but he'd expected someone smaller. Someone gentle. That had been one of the words she used to describe him. Gentle.

Even the weight of the gun in his sweaty palm

didn't make him feel any safer. He edged back through the clothes to lean against the rear corner of the closet. There was no doubt about it. He would wait until Nick left before he made his move.

As the evening slowly passed, Jax's mind tormented him with images of the worst-case scenario. If Angela and Nick were about to notify the authorities, he would have to stop them—and fast.

Angela pointed at the computer screen. "Look at the dates of the money transfers." She entered a few more commands, and the Pampered in Paradise screen popped up. "Now, look at these airport fees. WK's cash always goes up the day after a return flight."

"Pretty big coincidence."

"Let's check Paradise Promotions." She found the right screen and pointed as she explained, "They get paid a flat monthly fee. Must do a hell of a lot of promoting to earn twenty thousand bucks a month from just one company."

"You realize what this means?" Nick asked.

The edge of excitement was replaced by apprehension as she said, "From the sound of your voice, nothing good."

"If this is how they're laundering money back into the States, it's just the tip of the iceberg."

Angela stood up, her eyes searching his. "Meaning?"

"Meaning, you don't throw all your illegal funds back into businesses that have to pay tax. You keep most of it out of the country. Preferably one that has strict banking privacy laws."

"Like Switzerland?"

"And Grand Cayman."

"Which is just a small hop from Jamaica." Angela leaned back in her chair, gazing up at Nick. "Two of the passengers I flew down with on the Pampered jet said they were going to Grand Cayman. . . . My God, you were right! We'd better go to the police, Nick. Our lives may really be in danger."

"But what if we're wrong? What if there's a perfectly logical explanation for all this, which we aren't seeing because we've convinced ourselves Will Kellars is up to no good? And if he is up to no good and we drag in the police too soon, they'll lose valuable evidence. As clever as Kellars is, there's no way he would leave any kind of trail. We aren't in danger unless someone knows we're on to them. As long as we're careful, we'll be all right. If they really are selling babies, someone's got to stop them."

"I think it's up to us. After all, if K and K is involved, I certainly don't want to work there one minute longer."

"Amen." Nick rubbed his forehead as he thought, then added, "Why don't we forget about all this for a while? I don't know about you, but I didn't sleep worth a damn last night."

Standing, she reached to circle her arms around his neck. "The voice of reason, as usual. Besides, I'm starving."

Burying his face in her hair, he groaned and nuzzled his face against her hair. "Starving? As in ravenous? Maybe I can satisfy your hunger."

Relaxing in his arms, she enjoyed the feel of

him, his strength, the lingering scent of his cologne. Suddenly, her stomach growled, long and loud. By the time she pulled away, her face was already tinged with red.

Laughing, he said, "You win. Food first, passion second. Agreed?"

Still embarrassed, she sheepishly replied, "Agreed. I'll zap the Chinese food in the microwave. Let's have a good meal, relax on the sofa, and try to figure out where we go from here. Besides, if I don't get out of this suit pretty soon, I'm going to scream."

"I was thinking the same thing. Why don't you change while I zap the food? Remember, I like that sexy black number you had on yesterday." He winked, pulling the door closed behind him as he left.

Loud enough to be heard through the door Angela shouted, "Sorry, that jogging suit hit the laundry this morning. You'll have to settle for something a little less risqué."

Without turning on the light, Angela opened the door of the closet and flipped each high heel into the darkness at her feet. Stretching, she tiptoed to reach the jeans that lay folded on the top shelf, then rummaged through the hanging clothes. With a tug a sweatshirt fell into her hands. Then she headed for the bathroom. Several minutes later, she was back at the closet, hanging up the suit and blouse she'd worn to work.

Just as Angela started to close the closet door to leave, she suddenly stopped. For some reason she had an odd feeling deep in the pit of her stomach. Like she'd forgotten to do something important. Hesitating, she was sure the feeling would pass, but it lingered. She cocked her head from side to side, staring at the clothes but seeing nothing peculiar. The sound of Nick's voice brought her out of the daze.

"What do you want to drink? A wine cooler?" he shouted.

Closing the closet, she ambled into the living room. "Thanks for offering, but I'll pass. I'm too tired for anything with alcohol. Besides, I think I need to keep my head on straight."

He held up the bottle of sparkling water he was drinking, dangling one in front of her. "Brilliant minds think alike."

"I don't know about you, but I'm not feeling very brilliant right now. How could anyone steal babies?" she asked. "How could they look in the mirror every morning, knowing the pain they've caused?"

"Questions like those will drive you crazy." Setting aside his drink, he added seriously, "Life is much easier if you concentrate on the things you can control."

"Such as?"

His eyes held a promise even stronger than his words as he replied. "Making me fall madly in love with you."

His remark touched her so deeply she caught her breath. Without a thought she leaned her body against his, her hand trailing slowly up his arm to rest on his strong shoulder. She kissed him cautiously, until she felt his intense response in his lips, in his hands as they stroked her hair and neck.

Feeling particularly bold, Angela crawled onto his lap, her legs straddling him. Even though they were both fully dressed, the new position was incredibly erotic. For the first time she felt the deep blue of his eyes penetrating hers. He gently kissed her cheeks, her eyelids, then ran his tongue provocatively along the side of her neck.

With tenderness he worked his hand under the heavy sweatshirt, finding her breasts. She moaned, moving even closer to him, her body rhythmically responding to the stimulating strokes of his hands. Suddenly he pulled back.

"Did you hear that?" he asked.

Angela was lost in a haze of passion, her lips still caressing his face as she mumbled, "Hear what?"

As she pulled away he tensed. "There was a noise. In your bedroom."

Jax froze. When he'd shifted positions to ease the cramp in his leg, he'd somehow jarred loose a shoe box from the top shelf of the closet. The noise had shocked him so much, he'd dropped his gun. Now he was frantically trying to find it in the darkness. Angela's closet floor was lined with shoes. Touching each one, he finally felt the cold metal and gripped it tightly.

"It sounded like it came from in here. I'll check the window," Nick said.

"Maybe something fell off the bathroom counter. I'll look."

"Why don't you let me go first?"

"What are you so worried about, Nick? No one can get in here without coming through the front door. And we both know no one came in just now."

"Right. The same way no one can get in Kellars' office? I'd feel better if you let me check it out first."

Exasperated, Angela replied, "I'm not sure if I'm insulted or flattered. I don't consider myself helpless."

"I didn't say you were." He walked by and pinched her playfully on the butt as she opened the closet door. "I happen to like you just the way you are, so I don't want anything to happen to you."

"I suppose I'll choose to be flattered, then. At least this time. Looks like we found the culprit."

"A shoe box?" Nick muttered.

"I must have unsettled it when I got my jeans down." She stretched to push the box back onto the top shelf.

Nick took it from her hand, easily placing it back where it belonged. "Being six and a half feet tall does have its advantages."

Jax's finger was shaking on the trigger of the gun as a bead of sweat suddenly burned his eye. He had watched as Angela reached down and grabbed the box off the floor, less than ten inches from his own black shoe.

After they closed the closet door, he stayed absolutely still, watching the lights go out as they left the bedroom. Five minutes later, he realized he had never loosened his grip on the gun. Stuffing it carefully in the belt of his trousers, he rubbed his numb hand and sighed.

Patience had never been one of his virtues.

"Maybe we were interrupted for a good reason," Angela said as she pulled the bedroom door closed.

Nick grinned. "Sounds like the voice of reason is getting ready to bite me on the butt."

"Tempting idea—"

The phone rang, and Angela rushed to answer it. After exchanging a few words with the caller, she covered the receiver and whispered to Nick, "It's my Auntie Edna from California. This could take awhile."

Kissing her cheek, he replied, "I'll pick you up in the morning. I love you."

Her eyes were wide as his words sank in. She tugged his shirtsleeve as he turned away. When his eyes met hers again, she replied, "I love you, too."

He squeezed her hand, then let himself out the front door. Twenty minutes later, Angela hung up. As much as she enjoyed talking to her aunt, it brought back a flood of family memories that were so painful they made her chest ache. Pushing the disturbing thoughts aside, she forced herself to concentrate on other things.

Nick loved her! Even though she had fallen for him the moment she saw him, she couldn't believe *he* actually loved *her*. Rushing to the telephone, she dialed his number, as excited as a teenager.

"I knew you'd call," he said as soon as he answered.

"That predictable, am I?" Angela laughed.

"No. That uncertain. Yes, I love you. You didn't dream it. I love you. I love you. I love you."

"That sounds so good. Say it again."

"I love you," he laughed. "Now, get some sleep, gorgeous."

In her sexiest voice she answered, "I will. And by the way, I love you, too. And I intend to show you exactly how much the next time we're together. Good night." Angela softly cradled the phone, feeling wicked but very happy.

As she walked back into her bedroom, the glowing computer instantly reminded her of the night's discovery. Somewhere out there valuable information on Pampered in Paradise and the other companies listed in the accounting program must be available. All she had to do was find it, soon. Corporations could dissolve into thin air faster than a morning dew, and they didn't want to risk the consequences of losing any advantage, especially the element of surprise.

By Friday afternoon the Dunn & Bradstreet reports, credit-bureau information, and ownership records she had electronically ordered on each company should be in. Newspaper accounts of missing children were being researched and assembled by various friends. With any luck the answers would be sent via modem directly to her computer, and the pieces of the puzzle would fall into place.

Nick would be at her side every step of the way. Just the thought of him made her heart race again. It took all her willpower to keep from grabbing the phone just to hear his voice one more time.

Angela turned off the computer, throwing the

room into darkness. Navigating in the moonlight from the windows, she found the nightstand, slipped off her watch, and placed it in a crystal bowl with her favorite diamond earrings. She was just about to peel off her sweatshirt when she heard the bedroom door close. Confusion was quickly replaced by terror when she heard a voice echo through her bedroom.

"So we are finally alone again, pretty lady."

Chapter 15

Angela started to whirl around, but froze when she caught the intruder's reflection in the mirror over the dresser. With the door closed, the bedroom was thrown into heavy darkness, making it impossible to see the man clearly. Only his silhouette was defined. Although he didn't appear to hold a knife or gun, he seemed large enough to overpower her.

Her mind raced as she scanned the room, searching for anything she could use as a weapon. A clock radio and a lamp were the only nearby choices, neither of which seemed like a very lethal weapon. Without turning any farther she slowly raised her hands above her head and said, "Take whatever you want. I haven't seen you, so you don't have to worry about me identifying you. What little jewelry I have is on my dresser. I have some money and credit cards in my purse."

"But it's only you I want, Angela," he said, his voice like a teasing Caribbean breeze.

Her mind reeled with images of brutal rape. His voice was familiar, but from a time that seemed so far away she couldn't grasp it in her panicked state.

"Your cooperation is what I need," he continued, his voice even softer, growing more relaxed until it almost held an amused quality.

She stood silently waiting, unwilling to agree to cooperate, yet still too frightened to confront him.

"I'm hurt. After all the good times we shared, don't you recognize my voice?" He stepped back and flipped on the light switch. "It's Jax. From Jamaica, mon. I'll not hurt you. It's help I need, pretty lady. *Your* help."

Relief flooded Angela's senses, but enough doubt still remained to make her cautious. Although she could see his reflection in the mirror, she slowly turned to study his face. A seed of anger began taking root. "What are you doing here? And why did you have to scare the hell out of me?"

He sighed, then said, "Long story, pretty lady. Put your hands down, for goodness' sake. While I explain my curious actions, you sit. Be comfortable. Rest."

Angela did as she was told, edging over to crouch precariously on the end of her bed. Jax rolled the chair by the computer forward, straddling it as he faced her.

He took a deep breath, his gaze so intent Angela felt as though he was somehow staring through her. During the week she'd spent with him in Jamaica, this side of him had never emerged. Although his accent was there, it was less pronounced. His gestures were sharper, more controlled. There was a threat in his eyes, a look of sober power as he spoke.

"I know this is an unconventional way to get your cooperation, but we couldn't risk an overt connection. Your actions are being watched. Possibly by several different organizations." Jax's words were chosen carefully. He spoke slowly, making an effort to speak in the sharper, more American tones he had been practicing.

"Like who?"

"We'll get to that. I'm with Interpol. I've been under cover in the Caribbean for over six years, investigating an international kidnapping ring." He relished the stunned look on her face as he continued. "I made contact with you in Jamaica specifically because of your connection to Kellars and Kellars. We believe your firm is heavily involved in this case."

Holding up his hands, he said, "This is a shock, I know. We do not believe you are directly involved in any way, and we have no intention of arresting any of the current legal staff." She seemed to relax slightly. "We're after Kellars himself. What we need is your cooperation. We're very close to determining the entire network of criminals involved, and we need your help to finally stop them after all these years." Jax edged closer to her, his eyes narrow as he convincingly pleaded, "In order to bring this organization down, we'll have to know all the players in the game. We want to arrest every single one simultaneously. From the top of the pyramid to the bottom. Do you understand?"

"Yes," she mumbled, still in shock.

Standing up, he asked, "Will you help?"

"Of course."

Scanning the room, he pointedly asked, "What happened to the package I asked you to deliver to Annissa Jamison? She's one of our undercover agents, and we haven't had a response. We're afraid she may be in danger."

"I—I'm sorry. We tried to deliver it, but she wasn't home. It's in the living room if you want it."

"We?"

"Nick was with me. Nick Hunter." Angela stood and began pacing. "You see, things haven't exactly been normal since I got back. My mother passed away while I was in Jamaica. First there was the funeral, and then we started suspecting..."

The familiar Jax, the one with the patient eyes and tender voice, spoke, "So sorry, pretty lady. I know how close you were to her. I will miss my own mother terribly when she passes." He stood and went to Angela's side, pulling her into an embrace. She was tense, too tense.

When he finally let her go, he was serious once again. "What I'm asking you to do is dangerous. You do understand that, don't you? These are criminals, and they can be violent if provoked."

She nodded, then stopped and asked, "What about Nick? We've been trying to work this out together."

"The more people involved, the more risk we each take." In his practiced persuasive tone he asked, "Can you convince him to stop probing for a while?"

She shook her head. "I don't see how. Even though we agreed to solve this together, I'm sure he would keep looking for answers even if I asked him to stop. He'd be suspicious of such a sudden change."

"Can we trust him?"

"Yes. I'd trust him with my life."

With a hint of menace in his eyes, Jax replied, "You may have to, pretty lady."

It was six a.m. when the phone beside Nick's head startled him out of a deep sleep. Reaching over, he grabbed it. "What?"

"Nick, it's Angela. Are you awake yet?"

"Yeah. I'm getting there. Something wrong?"

"No. I need you to come over as soon as you can."

Nick sat up, rubbing one eye as he asked, "Why?"

"Please, it's unbelievably complicated, just come. I'll explain everything when you get here."

"Twenty minutes soon enough?"

"That would be great, Nick. Thanks."

He hung up and ran to the shower. Working as fast as he could, he showered, shaved, and dressed. He wondered why Angela was being so mysterious. Exactly twenty minutes from Angela's call, he was on her doorstep.

When she opened the door, she was already dressed for work, beautiful as usual. Her hair was braided elegantly, and the dark gray silk suit she wore perfectly matched her serious expression. She directed him to the kitchen table, where there were three coffee cups waiting.

"Are we expecting company?" he asked.

Before she could answer, Jax came out of the bedroom, still fastening his shirt buttons as he walked toward them. He was freshly showered, his khaki slacks and shirt crisply ironed. He extended his hand to Nick and said, "You must be Nick Hunter. I'm Agent Jackson. James Jackson. Interpol. Call me Jax."

Nick shot Angela an inquisitive, suspicious look before reluctantly shaking Jax's hand. "What's this all about?" he asked.

Angela answered, "He was working undercover in Jamaica. Remember? I told you about him escorting me around the island. He targeted me because of my connection to Kellars and Kellars."

Nick didn't like the sound of any of this. Something about Jax struck him wrong, filling him with distrust. After a few seconds Nick asked, "Exactly what did he target you *to do*, Angela?"

She exuberantly answered, "Help break up an international kidnapping ring! All our suspicions were right. Will Kellars *is* involved in illegal adoptions."

Jax held up his hands as he said, "I know our investigative methods may seem peculiar to you, Mr. Hunter, but you have to understand the broad scope of the criminal network involved. We even have reason to believe they have at least one contact at the FBI. That is why we are seeking your assistance instead of utilizing the normal agencies. We are so close now, we do not want to jeopardize our case."

Glaring at him, Nick asked, "I don't suppose you have any identification?"

Jax held back his excitement as they played into his hand. "I've been in deep cover for over six years. There is no place I could keep a badge that wouldn't risk detection by their people. Even my paychecks are deposited in an account here in the

States. In Jamaica I became Jax, the taxi driver. That is all the people there know me as. Nothing else. I contact Interpol through other agents, and only in emergency situations. My last contact was three weeks ago, when I was told to establish a way to communicate with my co-agent, the woman who runs Pampered in Paradise. The note I sent with Angela was our last hope."

Reading his gullible audience, Jax continued, "You must understand, we are dealing with people whose intelligence is only superseded by their tendency to be suspicious of everything and everyone. Otherwise they would not have successfully operated for so long. You will just have to trust me. Literally, hundreds of children are depending on us, not to mention their parents."

"I assume you have a plan?" Nick asked.

Inwardly Jax was celebrating. Containing himself, he stated, "The plan will depend on the two of you. We have two goals. The first is to obtain either the originals or copies of the documentation the ring maintains so we can not only find the children, but return them to their natural parents. The second is to get our agent out alive, if possible."

"And who would that be?" Nick asked.

"Annissa Jamison. You probably know her. She's a beautiful Jamaican woman. She's been posing as the manager of Pampered in Paradise for several years. We have reason to believe her life is in danger as we speak."

"What kind of help do you need from us?" Nick asked, watching Jax's every move.

"Mainly communication. Possibly some assistance in helping Annissa escape. They watch her very closely. We'll have to coordinate a diversion in order for her to slip past their people. That is, if she is still alive."

Angela excitedly said, "She is! I saw her last night at the office."

"Good. That will make our job easier. Time is of the essence. This is Friday. We expect to have all the pieces in place by Tuesday of next week."

"Only four days?" Nick asked, concerned.

"Timing is critical. We understand they are preparing another delivery, so to speak."

Angela asked, "What do we do today?"

Jax shrugged. "Go to work. Act normal."

She nodded and said, "We had planned to try and get Kellars to contact Nick about his secret organization today."

Jax frowned, wondering if they already knew too much for his plan to work. "And how were you going to do that?"

Nick answered, "We've heard our offices are bugged. We thought we could have a discussion about some friends of mine who are desperate for a child. Kellars already knows I'm very interested in their case. We thought we could make it sound like I'm desperate enough to handle the problem in a less than legal way. You know, imply that I am going to look for someone who might know a way around the existing laws."

Jax sat silently for a few seconds before answering. "We may need to do that later, if our initial plan doesn't work for some reason. Right now I want you to go to work and don't even hint that you know anything about this situation. Our first priority will be to notify Annissa that her assignment is almost over. But we must do it very carefully. As I said, she is watched constantly. We need to find a way to deliver the package I gave you in Jamaica without raising any suspicion."

"The UPS man practically lives in that office. I see him going in and out all the time. He could deliver it," Nick said.

"UPS?" Jax asked.

"United Parcel Service. They deliver packages."

"That would take too long. It could fall into the wrong hands. Personal transfer is best."

"I pass her in the ladies' room every once in a while. I could slip it to her there."

Nick said, "I have a better idea. I'll go talk to her about booking a trip for my parents again. I can give it to her while she's squirming."

Jax threw his head and laughed, his broad white smile contrasting with his dark brown skin. "You must be very talented. Not many people can make a woman like Annissa squirm."

After pulling away from Angela's apartment complex, Nick drove a few miles, then parked on the outer edge of a lot in front of a grocery store. "Thank God we're finally alone. We need to talk."

Turning toward him, Angela snapped, "I knew it! You're having second thoughts, aren't you?"

Nick hesitated, surprised by her sharp reply. "No. I'm still acting on my first impression."

"Which was?"

"That this whole thing doesn't sit right. Have you considered what Jax is asking us to risk? Our jobs, possibly our lives—"

"But innocent children are depending on us! Don't you see? This is our chance to make a difference! To do what's right!" Reacting to his unwavering gaze, she indignantly corrected herself by saying, "Make that *my* chance. You really don't have to get involved." Her voice cracked as she added, "In fact, it would probably be better if you didn't."

Softening, Nick tried to touch her cheek, but she jerked away. "Come on, don't do this, Angela. I never said I didn't want to be involved. I just think we should go into this with our eyes open. You know I've always defended the underdog, tried to help anyone who needs it. Even if I don't believe in Jax, I still believe in you."

Annissa's breath caught, and her heart pounded so furiously she was sure she would fall dead in the next few seconds. He was in her office, just a few feet away. The man from Will's office! His image was burned into her memory, along with the searing pain it had caused that night. His presence could only mean trouble.

She walked toward him, desperately trying to display an aura of confidence, even though she was acutely aware that her hands were shaking violently. "Good afternoon. May I help you?"

"I doubt if you remember, but I was here before to check on a trip for my parents. I've decided to actively pursue the idea."

"I'm sorry, Mr. . . ."

"Hunter. Nick Hunter."

"Mr. Hunter, I must not have explained clearly

enough what we specialize in at Pampered in Paradise."

His eyes held hers as he smiled and said, "I believe you were quite clear. Money is no longer an object. You see, I've recently inherited a rather large amount from a distant cousin in Jamaica."

"Really?" Annissa found it hard to believe that this mammoth young lawyer would have unlimited funds, and the reference to her homeland made her even more wary.

He held up his briefcase. "Do you have somewhere I could spread out my plans and show you what kind of trip I'm looking for?"

She stepped gracefully aside, her voice serious as she said, "I wouldn't want you to waste your time, Mr. Hunter."

"Trust me." He winked and flashed his killer smile. "No one's time will be wasted."

Annissa was truly confused now. This tall, handsome creature was obviously very happy about his decision to blow a fortune on his parents' vacation. Yet since he had broken into Will Kellars' office, he was definitely a threat. The problem was, she had no idea what kind of threat he posed.

After a long hesitation, she said, "We do occasionally charter trips for customers who aren't referred directly. Follow me." She led him into the conference room, then softly touched a hidden switch on the wall. The lights gradually came up, as if the sun were rising over the ocean. Music of gentle waves and tropical birds seemed to flow out of the fabric walls.

"Impressive." Nick said as he glanced around.

"Very impressive." Snapping open his briefcase, he pulled out a file folder and pointed at its corner as he spoke. "Are you familiar with my banker? You may have dealt with him before." Annissa leaned over, trying to make out the name. Written very lightly on the top corner were the words "Jax sent me. Be careful."

Annissa shifted uneasily. "Why, no, Mr. Hunter, I'm not familiar with him. We usually don't deal with bankers. Loans aren't typically needed by our clientele."

"He's quite a character. Travels extensively. I was lucky to catch him in town. He's willing to cover me on this, since my inheritance will be tied up for a few months. I've put together some information, with his help, of course." He pulled the manila envelope out of the file. "I'd be happy to leave this with you to review."

A mixture of panic and relief gripped her. "That would be fine."

"When can I get a decision—I mean, when can you have some options available for me to look over?" He slid the empty folder back in his briefcase.

"I—I should know something by early this evening. Why don't you stop by around five or six tonight?"

"I'll be here."

Annissa watched him as he crossed the foyer and went back into the offices of Kellars & Kellars. She locked the front door, leaning against it before making her way into her own office. For ten minutes she worked on the routine of daily operations, stacking papers on top of the envelope Nick had given to her.

After rechecking the reception area, she pushed the remote device that opened the hidden panel. She left it open long enough to check Will's office. Once she knew it was empty, she grabbed the pile of papers from her desk and closed the panel. Safely inside the secret room, she carefully opened the package. As she scanned the message, she realized it was coded in the same childish way they had devised on the beach so many years ago.

Twenty years after Jax got her into this mess, he was finally going to get her out. Or die trying.

Jax's fingers tapped rhythmically on Angela's kitchen counter as he anxiously asked, "How was she? What exactly did she say?"

Nick watched every move Jax made, still uncertain of his story. "She looked tired but okay. She said she understood the situation I was in, but that Pampered in Paradise would not be the company to help me book the trip for my parents. She handed me this piece of paper, and said that maybe this company would be better suited to my travel needs."

Jax snatched the paper from Nick's hand. Aloud he read, "Blissful Respites, Inc.—Daily Gala Excursions. Try them early tomorrow, their doors are always open."

Angela said, "That's a legitimate company. I've seen their advertisements. Low-budget specialists." She laughed. "Right up your alley, Nick."

With a smirk Nick said, "Thanks, Angela. Tomorrow I'll let *you* spring for dinner."

Angela mimicked Jax's accent. "No problem, mon."

"Maybe Annissa missed your point, Jax," Nick said.

Jax's mind was reeling. He stared at the message, certain Annissa would communicate more than just the name of some cheap travel agency. Finally, he recognized it. The first letters of each word in the agency's name spelled BRIDGE. Relief overwhelmed him when he realized Annissa was willing to work with him. "No. The code word was BRIDGE." He pointed to each capital letter. "We can pick something up tomorrow morning. She'll leave the door unlocked tonight when she goes home."

Nick had to admit he was impressed. Deciphering the message added a degree of credibility to Jax's story. "How will we know what we're looking for?" he asked, his voice a little less sharp.

Jax shrugged as he replied, "I don't know."

"Are you sure, Jax? I don't mean to offend you, but you seem to be inferring a lot from that short note. How can you be certain she means the pickup will be at Pampered and not at that other travel agency?" Angela asked.

"Pampered was the point of initial contact. Unless she specifies a different location, the exchanges will take place there," he confidently answered.

"Espionage 101?" Nick laughed.

Jax merely looked puzzled, so Angela interpreted, "He means, are Interpol agents trained to know to return to the initial contact point?"

Jax smiled and said, "No, mon. The shrewd ones plan for every possibility long before anything happens." He winked and added, "And there are none more shrewd than Annissa."

Chapter 16

Angela's computer received ten e-mail messages throughout the day Friday, each confirming their initial suspicions. Jax and Nick stood behind her while she sat at the computer, scrolling through them. "Looks like we wasted a lot of favors," she said.

Nick leaned close to Angela, wrapping one arm around her. "Not necessarily. The last child on the list of kidnappings was Amber Stover. Is she one of the children involved, Jax?"

"I have no way of knowing." Jax shrugged, resuming his incessant pacing. "The people I've been covering in Jamaica don't ever use the children's real names. The babies appear mysteriously, stay for several weeks, then disappear again." He stopped, his confidence growing as he talked his way to firmer ground. "Their physical appearances are changed as much as possible in a small infant. The few I have positively identified have been from photographs, not names. Usually their hair has been changed, and sometimes makeup is used to alter their skin color. We're almost certain their new parents, the ones who are adopting them, come to the island and take them directly home."

Angela turned to ask, "But how do they get out of the country? And how do they get past Customs and Immigration in the United States?"

"It's quite easy, really. Charter yachts, private planes. Cubans are especially willing to participate in the exchange. Enough money can bend laws when necessary. Officials simply look the other way."

Shaking her head, she asked, "What kind of people would *buy* a baby?"

Jax shrugged. "You'd be surprised. The instinct to bear children runs strong, especially once a couple is told they are unable to conceive. It becomes an obsession, blinding people to things others find quite obvious. These people believe they'll give these babies more of everything in life than their real parents ever could."

Angela's face drained, her color and spirit gone. "The birth parents will be overjoyed, but I can't help but feel for those poor children who have been raised by the people who bought them. They'll be taken away from the only families they've ever known. Their real parents are total strangers to them after all these years."

"All the more reason we have to stop these people before they destroy any more lives," Jax said, counting on their sympathy. "I'll need you to give me all the documentation you've accumulated. I'll ship it directly to our headquarters. Within forty-eight hours they can provide a detailed analysis of where we stand."

"What kind of information are you talking about?" Nick asked.

"Angela mentioned a tape of Will Kellars and

Annissa. Plus, the backup computer tape with the accounting records. Even copies of today's e-mail. Anything incriminating. We want this case locked up tight. Besides, if anyone gets suspicious, it would be safer for all the evidence to be out of Angela's possession. If they were to search this apartment and find any documentation, Angela would be deemed expendable."

Angela seemed more perplexed than convinced she was in danger as she asked, "They'd kill me?"

"So far they've operated without harming people whenever possible. But when it comes to kill or be thrown in jail for the rest of their lives, they'll choose to kill. I guarantee it."

Nick was agitated. "We should leave Angela out of this. I can help you alone."

Angela jumped to her feet, shouting, "Like hell you will! I'm the one who started all this, and I plan to finish it."

Nick rested his hands on her shoulders. "Calm down. I just don't want you to get hurt."

"And I don't want *you* to get hurt! So what's the difference between you and me?" Angela demanded.

Nick slid his hands down and lifted her to eye level. "I'd guess I outweigh you by a good hundred and twenty pounds. Plus some other obvious characteristics that we won't go into right now."

"Put me down!" Even though he did, Angela was still incited. She stormed across the bedroom. "I may be small, but that can be used to my advantage. I can hide better, blend into crowds easier, and I don't sound like a herd of buffaloes when I walk down the hall!"

Jax agreed with a muffled snicker. "She's right. You do tend to be a bit conspicuous, Nick. Especially in a crowd where you tower over everyone. Angela will probably need to be the one to help Annissa escape, but it depends on how and where we can pull it off." He flashed his best Jamaican grin and added, "Don't get me wrong, Nick. The agency appreciates your cooperation. You've already proven to be a valuable asset."

"In spite of my gangly appearance, I have an idea that might be useful. Instead of hinting and hoping they respond, I could talk to Kellars directly about my friend's case on cryopreservation. Tell him some bullshit about how badly it is going, and that he was right about me not representing them. I could tell him my friends have decided to drop their case against the fertility center and try for a private adoption. Ask if he knows anyone who can help them. Judging from the tape Angela made, they had one couple recently back out. Maybe they're searching for someone else to take that baby."

Angela's anger quickly turned into enthusiasm. "I like it. I'll bet they'd take the bait. It's better than having them eavesdrop on a conversation. You could hit him up directly. Then we could really nail them."

Jax held his hands up. "Slow down. You Americans always rush into things. Could Kellars check on the case and discover it really hasn't been dropped?"

Nick answered, "I suppose so."

"Are your friends wealthy? Can they afford to buy a baby? The going rate is three to five."

Angela asked meekly, "Thousand?"

"No, pretty lady. Three to five *hundred* thousand American dollars."

"My friends have spent every penny they have on trying to have a baby. That's definitely out of their ballpark."

Jax warily stated, "I'm certain they run extensive background checks on potential purchasers, including credit references. Your friends would be out of the running before the game even started."

Nick shrugged. "It was just an idea."

Jax shook his head. "I don't mean to discourage you. Quite frankly, I can use all the help I can get on this case, and your ideas are very good. But we have to be very, very careful."

Nick sighed and glanced at Angela. Their eyes held as he said, "Just tell us what you want us to do."

"Right now we have to wait for Annissa. She knows every angle of their business. We must follow her lead. Since timing is critical, is there any way either one of you can get her message to me in the morning?"

Nick answered, "I have an early meeting scheduled with Senator Holt. I could get it to you when I leave for his office."

"If I hide in the backseat of your car, would anyone be suspicious?"

"No. But it could be for several hours, and the backseat of my car isn't exactly comfortable."

"Trust me, mon." He leaned against the wall as if settling in for a long stay. "If there's one thing you learn living in Jamaica, it's how to wait."

With a sideways glare Nick muttered, "Like in Angela's closet?"

Jax grinned. "I believe they say, 'Desperate times call for desperate measures.'"

Annissa knew Tate was waiting in the reception room or nearby, working the same stinking crossword puzzle he had been staring at all day. As she had done since his arrival, she feigned an island blend of mellow composure and nonchalance whenever he was present, hoping to lull him into a false sense of security. In an uncharacteristically compliant voice she said, "My, it's later than I thought. Mr. Tate, why don't you bring the car to the front of the building? I'll lock up and meet you downstairs."

"Sorry, Ms. Jamison, Mr. Kellars wants me to stay pretty close to you all the time you're away from home. He's very concerned about your health."

Maybe the health of his frigging pocketbook, she thought. The envelope for Jax was in the center of her desk. It was addressed to Blissful Respites, Inc., stamped and ready to be mailed. She wanted to be alone, so she could move it to the reception area, where anyone behind the one-way mirror couldn't observe whoever picked it up. Hopefully, the tall, handsome man would be able to find it.

Annissa walked back into her office and retrieved her purse, casually laying the envelope on the reception desk as she passed. While she was flipping off the lights, she lowered her voice so he could barely hear her saying, "Could you ring for an elevator?"

"Sure thing," the man replied. He walked over to the desk and grabbed the envelope. "I'll put this in the mail drop."

"No!" Annissa snapped, her voice brimming with tension. Immediately forcing herself to regain her composure, she smiled and added, "It's too soon. There's a check inside that is post-dated. If they receive it too early, my client will be furious."

He dropped the envelope like it had burst into flames. "Excuse me. I didn't realize you were so efficient. I'll get the elevator."

"I'll be right out." She picked up the envelope, placing it exactly in the center of the reception desk as she hurried past. Once through the door, she inserted her key in the lock, twisting quickly counterclockwise to insure the door remained unlocked.

Holding the door open to the elevator, Tate asked, "Need help?"

With a genuine smile she answered, "No. Everything is fine. Just fine."

It was five-thirty a.m. when Nick rang Angela's doorbell. She answered immediately, her briefcase and pocketbook in hand. She wore a bright yellow dress highlighted with a wooden necklace and matching earrings in striking shades of navy, green, and yellow. Nick openly stared for several seconds, then wrapped her in a warm embrace. After a gentle kiss he pulled away, shaking his head.

"Something wrong?" Angela asked.

"Absolutely not. You just . . . Well, you strike

me as more stunning every time I lay eyes on you."

Stunning! Wow! Holding her head a little higher, she replied, "Thank you!" This time their kiss was anything but gentle.

When he finally pulled away, he exhaled loudly. "Forget the plan. Let's just stay here."

"No can do." She paused, then asked, "Did you sleep well last night?"

He shook his head. "I've been thinking about all this."

"Me, too," she said.

Nick sighed, worry furrowing his brows. "There's one thing that really bothers me."

"Only *one* thing?"

"Well, one more than the rest."

"And what would that be?" she asked as he unlocked and opened her car door for her. They were standing in the orange glow of the street lamp outside her apartment.

He flatly answered, "Jax."

"What about Jax?"

"I don't trust him," Nick said. "I haven't from the day I met him."

"Really?" She hesitated, realizing her first impression of Jax had been the same. "And I thought I was the only one who had bursts of intuition."

"I can't put my finger on it, but there's something not right about him. For one thing, the fact that he doesn't have any identification doesn't sit right."

She shrugged nonchalantly. "What if he had one? Supposedly any crook can come up with an official-looking badge. Would you know what authentic Interpol identification looked like?"

"Not even if it bit me on the nose."

Angela laughed and said, "I rest my case."

"Fine," he muttered, still not convinced. Holding up his hands, he said, "Let's *assume* he's legit. Where are the other Interpol agents? Why isn't this place crawling with them?"

"Maybe it is and we just don't know it. If they were any good, we wouldn't be able to just walk through a crowd and pick them out, now would we?"

"Do you have an answer for everything?"

She grinned sheepishly. "Well, no. It's just I've spent a lot more time around him than you have. I don't think an evil person could mask his true identity as well as Jax does. Even though I wasn't sure about him when I first met him, he earned my trust by always being there when I needed him."

Nick pinned her with a fatherly stare. "Because he needed your help. Why not kiss up? Especially when it's to his advantage."

"Come on, Nick. How could he have known I would go along with all this when he first approached me in Jamaica?"

"He couldn't, but if he really needed someone inside K and K, he could easily have had the agency run a background check on you. Before he even picked you up at the airport, he may have known everything from who you went to the prom with to what kind of dental floss you use. If he did, then he would've known you weren't the type to turn down a friend. So, presto, he becomes your friend."

Her nose crinkled. "You make it sound so deceitful."

"It *is* deceitful. This whole affair is downright sinister, if you think about it."

"Do you think we should quit helping him?"

Nick looked up, as if the right answer might suddenly fall from heaven and smack him in the eyes. After a few seconds he took her hands in his. "I don't know, Angela. If he's right about there being an informant at the FBI, then we could really blow their whole case if we report it now."

She squeezed his palms as she hesitantly asked, "So we stick with the plan?"

Staring at her delicate hands made him even more concerned for her safety, yet he knew they were trapped. "For now at least. I'll follow you to work and sneak inside Pampered while you stand guard." He pulled her against him and hugged her. "Just be careful, will you?"

"You're the one who'll be sneaking around a dark office. All I have to do is handle the hall. Not exactly a tough assignment."

"Tough enough." Nick watched her settle into her car, then gently closed her door for her. On the way to the motel, he stayed several car lengths behind, constantly watching his rearview mirror. It was too early for any substantial amount of traffic, and no one appeared to be following them. Jax was waiting outside when they pulled up. He waved to Angela and hopped into the backseat of Nick's car. In seconds they were back on the road.

"Good morning, Jax." *If that is really your name.*

"Irie. Are you ready for the day ahead, Nick?"

"As ready as I'll ever be. Let's just hope Annissa left whatever it is where I can find it."

Jax was showered and shaved, yet still seemed tired as he said, "She's a good agent. I'm sure you'll recognize it."

"There's a gray blanket on the floorboard." He nodded his head and Jax peered over the seat. "It's the same color as the car seat, so if you stay under it, no one will notice you're back there. We're going to park in a corner, so Angela's car will be on one side, and there'll be trees on the other. Most likely, no one will even come near. Are you sure you can hold out until lunchtime?"

"Absolutely. I've been up most of the night. A little nap will be no problem. Once you pass me the information, I'll catch a cab and meet you back at Angela's tonight."

Both cars pulled into spaces at the far corner of the parking lot. Nick and Angela casually walked into the building, greeting the security guard.

"You folks are up pretty early today." The guard was well over sixty and about as dangerous as a marshmallow, but he still had a gun strapped to his side.

Nick answered, "Important case going to trial today."

Angela said, "I'm still making up for the time it took to get this tan."

The guard laughed and waved them on. Once inside the elevator, Angela said, "Good luck." Nick winked and gave her a confident thumbs-up. When the doors slid open, he scanned the area, then quickly disappeared inside the dark

Pampered in Paradise reception area. He hurried past the receptionist's desk, checking the conference room first, since he considered it to be the point of his "initial contact" with Annissa. For several minutes he searched, glancing occasionally out the window to make sure Angela was still pacing back and forth in the space between the offices of Kellars & Kellars and Pampered in Paradise.

When he was about to give up hope, he noticed a piece of mail lying on the reception desk. The address made him certain it was the message he was looking for. Just as he was walking toward the door, he heard the ding of an approaching elevator, then the hearty ring of Angela's fake coughing. He instantly pressed himself against the back of the heavy mahogany door and waited.

Outside he could hear Angela talking to the old security guard.

"Need help, miss?"

"I have this awful cold. I coughed so hard, I dropped the computer chip I was cleaning."

Nick peeked through the glass. Angela was on her hands and knees running her hands through the carpet. The security guard joined her. When she glanced toward the window he signaled her, so she would know he was aware of the danger.

"Oh, look! I found it." She held out her palm, which had a tiny speck of black on it. "Thank goodness I found it. My boss will kill me if he finds out I took it home with me last night." She hopped up, extending a hand to the older gentleman. "Thanks for your help. What are you doing up here anyway?" She headed toward the doors to Kellars & Kellars, searching in her purse for her keys.

"Just making my morning rounds. I always check to make sure everything is secure before my shift ends."

"This floor couldn't be any more secure. You obviously do a good job . . ." Angela unlocked the double doors to the law office and flipped on the lights.

"Harry."

". . . Harry. Nice to meet you. My name is Angela. Angela Anderson."

"Pretty name. I guess I'll be going now. You keep those chips *in* your machine from now on, you hear?"

"Yes, sir."

As soon as he was gone, Nick rushed to her side and said, "I didn't know you had a microchip on you."

Grinning from ear to ear, she said, "I don't." She held out her hand and showed him the dark spot. "As far as I know, this is a piece of good old one hundred percent made-in-the-USA *dirt*."

"Where you headed in such a hurry, Hunter?"

Even though Will Kellars was the last person Nick wanted to see, he calmly said, "I'm leaving for a meeting with Senator Holt, Mr. Kellars. We're discussing the latest round of grand jury subpoenas."

"There are a few things I need to mull over with Bob, and Alice has been nagging me about taking her to lunch for ages. Mind if I tag along?"

"Not at all." Nick felt sweat break out across

his forehead. Jax was probably sound asleep in the backseat of his car. *Think! What would Jax want him to do?*

The elevator door closed, isolating them from the rest of the world. Nick cleared his throat, which had suddenly gone dry, and said, "I hear you have a new toy."

Kellars smiled, obviously proud. "You mean the Ferrari?"

"I'd say that's the *ultimate* toy. Maybe someday I'll be so lucky." The elevator came to the ground floor, and they headed toward the parking lot.

Kellars slapped him on the back. "Keep working like you do, and it won't take long. You've really been generating billable hours. I'm impressed."

"Thank you, sir. Are you impressed enough to do me a favor?"

"I still won't let you take on that cryo-whatever case in Arkansas. How's that going, anyway?"

Nick resisted the urge to make a plea for an illegal adoption on behalf of his friends. "You were right. They're bogged down in paperwork. Could be years before they even get to trial."

"Maybe your friends should consider adoption."

Nick's heart pounded in his ears. Maybe Kellars would do the dirty work for him. "They have. They're on every waiting list, but they say it could take years. They're considering every alternative, though."

"Such a pity. Sorry, I changed the subject on you. What favor did you have in mind?"

His heart sank, but he kept his voice steady as

he said, "I've never ridden in a Ferrari. Could we take your car to the meeting?"

"I'll do even better." He reached in his pocket and pulled out the keys, tossing them toward Nick. "You can drive it."

"Really?" Nick tried to sound enthused, even though he was too relieved to give a damn about driving anything. "I need to get something out of my car. I'll be right there. It is that beautiful red one in the far north corner, isn't it?"

"Damn right."

Nick ran full stride to his car, discreetly pulling the envelope out of his briefcase as he went. His leather dress shoes were slick against the concrete, making him slide when he finally tried to stop near the driver's door. Quickly unlocking it, he flung the envelope into the backseat, ducked his head inside, and muttered breathlessly, "No time for explanation. Stay down."

By the time he reached the driver's seat of the ruby Ferrari, he was breathing much easier, in more ways than one.

Jax didn't move. In fact, had the manila envelope not hit him in the eye, he probably could have convinced himself the voice he heard was part of a dream. Every muscle in his body ached from the awkward position his body was in as his senses came to life. When he couldn't stand it any longer, he squeezed the handle by his head and eased himself into daylight.

As nonchalantly as possible, he walked away from the building. Downtown Oklahoma City bustled with the lunchtime crowd. When he was a safe distance away, he found a bench near a fountain and sat down. Once he was certain no one was following him, he opened the envelope.

Inside were only two things. A computer diskette and a folded copy of the supermarket tabloid *The Probe*, with Amber Stover's picture blazoned across the cover.

Chapter 17

"I want to know who did this! Now!" Samuel Stover's fist landed on his desk, making the edges of the tabloid he smashed flutter. Glaring at his daughter, he walked around the desk and gripped her shoulders. "Who the hell did you tell?"

Susan was too shocked to move for a second. Then she twisted free of his grasp and hissed, "You're accusing *me* of leaking information about Amber?"

Still irate, he seethed, "We were *supposedly* the only people who knew about the ransom! I know I didn't tell a soul, so who else could have?"

"I should've known you didn't really have a heart! After all these years you fooled me the other day. I thought you cared as much about Amber and Sandra as I do."

Samuel was rapidly cooling down. "I do."

Susan shook her head sadly and said, "I don't think so. If you did, you'd know I'd never do anything to hurt her in any way." She hesitated, then added, "Sandra knew, too, and she didn't tell anyone, either."

Staring at the floor, he walked to his daughter and took her in his arms, in spite of her obvious lingering anger. His eyes were sincere as he held her and said, "I'm sorry, Susan. You're right. It's just this whole business is making me crazy. I can't sleep, can't eat. I never meant to hurt you."

She sighed, her eyes stinging. "It's all right, Dad. I'm tired and cranky, too. We all are." Pulling away, she added, "*Probe* employees aren't exactly known for their integrity. I think if we push them, we'll have a lead within a couple of days." Pacing his huge office, she shook her head and added, "I just don't get it. Who would start a rumor like this? The editor must have had some proof to go on, or a reliable source. I don't think even a cheap, disgusting tabloid would publish totally undocumented garbage when a child's life is at stake.

"The lab says the picture on the front page is easy. It was generated from the reward poster. Amber's face was computer-brushed a little, then transposed onto a different baby's body; then that composite was superimposed on a dingy garbage background. What I don't get is the ransom. The paper claims we've agreed to pay a million bucks to get her back. Where the hell did they get that figure unless one of us told them? Everyone else thinks the reward is a quarter million.

"How'd you send the money? Maybe someone at the bank leaked the information."

Samuel's skin was ashen as he slumped into his chair. "I'll check everyone. Whoever sold us out better pray that Amber doesn't suffer one bit because of their stupidity and greed."

* * *

Nick fumbled with the cord of the telephone outside Senator Holt's office as he quietly said, "Angela Anderson, please."

The receptionist at K & K discreetly answered, "She's on another line. Would you like to hold, Nick?"

From where he stood, he could see inside the senator's office. The men were all taking their seats around the conference table, getting ready to resume the meeting, but he needed Angela to check on Jax, since he had left him hanging without any explanation. Thinking fast, he merely said, "No. Just give her a message. Tell her I think I left the iron on in her apartment. She can use my car if she likes, I left it in the parking lot. Ask her to check over the lunch hour if she can get away."

"Sure thing."

Thanks to him, the office gossip factory had a juicy tidbit to discuss over lunch. He was beginning to wish his actual sex life was half as interesting as the one everyone at work believed he led.

Lesley Jaggers held up the tabloid, her tight grasp crinkling the pages as she raged, "Can you believe this crap? How can they get by with publishing such total garbage?" Several other agents looked quizzically over the tops of their cubicles to determine the cause of the commotion.

Ed glanced across his desk at her before calmly replying, "Remember the Constitution? Freedom of speech? Why are you so sure it isn't true? It could be, you know."

A little too hastily Lesley snapped, "The Stovers

agreed to cooperate. We'd know if anything was going down. We weren't notified of any suspicious activity, much less something as encouraging as a ransom note."

Casting her a wary look, he asked, "Put yourself in their shoes. Would you tell us? The omnipotent FBI. We've had fifteen years to solve this case, and we haven't done it yet. If it were my kid, I'd be tempted to pay the ransom and face the consequences later."

She sighed. "The Stovers know how important it is to stop these people. They wouldn't go behind our backs. And even if they did"—she shook the tabloid—"they wouldn't sell the story to a piece of trash like this. For God's sake, that family is worth millions, hell, maybe hundreds of millions. Why risk blowing their chances of rescuing Amber by splashing the ransom demand across every supermarket in America?"

"They wouldn't," he replied. "I'll bet you a hundred bucks someone they thought they could trust wasn't very trustworthy after all."

Angela left her office as soon as she got Nick's odd message. On her way to her car, she casually glanced in the backseat of his Cutlass, which was still parked next to hers. The blanket was crumpled on the floor. It didn't surprise her to see that Jax was gone.

After driving like a madwoman across town, she started to open the door to her apartment and froze. That nagging feeling hit her again, like a punch in the gut. Pushing open the door, she stayed outside, staring in.

Deadly silence wrapped around her. Everything appeared to be normal, so she forced herself to walk inside. Feeling like a scared child, she went from room to room, checking every hiding place she could imagine, until she suddenly noticed her computer's screen saver wasn't flashing through its normal array of geometrically designed shapes and colors. Either someone had recently used her machine, or something else was wrong.

Angela was shaking as she quickly checked her e-mail. No messages had been received since yesterday afternoon.

The gnawing uneasiness was piercing her every thought, making her want to run away. Holding her breath, she ran through a utilities program to verify her fears. There was no doubt about it—someone had not only been in her apartment, they'd used her computer less than twenty minutes ago!

Even though she'd been hesitant to believe Jax, it was becoming easier by the second. Her fingers trembled as she went to check on the one piece of evidence she had secretly hidden. Not even Nick knew that she hadn't sent everything to Interpol. . . .

She didn't have to open the tiny Velcro closure on the throw pillow resting at the head of her bed. Squeezing it to her chest, she felt the backup tape nestled deep inside. Knowing the cartridge was still there didn't make her feel any better. In fact, as she tossed it down and ran out her door, she wasn't sure she would ever feel safe again.

* * *

Jax was waiting in Angela's apartment for Nick and Angela when they came in just after six p.m. It was obvious from the lethargic way they ambled in that the last few days were taking their toll. Nick slumped onto the sofa, and Angela kicked off her high heels and collapsed beside him.

Jax's accent was thick as he teased, "So weak Americans can't handle a little excitement in their lives?"

Nick nodded, his eyes closed as he tiredly replied, "I guess not."

Angela yawned and agreed. "Too much turmoil, too little sleep . . ."

Jax laughed loud and long, then proclaimed, "The two of you are in luck tonight. I've prepared a Jamaican specialty, Jerk chicken, plus all the native trimmings, as a way to show my heart felt appreciation for your cooperation with this case." The smell of Blue Mountain coffee he'd prepared mixed with the fiery spices to fill the apartment with a tantalizing aroma. "Judging from how you both look, we might need to have the coffee before dinner to keep you awake. What happened today at lunch, Nick?"

Nick explained as he stretched. "Kellars invited himself to attend my meeting with Senator Holt. It took some fancy footwork, but everything worked out." He shot an inquiring glance over his shoulder at Jax. "It did work out, didn't it?"

"*Irie*, mon. Everything is fine. Did you have a good day, pretty lady?"

Angela was rubbing her temples. "I came home

for lunch, and someone had been on my computer. Scared the hell out of me."

Jax was barefoot, as if he were strolling on a sandy Jamaican beach, when he stepped into the living area. Grinning sheepishly, he admitted, "No need to worry, pretty lady, it was me. I got bored. Tried to play with your machine a little, then decided to take a walk. I must have just missed you. Come. Eat before it gets cold."

They grudgingly relinquished their comfortable seats and moved into the kitchen. Sitting down, Angela sighed, "Thank God it was you messing around on my computer. I had visions of kneeling in Kellars' office, waiting for him to execute me like they do in those Mafia movies."

"Too messy," Jax joked. "He'd never soil his carpet that way."

Angela stared blankly at him, too tired to find any humor in his joke.

Shaking his head, Jax lightly explained, "Just kidding. I think you Americans traded appliances for your senses of humor."

Nick asked, "What are you talking about?"

"Everyone in this country seems to have their own washers and dryers, not to mention phones, televisions, microwaves, and computers. In my country that would be quite extravagant."

Angela took a bite of the Jerk chicken. Her eyes instantly flooded with tears. She gulped down some water for relief. By the time she finally spoke, her voice was hoarse, barely a whisper. "Are you trying to kill us, Jax?"

His gaze was innocent as he answered, "With this *baybee* food? I toned it down for your delicate mainland palates. You have no fortitude. Associate Interpol agents must have strength of every kind. Physical and mental." He tapped his temple with one slender brown finger. "The spices are specially blended to awaken brain cells. Sparks set fire to new ideas and creativity."

Over her choking Angela managed to say, "Sorry, Jax. Associate Agent Anderson's brain cells exploded on impact. I guess I'm not cut out for the spy business."

Nick was enjoying the meal. "What gives this its unique flavor, Jax?" he asked.

"Jerk spices are used in Jamaica to make festive dishes of every kind. Apparently Angela's palate is not as sophisticated as yours, Nick." Jax winked at him. "Possibly you were right about the superiority of men in hazardous environments."

Angela pushed her plate away, opting instead for a container of yogurt from the refrigerator. Once the cool, soothing flavor of blueberries drenched the fire inside her mouth, she spoke, choosing to ignore Jax's latest dig against women. "What did Annissa have to tell us?"

"As I suspected, the organization's records are all maintained on a sophisticated computer network. There is no easy way to extract the information."

The mention of computers sparked Angela's imagination. "Could we access it by modem?"

"There are no outside links. For banking, international links are done on a separate system to insure the integrity of the main unit."

"Annissa could sneak out backup tapes."

Jax quickly weighed the consequences of telling

them everything Annissa had disclosed. Deciding it would do no harm, he stated, "The system only generates specially coded backups for the accounting records. The main information is apparently not backed up. System access by strangers was also anticipated, and protected. If the proper series of passwords are not utilized in two attempts, the entire system will self-destruct."

Nick watched Angela hang on Jax's every word. Leaning back, he was intrigued that Jax had acquired such extensive knowledge of the systems, yet couldn't help but wonder if the information was accurate.

"There are programs available that can retrieve erased data," Angela eagerly volunteered.

"Even when the hard drives are reformatted?"

"No. That would effectively eliminate any possibility of retrieval. What about the backup tapes? They must keep copies somewhere in case of system failures. Surely Interpol could decipher the codes, or Annissa could furnish the passwords."

Jax shook his head. "Will Kellars' unsuspecting employees handle the delivery of coded tapes to different banks scattered across the Caribbean. Annissa's message said they would be virtually useless without the decoding program. Apparently, it changes constantly."

"And it's on the main system?"

With a shrug Jax answered, "She didn't say. I would presume so."

Nick asked, "Sounds like a no-win situation. Where do we go from here?"

Angela responded, "It seems pretty simple to me. Downright obvious, as a matter of fact."

Jax's fork dropped, clattering against his plate before bouncing to the floor. "Then by all means tell us, pretty lady."

Angela's face tilted upward in mock defiance. "But I thought men were intellectually superior, Jax. Surely you already have a solution to this problem."

Tossing his napkin on his plate, he held his hands over his head in surrender. "*Irie*. You win. Provided your idea is worthy. Tell me, please."

"As I said, it's simple. While we're rescuing Annissa, we rescue the system."

Nick looked at Angela, his mind weighing her words. Slowly he began nodding his head. "It could work, Jax. When we get Annissa out of the country, we could take the computers as well."

Jax shook his head. "The entire network of machines?"

Angela gloated, "Of course not. Just the main hard drive."

"And how do you plan to do that?" he asked in wonder.

Angela smiled slyly. "Just have faith, Jax. Have faith in American ingenuity."

Angela paced nervously, waiting for the call a little before eight o'clock on Saturday night. Snatching the phone on the first ring, she cast a glance at Nick and Jax as she said, "Pizza Heaven. What can I do for you?"

The woman replied, "I'd like two medium supreme pizzas."

"Any drinks or salads with those, ma'am?" Angela asked.

"One draft beer, please."

Trying to sound official, Angela added, "Anything else?"

"No. Thank you."

"Delivery address?"

Angela jotted down the address, then hung up the phone. Grabbing her jacket, she said, "Looks like everything's going as planned. Annissa played her part perfectly."

Jax was already out the door. "Then let's go," he said, anxiously throwing it open and waiting for them to follow.

The three of them piled into Jax's rented red Ford. First stop was Pizza Heaven, where their two supreme pizzas were boxed and waiting. The large styrofoam cup of draft beer was topped with a plastic lid. Once on the road again, Nick carefully opened the lid and dumped in the contents of the vial Jax had given him.

"Are you sure he won't be able to taste that stuff?" Angela asked as she drove.

"Positive," Jax replied. With a sly grin he added, "It worked on you in Jamaica, didn't it?"

Angela's shock was apparent. "You drugged me? You lousy son of a bitch!"

Jax squirmed, but seemed more proud of himself than sorry. "Desperate times call for desperate measures."

"So I've heard," she snapped.

"I needed copies of your keys, pretty lady. And you needed authentic Jamaican braids to remember me by."

Angela was furious. He had lied to her over and over, and she had bought every stinking word of it. "Like hell I did! Next time just ask, and I'll give you the damn keys. No wonder I couldn't think straight for a few days."

"*Irie.*" He shrugged and smiled wryly. "The drug does have a hangover effect on some weaker individuals."

Nick interrupted them, "Okay, you two! Quit the bickering. We're almost there. Here's the sign." Angela turned off onto a side street while Nick placed the pizza-delivery sign Jax had somehow obtained on the roof of the car.

"You two stay down," she barked. "Her condo is just around the corner."

Angela sped around the corner, purposely screeching to a halt in front of Annissa's house. One last glance in the rearview mirror confirmed her appearance. No one would recognize her with the short red wig, heavy makeup, and thick coat. She grabbed the pizzas, balanced the beer on top, and bounded toward the house. From the corner of her eye, she caught a glimpse of the man in the car parked in Annissa's driveway but ignored him.

Ringing the doorbell, she shouted, "Delivery from Pizza Heaven!"

Annissa opened the door, a twenty-dollar bill in hand.

"That'll be sixteen-fifty, ma'am."

Stuffing the money in Angela's hand, Annissa nervously said, "Thank you. Keep the change."

"Wow! Thanks for the tip, lady! Have a good evening." Angela bounced back to the red car, hopped in, and squealed off.

* * *

Without even walking back into her house, Annissa headed toward the private investigator's car. He rolled down his window as she approached.

In her best Caribbean lilt she said, "I ordered enough for you, too. Have you had dinner yet?"

"No, ma'am. That was mighty nice of you."

"I hope you like it. It's been true comfort knowing you're around, just in case."

He smiled, warming to her generosity. "That ticker of yours seems to be working fine now."

"I hope so. It still concerns me, though. The doctors say I could have another attack at any time." She handed him the pizza and beer, for the first time noticing the butt of a shotgun protruding from the passenger-side floorboard. Flashing another sugary smile, she added, "Have a good evening."

"I will, ma'am." Toasting her with the beer, he added, "And thanks again for dinner."

Annissa strolled back to the house, then placed the other pizza on her kitchen table. Without opening it, she walked back into the dark living room and peered through the edge of the curtains. He seemed to be enjoying his feast. Every bit of it.

Jax could see Annissa in the moonlight reflected on the calm lake waters behind her elegant home. From a distance she looked the same as she always had. Exotically beautiful, a regal air to her. But as he drew closer, his muscles tensed. Her eyes were drained of life, her cheeks gaunt. Even in the dim light he could see the radiant ebony of her smooth skin had been betrayed by time.

With outstretched arms he greeted her. "Annissa" was all he said as he held her in his arms. Finally, he pulled back and wiped the tears from her eyes. "It's almost over."

Her voice was cold, her words calculated as she asked, "Are you sure the man out front is unconscious? He had a shotgun beside him."

Jax used his soothing grin and deepest accent to regain her trust. " 'Tis sleeping like a *baybee*. Will be for at least five hours, probably all night if he drank every drop. How are you feeling?"

Annissa turned away, overwhelmed by how little he had changed. Certainly he was older, yet she could still see the wheels cranking in his head before each word was spoken. His need to manipulate even his own sister disgusted her. She knew she was still only a pawn in some bigger scheme, yet playing his game might be the only way to make the last few years of her life tolerable. Her voice was deliberately soft as she said, "I meant what I said in my message about being sick, Jax. I may not make it through this alive."

"You'll make it. As always, I've planned for everything."

"And the rest of the family? Where are they?"

"Safely tucked away. We all agreed this was our only chance."

She nodded, eyeing the moon's reflection on the black water. Many nights had been spent staring at those luminous ripples, wondering how it all would end. Sighing, she realized she would soon have her answer. Turning toward him, she asked, "Did you ransom the Stover baby?"

"Yes."

"But why? With the bank codes I'll have, we'll

be millionaires. It was too risky." Shaking her head, she was suddenly overwhelmed with exhaustion. "Haven't you learned yet that your damned greed is going to get us all killed?"

"And what if something goes wrong?" he asked. "Even when we were kids, you always took the easy path, Annissa. That's how you ended up here in the first place, remember? Well, maybe this time the easy way won't work."

Keeping her voice low, she hissed, "Go ahead, say it. Or what if I don't make it through this *alive*."

He merely shrugged. "I have to think of Tica. And Maya. Your life isn't the only one at stake."

"I know." Sighing, she thought, *After all these years, his words still make me bleed, just as they always have.*

"Then you are ready to go through with it?" Jax said, his voice more challenge than question.

"Tuesday. I can have everything arranged by Tuesday afternoon," Annissa tiredly answered.

"Four o'clock?"

"Fine. Have the pizza midget meet me Monday at three in the ladies' room. I'll pass her the final information."

"Thanks." Jax backed slowly away. "Stay with me, Annissa. I know you've paid dearly for my mistakes in the past, but from now on I'm going to make it up to you. I promise."

Annissa exhausted what little remained of the night watching moonlight glitter on the lake. Most of the time she wondered why all the men in her life were such manipulative bastards. But deep down, she knew she could have stopped them. She just hadn't ever tried.

Angela spent her Sunday afternoon sitting cross-legged on the floor of her bedroom, watching Nick sweat. When he finally pulled the square metallic box out for the fourth time, she punched the stopwatch. "Three minutes flat. You're getting better, Nick."

"Still not close to your minute-twenty. I don't see how you can take these blasted machines apart so fast," he answered.

Touching his wrist, she aligned her hand with his palm. His fingers overlapped hers by more than three inches. "Small hands help. But you'll catch on. I'll put this machine back together while you try a different one."

Angela's bedroom was a virtual showroom of computer hardware. Since they didn't know what kind of machines they would be working with, they had rented one of each major brand. The room was cluttered with computers in various stages of disassembly, and a smattering of assorted tools accompanied the electronic gadgetry.

Nick looked at Angela, his eyes begging for mercy. "I still think you should handle the computer end, Angela. You know a thousand times more about it than I do. Besides, I always liked being computer illiterate. It gave me a chance to bug you."

She shrugged apologetically. "You'll learn. I agree with Jax on this one. My talents are better utilized elsewhere."

"You're beginning to sound like an Interpol agent," he laughed.

Angela's eyes brightened. "This *is* exciting, isn't it?"

"Just remember, these guys play with real bullets."

"So far I think all they play with is money."

"Which is not a bad choice of hobbies." Nick kneeled behind Angela, watching as she slid screws into place and piece by piece reconstructed the machine he had just disassembled. His breath was warm against her ear as he asked, "When is Jax supposed to be back?"

She nuzzled into his warmth, then slowly turned to face him. "I have no idea. Did you have some other sort of practice in mind?"

"I seem to recall a promise you made." His eyes burned through her as he softly added, "If I remember right, it had to do with showing me exactly how much you loved me."

She answered with her hands, her lips, her tongue, as he provocatively wrapped his entire body around her. In one swift motion Nick stood up, sweeping her into his arms. She felt every muscle in his powerful chest, his strong arms surrounding her, as he carried her to the bed and gently lowered himself over her, his mouth never leaving hers. His hands ran the length of her body, lighting fires everywhere they touched.

Angela pushed him away, long enough to roll on top and tug the bulky sweater over her head. Her body ached for him as she watched his eyes drink in the sight of her naked breasts. In an instant his mouth found one, his hand the other.

The sound of the front door banging open was followed by Jax's voice. "Are you a computer expert yet, my friend?"

Nick moaned in reply, shifting quickly toward the door so his body would block Jax's view of Angela. As she squirmed back into her sweater, he kissed her one last time and whispered, "I'm really starting to hate that man!"

"Me, too," Angela answered breathlessly. "It could be worse, you know."

"How's that?"

"He could've barged in five minutes from now."

Susan Stover carefully placed the latest ransom demand on her father's desk, then stepped back as he read it aloud.

" '*Probe* article interesting. Obviously you can't be trusted. Advance transfer of additional money now required. Deposit two million in Zurich Deutschebank account number 495-15MN-840. Further instruction to be forwarded upon confirmation of receipt to you on your arrival at Jamaica's Wyndham Rose Hall. No transfer, no baby. Any more leaks and Amber will die.' Damn them!"

Pacing in front of his desk, she asked, "Are you sure nothing else will be leaked?"

Samuel stood as he stoically said, "Positive. The bank teller who contacted the *Probe* about the first wire transfer was fired."

"What do we do now?" she asked.

"We pay the bastards," Samuel answered.

Susan shook her head, at odds with the way the

kidnappers were being handled. "What will we bargain with if we give them more money? They'll have everything they've asked for."

"They already do. And believe me, they damn well know it."

Chapter 18

The irritating grind of the rented Ford's brakes splintered Tuesday's early morning silence as Nick parked behind the Twin Peaks office complex. Both he and Jax watched for any sign of life for several minutes before Nick nervously whispered, "Looks clear to me."

"Let's hope 'tis so," Jax replied. Opening the passenger door, he winced when it creaked. Cradling the device, he carried it with a degree of respect he hoped it didn't deserve. A hint of a smile touched his face as he glanced at the nervous man at his side. Jax knew Nick would never have agreed to come along if he had known the plastic explosives contained in the simple but effective bomb had been purchased from an unreliable Cuban whose knowledge of explosives was directly related to the size of the purchaser's pocketbook. He could only trust the makeshift bomb truly was what he had asked for—equivalent in explosive power to a large firecracker, just enough to cause a little havoc, knock out the building's electricity to create a diversion. But deep down he knew the chances of trusting Juan's technical abilities were about as good as having a snowstorm in Jamaica.

Last Sunday, when Jax checked the main power supply going into the building, he had scraped off a paint sample and painstakingly matched it. Now, as he held the small metal case against the electrical box, he saw the fruit of his efforts. They were exactly the same color. Peeling off the adhesive paper on the back of the bomb, he positioned it, giving it a firm, steady push to seat it properly. When he drew his hand away, the bomb firmly held its place.

Carefully, he slid the small black switch to the On position. Inside the steel gray case the red digital lights on the timing device started counting down. Twelve hours, second by second.

The hidden office seemed to grow smaller every day, its bare walls closing in on her. Each moment dragged like hours. Finally, it was time to place the call, and she dialed the first number with relief. "This is Annissa Jamison. I'm calling to confirm the change in today's flight schedule for Pampered in Paradise Flight 26."

"Private hangar number?"

"Thirty-eight," she answered, surprised her voice sounded so calm when every nerve in her body was screaming.

"Yes, ma'am. Your nine a.m. flight takeoff time has been changed to five p.m."

"And we are cleared to land in Montego Bay, Jamaica, as well?"

"I'll check." Annissa could hear the sound of computer keys in the background. "Yes, Ms. Jamison. You are confirmed to arrive at Jamaica's MoBay Airport at nine p.m. this evening."

"Thank you." Annissa hung up. This time she dialed each of the three employees of Kellars & Kellars scheduled for trips that day. She apologized once again for the inconvenience of the delay, and wished them safe, pleasant trips aboard the afternoon flight to Montego Bay. After she hung up, she leaned back, realizing how many hours she had spent in this small, windowless, barren room for the last twenty years.

Staring at the equipment, Annissa wondered if the nightmare was almost over. Every muscle in her body protested when she crossed into her own office. The beautiful furnishings that once thrilled and comforted her held no meaning. As she ran her hand along the brightly woven fabric wallpaper, she realized exactly how high a price she had paid to surround herself with expensive things. Things that were now as worthless as her own life.

With slow, patient steps she crossed to the window. Outside, a few scattered clouds were gracefully sliding across the sun. Slowly, deliberately, Annissa reached first one hand, then the other over her head—stretching, relaxing. In only a little while it would be over. If she lived, she might finally be free.

It was the last luxury car the agency had in stock, a rose-colored Lincoln Continental the rental agents jokingly referred to as the "pimp mobile." Every businessman had politely decided a compact model was preferable to the only available Lincoln.

Jax didn't blink an eye when the pretty young agent led him to the car and looked at him for approval. He happily accepted it, then held his breath as the credit card he'd stolen that morning was scanned. When she handed back both his card and the car keys, he inwardly sighed.

The new rental car needed to be thoroughly checked. Too much was at risk for them to have car trouble tonight. With white knuckles Jax gripped the steering wheel, weaving in and out of traffic. Twenty minutes later, he was at ease with both the car's performance as well as driving on what he considered the wrong side of the road.

Satisfied the situation was under control, he abruptly crossed two lanes of traffic, barely making the exit he needed. Behind him, to his delight, brakes squealed and horns honked. A few minutes later, he pulled into a parking spot in front of the Days-n-Nites Motel. His luggage was already packed.

In fact, he was pleased with his choice. So far Angela had performed exceptionally well. A flash of guilt hit him as he thought of her precious computer equipment resting at the bottom of Lake Hefner, along with the other incriminating documentation she and Nick had so generously provided. After loading his luggage into the spacious trunk, he went back in and placed what he hoped would be his last call from the United States.

Maya answered on the seventh ring. "Hello."

"It's me."

The operator interrupted, "Will you accept collect charges from James Jackson?"

"Yes, operator. Put him through," Maya replied.

Jax began, "Are you ready?"

"I'm ready."

"Contact Deutschebank in the morning to confirm receipt of another two million dollars. If it is there, transfer it immediately."

Maya briefly hesitated, then asked, "Two million?"

"Yes, two." He sighed, impatiently twisting the cord of the old telephone. "Just listen and don't ask questions, Maya. Confirm Annissa's wires to Grand Cayman as well. Next, I need our Cuban friend to be ready around midnight tonight at the agreed location. Last, get on the Internet and book James Jackson on four different flights out of Oklahoma City, then four more out of Jamaica in the morning. One to somewhere in Europe, another to Canada, etc. Get the picture?"

"*Irie.* When will you be here?"

Jax thought for a second, running his free hand through his short, curly hair. "With any luck, a few days from now we'll all be sipping Tica's pineapple coconut concoctions and applauding the assistance of our trusting American friends. Of course, that depends on how well Annissa can travel. She'll be arriving shortly before I do."

Maya's voice was filled with concern as she asked, "Is Annissa sick?"

"Don't tell Tica. She had a heart attack last week. She doesn't look well."

"Then we should wait, Jax!"

He resisted the urge to explain the stakes to his little sister, to tell her he didn't give a damn as long as they managed to get out with the money. Instead he merely hissed, "Things have gone too far to turn back now. Much too far."

"If anything happens to her, it will kill Tica."

"I know. I told you, I'll take care of her. How do you like the remote island of Saba? It's one hell of a secluded place, isn't it?"

"I've never been on an island without beaches." She sounded tired, like a caged animal as she added, "Saba is a beautiful place in its own way, but it just doesn't feel right. . . . Like it will be sucked back into the ocean any second. The house you rented is nice, but it sits atop a steep hill, and the other side looks over a cliff. It frightens me."

"Quit worrying, Maya. Everything is going to work out. At least you're safe there. Right now we need to concentrate on executing the plan. We can worry about creature comforts later."

"All these stairs are hard on Tica. She had to rest many times the day we arrived. I couldn't believe she made it."

"I'm sorry, Maya. Tell her the next place we stay will be flat, near a beach. It's already lined up. You'll receive instructions on when and where to go next whether Annissa and I make it out of this mess or not. I promise."

"You've been making an awful lot of promises lately, Jax."

"I know," he snapped as he slammed down the phone. "Believe me, I know."

Angela smiled when Nick stepped into her office. The anxious look they exchanged expressed more emotion than words could ever hold. Finally she asked, "Are you as tired as I am?"

Nodding, he replied, "We both need a vacation." With a wink he added, "If I don't get more billable hours in this week, that may be easily arranged."

"By the way, it should be quiet today. Did you know Mr. Kellars went to Tulsa on business?"

"So I hear."

She added, "And I'll be out all afternoon. I'm screening actors for the estate campaign commercial."

"Sounds like fun." He leaned over her desk, quickly kissing her. "Any parts for dashing young lawyers?"

"No, just an old, grandfatherly type. Come to think of it, you'd be perfect for the role."

Their eyes met and held again as Nick said, "Good luck this afternoon, Angela."

Angela squeezed his hand, sharing one last moment as she whispered, "Good luck to you, too."

Annissa stayed at the window most of the afternoon, watching the clouds and the people passing on the sidewalks below. Her scheme had worked on Tate—he no longer felt it necessary to be in her office all day, and he never even suspected he had been drugged. She was sure he simply wanted an excuse to nurse his aching head in private when he resumed his watch from the parking lot, merely guarding the front door instead of sticking so close to her side.

Every five minutes Annissa checked her watch and wondered if these were the last few seconds of her life ticking away. Her end of the deal was complete. Wire transfers had been made to the accounts Jax specified. Kellars wouldn't realize his Grand Cayman accounts had been wiped out for

DEADLY SILENCE

at least twenty-four hours. Three hundred thousand dollars from the safe had been divided into equal parts, wrapped in brown paper packages, then shipped to blind post office boxes on the tiny Caribbean islands of Saba, St. Eustatius, and Dominica.

Finally, it was three forty-five. Right on schedule Annissa picked up the phone and dialed 911. Before she left, she looked around the small hidden room one last time. Almost as an afterthought, she opened the safe and withdrew the only existing PLACE documentation. Although it appeared to be an expensive oversized book of her homeland, inside were the portraits of teens and babies used in the last presentation. She ran her fingers along the glossy jacket, marveling at the magnificent photo of Dunns River falls near Ocho Rios—a sight she was sure she'd never see again, in this lifetime anyway.

Annissa started to put the book back in the safe, then placed it gently on the table closest to Will's office instead. After closing the safe, she slipped through the secret panel and went into the reception area to wait.

Tate watched the ambulance pull up in front of the Twin Peaks building, its red and blue strobe lights bouncing off the black glass to create an ominous image.

When the attendants rushed inside, he climbed out of his car, stretched his legs, then walked slowly to the entry. A small crowd formed, but split apart to let the stretcher emerge from the elevator. There was no doubt—even though her face was partially covered by an oxygen mask, it was Annissa whose head bounced limply back and forth as the attendants wheeled her quickly past him.

Rushing back to his car, he grabbed his cell phone and dialed Will Kellars' private number. When there was no answer, he left a message as he discreetly started to follow the ambulance. Two miles later, with sirens blaring, it bumped over the center medians to cross an intersection with a red light. Slamming his fist against the steering wheel, he shouted, "Shit!"

By the time the light turned green, the ambulance was out of sight.

As planned, the door to Pampered in Paradise was unlocked when Nick arrived at four o'clock. No one answered when he called, "Hello . . ." Slinking into Annissa's office, he silently laid his briefcase on her desk and glanced at his watch.

Now that he was here, he really couldn't believe he was a part of this scheme. It had all seemed very logical and well planned when they'd discussed it in the wee hours of the morning in Angela's apartment. But discussions were different from actually breaking into a stranger's office and stealing valuable equipment. Doubts plagued him. Was he too tired to think straight? What if Jax wasn't who he said he was? Would he hurt Angela?

Staring at his watch, he counted down the seconds as he paced. Anxiously he waited for the power to fail, the lights to die, so he could finish playing this game and get both Angela and himself out of this insane nightmare once and for all.

Exactly two minutes after four o'clock a violent blast knocked out twenty square feet at the base of the Twin Peaks building. Windows shattered throughout the first two floors. The rest of the building shook so violently, the occupants were sure they were experiencing another horror like the bombing of the Murrah Federal Building. An eerie silence closed around them as all the noise from electronic devices slowly faded. Without power the building was eerily dim and quiet. Too quiet.

The blast sent bricks and debris flying in every direction. One brick flew upward, as though it were attempting to escape from hell. Its flight was slowed by an electrical junction box two floors above the main circuit breakers. The metal box shirred easily, unleashing a display of hissing sparks that fell in great arcs through the gaping hole to the floor below.

The fire started slowly at first, consuming a tiny storeroom filled with varnish and paint on the second floor. Jumping across the hall it found layers of carpet and room after room of furniture to feast on. A little over four minutes after the blast, fire alarms began ringing through the stifled hallways.

In a newer building, automatic sprinklers would have quickly doused the flames. But this office building was one of the last to be constructed before the law requiring sprinkling devices was added to Oklahoma City's safety codes. Consequently, the flames carried on, undisturbed by human intervention. Black smoke began to curl out windows, seep through walls. Panic-stricken people poured into stairwells, which quickly turned into chaotic vertical tunnels swirling with occasional bursts of smoke.

Five minutes after four o'clock on Tuesday afternoon the elevators automatically shut down, leaving over a thousand people trapped inside the Twin Peaks building.

For a few seconds after the shock waves rocked the building, Nick could hardly breathe. As the rattle of the furniture died around him, a primal rage ignited deep within his soul. So fierce was his anger that it momentarily made him nauseous. Jax had obviously miscalculated the strength of the blast. The power was down, as expected, but he suspected far more damage had been done than necessary. Silently he cursed Jax, praying no one was hurt. The hammering of his heart against his breastbone made him realize his instincts about Jax had probably been right. Still, at this point he had no choice but to continue as planned—Angela's life was at stake.

The remote-control device was exactly where Annissa had said it would be in the note she slipped to Angela that afternoon. It should have activated the secret door, but when Nick pushed the button, nothing happened. He tried again, in his fury pressing hard enough to crack the plastic casing, but still nothing. Then he realized something they should have thought of sooner—the door operated on electricity. He'd missed his chance to open it while the power was still on. In exasperation he hurled the remote across the room. The sound of it shattering echoed in the silence.

Nick tried to calm his rattled nerves, willing himself to relax his clenched jaw and hands. He knew exactly where the door should be from the map Annissa had sent to Jax. Prying it open with his fingertips didn't work. Glancing at his watch, he realized valuable time was ticking by. He stepped back, took a deep breath, and with all his strength threw himself against the paneled wall. At first he wasn't sure if it was his shoulder or the door he heard crack. But when he stepped back, he saw a tiny sliver of an opening, and heard the faint hum of equipment.

Angela paced back and forth, trying to fit into the unfamiliar routine of the hospital's emergency room. The nurse's aide uniform she wore was crisply starched, perfectly matching the other employees milling about. Yet she felt as though someone was watching her every move. She tried to ignore the nurse standing behind the counter frantically signaling her, but finally acknowledged her presence by closing the gap between them.

"I asked, are you new?" the nurse said impatiently.

Angela nodded.

"How long have you worked here?"

"Two days," Angela replied.

"Do you know where Radiology is?"

She shook her head.

"Do you speak English?"

Her cheeks flushed as she muttered, "Yes."

"Radiology is on the fourth floor, west wing. I need these X rays taken up there. Stat! Just go down this hall, take the elevator to the fourth floor, and follow the signs. You can't miss it."

Angela reached over and grabbed the X rays. "I'll get right on it."

The nurse shouted from behind her, "Don't forget your hospital identification badge when you come to work tomorrow, young lady."

Angela called over her shoulder, "Thanks for reminding me." She practically ran down the hall, her long stride abruptly interrupted when Annissa was wheeled through the emergency room doors directly in front of her.

Thinking fast, she pushed the button for the second floor. Hobbling off the elevator, she clutched the wall for support as she approached the nurse's station with the large manila envelope of X rays tucked under her arm. The head nurse peered over her glasses, watching her as if she might be spreading some deadly disease.

"May I help you?" she asked, clearly much too busy to be expected to perform any additional duties, especially for a mere nurse's aide.

Angela hopped over to lean against the circular desk. "I think I just sprained my ankle when I rushed to get on the elevator. The nurse in the emergency room said these X rays needed to be in Radiology right away. If you could run them upstairs for me, it would really help."

The nurse was clearly skeptical, but then seemed to relax a little. "I'll get you some ice for your ankle first, dear."

"That's okay. It can wait. I think this patient is

in pretty bad shape." She held out the X rays, raising her eyebrows like a starving puppy. "I'd really appreciate your help with these."

The nurse came around the corner and looked at her ankle. "No swelling yet. That's a good sign. I'll be right back. Make sure you cover the phones while I'm gone. Tell anyone who calls I'll be back in five minutes."

"Sure thing." Angela watched as the woman disappeared into the elevator. As soon as the doors slid closed, she took off running toward the stairway. Slamming into the heavy metal door, she practically hurled herself down the stairs and out the first-floor exit.

As she rounded the corner to the emergency room, she took a deep breath and consciously slowed her pace to match the other people in the area. As though she had every right to cross into the restricted area, she walked boldly through the pneumatic silver doors that read *Hospital Personnel Only*.

A room near the front of the line of small cubicles held a vast array of medical equipment, including crutches and wheelchairs. Angela nonchalantly grabbed a wheelchair, unfolded it, and headed down the hallway, confidently pushing it. As she passed each partitioned area, she peeked in. On her sixth attempt she found Annissa. Alone.

"Excuse me. Are you Annissa Jamison?" Angela asked, even though her bright red, yellow, and green silk dress was unmistakable. From the sallow look of her, either she was actually quite ill, or she was playing her role perfectly.

"Yes?" Annissa asked with questioning eyes, then recognition crossed her face.

Angela grabbed the silver medical chart at the foot of the bed. "I'm supposed to take you to Radiology for tests. Please hurry, ma'am."

Annissa climbed off the table and into the wheelchair. In a matter of seconds, the heavy metal doors whooshed closed behind them.

Inside the insulated hidden room on the twenty-second floor of the Twin Peaks building, Nick couldn't hear the rhythmic whine of the fire alarms. The main computer was still humming, its battery backup unit blaring the warning signal for power interruption. He took out Angela's array of screwdrivers and other tools, spreading them quickly on the table before him. Just as they'd practiced, he switched off the machine, then unplugged it from the battery unit. He carefully removed the outer cover, only dropping one small screw as he worked.

His forehead was drenched in sweat when he realized he'd hit another snag. The machines he'd practiced with were cool. This machine had been on for hours—its components were hot.

Nick thanked his lucky stars when he touched the first tiny screw inside. Even though it was quite warm, it wasn't too hot to handle. In a matter of seconds, he removed the computer's hard drive, replaced the cover, and gathered his tools. Carefully he placed each item in his briefcase. Glancing around, he checked to make sure everything was in its proper place. He was about to leave when he noticed the Jamaican book on top of the far desk. It struck him as odd, since the rest of the room was conspicuously void of anything besides machinery.

Crossing the room in three strides, he stuffed it in his briefcase alongside the other things. Abruptly he froze. He was standing directly in front of the one-way mirror into Will Kellars' office. It was a weird sensation, like looking at a familiar world distorted by someone else's eyeglasses. Then his stomach clenched violently.

Outside the tall windows were rising curls of thick black smoke.

Lesley waited impatiently on hold, wondering what the clerk in research could possibly be doing that would take so long. Her gut instinct told her the Stover family was up to something. Susan Stover's voice had been a bit too haughty when she categorically denied any knowledge of the story run by the *Probe*.

Finally, the woman came back on the line. "Stover family's personal accounts are clean. No large transfers in or out in the last six months."

"What about the corporate accounts? Stover Enterprises would have access to millions on a daily basis. Did you check the campaign funds for Susan Stover?" Lesley asked.

"Yes. There have been eighteen wires in excess of one million dollars out of the Stover Enterprises bank accounts. Most are to their Canadian subsidiary, but two recently went to Zurich. The first was one million, transferred on the sixteenth, then this morning another two million."

"Both to the same account?"

"No. Different accounts. But both were to Deutschebank."

Lesley's heart was pounding. "Any other account activity?"

"Nothing. Susan Stover doesn't have signatory power over campaign funds. Even if she did, the account has been virtually inactive for several months."

"Good work, Turner. I really appreciate it."

Lesley sat back for an instant, then grabbed the stack of files in front of her. Flipping furiously through the pages, she finally found what she was looking for—her interview notes with key employees of Stover Enterprises. She remembered the pilot because he was handsome and had been very cooperative. Jotted in the margin she found the airport's telephone number, and the call letters for the Stovers' private jet.

Angela pushed Annissa slowly down the halls of the hospital, careful not to draw unnecessary attention to their presence. They were approaching the front entrance when Angela heard brisk footsteps rapidly gaining on them. One quick glance over her shoulder confirmed her suspicions. The man she'd seen watching Annissa's house was running like a madman toward them.

"We've got trouble," Angela said as calmly as she could, increasing her own gait. She was surprised how easy it was to push Annissa, who she guessed weighed less than a hundred pounds.

Angela's mind raced. Knowing Annissa couldn't possibly survive a struggle didn't make things any easier. She had to detain the man while

Annissa went on alone. When he was only a few feet behind them, Angela abruptly stopped and yelled, "Run, Annissa. Go on without me."

As soon as Annissa jumped from the wheelchair, Angela swung it around, smashing it into the man's legs just as he tried to grab the back of her uniform. When he and the tangle of wheels and metal finally stopped sliding across the slick tile, Angela reached into her pocket and grabbed the cylindrical tube of pepper gas she'd brought along in case of an emergency. Before he could regain his senses, she fired a long stream of the fiery liquid into his face and ran. Behind her, Angela could hear him gagging and screaming, but she never stopped or looked back.

Sprinting, she reached the curb where Jax was waiting. He was anxiously holding the back door open. After diving inside, Angela sucked in her breath when she felt a sharp sting on her thigh.

The last thing she saw was Jax's smiling face as he plunged the syringe through her clothes into her flesh.

Chapter 19

"Are you feeling all right?" Jax asked Anissa as he crawled behind the wheel.

"I think so." Looking at the small, lifeless woman buckled in the backseat, she asked, "What about her?"

Jax laughed. "Angela will be fine if she chooses to cooperate. She has spunk, that one. An excellent choice on my part."

Annissa shot him a disgusted look. "And I'll bet you don't even feel guilty about using her."

Feigning concern, he said, "That's where you're wrong, sister. I'm truly bleak about this whole mess."

Jax pulled into a parking lot.

Annissa snapped, "Why are you stopping?"

"Nick is to meet us here with the computer's hard disk from your office. Remember? Once we have it, we're home free. All the evidence that could incriminate us will be destroyed."

Shaking her head, she said, "It would've been much easier for me to simply destroy the computer, Jax. Then we would know for certain it was disposed of properly."

Jax impatiently stated, "We already discussed it. How do you know the machine wasn't wired somehow by that CompuCorp firm to set off an alarm? This way you'll be long gone even if they do discover something is amiss."

"The emergency room personnel were talking about an explosion in a nearby office building. I don't suppose you had anything to do with it?"

Jax shifted nervously. Trying to downplay the significance of the blast, he replied, "A little boom. Just enough plastic explosive to knock out the building's power supply."

"Guess again. They said there were injuries. And a fire."

Jax's face hardened. "We'd better check," he muttered, then drove toward the building. They were stopped by police blockades several blocks away. Even from that distance it was easy to see the smoke pouring out of the first two floors. Overhead, two news helicopters circled.

Annissa hissed, "How much explosive did you use, Jax?"

"Exactly what Juan gave me."

Wide-eyed, she shouted, "You trusted that stupid Cuban? I'm surprised it didn't blow up in your face long before you triggered it. Now what are we going to do?"

He threw the Lincoln into reverse and said, "Get the hell out of here."

"What about the rest of the evidence?" she asked, her hands shaking with fury.

"Hopefully it'll burn." He shrugged and added, "The fire may be a blessing in disguise."

Annissa thought of all the people she passed every day. Repulsed, she cried, "There are hundreds of people in that building, Jax! Have you lost all sense of decency?"

His voice revealed no feeling whatsoever as he answered, "I had one job to do, and I did it. You're out. And you're alive. That's all that's important."

His attitude was so callous she wanted to slap him. "If the police get their hands on that computer drive, they'll have more than enough evidence to convict us."

"They'll have to break through your almighty security system first. I thought you said it was virtually foolproof," he said.

Annissa hesitated.

"It *is* foolproof, isn't it?"

She looked out the window at the passing buildings. "It was until I disarmed it."

"You did *what*?" he shouted.

"You heard me. Will Kellars was trying to cover his ass in case anything happened to me. I was afraid he'd destroy the whole system, so I temporarily disarmed the reformatting feature. I intended to reinstate it once things settled down. Then you showed up with your clever scheme to escape."

"So if the building doesn't go up in smoke, how much will they know?"

"Everything." Deep down, Annissa knew Jax would never understand. She hadn't replaced the security codes because she secretly wanted the children listed in those files to be found. A quick glance at Jax made her certain she had made the right choice. Her soul could no longer bear the weight of trapping babies in families where greed and money were used to buy dreams.

Nick knew better than to try the elevators. Instead, he headed directly to the staircase. When he opened the door, he could hear voices from the floors below echoing up the stairwell.

Walking down each step like a robot, he placed one foot deliberately in front of the other. Nick wasn't thinking about being trapped on the twenty-second story of a high-rise building that was on fire, or about missing the rendezvous with Jax. He was cursing himself for not trusting his gut instincts.

A new fear made him suck in a ragged breath. If he didn't show up as scheduled, would Jax panic and harm Angela? If Jax was half the criminal Nick suspected, he would destroy every ounce of evidence, and every person who could identify him.

When he reached the tenth floor, the stairway was packed. Seeing the terrified look on people's faces as they stood waiting suddenly made him instantly realize what he had to do. Shouting as loudly as he could, he said, "Everyone, listen. Very slowly, we need to walk upstairs. We can get to the roof. There'll be fresh air and plenty of room to wait. Breathe through a piece of clothing and follow me."

To his surprise, the people did what he said. There were a few disgruntled rumblings over the coughing, but as he looked over his shoulder, most of the people were methodically plodding up the stairs behind him.

As they approached the top of the stairwell, the crowd began moving slower and slower as they tried to complete the long climb. The small amount of smoke that was seeping into the stairwell was rising along with them, making breathing more difficult. Once he finally reached the top, Nick pushed the handle on the door marked ROOF. He wasn't surprised to find it locked. Snags seemed to be par for the course today.

Nick was in a rare mood. The mixture of anxiety, frustration, and anger had pushed him to his limit. He politely asked the few people who had climbed the stairs as quickly as he had to stand aside. With closed eyes, he took two deep breaths, then kicked the door hard enough to dent it. Three more irate jabs sent the heavy metal door flinging open so violently that it snapped back and forth before stopping. As the people slowly filed past him toward the welcome fresh air, Nick headed back downstairs to see if anyone below needed help.

Hovering over the Twin Peaks building, helicopters filmed people pouring out of the stairwell, their live news reports interrupting programming across the nation. Over a loudspeaker the victims were told to sit and wait; the fire posed no immediate danger. It would be under control in a few more minutes, and firemen would get them out of the building as soon as possible. Even though the main part of the blaze was doused quickly, it was almost another half hour before the trapped employees were led single-file past the tangle of hoses that lined the dripping stairwell.

Nick was one of the last people out of the building. When he stepped into the parking lot, he knew he was probably too late to meet Jax. But he also knew he had to try. Running as fast as he could, he dodged chunks of debris as he crossed the chaotic parking lot.

Angela's car was still parked next to his Cutlass, which was blocked in back by a fire engine. After what he had just been through, he didn't intend to let anything stop him. He crawled inside, revved the engine, and bumped the car over the curb in front of him. Dodging several trees, he drove across two flower beds, then fishtailed into the street.

His only hope was to make it to the airport in time.

Jax parked the rented Lincoln at the far corner of Hangar 38. Leaving the keys inside, he transferred the luggage into the red Ford. With Annissa's help he buckled Angela into the backseat, carefully positioning her limp body so she appeared to be napping.

Annissa casually boarded the plane, greeted the passengers, then told the flight crew how excited she was to finally be on board as a passenger instead of merely doing her routine inspections while watching everyone else have all the fun. After confirming the flight was scheduled to take off in ten minutes, she offered to secure the passenger door on the way to her seat.

Annissa walked toward the elegant passenger compartment, carefully closing first the lightweight door that separated the small galley from the cockpit, then the set of curtains that blocked the view from the galley into the passenger seating area. Slinking into a blue mechanic's jacket and hat that she had stashed under the galley's counter, she slipped out the main door, pushing it closed behind her. In an instant she deplaned, ducked under the belly of the plane, and crossed to where Jax was waiting in the red car.

"Everything set?" he asked.

"It went smoothly," she said, her voice cold.

Jax slammed the car into drive and sped away. Even though it was a much longer route, he circled wide, making certain he wasn't spotted at this point in the game.

Annissa wiggled out of the smelly mechanic's clothes, rolled down the window, and tossed them into a ditch. She sighed as she said, "The pilot won't know I'm gone until they're airborne. If anyone asks, they'll confirm I'm on board."

"Perfect," Jax said.

Nervously twisting several exquisite rings around her fingers, she nodded toward Angela, who was still unconscious. "I think we should leave her."

"Which do you prefer, leaving her body here or taking her with us to Jamaica?"

Annissa didn't miss the implication. Too tired to argue, she merely replied, "You cold bastard."

Jax glanced at her as he confidently said, "I've thought about the information on the computer. I have new identities for all of us. We'll only stay in Saba for a few days, then our next stop is St. Eustatius. After a month there we can settle in Dominica for a little longer, maybe a year. Even if the authorities are searching for us, they'll never find us. So, don't worry, sister. As usual, I've thought of everything."

Jax reached into the backseat. "I brought you a pillow. You'd better get some rest. It's a long drive."

Amazed at his chameleon-like ability to adapt, she stared out the window, trying to push the ghastly image of Will from her mind. "You really think we'll make it out of the country tonight, don't you?"

Jax merely threw his head back and laughed.

Tate sat in his car for a while, his eyes tearing so much he could barely see to use his cell phone. He dialed Will Kellars' direct line at work, but a recording from the phone company said it was temporarily out of service. Assuming he'd misdialed, he tried again, reaching the same notice. The only number he could get to go through was at Kellars' home.

The message he left was brief. "Annissa ran. My attempt to stop her failed."

Leaning back, he breathed deeply, the chemicals still burning his eyes and nose to the base of his lungs. Then it dawned on him. He might still have a chance, if he hurried. Through the veil of tears he drove like a maniac out of the hospital parking lot until he pulled into the private airport.

Slamming on his brakes, he almost skidded into the ugly pink Lincoln parked alongside Hangar 38. A small jet with PAMPERED IN PARADISE blazoned in bold colors along the side was pulling slowly away, headed toward the main runway.

Running inside the hangar, he found a mechanic working beside an open cowling. He was a cocky young kid, covered with grease and reeking of airplane fuel. His hair was pulled back in a ponytail, and he rhythmically popped a wad of bubble gum between his back teeth as he worked.

Tate breathlessly asked, "Did you see a pretty black woman in a bright red and yellow dress board that plane?"

"Sure did," the mechanic muttered.

"Thanks," he called as he ran back to his car.

The kid watched him run away, a smile making a dimple in one cheek. He quietly said to no one in particular, "Saw her get back off, too," before he bent down to resume his work.

Nick parked alongside the pink Lincoln and hesitantly searched the car. The keys dangled from the ignition. Opening the driver's side, he reached in and popped the latch to open the trunk. It automatically rose. With great relief he found the trunk empty. No dead bodies, or anything else, for that matter.

He knew it was too late to catch the airplane, so he stood on the tarmac gazing at planes as they soared over the dark green field of winter wheat. Nick jumped at the sound of the voice directly behind him.

"You looking for the black lady, too?"

Nick turned and saw the scruffy mechanic wiping his hands on a dirty pink rag. He answered, "I suppose so. Has someone else already been here?"

"Yeah. A real uptight guy. Looked like he'd

been crying. Took outta here at ninety miles an hour."

"Did you happen to see everyone who boarded the Paradise plane?" Nick asked.

"Sure did."

"Was there a small woman with either auburn or bright red hair on board?"

"The only woman who got on that plane was an older black lady. The rest were all stuffed suits. If that last guy had stuck around long enough to listen, I'd have told him what I'm gonna tell you. That lady got back off the plane before it left. Took off with a black guy in a red Ford, and a red-headed woman."

"What was the other woman wearing?"

"Maybe a nurse's uniform, but I wouldn't bet my life on it. She looked pretty out of it, like she was sleeping. What's this all about anyway?"

Nick's voice was grim as he said, "You wouldn't believe it if I told you."

Lesley had just finished talking to one of the pilots for Stover Enterprises when her phone rang. "Agent Jaggers."

"My name is Nick Hunter. I'm a lawyer with Kellars and Kellars. We talked on the phone a few weeks ago shortly after the Stover baby was kidnapped."

Sliding forward, Lesley grabbed a pen so she could take notes. "What can I do for you, Mr. Hunter?"

He breathlessly answered, "I know you have no reason to trust me, but it is imperative that you do. I'm afraid I've inadvertently helped the people who are responsible for kidnapping countless babies escape—"

Lesley's heart pounded. "Slow down, Mr. Hunter."

"Angela Anderson, who also works at Kellars and Kellars, and I became suspicious that our firm might somehow be involved several weeks ago. When a man approached us who claimed to be an Interpol agent working on the kidnapping case, we helped him, thinking we were doing the right thing. I'm at Angela's apartment right now, and I think he may have hurt her."

"Why?"

"She would've met me or left a message if everything had gone as planned. Her computer's been disassembled, the hard drive stolen. The bastard even had the audacity to leave this note: 'Nick and Angela, thanks for all your help. I'm sure Interpol will reimburse you for your time and trouble. I couldn't have done it without you. Jax.'"

Lesley was sure the man was telling the truth. He sounded far too agitated to be fabricating a story. "Would you mind telling me exactly how you helped these people and who they are?"

Nick ran through everything they'd been through as quickly as he could, then added, "I have the main computer drive from Pampered in Paradise's office, plus a book I found on the table. I don't think these people would want anyone to have the kind of evidence they must contain, unless Annissa erased everything before she left, or they're egotistical enough to think their security system is unbeatable. It's possible Jax planned to destroy the whole building with the bomb."

"Could you hold on for a second?" Lesley dropped the phone and ran to Ed's office. She anxiously asked, "Has there been any report of a bomb in Oklahoma City?"

Glancing up, he said, "I thought you were on your way to the airport." Reacting to her impatient look, he answered, "About an hour and a half ago. Very small, only a few casualties. Why?"

"Oh, my God! I'll tell you in a minute," Lesley called as she ran back to her desk. Grabbing the phone, she said, "Mr. Hunter, can you give me a number where you can be contacted?"

"Why?" he snapped.

"So I can send an agent to retrieve the information—"

Interrupting her, he shouted, "The damned information can wait! I'd bet that Jax and Annissa are on their way to Jamaica right now!"

The pieces of the puzzle were falling together. Lesley had just confirmed the Stovers' private jet was on its way to Jamaica. She knew they had already paid three million dollars in ransom money. Her mind was racing as she said, "You're probably right, Mr. Hunter. I'll see what I can do. These things take time—"

"What!"

"Unfortunately, I need approval to—"

"Bullshit! The woman I love may be dead, and you're worried about getting approval? We've got to catch the bastards! For God's sake, they've stolen babies, bombed a building, and God only knows what else! Every second counts at this point! If you won't do anything, then I will!"

"Calm down, Mr. Hunter!" In a flash Lesley knew what she had to do. "I'll help you, but you've got to promise to help me in return."

He still sounded furious as he asked, "How?"

"Stay where you are. I'll send a task force to help. If Kellars and Kellars is involved, we'll have to act fast to catch whoever's responsible."

"What about Angela?"

"If you'll fax me her picture and description, I'll do everything in my power to find her."

"What if they took her to Jamaica?" Nick asked.

"That's exactly where I'm headed."

Chapter 20

Will Kellars was more relaxed than he had been in years when he pulled into the garage of his luxurious home. The short business trip to Tulsa had proven to be even more profitable than he had hoped. Driving the Ferrari was a pleasure—the CD player surrounded him with Beethoven and Tchaikovsky while the car powerfully attacked the road. Following his normal routine, Will fixed himself a dry martini, went into the study, then checked his answering machine.

As he listened to Tate's messages, the words stung as though he'd been slapped. The martini fell to the floor, the fine crystal shattering on impact. There were more messages, but as he looked at his watch, he realized how late it was, and how little time was left.

After stopping the machine, he flipped through his Rolodex to find Tate's phone number. When he finally answered, Kellars angrily asked, "What the hell is going on?"

"Like I said, Annissa ran. But I know where to."

"So bring her back. Your job was to stop her!"

"It's not that easy. I followed her. She's on the Pampered in Paradise jet heading for Jamaica right now."

Kellars' hand was shaking, his voice weak as he asked, "Are you sure?"

"Talked to the pilot myself from the control tower. They're scheduled to land around nine tonight in Montego Bay."

"Fine. I'll have someone waiting for her when she lands. Good work."

Will's hands were shaking severely as he punched the next telephone number. He desperately wished he hadn't dropped his martini. A stiff drink would do him good right now.

"Hello."

"Annissa ran. She'll be landing in Jamaica on the Pampered jet at nine tonight. Can you get anyone that fast?" he asked.

"I'll take care of it. Have you checked the files?"

"Not yet." He hoped his voice didn't carry the dread he felt. "I'm at home."

"Aren't you glad I suggested you change the account requirements last week when she got sick? If I hadn't insisted you add a secondary approval requirement on every wire-transfer order, she could've stolen all our money."

He sighed. "You were right. As usual."

"Are you going to the office to make sure the computer records were destroyed by the fire?"

"What fire?" he snapped.

"You haven't heard? Where the hell have you been all afternoon?"

"In Tulsa on business." Gripping the phone so tightly his knuckles pulsed white, he shouted, "What goddamned fire?"

"There was an explosion on the first floor of the Twin Peaks building. Gutted the first couple of floors, but no one was killed. The twenty-second floor probably just has smoke damage."

Kellars grimly said, "I'll find out soon enough."

"Call me when you're finished."

"I will."

"I guess I'll destroy the documentation I've kept. It's obviously useless now. Like it or not, we're all out of the kidnapping business for a while."

Across town, the sound of Kellars' voice was still fresh as a special number was dialed. For other people sentimentality might have played a part in the decision, maybe even tipped the scales toward a more tolerant solution.

The orders were given in a clear, sharp voice that bore no sign of regret or remorse. "I have three jobs for your organization, similar to the one performed for me not long ago in Chicago. The first one is in Jamaica. There's a Pampered in Paradise charter flight landing at MoBay airport tonight at nine o'clock, Central Standard Time. I need someone to meet it and make sure Annissa Jamison doesn't leave the airport alive. . . . Tall, thin black woman about sixty years old. The first job is worth seventy-five thousand dollars.

"The second job needs to be done before morning. On the top floor of the Twin Peaks building, there are law offices for the firm Kellars and Kellars. The target is the owner, Will Kellars. There's a photograph of him with his son hanging in the entryway, so he'll be easy to identify. He should be in his office, or in an office hidden behind the large bookcase. Be careful, the mirror is one-way.

If you miss him there, he lives alone at 319 Sparrow Road. Either way, it needs to look like a suicide. The second job is worth a hundred thousand dollars.

"The last is in Manhattan. I want the apartment above a business called Paradise Promotions on Fifty-seventh rigged to explode after entry with no telltale evidence, just like Chicago. The third job is worth fifty thousand dollars."

Angela emerged slowly as she fought her way through a drug-induced sludge. When she finally managed to open her eyes, she had no idea where she was, only that her head ached so brutally she was sure it would roll off if she dared to move. Trying to focus, she concentrated on what she could see—a single beam of sunlight slicing the darkness from a split in a rusted tin roof.

Shifting only her eyes, she realized she was in a dilapidated shed. Her hands were bound behind her back, her fingers pressing into warm, sandy earth. As her senses returned, she could not only hear the ocean nearby, but smell it along with an occasional whiff of something else, something vaguely familiar that she couldn't quite place.

Stretching carefully as she scanned her surroundings, she found she was barefoot, her legs tied at the ankles with thick silver duct tape. Although waves of pain knifed through her body, she rolled to one side and managed to sit up. The effort made her realize for the first time how hot it was. Sweat dripped from her face. She licked her swollen, cracked lips, wishing for water. Memories were flooding back—the hospital, Jax and

Annissa, a hazy boat ride stuffed in a small wooden crate. . . .

When she heard a car pull up, she quickly resumed the position she had awakened in. Sunlight fell across her face, but she stayed still, listening to every sound.

Jax's voice cooed as he said, "See, little one. I told you she'd be okay."

Angela could hear the gurgling sounds of a child, and suddenly realized that the other smell in the shack was baby powder. Barely cracking her eyelids, she tried to see them, but his back was to her until he turned around, placing the infant on a blanket just a few feet from her face.

A lump in her throat threatened to choke her as she realized that the child looked just like the picture on her poster. Jax had Amber Stover!

Susan Stover returned from the ladies' room, adjusted the beach chair, and pulled it across the sand until it was back in the shade. Picking up the paperback novel she'd been pretending to read for the last two hours, she opened it to the same marked page. Only this time a piece of paper fell into her lap.

Certain it was finally a note from the kidnappers, her heart raced as she opened it.

Act natural. They are probably watching. I know about the ransom and am here to help. I will not interfere until Amber is safely in your possession. Please trust me. I need your help as much as you need mine. Will you ever feel truly safe if these people aren't caught?

Lesley Jaggers, FBI Room 217

At first disappointment overwhelmed Susan. But as she listened to the sound of the ocean and felt the warm breeze, she knew what was right—she had to cooperate. But she also knew that she couldn't, and wouldn't, tell her father.

Annissa stepped out of the cab and stared at the column of steep steps before her. She had never traveled to the Caribbean island of Saba before, and was amazed at how different it was from Jamaica. There were no beaches, just rain forests and bushlands spread over the three-thousand-foot peaks of the volcanic mountaintops.

One by one she climbed the steps, stopping several times to rest and admire the breathtaking view. By the time she made it to the top, the sun had fallen below the ocean. It was a quaint village house, even smaller than the tiny one she had grown up in. She walked around to the back, and found Maya and Tica sitting on a rock patio, surrounded by lush ferns and tropical flowers in the dwindling light.

It was a strange reunion. The love was there, but it was buried beneath years of pain and anger. Tica was the first to act. Moving slowly, she wrapped her arms around her daughter. "Is it finally over?"

"I hope so," Annissa hoarsely replied.

"Where is my boy? Where is Jax?" Tica softly demanded.

Annissa buried the hatred that threatened to spill from her, controlling her voice as she answered, "He had one last thing to clear up. He'll be here in a few days."

Walking away, Tica flatly said, "No, he won't. All my children will never be with me again before I die. 'Tis my punishment for letting this happen."

Annissa glanced at Maya, who shrugged her shoulders as if Tica's rambling was commonplace. Annissa said, "Jax will come. I promise."

"Don't make promises you can't keep. Didn't I teach you that?"

Annissa struggled, trying to reconcile the woman of her childhood to the ravaged person before her. "Yes, Tica." She spoke as if she were addressing a child. "But you must have faith."

"Faith in what? And for how long? I've prayed for you to come back every day for over fifteen years."

"And here I am."

"I don't have another fifteen years to pray for Jax. His soul is lost, as is my own."

An hour later, after Tica had finally been convinced to rest, Maya whispered in her sister's ear, "I called to confirm the money was wired like Jax told me to. The ransom money arrived, but the bank in Grand Cayman says it hasn't received any transfers."

Annissa shook her head, her grim face only a tiny reflection of her concern. "There must be some mistake. I sent it yesterday."

Maya handed Annissa the phone number. "Maybe you should call tomorrow."

She snatched the paper, stating, "I will. Have you heard from Jax?"

"Not yet."

"When he calls, don't tell him about the wire. At least not until we know what went wrong."

"Where are you?" Nick asked as soon as he recognized Lesley's voice on the line.

"Wyndham Rose Hall, near Half Moon Bay in Jamaica. I'm a few doors down from Susan and Samuel Stover," Lesley replied.

"So the Stover baby is connected to all this after all," Nick quietly said.

"Apparently so. I thought we had a deal."

"We do," Nick replied. "That's why I'm checking with you every four hours. Did the lead I gave you on Paradise Promotions in Manhattan turn up anything?"

"Not yet. Why haven't you met with the task force? They've been waiting outside your apartment for hours. In fact, half the FBI agents in Oklahoma are looking for you right now."

Nick shifted the cell phone to his other ear, then cleared his throat. "I've been busy. First, I tried to find Angela, but she's disappeared. I'm sure she's with Jax."

"Most likely," Lesley agreed, although he could tell from the tone of her voice that she was irritated.

Nick continued, "Since I couldn't find her, I started working on how to keep Kellars from getting away with this."

"Kellars is no longer a problem," Lesley said.

"Did your team already arrest him?" he asked eagerly.

"Couldn't. He's dead."

Nick stared at the phone in disbelief, the shock apparent when he finally spoke. "I don't believe it." Shaking his head as if he could take himself back to a less complicated time, he muttered, "How'd it happen?"

"Hung himself," Lesley replied.

"When?" he asked.

"Sometime last night, probably right after he realized his world was falling apart. What difference does it make?"

"Because he's not the suicidal type," Nick replied.

"What makes you so sure?" Lesley asked.

"If he was, he would've done it when his son was killed. From everything I've heard, the man was totally devastated. Supposedly, he turned to the bottle for a while, then cleaned himself up and got back to business."

"Maybe the thought of going to prison was more than he could handle," Lesley suggested.

Shaking his head, Nick sighed. "Kellars was the kind of guy who probably plotted a sensational defense before he ever got involved in this scheme in the first place. He would've had a plan ready, or he'd just post bail and skip the country. Considering the money these guys have been making, I'll bet he has quite a stash somewhere." Nick thought for several seconds, then added, "Angela and I may have been wrong about something...."

"What's that?" Lesley asked.

"There may be someone even higher up the pyramid than Kellars."

"And who would that be?" Lesley asked.

Nick's voice was distant as he replied, "The person who had him killed."

When night fell, the shack was finally cool. Jax had come and gone all day, leaving Angela time to search for a way to save not only herself but Amber Stover as well. When he left again just after dusk, Amber was sleeping on the floor, only inches from Angela's face.

Now that they were alone, her goal seemed simple enough—free her hands and feet so she could grab the baby and run. Yet the shed was basically empty. There were several blankets on the sandy floor, a package of disposable diapers, a box of canned baby formula, two baby bottles, and a jug of water.

As she scooted toward the door, hoping to have better luck outside, something dug into the flesh on her knees. Looking down, she realized it was a broken seashell—a *sharp* broken seashell. Scurrying backward, she worked furiously until she had it in her right hand. It was barely long enough to reach the tape that bound her wrists, and she focused all her effort on cutting it with short, sawing strokes.

Only seconds after she felt something snap, she heard Jax's van return.

Nick turned down Will Kellars' dark street, his headlights occasionally reflecting off a mailbox or a stray animal roaming the night. Driving past, he slowed to less than five miles per hour. There were no cars parked in the street, none in the driveway. Only yellow POLICE—DO NOT CROSS ribbon made the elegant house stand out from the others.

After parking around the corner, he eased out of the car and practically crawled across the back edge of the immaculately manicured lawns. Several houses away, a lone dog barked a few times, then went back to sleep as Nick crouched and ran the short distance to the back of the house. Shining a light through the French doors, he watched the artificial moon created by the flashlight's beam bob around the room, erratically falling across four elegant wing-back chairs, an ornately carved table, and original oil paintings. On the far wall, Nick finally saw it.

There was an electronic keypad on the wall. Beside the number keys was a solid green light that he was certain meant the security system wasn't armed. Standing back, he found a small rock and launched it through the pane of glass closest to the lock on the French doors. Carefully pushing away the remaining glass, he reached in and popped open the doors. For a few seconds he stood motionless, making certain the noise hadn't drawn any attention. Moving silently from room to room, he didn't see anything suspicious until he entered the study. Scanning the room with the flashlight, he walked to the desk, stopping suddenly at the noise of glass crunching underfoot.

Nick aimed at the parquet tiles near his feet. The crystal stem of a glass was still intact, though the rest of it was shattered. "Looks like Kellars dropped his drink," Nick muttered to himself. He illuminated the desk, the combination telephone-answering machine catching his attention. "Must have got a message that upset him."

Reaching over, he punched the Playback button with his gloved finger. The message seemed to roar out of the machine. He listened intently to the description of Annissa's escape.

Turning off the flashlight, he leaned against the desk, trying to overcome the most violent wave of hatred he had ever experienced. Taking several deep breaths, he forced himself to think logically. *Kellars gets home from his trip, fixes himself a drink, then listens to his messages. He's unnerved by what he hears, drops his drink . . . then calls to warn his partner!*

Glancing down, Nick saw the automatic redial button on the telephone. He knew that unless the police had used the phone when they picked up his body, it would dial the last person Kellars had called before he died. After he pushed the Speaker button, the dial tone filled the air followed by the beeping numbers as the machine dialed. The call rang through, loud and clear.

"Hello. Hello. Who the hell is this anyway? How'd you get this number?"

Nick silently disconnected the line. He had easily recognized the voice. "Oh, my God!"

Evan was exhausted when the taxi dropped him off in front of Paradise Promotions. It was well after midnight, and he desperately needed a good night's rest after the long trip back from Grand Cayman. The stitches healing behind his ears and along his hairline were itching like crazy. When he stepped inside, he flipped on the lights. One of his favorite things about this office was watching the neon snap and flicker before it settled into its effervescent glow. He dropped his luggage onto the carpet, sadly realizing how much he would miss this place.

A voice cut through the night's silence, its threat unmistakable. "Who the hell are you?"

Evan froze. He couldn't see anyone, but the sound was close—from behind the counter.

Thinking fast, he answered, "I'm Eric. Evan's brother."

"Which makes me the queen of England!" the man shouted.

Evan couldn't quite place the familiar voice. He knew better than to show fear, so he boldly called, "Who the hell are you? How'd you get in here? And why are you hiding?"

"Because there's a window behind you, and I have a gun aimed at your pointed little head. We wouldn't want anyone to interrupt us, now would we? I need to know where Evan is, and if you don't tell me, I'm afraid I'll just have to kill you."

Finally Evan recognized the voice. "Tony? That is you, isn't it, Tony? I *am* Evan."

"Make up your mind. A minute ago you were Eric."

"That was before I realized who you were. What are you doing back in the country? It's too soon. The police are still looking for you."

"I don't know who you are, but you'd better tell me where Evan is! Now."

"Damn it, *I am* Evan. I just had plastic surgery

at a private clinic in Grand Cayman. Let me think for a second. Who else would know that you love playing roulette in Monte Carlo? Or that when you pulled off the Stover job, you felt like holy shit from a bout with the flu? Or that you screwed up and left your thermos in the car?"

Tony raised his head above the counter, where he could see Evan better. "Must have been one hell of a plastic surgeon. You look fifteen years younger."

"Thanks. Now could you put the damned gun away? You're making me break out in hives."

Tony laughed. "You definitely are Evan."

"So, are you going to tell me what you're doing here?" Evan impatiently asked.

Lowering the gun, he shrugged. "At first I came to kill you." Tony watched Evan's face, which showed no emotion, no sign of remorse, so he added, "I figured you were in on it."

"In on *what*?" Evan asked.

"Someone tried to kill me. The head honchos must have decided they didn't want any dead weight around after the problems we had on the Stover job. I thought you were in on it, so I never left the country like we agreed. Instead, I hid for a while, then decided to pay back the bastards." Tony nodded toward the spiral staircase, adding, "Since you've handled the contacts for the last ten years, my original plan was to get the information from you, then watch you swing from your balcony."

Evan tensed again. "I'm glad you changed your mind. How do you know they were trying to kill you?"

"Because they killed my baby brother by mistake. Blew my apartment to hell, toasting him like a marshmallow."

"I didn't know, Tony. I swear I didn't know." Evan started to move toward him, but Tony held up his hand. Evan froze and continued, "I thought you'd slipped out of the country like we discussed. I'm really sorry about your brother." Hesitating, he asked, "What changed your mind about killing me?"

"I've been trying to track you down for a few weeks. I even flew to Grand Cayman to see if I could dig up Elaine Patterson and find out if she knew where the hell you were. Who is that bitch, anyway?"

Evan laughed so hard, the stitches around his face pulled painfully. After catching his breath, he said, "Me, you idiot. She's one of my more interesting personalities, so to speak."

"Shit, I should've known. Well, when I couldn't find her, I came back here. I've been watching this place for a few days. Two nights ago a couple of thugs broke in. They spent a long time upstairs. I guess I was just damned lucky they didn't find me hidden under this counter. At any rate, I checked out their handiwork. The place is wired to blow as soon as anyone sets foot upstairs. Obviously, you've become dispensable, too, Evan. I figure that makes us on the same side again."

"We should get the hell out of the country," Evan said. "They won't give up until we're both dead."

"They already think I'm dead. Now all you have to do is tell me where to find the bastards, and you won't have to worry about them bothering you, or anyone else, for that matter, ever again."

Evan quickly weighed his options. "They're in Oklahoma City. But before we get down to details, we need to clear out of here," he said. "If this place is wired, I personally don't care to hang around any longer than I have to."

"I've got a van parked up the street. We can figure out what the next step is later," Tony said, heading for the door.

Evan picked up his suitcases and replied, "I agree."

Following Tony outside, he stopped to lock the door. A tall man with dark brown eyes and slicked-back hair bumped into Tony as he hurried past him on the street. Tony whirled around, only to be face to face with the man's badge. "FBI. Hand over the gun," was all he said. Tony reached in with only his fingertips, easing the gun from under his coat. In a matter of seconds, Tony was handcuffed and being pushed into a nearby van.

A different FBI agent had stopped Evan at exactly the same moment. He slammed him against the brick storefront and shouted, "Who are you?"

"Just a friend of his. Eric Hopkins. You can check my driver's license if you like. It's in the front pocket of my jacket."

"Funny, but when you were inside talking, your name was Evan and his was Tony. And I believe the Stover kidnapping was mentioned, too." The agent twisted Evan's arms painfully behind his back and slammed handcuffs onto his wrists. "To tell you the truth, I don't give a damn what you call yourself." He jerked the cuffs tightly. "Whoever you are, you've got a lot of explaining to do."

Angela waited for what seemed like an eternity before she tried to pull her wrists apart. When they finally broke free, she stopped and listened. The steady rhythm of Jax's breathing made her certain he was sound asleep.

Moving at all was difficult; doing it silently seemed almost impossible. Every muscle in her body screamed in protest. By the time she sliced through the duct tape around her ankles with the seashell, she was exhausted. For several minutes she simply stretched her legs and concentrated, uncertain if she could stand at all, much less manage to pick up Amber and escape without waking her.

Yet she knew she had no choice. Whatever scheme Jax had in mind would be over soon. He wasn't one to tempt fate by wasting precious time.

With every ounce of energy she could muster, Angela rolled to her feet. Moving next to Amber, she wedged her arms under the blanket on which she slept, lifting her smoothly into her arms. Holding her breath, she waited for the child to cry.

Amber shifted, one tiny arm flailing momentarily before she settled against Angela's chest. Ever so slowly Angela stood, then shuffled toward the door. She managed to push it open, slide through, then ease it closed without making a sound. The sand was soft and cool beneath her bare feet as she searched the darkness. Moonlight illuminated the unfamiliar country—a stretch of endless beach against a tangled overgrowth of bushes.

Spotting the van, she wondered if she could use it to get away. Tugging the driver's door handle quietly, she realized it was locked. The beach offered little cover, so she began following the trail left in the sand by the van's tires. They walked slowly, softly for a while, until she heard something snap behind her. Clutching the baby, she broke into a frantic run.

Amber's cries pierced the night, forcing Angela to slow her pace. Rocking the child, she cooed, begging her to be quiet as she lightly covered her face with the blanket to muffle her screams. Knowing Jax could simply follow her trail on the sandy road, she headed into the trees to hide. Bushes scraped her bare legs, while underfoot twigs snapped and dug into her flesh. She quickly wished she had stayed on the path.

Suddenly she stopped. Illuminated by the moon, Jax stood in front of her, his gun aimed directly at her head. With a hearty laugh he declared, "That *baybee* loves to cry, doesn't she, pretty lady?"

Susan Stover spent the entire night sitting outside the luxurious hotel room on the small patio overlooking the beach. As she watched the sun peek over the horizon, she wondered if today would finally end their ordeal.

When the phone rang, it startled her. She ran inside, frantically searching in the unfamiliar room for the telephone. After fumbling and dropping the receiver, she managed to answer it. The voice on the line was obviously disguised, the message simple:

> "Be at the open market in Ocho Rios today at noon. No police or Amber dies."

The ringing awakened Samuel, who emerged from his adjoining suite. Moving slowly, he tied a thick terry-cloth robe around his waist while he rubbed the sleep from his eyes. He sat down next to his daughter, his unspoken question obvious.

Staring into her father's eyes, Susan carefully repeated the kidnapper's message word for word. For several minutes, they sat in silence. Susan hugged her father, saying, "I'm afraid, Dad. I keep going over this in my head, and I can't make any sense out of it. They already have the money. Why would they risk being caught now?"

His haggard expression was laced with anguish and fear. "God only knows. Maybe they couldn't live with themselves if they didn't give her back. Deep down, I think everyone has a conscience. At least I hope they do, for our sakes."

Susan sighed, stroking her arms as she said, "I used to think that, too. Then I became a lawyer. I've seen people rape and kill a grandmother for a twenty-dollar cocaine fix. A few hours later when their buzz has worn off, they do it again. The world is full of sick people. Who else would steal a helpless baby?"

"Someone who's more interested in money than anything else." Samuel looked into his daughter's eyes. "I'm really sorry about all this. You know that, don't you?"

"Sorry about what?"

"The kidnapping. If it weren't for all my goddamned money, they wouldn't have taken her."

Susan's eyes softened, her voice reassuring as she said, "We don't know that. But there is one thing I know for certain. Without all your so-called 'goddamned money,' we would never have had this chance to get her back."

Lesley welcomed the morning with a walk down the beach. Aimlessly wandering back toward the hotel, she was surprised to see Susan Stover heading her way. They greeted each other cordially, as vacationing strangers would. When Susan accidentally dropped her hat, Lesley politely bent to pick it up, instantly spotting the small piece of paper tucked inside the inner straw rim. Slipping it casually into her palm, she handed the hat back. The women wished each other a pleasant day, then headed in opposite directions again.

Once safely inside her hotel room, she read the note Susan had passed to her.

Open market—Ocho Rios—Noon today

Grabbing the phone, she called Ed to report the news. Before she hung up, she asked, "Did they find anything incriminating in Will Kellars' office?"

"Not directly. But we came up with a list of bank accounts and current wire-transfer codes. Some are in Grand Cayman, others in Switzerland.

If he was running the kidnapping show, he kept it clean. Meticulously clean."

"Supposedly, he was very intelligent. What about his house?"

"They're working on it today. This kidnapping scam went on for so many years, they're sure to find something. Oh, yeah, Nick Hunter was right about his death. The coroner's preliminary report confirms it wasn't a suicide."

"Has Nick turned up yet?"

"No. I get the distinct impression he doesn't trust us."

Lesley was quiet for a moment, then replied, "Why should he?"

"Not hungry, little one?" Jax asked.

Angela could barely see Amber from the backseat of the van. As inconspicuously as she could, she tried to keep her bearings by watching the tropical countryside as they drove. When she recognized the outskirts of Ocho Rios from her recent trip, she relaxed against the torn seat, thankful that he had tied her hands in front this time. At least she could run for help, or possibly grab a rock and bash him in the head.

When the van slowed, she dared to barely raise one eyelid. Jax parked the van in an alley, then turned to face her. "I'm giving the *baybee* back this day. In spite of what kind of beast you think I am, I'm no killer."

Angela didn't react. Keeping her eyes steady, she prayed he would believe she was still too drugged to fight.

As though they were engaged in brisk conversation, he continued talking. "Not to worry, pretty lady. Soon I'll quit being so greedy with your food and water. You must forgive me for wanting to keep you weak. I knew you would find a way out, somehow, someway. You're a fighting soul, Angela."

She still didn't respond. Instead she focused all her energy on breathing as if she were unconscious. Each time Jax drugged her, although it took longer to knock her out, she had always pretended to be immediately affected.

She heard him open the door next to her, felt him tug open one of her eyelids. Even though her heart was pounding, she met his intent scrutiny with eyes glazed and unseeing.

Seconds passed. She knew Jax had left her door cracked wide as he opened the passenger door to the front seat. Hearing something rustle nearby, she dared to steal a glimpse. Jax was pulling a cap adorned with dreadlocks over his own short hair. Relief washed through her. He must have believed she was asleep!

Just seconds later, Angela felt the familiar sting of a needle burn her thigh as he said, "I would never trust you, pretty lady. Sleep well." A mournful groan escaped her parched lips—not from the pain but from overpowering disappointment. The bastard had won! Half opening her eyes, she watched him lift Amber from the front passenger floorboard, then step into the sun.

"Don't go anywhere," Jax laughed as he hurried across the street into an area filled with vendors and tourists.

Angela recognized the open market. She knew

she had only minutes, if not seconds, before the shot would knock her out again. *I've got to do something!* Searching the van, she studied the few things Jax left behind—Amber's blankets, a rattle, and a full bottle of baby formula. Grabbing the plastic bottle between her bound hands, she bit the nipple, letting the bottle dangle from her teeth so her hands were free. As she unlocked the door, she was thankful Jax hadn't tied her ankles this time.

Out of the van, she grew more light-headed as she worked to unscrew the cap to the gas tank. Clutching the baby bottle, she pushed it into the hole and started squeezing. In a few seconds it was empty. After replacing the gas cap, Angela quickly weighed her options.

It took only a second to decide to take her chances in the open market. Rushing as fast as she could, she stumbled across the street and drifted into the crowd. It was obvious from the stares of each person she passed that her filthy nurse's uniform, tied hands, and bare feet made her quite conspicuous. Swaying back and forth, the crowd seemed to float around her.

Stopping at a woodcarver's booth, she leaned against his table, trying to focus her eyes. The old vendor merely smiled as he stared at her bound hands. Without saying a word, he reached for a long, ornately carved wooden object on the table before him. In a flash he separated a slender sword from the wooden sheath. Winking, he gently sliced the tape from her wrists.

Before she weaved back into the crowd, Angela gruffly whispered, "Thanks."

The world around her seemed so outrageous, so filled with bold colors and sounds drifting from far, far away, she was sure she was wrapped in the protection of a strange, puzzling dream.

Lesley arrived at the Ocho Rios open market dressed in native Jamaican style—a T-shirt dress barely covering a fluorescent orange bikini, plus flip-flop sandals. "They obviously don't call it an 'open' market for nothing," she said to the taxi driver as she stuffed a twenty-dollar bill in his palm.

Scanning the area, she knew the kidnapper had picked a perfect place to make a drop. Hundreds of people milled around the hot, crowded place. There were no real walls, just canvas dividers, and all the vendors looked pretty much alike. Heaven for a criminal.

Glancing nervously around, she spotted the Stovers. They had stopped to admire necklaces made from polished seashells. Lesley maintained a safe distance, but found it hard to keep the local vendors from getting in her way. They were constantly running out of their canvas booths, waving T-shirts and jewelry under her nose, demanding the chance to braid her hair. Jamaican vendors were definitely not shy.

The drop happened so fast, Lesley almost missed it. One second the Stovers were admiring a large handwoven basket; then suddenly the basket had a baby lying in it. Lesley looked up in time to see a black man running away from them, his mass of long, tangled black braids bobbing from under a green and orange hat as he weaved through the crowd.

"Stop! FBI!" she shouted as she began to chase him. Flipping open her purse, she pulled out her gun. Chaos followed as frightened tourists tried to dive into the booths to keep out of the line of fire. Vendors screamed when their merchandise was knocked into the dirt. As suddenly as the man had appeared, he was gone.

Lesley slowed to a walk, her elbow bent so her gun pointed directly in the air. She had no idea which way to go. Stepping cautiously, she searched each stall as quickly as she could. When she saw the green and orange cap lying in the dirt at her feet, she knew the search was hopeless. It was a souvenir she'd seen for sale in all the local shops, a cap with fake black braids sewn around its edges so they dangled down, making it look as though the person wearing it had dreadlocks like the natives.

Lesley snaked back through the people, knowing any one of them might be the kidnapper. Susan Stover was holding Amber with a look of joy on her face. Samuel laid his hand on her shoulder and said, "Susan just told me you came to help us."

Shaking her head, she muttered, "The bastard got away."

"But Amber's safe." He was openly crying as he said, "Thank God, Amber's safe."

As if the baby girl understood, she smiled and grabbed a handful of Lesley's long, beautiful hair, pulling her closer. Tears flowed down Susan's cheeks as she speechlessly hugged Lesley. Amber cooed and smiled between them.

"I can help you catch the man who did this."

All three turned to face the woman who had spoken. Her eyes were shallow, her skin pale as she swayed, then collapsed.

Lesley and Samuel caught her, easing her safely to the ground while a nearby vendor summoned help. Lesley instantly recognized Angela from the picture Nick had faxed. "Ms. Anderson, are you all right?" she asked.

Just before she lost consciousness, Angela smiled and hoarsely replied, "I made sure Jax won't be going far. . . ."

Nick hadn't slept in days. Standing in a men's room at the Capitol Building, he splashed cold water on his face, then wiped his damp palms on a paper towel. He looked like hell and felt even worse. Every minute that passed made him more certain something horrible had happened to Angela. As he headed for his meeting, he knew she would have found a way to call or get help, unless . . .

Shaking away the revolting thought, he took a deep breath and walked into the senator's office. He wasn't surprised to see Alice Holt behind the bar, fixing herself a drink. "Good morning, Mrs. Holt," he said, trying to sound normal.

"Mr. Hunter. I'm so glad you called."

"I wanted to come sooner, but with things so hectic since Will's death . . ."

"I understand completely," she replied.

"Will the senator be joining us soon?"

Shaking her head, Alice said, "No. He wanted me to handle you myself."

Nick didn't miss the sexual innuendo in her voice, or her eyes. Returning her provocative stare, he said, "At least things have finally slowed up with the grand jury investigation. It looks like Susan Stover has backed off."

"It's about time that bitch realized she was playing with the wrong people." She took a deep breath, leaning toward Nick as she said, "It's a real shame about Will. Have you heard what's going to happen to the law firm?"

"No. No one seems to know where to turn. I thought maybe we could strike a deal."

"I suppose you want me to put in a good word for you with the senator." Alice ran her hand over his shoulder suggestively. "I might just be convinced we need a staff lawyer. Bob always does what I ask him to, if you know what I mean. . . ."

"To tell you the truth, Alice, that isn't exactly the arrangement I had in mind."

She moved closer, blatantly eyeing him as she asked, "Then what exactly is it that you want?"

After clearing his throat, he asked, "Did Will ever talk to you about me?"

She nodded. "He told Bob and I that you were the best lawyer he'd ever had work for him. That's why he put you on our case."

"But did he tell you about our *relationship*?"

Sipping her drink, she asked, "What relationship?"

Nick stared at his feet as he spoke, afraid he couldn't effectively carry off the lie if he looked her in the eye. "I can't believe he didn't tell you. He promised he would."

"Tell me what?" she snapped.

"That he wanted to bring me in on your deal."

She froze. "Our deal? I don't know what you're talking about. I didn't have anything to do with his law firm. Except for paying those ridiculously high bills of yours."

Nick laughed. "Come on, Alice. You know what I'm talking about. You don't have to pretend. It's me. Nick. I know about PLACE, the whole underground adoption thing, Paradise Promotions, the portraits of kids. Will told me all about it. Even showed me the secret office behind his bookcase. Introduced me to Annissa. It's quite a setup."

Alice grabbed her glass, gulping the last half of her drink. Staring at him, she was wide-eyed yet cautious.

Nick moved closer as he said, "It's okay, Alice. I know Annissa ran off, but we can rebuild the organization. We'll make it bigger and better than ever."

Her breath caught as she spoke. "I need to think about it. So much has been lost, with Will dead. We'd have to start again from scratch. Rebuild the network."

"Could we at least try? Isn't it worth thousands of dollars?"

Alice laughed. "More like millions. Annissa tried to steal the funds in the Cayman accounts, but I stopped her. The greedy bitch got exactly what she deserved." She stared at Nick as though she were assessing every inch of him. Finally, she leaned close and throatily said, "I think we would make excellent partners . . . in every way."

Nick slid his hand into his pocket, his fingertips resting on Angela's mini-recorder as he said, "I can't tell you how much this means to me."

Alice Holt was still screaming obscenities at Nick from the backseat of a police squad car when an FBI agent tapped him on the shoulder. Handing him a cell phone, he said, "Agent Jaggers needs to speak to you."

Grabbing the phone, Nick hesitantly answered, "Yes?"

"I've got someone with me who'd like to talk to you."

In a second Angela softly said, "Hi, handsome."

Nick's heart was in his throat as he held the phone, tears of relief springing to his eyes. "I . . . thank God you're alive! Are you all right?"

"A little weak, but I'm doing great. I hear you just cracked the case for the FBI."

Smiling broadly, Nick said, "As a matter of fact, I used one of your favorite techniques to trick Alice Holt into confessing on tape."

"*Alice* Holt was behind all this?" Angela asked.

"Hard to believe, isn't it? What about Jax and Annissa?"

"I'm not sure about Annissa, but I helped them nail Jax."

Nick proudly exclaimed, "That's my girl! How'd you do it?"

"All I did was put baby formula in his gas tank. They caught him walking down the highway on the outskirts of Ocho Rios."

"When will you be back?"

"They tried to convince me to stay here until I was stronger, but I told them to go to hell. Lesley pulled some strings with Customs, and I'm leaving on the next flight. Would you meet me at the airport?"

"A trigger-happy SWAT team couldn't keep me away!"

Epilogue

"Need help carrying anything?" Nick asked.

Angela searched the office she'd worked in for so many years, realizing as she inhaled the lingering odor of smoke that the past few weeks seemed like something out of a bad dream. "No. I guess I've got it covered," she said. Gazing at Nick, she wondered why he seemed to grow more handsome every time she saw him. Smiling, she added, "You look awfully . . . relaxed."

"I guess I am. I talked to my friend Jim. He and Peg are really excited to have more legal help." Moving closer, he touched her cheek. "For the last few weeks I kept wondering where all this would lead. At least now we know."

"Do we?" Angela turned away from him, pretending to look for some mysterious misplaced item.

Nick asked, "Are you okay? You still seem a little puny."

"Gee, thanks. Puny was the look I was going for."

"Did you get any sleep at all last night?"

"Not much. My head feels like it may explode. To tell you the truth, I don't know what I am right now. I feel like someone threw my life in a blender and hit the pulverize button. Every stable aspect of my existence is gone." Tears spilled down her cheeks as she added, "My mother, my job . . ."

Nick pulled her into his arms, tenderly wiping the tears with a gentle swipe of each thumb. His hands cupped her face as he smiled. "You still have me."

"Did it ever occur to you that your arrival sort of started the proverbial ball rolling in this mess? Before you came along I was blissfully ignorant of the fact that I was working for one hell of a bastard."

Nick innocently asked, "You're not going to blame me for all this, are you?"

With a hint of a grin, she replied, "No. I'm just saying you seem to be a catalyst."

"Dozens of children will be returned to their birth parents. A lot of good has already come out of all this." He scanned her office, then added, "And some long overdue changes."

"I know." Pulling away, she looked around the small, empty room, tears threatening to flow again. "I've always had a hard time dealing with change." With the back of her knuckle she forced the tears back, then lifted her head high. "After all, things will turn out better than ever. You just have to have faith. Right?"

Nick wrapped her in his arms again. "People who work hard always come out on top. You just need rest. It'll probably take awhile for the drugs Jax gave you to wear off completely. A few good nights of sleep will work wonders. I promise."

Marilyn poked her head into Angela's office. "Excuse me."

Nick and Angela pulled slowly apart, neither

embarrassed by being caught in an embrace, since for all intents and purposes, there was no office anymore. Even though Will Kellars had lectured Angela on the evils of dying intestate many times, he apparently had died without a last will and testament. The law firm's employees were spending their last day together, packing their personal belongings and wondering where the next step would take them.

"These just came for you." Marilyn set a huge bouquet of pink and white carnations on Angela's empty desk, then slipped back out of her office.

Angela smiled tenderly at Nick, who shook his head and held up both hands. "Don't look at me. I didn't send them. I'm unemployed. Remember?"

She plucked the card off the plastic stem and opened the small envelope, reading the message aloud. "Angela, thanks for the delicately handled press release on Alice's arrest. I owe you one. Senator Bob Holt."

"I guess he's not such a bad old geezer after all," Nick said.

"He told me he was going to retire this fall when his term runs out. I think deep down, he really cared about Alice."

"Either that or he realized how much he was depending on her to make his business decisions for him."

Angela sighed, leaning back against Nick. She was too tired to care about the senator or anything else. "What are we going to do? Do you think Alice Holt will really hunt you down like she threatened when they arrested her?"

Nick held her, gently stroking her hair. "I doubt it.

She always had money to pay people to do her dirty work." Looking into her eyes, he added, "Speaking of money, I've been thinking about that cryopreservation case. You could go to law school, or start that computer business you've always dreamed of."

Lesley Jaggers rapped gently on the door as she leaned in. "Excuse me. They said I could just come back."

Angela smiled and replied, "You bet. Pardon the mess. We're moving out today."

With a firm handshake Nick added, "Nice to finally meet you."

"Believe me, the feeling is mutual," Lesley replied. "For a while I was afraid you were a figment of my imagination. I never heard why you didn't meet with the team."

"Let's just say I'd been burned once."

Lesley smiled and warmly said, "You certainly came through. The evidence you turned over should easily convict everyone involved. I can't tell you how much we appreciate the help both of you have given us."

Angela asked, "Would you mind clearing up a few things?"

Lesley laughed. "That's the least I can do!"

"Have you found the families where the children belong?" Angela asked.

"The backup tape you kept, plus the disk drive and book Nick had taken from the hidden office, contained a wealth of information. There were lists of each child kidnapped, the date they were first taken, the date and location they were delivered to the purchasing parents, and all their payments. The related companies were also listed, as well as how much money had been laundered through each one."

"What will happen to the pregnant teenagers who are currently staying at the PLACE Foundation?" Nick asked.

Lesley answered, "There isn't such a thing. The whole adoption organization was pure fiction. The book you found was just a very creative part of a scheme used to make the prospective purchasers feel justified in paying money for a baby. They were led to believe that their money was helping poor, innocent teens who had nowhere else to turn."

"I can see how people might have believed a story like that years ago when teenage pregnancy was considered shameful, but these days it's pretty socially acceptable," Angela said.

"Even after all these years, one thing hasn't changed. There are still couples out there who desperately want a baby, and can't have one of their own. To them the story about PLACE was totally believable, because they needed to believe in something, anything. Legal adoptions were available to them, but they would have to wade through paperwork and waiting lists. Surrogate mothers present a whole different set of problems. Keep in mind, today so many unwanted babies are hurt before they're even born by their mothers' addictions and physical abuse. It was comforting to these couples to believe the pregnant teens at the fictional PLACE Foundation were healthy and received proper prenatal care.

"Time was a big factor, too. This organization moved fast. As soon as they heard about a prospective couple, they arranged for an immediate presentation. Promising desperate people they could have a baby in a matter of a few short weeks was like a godsend. After years of waiting and worrying, it was just too good to turn down."

Angela sighed. "Surely they realized paying so much money was out of line."

"The presentations were flawless. All the people approached could easily afford to make huge donations to such a worthy cause. To them it was no different than writing a check to a local church or the Salvation Army. They were helping needy teenagers and unborn children. Quite a noble cause, as long as they didn't try to get too rational about it. I suspect most of them had their doubts at first, but the excitement of finally having a child pushed the doubts out of their minds."

"Will the people who bought the babies go to jail?" Angela asked.

"It's too soon to tell. So far every couple we've located has given the child they supposedly adopted an excellent home. Their lives are being ripped apart. They've raised these babies as their own, and there's a good chance they'll never see them again. Now that they know the truth, that most of the children were actually stolen from parents who loved them very much, their guilt is overwhelming. They realize how much pain has been caused by their selfish actions. The couple we saw yesterday acted like they had nothing left to live for. Since there was no criminal intent, they probably won't go to jail. At this point I don't think they care what happens."

Angela glanced at Nick, then asked, "Have you returned any of the children to their real parents yet?"

"Did you hear about the Nelson kidnapping in Georgia a couple of months ago on the news?" Lesley asked.

Both Nick and Angela nodded.

Lesley beamed. "The baby was still in Jamaica with the woman who was going to adopt him. He was flown back to the United States, and yesterday morning I had the privilege of putting Mary Nelson's baby boy back in her arms. I'll never forget the look on her face as long as I live."

"What about Jax and Annissa?" Nick asked.

"Jax is still in jail in Jamaica, and his sisters, Annissa and Maya, were apprehended on another Caribbean island called Saba. With Nick's help we traced a phone call Jax made to them from a hotel here. The women were arrested as they left their mother's funeral."

Nick and Angela exchanged a glance, obviously pleased with their capture yet still saddened by their loss.

Lesley extended her hand as she moved to the door. "I really have to go. I just came by to thank both of you again for all your help."

"No problem," Angela replied.

Once she was gone, Nick closed the door to Angela's office and leaned against it. He held out his arms, and Angela leaned into him. "Can you believe it?" she said. "We helped stop an international kidnapping ring!"

Nodding, Nick skeptically added, "I just hope the Jamaican police guard Jax well. He has a way of slipping out of sticky situations." Pulling her tighter, he said, "I have a haunting vision of spotting him someday when we're honeymooning on a romantic Caribbean island."

"Honeymooning?" Angela excitedly asked.

Nick smiled and winked before kissing her. "Yes, honeymooning. It's a technical term used to describe the first few years after two people get married. I can't imagine life with you not being exciting. If the last few weeks are any indication, we'll have quite an interesting marriage."

"Is this some sort of backward proposal?"

"No." He dropped to one knee. As he kissed her hand, he asked, "Angela Anderson, will you spend the rest of your life with me?"

"That depends."

"On what?"

Slipping into his embrace, Angela answered with her body. After a long, sensual kiss, she pulled away to look into his eyes. "It depends on whether you expect this kind of excitement all the time."

In one swift motion he swept her in his arms. He looked lovingly into her eyes, then began slowly kissing her cheeks, her neck. His breath was ragged when he finally whispered, "This is the only kind of excitement either one of us needs for a long, long time."

Jerking back, Angela sternly said, "Nick, no!"

"Oh, God! You're not going to back out on me, are you?"

"Of course not!" Reaching across her desk, she unplugged the telephone. Next, she flipped the lock on her office door and pushed a chair in front of it for good measure. With a sly smile she slid back into his embrace as she said, "I never break a promise . . ."

TERROR ... TO THE LAST DROP

☐ **A DESPERATE CALL by Laura Coburn.** Kate Harrod will risk sacrificing her own family in her obsessive search for one unlucky young boy. And she'll willingly walk into the sights of a practiced killer ... and dare to cross the line no woman—and no cop—must ever cross.
(182944—$4.99)

☐ **STRIKE ZONE by Jim Bouton and Eliot Asinof.** A big league thriller in which an underdog pitcher, against all odds, must win the most important game of his career. "Enjoyable ... suspenseful."—*Chicago Tribune*
(183347—$5.99)

☐ **NO WAY HOME by Andrew Coburn.** Filled with insight and irony, this electrifying thriller blends roller-coaster action with the sensitive probing of men and women driven by private demons of love and hate, need and desire. "Extremely good ... vivid ... one of the best suspense novels."—*Newsweek* (176758—$4.99)

☐ **UNIVERSITY by Bentley Little.** Something Evil has invaded the California campus once praised for its high honors. Now violent death is crowding out pep rallies for space on the front page ... and leaving streaks of bloody ink in its wake. (183908—$4.99)

*Prices slightly higher in Canada

Buy them at your local bookstore or use this convenient coupon for ordering.

PENGUIN USA
P.O. Box 999 — Dept. #17109
Bergenfield, New Jersey 07621

Please send me the books I have checked above.
I am enclosing $_____ (please add $2.00 to cover postage and handling). Send check or money order (no cash or C.O.D.'s) or charge by Mastercard or VISA (with a $15.00 minimum). Prices and numbers are subject to change without notice.

Card #_____ Exp. Date _____
Signature_____
Name_____
Address_____
City _____ State _____ Zip Code _____

For faster service when ordering by credit card call **1-800-253-6476**

Allow a minimum of 4-6 weeks for delivery. This offer is subject to change without notice.

① SIGNET   **Ⓑ ONYX**

TALES OF TERROR

☐ **THE WEATHERMAN by Steve Thayer.** When Andrea Labore, a beautiful, ambitious Twin Cities TV newscaster, goes after the story of a serial killer of pretty women, it soon becomes clear that the monstrous murderer is after her. As the clouds of suspicion darken, the only sure forecast is that death will strike like lightning again and again ... closer and closer.... (184386—$6.50)

☐ **SAINT MUDD by Steve Thayer.** The gruesome double murder was not unusual for St. Paul, wallowing in the Great Depression. Even a hard, seasoned reporter like Grover Mudd couldn't get used to dead bodies. With the reluctant help of the F.B.I., the conflicted loyalty of a beautiful blond moll, and the hesitant encouragement of his own gentle mistress, Mudd targets the sociopathic killers with his own brand of terror. (176820—$6.50)

☐ **BONE DEEP by Darian North.** A beautiful woman runs for her life in a vortex of passion, lies, betrayal, and death ... all intertwine in this stunning novel of knife-edged suspense. (185501—$6.99)

☐ **FLAWLESS by Adam Barrow.** A woman is found brutally murdered, the pattern all too familiar. Her killer, long gone from the scene of the crime, is Michael Woodrow, a flawlessly handsome and intelligent thirty-year-old. He is a man who cannot control his compulsion to kill and kill again. "A nail-bitter."—*People* (188497—$5.99)

*Prices slightly higher in Canada

Buy them at your local bookstore or use this convenient coupon for ordering.

PENGUIN USA
P.O. Box 999 — Dept. #17109
Bergenfield, New Jersey 07621

Please send me the books I have checked above.
I am enclosing $_____ (please add $2.00 to cover postage and handling). Send check or money order (no cash or C.O.D.'s) or charge by Mastercard or VISA (with a $15.00 minimum). Prices and numbers are subject to change without notice.

Card #_____ Exp. Date _____
Signature_____
Name_____
Address_____
City _____ State _____ Zip Code _____

For faster service when ordering by credit card call **1-800-253-6476**

Allow a minimum of 4-6 weeks for delivery. This offer is subject to change without notice.

FEAR IS ONLY THE BEGINNING

☐ **PRECIPICE by Tom Savage.** The house is named Cliffhanger, a bit of heaven perched high on a hill in a Caribbean paradise. It is the home of the perfect family—until bright and beautiful Diana arrives, the ideal secretary-au pair. Now suddenly, everyone in this house is on the edge of a hell where nothing is what it seems, and no one is who they pretend to be. (183339—$5.99)

☐ **THICKER THAN WATER by Linda Barlow and William G. Tapply.** A precocious teenager's abduction leads to a seductive voyage of danger and self-discovery as he and his family must at last confront the very essence of evil.
(406028—$5.99)

☐ **JUST BEFORE DAWN by Donna Ball.** When Carol Dennison received the call after midnight, she knew without a doubt that the voice pleading for help was her teenage daughter's. Though the police had written her off as a runaway teen, Kelly's mother, Carol, had always suspected far worse. Now one parent's most fervent prayer has been answered. And her greatest nightmare is about to begin.
(187342—$5.99)

EXPOSURE by Donna Ball. Jessamine Cray, Philadelphia's most poised and glamourous TV talk show host is being stalked. The police think she's faking the campaign of terror out of a twisted hunger for public sympathy. But her tormentor is using her own darkly buried secrets as a cunning weapon to destroy Jess's peace of mind—before destroying her. (187334—$5.99)

GAME RUNNING by Bruce Jones. A stranger comes to your door, claiming he once knew you. You invite him in, and he drugs you. You wake the next morning to find your home has been stripped clean and your wife has been kidnapped. Your life has suddenly spiraled out of control. (184068—$5.99)

*Prices slightly higher in Canada

Buy them at your local bookstore or use this convenient coupon for ordering.

PENGUIN USA
P.O. Box 999 — Dept. #17109
Bergenfield, New Jersey 07621

Please send me the books I have checked above.
I am enclosing $_____ (please add $2.00 to cover postage and handling). Send check or money order (no cash or C.O.D.'s) or charge by Mastercard or VISA (with a $15.00 minimum). Prices and numbers are subject to change without notice.

Card #_____ Exp. Date _____
Signature_____
Name_____
Address_____
City _____ State _____ Zip Code _____

For faster service when ordering by credit card call **1-800-253-6476**
Allow a minimum of 4-6 weeks for delivery. This offer is subject to change without notice.

SIGNET   **ONYX**

PROVOCATIVE SUSPENSE NOVELS

☐ **A SOUL TO TAKE by C.N. Bean.** Homicide investigator Rita Trible has seen many hideous crimes—but none like the eleven-year-old altar boy who was sexually abused, murdered, then embalmed. And worse, he is but the first victim of a serial slayer out to make Milwaukee a killing ground. Now Rita's own little boy has been targeted by the killer who seems to read her mind and mock her every move. (406648—$5.50)

☐ **BRIGHT EYES by Preston Pairo, III.** Four years ago, Baltimore's sickest serial killer, known in the press as "Bright Eyes," savagely murdered the wife and son of Jimmy Griffin's best friend. Four years ago, "Grif" thought he blew away the city's worst nightmare on a rain-slick bridge. Suddenly Bright Eyes is back and Grif seeks to take the killer down before he snares his next prey. (407067—$5.99)

☐ **THE RETURN by Joe de Mers.** Brian Sheridan is the charismatic leader of a Mid-western parish, currently on leave. But he is called back to service by his mentor to uncover the truth about a man claiming to be Jesus. At Brian's side is Marie Olivier, a passionate journalist determined to unmask this imposter, and a woman who tempts Brian with love. "A fast-paced thriller that kept me guessing and on the edge of my seat."—Phillip Margolin, bestselling author of *After Dark* (407296—$6.99)

Prices slightly higher in Canada

Buy them at your local bookstore or use this convenient coupon for ordering.

PENGUIN USA
P.O. Box 999 — Dept. #17109
Bergenfield, New Jersey 07621

Please send me the books I have checked above.
I am enclosing $_____ (please add $2.00 to cover postage and handling). Send check or money order (no cash or C.O.D.'s) or charge by Mastercard or VISA (with a $15.00 minimum). Prices and numbers are subject to change without notice.

Card #_____ Exp. Date _____
Signature_____
Name_____
Address_____
City _____ State _____ Zip Code _____

For faster service when ordering by credit card call **1-800-253-6476**

Allow a minimum of 4-6 weeks for delivery. This offer is subject to change without notice.

D SIGNET   **B** ONYX

MICHAEL SLADE TAKES YOU INTO THE DEPTHS OF *HORROR*

- **RIPPER** Grisly lust and murder scripted by the world's most heinous killer. **"A master of horror!**—*Toronto Sun* (177029—$4.99)

- **CUTTHROAT** The hunt for a savage serial killer—in a thriller that embraces man's darkest fears.... "Would make de Sade wince."—*Kirkus Reviews* (174526—$5.99)

- **HEADHUNTER** When a beautiful woman is found dead, Detective Robert DeClerq must comb the underground of two continents ... to find a killer whose lust for women goes far beyond twisted sex.... "A real chiller!—Robert Bloch, author of *Psycho* (401727—$4.99)

- **GHOUL** The bodies were all the same. First they had been stripped naked. Then the blood had been drained from them while they were still alive. Then their hearts had been cut out. The police looked for a psycho killer. The press screamed that a vampire was loose. But they were wrong. It was worse.... (159594—$6.99)

*Prices slightly higher in Canada

Buy them at your local bookstore or use this convenient coupon for ordering.

PENGUIN USA
P.O. Box 999 — Dept. #17109
Bergenfield, New Jersey 07621

Please send me the books I have checked above.
I am enclosing $_____ (please add $2.00 to cover postage and handling). Send check or money order (no cash or C.O.D.'s) or charge by Mastercard or VISA (with a $15.00 minimum). Prices and numbers are subject to change without notice.

Card #_____ Exp. Date _____
Signature_____
Name_____
Address_____
City _____ State _____ Zip Code _____

For faster service when ordering by credit card call **1-800-253-6476**

Allow a minimum of 4-6 weeks for delivery. This offer is subject to change without notice.

① SIGNET ⒷⒷ ONY

CONTEMPORARY ROMANCE AND SUSPENSE

☐ **SLOW DANCE by Donna Julian.** Lily Hutton is going home to the close-knit Southe town where she grew up. But along with her past, Lily must face again t' heartbreakingly handsome, darkly driven man whom she never forgot, and who now desperately trying to drive her away. (186710—$5.5

☐ **RIVERBEND by Marcia Martin.** As a dedicated young doctor, Samantha Kelly w ready to battle all the superstitions and prejudices of a Southern town seethi with secrets and simmering with distrust of an outsider. But as a passiona woman she found herself struggling against her own needs when Matt Tyler, t town's too handsome, too arrogant, unoffical leader, decided to make her his. (180534—$4.9

☐ **SILVER LINING by Christiane Heggan.** Diana Wells was a beautiful woman, brilliant success, and a loving single mother. Was she also a murderer? T police thought so. The press thought so. And the only one to whom she cou turn for help was dangerously attractive Kane Sanders, the lawyer who was h worst enemy's best friend ... the man whose passion threatened the defense the last thing left she could safely call her own—her heart.... (405943—$4.9

☐ **BETRAYALS by Christiane Heggan.** Stephanie Farrell appears to have it all, one of television's most in demand actresses and the mother of a beauti daughter. But beneath her carefully constructed image is a girl whose childho was scarred by a tyrannical father and whose one chance at happiness w overturned by a shocking betrayal. "Dazzling romantic suspense!"—Judith Go (405080—$4.9

*Prices slightly higher in Canada

Buy them at your local bookstore or use this convenient coupon for ordering.

PENGUIN USA
P.O. Box 999 — Dept. #17109
Bergenfield, New Jersey 07621

Please send me the books I have checked above.
I am enclosing $_____ (please add $2.00 to cover postage and handling). S check or money order (no cash or C.O.D.'s) or charge by Mastercard or VISA (with a $15 minimum). Prices and numbers are subject to change without notice.

Card #_____ Exp. Date _____
Signature_____
Name_____
Address_____
City _____ State _____ Zip Code _____

For faster service when ordering by credit card call **1-800-253-6476**

Allow a minimum of 4-6 weeks for delivery. This offer is subject to change without notice.